CHINA BLUE

— ·—· ···· ·· —· ·— —··· ·—·· ··— ·

CLAIRE, THE THIRD DUDLEY SISTER

by

MADALYN MORGAN

To Cathy
with best wishes.

Hope you enjoy China Blue.

Love Maddie

British Library Cataloguing in Publication Data.
A catalogue record for this book is available
from the British Library.

ISBN: 978-1512089783

Book Jacket Designed by Cathy Helms
www.avalongraphics.org

Proofreading by Alison Thompson
www.theprooffairy.com

Formatting by Rebecca Emin
www.rebeccaemin.co.uk

Author Photograph: Dianne Ashton

Madalyn Morgan

ACKNOWLEDGMENTS

My thanks as always to my mentor, Dr Roger Wood, for his brilliant critique.

My family and friends for their love and support.

My author friends, Theresa Le Flem, Jill McDonald-Constable, Pauline Barclay at Chill With A Book, JB Johnson at Brook Cottage Books, Sarah Houldcroft at Authors Uncovered, and Gary Walker at Look 4 Books. Thank you for your friendship and encouragement – and for the help you have given me in promoting Foxden Acres and Applause, while I was writing China Blue.

China Blue is dedicated to the memory of my mum
and dad, Ena and Jack Smith.

And to my beautiful friend, Debbie Seepersad.

*

I also dedicate China Blue to the brave men and
women of The Special Operations Executive, The
French Resistance, the WAAF, RAF, RCAF.

To all the servicemen and women of the British,
Commonwealth and American armed forces. The
home guard, air-raid wardens, nurses, doctors,
hospital auxiliaries, volunteers, ambulance drivers,
men and women of the fire brigade, factory workers,
farmers, land army girls and wartime
correspondents.

Last, but by not least, the mothers, daughters, sisters
and wives who kept the home fires burning, so our
heroes had a home to come back to.

CHAPTER ONE

'Damn fog.' Claire rubbed her eyes and strained to see the road. 'Morecambe station would have to be closed in a pea-souper like this. What time is it, Ed?'

Eddie lifted her arm and squinted at her wristwatch. 'Too dark to see, darling, but your train came in to Lancaster at half past seven, so it must be quarter to eight.' Eddie leaned back in the passenger seat and put her feet up on the dashboard. 'How do you say, "Hello, good looking" in French?'

Claire laughed. 'You're incorrigible, Edwina Mountjoy. Can't you think of anything else?'

Eddie put her forefinger to her chin. 'Now let me think... No! Be a pal, Dudley and *parler Français.*'

'*Bonjour, mon beau!* But you won't need phrases like that when we get to France.'

'Maybe not with the RAF, but we will when we're out on the town with the local *Monsieurs.*'

'Out on the town? There's a war on, Eddie. We'll be going to France to work, not to fraternise with the locals.'

'Don't be a bore, darling and tell me how to say, "Would you like to take me to a dance?"'

'If you don't shut up and let me concentrate, you can drive back to Morecambe.'

'Not me!' Eddie said. 'I hate driving in fog.'

'And I love it, I suppose?'

'No, but you're better under stress than I am.' Eddie began to sing, '"*Frère Jacques, frère Jacques, Dormez-vous? Dormez-vous?"* Come on Dudley,

"Morning bells are ringing! Morning bells are ringing! Ding, dang, dong. Ding, dang, dong."'
Eddie poked Claire in the ribs. 'You're no fun at all, Claire Dudley! *"I hear thunder, I hear thunder, Hark don't you? Hark don't you?"'*

'Shush, Ed. I hear something that sounds like thunder, but I don't think it is. Listen!' Eddie took her feet from the dash and sat up. She wound down the passenger window and leant out, while Claire peered through the windscreen. She looked up. 'Is it an aircraft?'

Eddie twisted round to look out of the back window. 'It can't be a plane, it's on the road behind us. Good God, it's as big as a bloody tank.'

Claire looked in the rear-view mirror and put her hand up to shade her eyes. 'Whatever it is, its headlights aren't hooded.'

'They are, but it's a ruddy big lorry, and it's hellishly close. Put your foot down, Dudley, it's almost on top of us.'

At that moment there was a loud crunch as metal collided with metal, followed by a violent shunt, sending the Wolsey into a skid. 'Brace yourself, Eddie, we've lost the road,' Claire shouted, as the car hurtled over a ditch, stopping with a jolt against the exposed roots of a huge oak tree.

'Good God, that was close. Are you all right, Ed?'

'I think so.' Eddie rolled her shoulders and flexed her hands. 'Ouch! I think my left wrist's had it. You?'

'Jarred my neck.' Claire inhaled, and coughed. 'The steering wheel's knocked the wind out of me. Still, it stopped me from going through the windscreen.' She pressed on her ribcage and struggled for breath. 'Damn! That hurt.'

'Someone's coming,' Eddie said, getting out of the car. 'Careless bugger will get us bombed as well as ditched the way he's waving that flashlight about.'

Claire struggled to open the driver's door and stumbled out. 'What the hell were you doing pushing us off the road like that?' she gasped, holding her ribs.

'I'm sorry, Miss. I didn't see you till it was too late. Are you all right? I'm a first-aider with St John's Ambulance. If there's anything I can do?'

'I think you've done enough!' Claire said, and lost consciousness.

'Excuse me?' Claire called, as a nurse passed the half-closed curtains surrounding the bed she was lying on. 'Where am I?'

'The Royal Infirmary, Lancaster.'

'Lancaster?'

'You were involved in an accident on the Morecambe road.'

'Is my friend here? Her name is Edwina Mountjoy. She was in the car with me.'

Before the nurse had time to reply, Eddie shouted, 'I'm in the cubicle next to you, Dudley.' A second later she was at Claire's side.

'Thank God you're all right. Help me to sit up, will you? My neck and chest hurt when I move.'

'Wish I could.' Eddie lifted her arm to show Claire a white sling. 'I put my hand out to stop my head from hitting the windscreen. It might be broken. I'm waiting for the dishy doctor to confirm and administer,' she giggled. 'Crikey, if it's broken, I'll be in plaster for God knows how long. It'll be *au revoir pour le moment, France*,' Eddie said, frowning.

'I'm sorry, Eddie.'

'It isn't your fault, Dudley.'

'Maybe not, but as you say, it will be goodbye to France until your wrist heals.'

Eddie wrinkled her nose. 'Well, it was always going to be you who got first bite of the *cerise*. You came top in the written exam, and you speak better French than I do. I danced my way through Christmas leave.' Eddie dragged a chair from the head of Claire's bed and sat down. 'I expect you spent the holiday swotting.'

'I did a bit, yes.'

Eddie shrugged. 'Anyway, your accent is better than mine. I'd be able to blag my way through the interview, but I'd muck up an oral exam.'

'I'd forgotten about the exam tomorrow.'

'Today!'

'What?'

'Today. The oral exam: It's today, after the interview.' Eddie took her wristwatch from her pocket. 'In four hours, to be precise.'

Breathing heavily, Claire pushed herself up into a sitting position and swung her legs over the side of the bed. 'I need to get to Morecambe.'

'The lorry driver's around somewhere. He said he'd wait to make sure we're all right.'

'Wait to see if we're going to shop him for shoving a WAAF staff car off the road more like. I've got to get out of here. You stay and have your arm seen to.' Claire buttoned her shirt, grabbed her jacket, and struggled into it with Eddie's help. 'Goodness, my ribs hurt.'

'You shouldn't leave until you've seen the doctor.'

'Tell him I'll be back this afternoon.' Claire lifted her arms and put on her hat. 'Ah! Damn!'

'How are you going to fake "fit and ready to fight" at the interview when you're in such pain?'

'I'll be fine by the time I get there. I've worked too damn hard to miss this interview.' She looked at her reflection in the window. 'My hair's a bloody mess. I'll do something with it before I go in,' she said, pushing a rogue strand under her hat. 'Will you be all right if I go?'

'Of course.' Eddie hugged Claire with her good arm.

'Ouch!' and 'Argh!' they said at the same time, laughing.

'Don't make me laugh, it hurts,' Claire said, leaning on the metal bed frame.

'Sorry, darling. Give that damn driver what-for from me, will you?'

Claire found the lorry driver slouching against his lorry smoking a cigarette. 'I think you owe me a lift.' The driver's cheeks reddened. 'Can you take me to WAAF headquarters?'

'Where is it?'

'The Clarendon Hotel in Morecambe. I've got an interview at nine, but I'll need to be there by eight, to tidy myself up.'

'I'll try,' he said, straightening.

'You'll do more than try,' Claire snapped. 'If I'm not at that interview by nine, you'll be in trouble for shoving the vehicle of one of the

WAAF's top brass off the road.' The lorry driver threw down his cigarette and stamped it out. 'Come on then, give me a shove, so I can get into the cab.' With the driver pushing her from behind, Claire managed to pull herself up and swing onto the passenger seat. 'Well?' She looked down at him. 'What are you waiting for?'

Claire arrived at the office of her superior, Flight Officer Bingham, and reported to her secretary. Before acknowledging Claire with a scowl, she looked at the clock on the wall. It was two minutes to nine. She knocked on the FO's door and disappeared inside. A couple of seconds later she reappeared. 'Aircraftwoman 2nd Class Dudley?' Claire stood to attention. 'Flight Officer Bingham will see you now.'

Claire saluted and marched into the office. Her ribs felt as if they were in a vice that was being slowly tightened. Pretending to clear her throat, she put her hand up to her mouth and wiped perspiration from her top lip.

'At ease, Aircraftwoman,' the FO said, reading Claire's notes.

Simultaneously, Claire moved her right foot to shoulder width and put her hands behind her back. Instead of placing them palms out, one on top of the other, she clasped them tightly. Her nails, as short as they were, dug into the fleshy backs of her fingers, but she didn't relax them. The pain in her fingers took her mind off the pain in her chest.

'For the short time you've been here your service record is exemplary. Top of your class in French. Not only do you speak the language, but you read and write it. Ninety-nine percent fluent, it says.' The FO looked up. Claire nodded once in acknowledgement. 'Do you have family in France?'

'No, Flight Officer Bingham.'

'Was any part of your education in France?'

'No, Flight.' If she hadn't been in so much pain, she'd have laughed. Lowarth was about as far away from France as you could get, in every respect. The FO looked at her and tilted her head. She's expecting me to elaborate, Claire thought. 'My language teacher said I have an ear for languages.'

The FO nodded. 'It isn't often we get someone who is fluent in a language that isn't their mother tongue.' She continued reading. 'If you speak French as well as you read and write it, you'll be a perfect candidate. An asset,' she said, more to herself than to Claire. Her eye was caught by something on the page. 'Languages?' she queried. The FO looked up from Claire's notes. 'Which other languages do you speak?'

'A little Polish and some German. I--' A spasm of pain took her breath. It was so severe, Claire thought she'd faint. She gripped the back of the chair in front of the FO's desk with both hands and tried to keep her balance. She looked down at her feet, took a shallow breath, and looked back at the FO. 'Argh!' She had looked up too quickly. Her head was spinning. She tried to focus on her superior officer, but the light from the window behind her was suddenly bright and shimmering. It hurt her eyes. She closed them and slid to her knees.

'Aircraftwoman Dudley?' Claire was aware that the FO had left her seat and was crossing the room to the door. 'Call the medics!' she shouted to the WAAF who had shown Claire into the office.

Flight Officer Bingham helped Claire to her feet. 'Sit down, Dudley,' she said, prizing Claire's hands from the back of the chair and helping her into it. 'We'll resume this conversation tomorrow.'

Feeling nauseous, Claire nodded. She daren't speak in case she was sick. Shortly afterwards two medics arrived and after a few simple tests – holding one finger up, and then two, and moving them across Claire's line of vision to make sure she was able to follow them – they agreed she wasn't concussed. Arming Claire out of the FO's office, the medics took her to the sickbay; and from there to the Royal Infirmary, in Lancaster.

With her ribs tightly bandaged, Claire walked slowly and stiffly to the appointment with Flight Officer Bingham.

'I have the maintenance report for my car!' the FO said, as soon as Claire was shown into her office. There was nothing Claire could say or do to get out of the inevitable ticking off that awaited her, so she braced herself to take it. 'What the hell happened to cause you to career off the road into an oak tree? Have you seen the damage you've done to the Wolsey?' Claire opened her mouth to apologise, but the FO cut her off. 'It needs a right wing, headlights, bumper, and God knows what else. Apart from which, you and Aircraftwoman Mountjoy could have been killed. Well? What do you have to say for yourself?'

'I'm sorry, Flight. A lorry drove into the back of us, and there was nothing I could do. The driver admitted responsibility. He said he didn't see us. It was very foggy.' The FO didn't comment. 'He did what he could to help at the scene, and then drove ACW Mountjoy and myself to the hospital in Lancaster, later bringing me here for my interview.' Claire could have bitten her tongue. She wished she hadn't mentioned the interview. She shot the FO a sideways glance. She was making notes on a large writing pad. Eyes front again, Claire hoped she'd said enough to get herself and Eddie off the hook; the lorry driver too.

The FO finished writing. 'Continue.'

'That's it really, Flight. He said that, because his cab was high and the car low, he hadn't seen it until it was too late. The Wolsey, being black, wouldn't have been easy to see in thick fog, especially at night. From the position of the lorry after the accident, I --'

'All right!' The FO put her hand up. Claire waited for her response. It was some time before she spoke. 'I can't think why you would want to, but you've made a good case for the driver of the lorry, so I won't be taking the matter any further. We'll leave it to his employer to reprimand him.' Flight Officer Bingham pushed the maintenance report to one side, put her elbows on the desk and clasped her hands. 'As for not informing me about the accident, I should put you on a charge. What the hell were you thinking of?'

'I'd hoped--'

'I haven't finished.' Claire stopped speaking immediately, lifted her head and, in agony, stood to attention. 'You have several severely bruised ribs after an accident in a WAAF staff-car that Aircraftwoman Mountjoy had signed out as the driver, which means you were not authorised to drive it.' Claire opened her mouth to explain why she was driving, but the FO put her hand up again. 'ACW Mountjoy has explained that she is nervous of driving in fog.' The FO raised her eyebrows. 'If I am to believe that, I must also believe that it was not foggy on the journey to Lancaster, only on the way back! And why Lancaster railway station?' Clearly exasperated, she said, 'No matter!' and shook her head. 'Apart from making me look as if I don't know what my WAAFs are doing, you have ruined your chance of working with the RAF's Advance Air Strike Force in France.'

Claire bit back tears of disappointment. 'I'm sorry, Flight.'

'I'm sure you are. What the hell were you thinking of, Dudley, attending the interview in the state you were in? Were you going to inform me about your injuries?' Claire didn't answer. 'Or were you going to go ahead with the training and get yourself, or someone else, killed?' Claire's head was pounding and her cheeks burned with embarrassment. 'Pretending there was nothing wrong after injuring yourself as severely as you had was a stupid thing to do. Well?'

'I didn't think I was that badly hurt. And,' Claire lowered her eyes, 'I didn't think I'd be lucky enough to be chosen to go to France with the first batch of recruits.'

The FO pushed her chair back, stood up, and stormed across the room towards the door. 'That's the problem, Dudley. You didn't think at all!'

'Flight Officer Bingham?'

Claire's superior stopped in her tracks. 'Will I be able to sit the French oral exam, and try for the

RAF's Advanced Air Strike Force the next time they're recruiting?'

The FO spun round. 'You've got balls, Dudley, I'll give you that.' She looked at Claire, her face set in a scowl. 'I don't know. For now you're on seventy-two hours sick leave. You'll also be mentoring new recruits for six weeks.'

Claire opened her mouth to protest.

'If you persist in interrupting me when I'm speaking, you'll be mentoring for six months!' the FO bellowed. 'Is that clear?'

Claire acknowledged the rebuke with a nod.

'The answer to your question,' the FO said, sighing loudly, 'is yes! And you will still be going on study leave with a French family. You're damned lucky it has already been arranged. When the doctor signs you off as fit, come and see me.' The FO looked at Claire with steely eyes. 'Not a day sooner.'

'Flight!'

'Dismissed, Aircraftwoman 2nd Class!'

Claire saluted, turned on her heels and marched out of the office. In the corridor she leant against the wall and held her ribs. She was exhausted and disappointed, and she felt like crying. A stripping-down from Flight Officer Bingham was something everyone dreaded. It could have been worse, she supposed. If the FO wanted to see her when she had recovered, it sounded as if she would get another crack at the French oral exam, and the RAF's Advanced Air Strike Force. Until then she needed to keep her head down, her nose clean, and hope her ribs healed quickly.

CHAPTER TWO

'You packed, Ed?'

'Almost.' Eddie ticked off clothes items on her fingers. 'I think I have everything. Oh, not quite,' she said, grabbing a pair of fully-fashioned silk stockings from the makeshift washing line that stretched across the room from the edge of the window to the corner. 'Where are you staying?'

'In a small town called Cullercoats. It's on the coast about ten miles from the centre of Newcastle. The father of my French family,' Claire took the briefing notes from her bag and read, '"Professor Auguste Marron, is a lecturer at King's College. He specialises in European studies, history and languages. He has a sixteen-year-old son called Éric and a ten-year-old daughter, Mélanie."' She looked down the page. 'There's no mention of a wife. Perhaps the professor is divorced, or widowed. Anyway, I am to familiarise myself with their customs, pick up habits that are indigenous to the French way of life, study the map of France – occupied and unoccupied zones. And listen to this, Ed: the FO suggests I learn as much German as possible. She says if my understanding of the language is good enough, it will stand me in good stead.'

'In good stead for what?'

Claire scanned the rest of the page. 'She doesn't say. What about you?'

'Same as you, but without the German. My French family live in a suburb of Newcastle called Gosforth.' Eddie sighed.

'What's the matter? Living in the city will be

18

just up your street. Think of all the dances you can go to.'

'I suppose.' Eddie frowned.

'So why the long face?'

'I'm worried about poor George. It's so unfair. He could lose his job over the accident.'

Claire had seen the 'poor George' look before when her friend had fallen for poor Stanley, and a few months earlier for poor Freddie. 'Are you walking out with George?'

Eddie gave Claire a haughty look. 'Yes, if you must know. He's very nice,' she said, defensively, 'and loyal. He said he'll wait for me while I'm away.'

Claire burst into laughter. 'Anyone would think you were going to the front for six months, instead of to the North East of England for a few weeks.'

Eddie started to laugh, but quickly regained her serious face. 'I know you don't think much of George, because he's a lorry driver…' Coming from an upper-class family, rank and position were important to Eddie. As the daughter of a groom who was born and brought up in a tied cottage on a country estate, Claire had never considered such things. 'But he won't be driving a delivery lorry for much longer. He has joined the Army; The First Armoured Division. He's waiting for his papers. They could be here any day, which is why I don't want to leave him.'

'Unfortunately, Eddie, you don't have a choice.' Claire put her arm around her friend's shoulder. 'I suggest you pack your twilights. Wearing them will make it easier for you to save yourself for poor George.' Eddie pretended to be sick. Neither she nor

Claire had worn the WAAF-issue long grey woolly bloomers since their first week at Morecambe. 'Chin up! Absence makes the heart grow fonder.'

'It does, doesn't it?' Eddie said, brightening.

Claire picked up her suitcase. 'I'll wait for you outside. Get a move on, or we'll miss our lift to the station.'

The train journey was uneventful. Eddie spent her time gazing out of the window, looking into the mid-distance and sighing, while Claire brushed up on her French. The train was late getting into Newcastle upon Tyne's Central Station, so they went straight to the Enquiries Office.

'Excuse me, I'm Aircraftwoman Claire Dudley, and this is Aircraftwoman Edwina Mountjoy. Has anyone asked for either of us?'

'Hello?' Claire and Eddie turned to see a good-looking chap in his early twenties with chestnut-brown hair, tanned skin, and big brown eyes. 'I am Bernie Le Foy. My father has been detained and asked me to collect, Miss Mountjoy.'

'I'm Edwina Mountjoy,' Eddie said, batting her eyes and smiling for the first time since leaving Morecambe.

'So you must be Miss Dudley?' Claire turned to see a tall distinguished-looking man in his early fifties. His hair was black and peppered with silver, as was his close-cropped beard. He walked towards her, arm outstretched.

'Yes, Claire Dudley,' she said, shaking his hand. 'Pleased to meet you, Professor Marron.'

The two men introduced themselves and talked about France, while Claire and Eddie said goodbye.

Claire put her arms round her friend. 'See you in a couple of weeks.'

'Poor George. He will get over me, won't he?' Eddie giggled.

'You're incorrigible,' Claire said, her arms still round her friend.

'Absence also makes the heart wander,' Eddie whispered.

'Enjoy Newcastle,' Claire said, hitching the strap of her gas mask further onto her shoulder, 'and keep your twilights on.'

'You too. I mean enjoy Culler-thingy, whatever it's called'

'Did you sleep well, Miss Dudley?' Professor Marron asked, when Claire came down for breakfast the next morning.

'Yes thank you, Professor.' She looked at the Marron siblings, who had empty plates in front of them. 'I hope I'm not late.'

'Not at all. Mélanie, Éric, this is Miss Dudley. Is Miss Dudley the correct way to address you, or would you prefer Aircraftwoman Dudley?'

'I'd prefer Claire. Miss Dudley sounds so stuffy, and I don't intend to wear my uniform until I go back to RAF Morecambe. I'm pleased to meet you Mélanie, Éric.' Both children said hello with welcoming smiles.

Professor Marron poured coffee into Claire's cup and Éric passed her a dish of croissants.

'Butter?' The professor's ten-year-old daughter handed Claire the butter dish.

'Thank you, Mélanie.'

'Why are you speaking English? Papa said we

21

are only to speak French while you are here.'

Mélanie was bright, forward too. 'You are quite right. From this minute I will only speak French, *d'accord*?'

'Okay.' Mélanie put her hand up to her mouth and giggled. 'I mean, *très bien*.'

'I think you and I are going to get on well, Mélanie,' Claire said.

'You know Claire is a French name?'

'Yes. I don't know why my parents chose it. I don't think we have any French connections.'

'You should ask them.'

'That is a good idea, Mélanie, I shall.'

That night when chatter-box Mélanie had gone up to bed, Claire asked Professor Marron if she could see the library.

'But of course. Are you looking for a specific book?'

'No. I'd like to browse, if that's all right.' Claire pushed open the heavy panelled door and breathed in the smell of polished wood, old books and leather. She looked around. It reminded her of the library at Foxden Hall, where her father had been head groom before the war, and where her sister Bess, with a team of land girls, was turning the estate into arable land. Foxden Hall's library was considerably bigger. It had one of the largest collections of rare books in the country. The Professor's bookshelves held fewer books, but many were as rare and beautiful as those at Foxden. It was books by French authors that interested Claire. She walked the length of the bookshelf, fascinated by the Professor's collection of nineteenth century books. She turned at the sound of the library door opening. 'I'm admiring *Le Comédie Humaine*,' she said, as Professor Marron entered. 'Do you have the complete works of Balzac?'

'I wish,' the Professor said, putting his hands together as if in prayer, 'but sadly no. There are more than ninety volumes. Is it Balzac that you're interested in?'

'Not especially. I want a break from learning German and reading French history books – and thought I'd read a novel for a change.'

Professor Marron stroked his neat beard as he walked along the bookcase, stopping every now and then to peruse a title. 'You may like this author,' he said, pulling two novels by Anne Louise Germaine de Staël from the shelf. He handed one to Claire. '*Delphine*. I think you'll enjoy it.' He turned the remaining book over in his hands. '*Corinne*! One of my wife's favourite books. You and she have a lot in common I think – with Madame de Staël too. Goodnight.' Replacing his wife's favourite book on the bookcase, Professor Marron left the library.

The following morning Claire tied her scarf tightly under her chin and lifted her face to the sky. She inhaled deeply, filling her lungs with salt air and ozone. With her coat buttoned up to the neck, she braced herself against the blustering wind coming off the North Sea and walked along the beach at Cullercoats. She stood at the water's edge, overwhelmed by the vast expanse of grey-green sea in front of her. Bending down, she picked up a shell and put it to her ear.

'Can you hear the sea?' Éric Marron shouted.

'Éric! You made me jump. No, I can't hear anything except the wind.'

Éric picked up a much bigger shell. 'Try this.'

Claire put it to her ear. 'Yes!' she shouted. 'I can hear the sea. It's amazing. It sounds… Well, it doesn't sound anything like I imagined.'

'Don't you go to the sea front where you're based?'

'Yes, we do our physical training on the beach. It's mostly sand. I haven't seen any shells on it. My favourite pastime is walking along the promenade. I do it every chance I get.' She picked up a pebble and skimmed it across the choppy sea. 'Two bounces. Whoohoo!' She bent down and found another flatter, rounder stone. 'See if you can do better,' she said, dropping it into Éric's hand. He threw it and it sank without bouncing. 'I win,' Claire cheered.

'Do you get excited about everything, Miss Dudley? Sorry, Claire. Or is it just the sea?'

Claire thought for a moment. 'I don't get excited about everything, but I suppose I'm enthusiastic about most things. What are you enthusiastic about, Éric?'

'France,' Éric said, 'and my mother.' He turned into the wind. It tousled his hair and made his eyes water. 'My mother is in Paris with my grandparents.' He picked up a pebble and lobbed it into the waves. 'She insisted Papa brought Mélanie and me to England, so we would be safe. Huh!' Éric kicked out at a piece of driftwood.

'I know there are munition factories and bomb factories and of course the docks in South Shields, but here in Cullercoats you're pretty safe,' Claire said, reassuringly.

'I know.' Éric looked at Claire and held her

24

gaze.

'What is it, Éric?'

'It isn't that kind of safety my mother was concerned about. It is because we are Jewish that she made Father bring us to England.' Éric talked and Claire listened. 'Jewish people, entire families, are being persecuted. The persecution of the Jewish people began in Germany ten years ago, longer, and now it is happening in France. As the Germans march through my country, Jewish people are disappearing. The official line is that they are being relocated, but,' tears filled the boy's eyes, 'it is a lie, Claire. They are being sent by the thousand to camps in Germany. They say it is to work, but many are too old to work, or too sick – and some are only children.' Éric broke down and cried and Claire wrapped her arms around him. She tried to imagine what it would be like if England was occupied by the Germans – if her parents and her brother and sisters were taken to work camps in another country – but she couldn't. Éric lifted his head and wiped his eyes on the sleeve of his jacket. 'I will go back and liberate my country, and the Jewish people, as soon as I am old enough. I will join the Army and I will fight the Germans until France and her people are free again,' he cried.

Éric had an old head on young shoulders. He reminded Claire of her older brother, Tom, who was in the Army. He had joined up as soon as he was able, before war was declared. In his last letter, Tom said he was somewhere in France. Claire shivered. 'I wonder where my brother is.'

'Excuse me?'

Claire looked up at her young friend. 'I was

thinking aloud. You were talking about joining the Army and fighting in France, and it reminded me that my brother Tom is doing exactly that.' Claire pulled the lapels of her coat up to her chin and held them tightly. 'I'm cold. Shall we go back?' Éric looked disappointed. 'Come on. I'll tell you about my big brother as we walk.'

That evening, when Claire was reading in the library, Éric poked his head round the door. 'Is it all right if I do my homework in here with you?'

'Of course.' Éric lumbered in and sat at his father's desk. He spread out his books and took a pen from his pocket. 'You're keen, working at the weekend.'

'We have so much homework, we have to. And I need to use Papa's reference books when he doesn't need them. Politics!' he grimaced.

'I suppose I ought to know about French politics from a young French person's perspective. If you do the studying tonight, can I pick your brains tomorrow?' Éric didn't reply. 'I'll buy you coffee and cake in the Beach Café.'

'All right!' Éric said, his eyes wide and sparkling.

'Good. You can tell me what someone who isn't interested in politics needs to know.' Claire finished reading de Staël's *Delphine*, and returned it to the bookcase. She looked at a dozen other novels, read the information on the fly-leaf of several, and settled on Madame Marron's favourite book, *Corinne*.

After supper Éric said he had a little more work to do and returned to the library. Claire joined Mélanie and her father in the parlour. While they played cribbage, Claire read her book. Mélanie, obviously an expert at the game, won almost every match. Eventually the Professor put his hands up and called time on the game. Kissing her father and calling goodnight to Claire, Mélanie danced out of the room the victor.

Claire rubbed her eyes and yawned. 'I am going up too,' she said, closing her book. After wishing each other goodnight, the professor moved to an armchair by the fire and put on the wireless, and Claire went to the library. Éric wasn't there and the fire had gone out. Coming from the warm parlour, the library felt quite cold. She shivered and quickly placed the book she'd been reading, *Corrine*, on the bookshelf next to its sister book, *Delphine*. Then she switched off the light and left.

Crossing the hall she noticed a couple of books on the post table. She read their spines. The book on top was an atlas called *Maps of France*, the one underneath *France and its Bordering Countries*. She blew out her cheeks. 'Tomorrow will be soon enough,' she said out loud. As she turned to leave she saw something white sandwiched between the two volumes. She lifted the book on top to reveal a sheet of note paper. Written in a neat hand was a list of occupied and unoccupied zones. Beneath it, in Éric's casual scrawl, it said *65 Avenue St. Julien, 8th Arrondissement, Paris.* Guessing it was the address of Éric's grandparents, where his mother was living, Claire committed the address to memory, replaced the note, and went up to bed.

The next morning, when Mélanie had returned to her bedroom to finish dressing and Professor Marron was in his study, Claire asked Éric about the address.

27

'It is my grandparents' address. I thought if you were ever in Paris you might look my mother up.' Éric pressed a piece of folded paper into Claire's hand.

Without opening it, Claire gave it back to him. He looked crestfallen. 'I've memorised it. If I am ever in Paris, I will visit your mother and give her your love.' Éric looked at her through sad eyes. 'I promise!' she said, and her young friend smiled. Grandma's house is only a couple of stops from the Champs Élysées, on the Métro. Take this,' he said, giving Claire a book of the underground stations. 'It was mother's. The last time we visited my grandparents we went sight-seeing. She gave it to me in case we got separated.'

Claire opened the small square red and blue *Paris Nouveau Plan*. 'It's lovely, Éric. Are you sure you want to part with it?'

'Yes, if it will take you to my mother.'

'*Repertoire Des Rues Métro*,' Claire read. 'Directory of Streets and the Métro.'

Éric cuffed a tear from his cheek. 'You must think I'm a baby, always crying.'

'I don't think anything of the sort. I can't begin to imagine what it was like for you, and your sister and father, to have to leave your home and move to another country--' Claire's voice faltered and she cleared her throat. 'And to leave your mother and grandparents behind... I think you are very brave, Éric.'

Éric glanced at the door. 'My father would be furious if he knew I was asking you to put your life in danger when you are… I mean, if you are ever in France.' Claire smiled. Éric had worked out that she hoped to go to his country. It wouldn't have been difficult.

Mélanie tested her almost every day. She asked questions about France and the different zones, regions and borders. She changed her accent, impersonating her father and brother, as well as Prime Minister Pétain and a dozen celebrities that Claire had never heard of. And while they walked along the seashore, or drank coffee in the Beach Café, Éric told her about the people he knew and the place where he was brought up, which Claire used to invent her French family. With discussions on politics, French history, and the Professor teaching her how to read maps, Claire's stay with the Marron family was busy and productive. She had read French novels, listened to French music and eaten French food, when rationing allowed. For two weeks she had enjoyed everything French. She had even started to think in French. It was a happy time. She wasn't looking forward to leaving.

On her last morning, the Marron family sat down to a special breakfast of French coffee, buttered croissants, crusty bread and soft creamy Brie. 'Will you write to me, Claire?' Éric asked. 'When you return to the WAAF, I mean.'

The request took Claire by surprise. 'Yes, I shall write to you,' she said, smiling at Mélanie, so she didn't feel left out. 'But don't expect me to write for a while, or often. I shall be busy when I get back.'

When they had finished eating they all piled into the Professor's car and set off for Newcastle. Éric and Mélanie got out at their respective schools and Professor Marron took Claire on to Newcastle Central. Her train was in the station when they

29

arrived, so there wasn't time for a long goodbye. Kissing him on both cheeks, which was the French custom, Claire thanked Professor Marron for his hospitality and set off across the platform. As the attendant blew his whistle, Claire spotted Eddie leaning out of the window, waving. A second later Eddie flung open the door and Claire jumped in.

Arriving at the house in Morecambe where she and Eddie shared a room, Claire found several letters. One was from her sister, Bess. She read it and squealed. 'Tom's alive, Eddie!' she shouted. Crying and laughing at the same time, she shouted again, 'My big brother is alive. He got out of Dunkirk in one piece. Bess said he telephoned her from a hospital in Kent. He said he'd been ill, but was better, and was going up to Foxden to recuperate.' Tears spilled onto Claire's cheeks.

Eddie put her arms round her. 'Come on, Dudley, no blubbing. Your brother's home and safe.' Eddie looked at her wristwatch. 'I'm starved. Let's go to the NAAFI and have tea.'

'And afterwards we'll put on our glad rags and go to the pub in town. I feel like a gin and orange.'

'Atta girl. Can I borrow your white belt?'

CHAPTER THREE

Eddie leapt from her bed. 'Well?'

'RAF Coltishall.'

'Me too.' The two friends danced around hugging each other.

'Bomber and fighter squadrons are stationed there. We'll see some action, Ed.'

'What? With all the scrummy pilots?'

'No! With the aerodrome being on the east coast. Oh, I give up!'

'Only joking, Dudley old thing. Come on, let's go to the flicks.'

'I think not!' someone barked from the door. Claire and Eddie stood to attention as a corporal marched into the bedroom of their billet. 'Get your kit together. You leave for RAF Coltishall in the morning at 0:600 hours.' She looked at Eddie. 'I suggest you get your beauty sleep, ACW Mountjoy. They're still building the WAAF's quarters at Coltishall; you'll need all your strength for cleaning them. Goodnight!'

'Miserable old besom.' Eddie flopped onto her bed and let her shoulders sag.

'Come on, Ed, let's pack. We'll go to the pictures next week, in Coltishall.'

Too excited to sleep the night before, and up early to be at the administration building at six, Claire and Eddie dozed as the train from Morecambe to Norwich chugged its way south to Peterborough, before going east to Norwich, where they changed to a local train that took them the last eight miles to

Coltishall.

Outside the station, Eddie dropped her kitbag, sat on it, and with her face turned to the sun, closed her eyes. Claire put her bag down and sat beside her. After three-quarters of an hour – and not a sign of transport to take them to the RAF base – Claire suggested they walk. 'The train was late getting in. I bet we've missed our lift.' Getting to her feet, she picked up her kitbag and hauled it onto her shoulder.

Eddie opened her eyes. 'We're sitting in view of the bus stop, Dudley. So, since we don't know which way to walk, I suggest we hang on for…' she looked at her watch, 'fifteen minutes. There's bound to be a bus on, or around, the hour – and it's bound to go to the aerodrome. If not, I'll ask the station master how we get there.' She closed her eyes again. Claire put her bag down and sat on it again. 'These damned bags are so heavy we probably wouldn't get very far walking anyway.' Eddie sighed.

Still agonising over whether they should walk or wait for a bus, Claire spotted an open-topped sports car drive into the station car park and pull up in front of the bus stop. The driver, a tall good-looking chap of about thirty, got out of the car, walked jauntily round to the passenger door, and opened it. Claire nudged Eddie. She tutted and opened her eyes. A beautiful blonde who could easily have been looking out from the cover of *Vogue* magazine swung her long slim legs out of the car. Wearing the sheerest of stockings, a blue silk dress and jacket, navy high heels and matching handbag, she offered one white-gloved hand to the man, while holding onto a white pillbox hat with the other. Helping her out of the car, the man slammed the door and slipped his arm round her waist. Oblivious to a couple of WAAFs scrambling to their feet, the couple strolled into the station.

'Bet you five bob he's RAF.'

'I think you're right, Ed. He's got the swagger.'

'When he comes out I'm going to ask him if he knows which buses go to Coltishall.'

'Bet he doesn't. By the look of that sports car he's probably never taken a bus.'

Eddie smiled wryly. 'Tactics, Dudley. I was thinking more along the lines of him taking pity on us and giving us a lift. We haven't seen a ruddy bus in an hour. They might have stopped running.'

Claire put her hand up and shaded her eyes. 'I'd rather ask the ticket clerk than ask him. If he is RAF, he'll be an officer--'

'Shush, he's coming.'

'How do you know it's him?'

'He's got a distinctive walk. Listen.'

As the man stepped out of the station's dark entrance into the Norfolk sunshine, Claire and Eddie saluted. He took a step back. They had clearly taken him by surprise, but he recovered quickly, returning the salute with a rakish smile. Eddie's mouth fell open. Claire looked at her, expecting her to speak, but she was just staring at him. 'Excuse me, sir,' Claire said. His eyes twinkled and Claire felt herself blush. She stood as tall as she was able and began again. 'Excuse me, sir, my friend and I were expected at RAF Coltishall this morning. We were told an RAF vehicle would collect us, but there must have been a hold up because we've been here an hour and no vehicle, other than yours, has stopped at the station, not even a bus.' She felt flustered and knew she was waffling.

'What my friend is trying to say,' Eddie said, having at last found her tongue, 'is do you know if this is the right bus stop for RAF Coltishall, and if it is, do you know the times of the buses that go there?'

The chap looked around the car park and back at Eddie. 'It appears there is only one bus stop. As for buses going to Coltishall, I haven't a clue. But there's a bus coming,' he said, looking in the direction of the road. The girls followed his gaze. 'You could ask the driver. Ooops! I'd better move the old jalopy from the bus stop.' He ambled over to his car, saluted, swung himself onto the driver's seat and sped off.

'Scrump-tious!' Eddie said under her breath as she returned the salute.

'Too cocky in my opinion,' Claire said, before running over to the bus. 'Do you go to RAF Coltishall?'

'Yes, but we've got to wait for the ten-past train to come in,' the clippie said, pushing past them. 'Just going to refresh my lipstick,' she winked.

Eddie stepped onto the bus, threw her kitbag and gas mask into the luggage compartment and took a seat. Claire did the same. 'Oh well, we're one step nearer. Shouldn't be long now,' she said, joining Eddie. Looking out of the window, Claire saw the small red sports car heading towards them. 'What on earth…? Look Ed, the RAF officer has come back.'

'Well?' he shouted from the driving seat. 'Do you want a lift to Coltishall or not?'

Like a pair of giggling schoolgirls, Claire and Eddie pushed and shoved each other, took their belongings, and left the bus. By the time they got to the car the officer had opened the boot and was back behind the wheel. They hauled their bags in and ran to the passenger door.

'Oh dear,' Eddie said, 'it's a two-seater.' She looked at Claire. 'Shall we toss for it?'

'No need,' the officer said, pushing the passenger seat forward. 'Clever, isn't it? I can't do it with mine, I need the leg room, but now there's space for one in the back, if you don't mind sitting sideways.'

Eddie stood to the side, grinning. 'I'll sit in the back then, shall I?' Claire said, pointedly. The officer didn't get out of the car to open the door for her, so she opened it herself and clambered in. Eddie demurely slipped into the passenger seat and closed the door. With his unlit pipe in his mouth, the man put the car into gear and it roared off.

Holding onto her cap with one hand and clinging onto the back of Eddie's seat with the other, all Claire could see from her half-sitting, half-lying position was sky. The car raced through the Norfolk countryside at such speed that every time she attempted to sit up she was thrown backwards. She closed her eyes and squealed each time the car flew round a bend, and shook her head when Eddie turned to speak to her. She couldn't hear anything above the roar of the engine. When they arrived at the aerodrome, Claire was white-knuckled and windswept.

'Out you get, ladies. This is the administration block, where you report for duty,' the chap said. 'I'd tidy yourselves up before you go in, if I was you.'

'Yes, sir. Thank you, sir,' they said in unison. Eddie opened the passenger door and, as the blonde woman had done at the station, swung her legs out, leaving Claire to climb over the seat. Pulling her skirt down so the chap didn't see her blackouts, Claire almost fell out of the car. Her instinct was to thank him for the lift, but she was so embarrassed by her ungainly exit she ran to Eddie, who was standing by the car's boot with the kitbags.

'What did you have to do to get a ride in old Dogsbody's car?' a passing WAAF asked as the car sped away.

'Whose car?'

The WAAF looked at Claire as if she had arrived from another planet, instead of the railway station. 'That was Acting Squadron Leader Bader. He's a fighter ace. Didn't you know?'

'No,' Claire said, 'neither of us knew, did we Ed?'

Eddie shook her head. 'How kind of him to give us a lift.'

The WAAF guffawed. 'He wouldn't have been kind, if you hadn't been pretty. Come on, I'll take you in and get you registered, and then I'll show you where to go for lunch. If you come back here afterwards, I'll take you to your quarters.'

'This was on the hall table when I came in,' Eddie said, as Claire joined her in the billet. 'It's addressed to you. I bet it's the results of your French oral exam.' Eddie pressed a buff envelope into Claire's hand and followed her upstairs to their bedroom. 'Well? Aren't you going to open it?'

'Give me time to get through the door.' After taking off her coat and hanging it up, Claire ran her forefinger along the flap of the envelope and took out a sheet of white paper.

'Come on, Dudley, don't keep me in suspense,' Eddie said. 'Have you passed?'

'Yes.' Claire fell onto the bed and exhaled loudly, making a raspberry sound as air reverberated between her lips. 'That's a relief.'

'What percent?'

'Does it matter?' Eddie snatched the letter out of Claire's hand. 'Give it back, Ed.'

Eddie sat on the bed beside her. 'You don't mind, do you?'

'Would it make any difference if I did?'

'I knew it. You clever old thing, Dudley.'

'Flight Officer Manders said I'd be promoted to Aircraftwoman First Class if I passed.'

'And about beggaring time,' Eddie said. 'Come on, let's celebrate. We'll go to the dance at the mess hall. There's a local band on tonight that play jazzy tunes. It'll be fun.

'I don't know, Ed, I'm tired.'

'Be tired tomorrow. Tonight we're celebrating.'

'If you say so. With all the bloody air raids here, I wouldn't get any sleep anyway.'

'Good decision, ACW – soon to be First Class – Dudley. You must mark the occasion, you lucky blighter. Not that you don't deserve it,' Eddie chatted on. Claire dropped onto the bed and closed her eyes. 'And, starting now, we have forty-eight hours of glorious leave. You can sleep all day tomorrow if you want, but you are not sleeping now,' Eddie said, pulling Claire up into a sitting position. 'We'll put on our best frocks... Can I borrow your white belt again?' Opening Claire's cupboard, Eddie took out the belt. 'It'll look top-hole with my pink and white floral. What are you going to wear? I know, the blue,' she said, before Claire could answer. 'The skirt on your blue dress was made for dancing,' she said, twirling round. 'Oh,' Eddie stopped suddenly. 'I almost forgot. A squadron of Canadians arrived today – and they're all scrumptious.'

Claire laughed. 'How do you know they're *all* scrumptious?'

'I went up the tower with one of the girls from meteorology. We watched them land, but don't change the subject! You are coming to the dance, aren't you? Dudley, don't be a bore...'

'All right! Yes!'

Eddie hooted and clapped. 'That's settled then. And the best of it is we don't have to get up early in the morning. I'm going to dance and dance,' she said, waltzing out of the room.

Eddie was right, the dance was fun. The band played jazzy tunes, as Eddie called them, and there was no shortage of good-looking RAF and RCAF airmen to dance with. Claire danced so much she thought her feet would drop off. At ten o'clock she'd had enough and decided to leave. She scanned the room and spotted Eddie dancing with a Canadian pilot. She caught her friend's eye and pointed to the door. Eddie waved over the airman's shoulder as he buried his head in her neck. Claire waved back. Tomorrow, Claire thought, Eddie will be talking about 'poor Chuck' or 'poor Cliff'. Laughing, she pushed her way through crowds of smooching dancers to the cloakroom. She gave the young WAAF on duty her ticket and, goodness knows how, she found Claire's coat among the dozens of coats hanging up in the small room. After putting it on, Claire made her way to the exit. She had enjoyed the dance, but her mind was on her exam results. A pass meant the RAF Advance Strike Force was now within her grasp.

As Claire reached for the handle of the mess door, it flew open, knocking her off her feet. An RAF pilot ran to her aid, while a couple of handy-looking lads went to the door. 'Are you hurt, Miss?'

'No, I'm fine,' Claire said, as the pilot helped her up.

'Hey, English,' the Canadian airman who had barged through the door shouted to Claire, 'are you falling for me? All the girls do, English, all the girls do,' he said, staggering towards her.

'Move on, Airman, the lady doesn't want you slobbering over her.'

'Who the hell do you think you're talking to, buddy?'

'I'm talking to you, and I'm not your buddy. I'll ask you again, politely, move out of the way and let the lady pass, or--'

'Or what, Big Shot?' The Canadian airman took a swing at the RAF pilot. The pilot ducked the blow and the Canadian's fist connected with Claire's nose, sending her stumbling backwards into the arms of a Canadian captain who had come to see what the fuss was about.

'What the hell is going on here?' the RCAF captain bellowed, pushing Claire to her feet.

'Hey, you!' he shouted to his fellow

countryman, 'the party's over.' He jabbed a finger at the RAF pilot. 'For you too. And you--' he said, turning to Claire. 'Get out, before I put you out.' Claire opened her mouth to tell him what she thought of his bullying, but he ignored her. 'Get our men out of here and sober them up,' he shouted to the Canadian officer who had arrived with him. 'And you,' he said into the ear of the airman who had insulted Claire, 'are a disgrace to the RCAF uniform. Take him to the guard house,' he shouted, pushing the airmen towards the door. 'Are you still here?' he said to the RAF pilot.

'It wasn't his fault!' Claire protested. 'He helped me when the drunk knocked me to the ground.'

The Canadian captain turned from the RAF pilot to Claire. She saw his eyes settle on her nose, and he looked for a moment as if he was going to apologise for the behaviour of one of his men. Instead he said, 'I have no jurisdiction where RAF girlfriends are concerned, but if you know what's good for you, you'll stay out of my way!' Marching towards the door he shouted, 'Let's get out of here.'

Tears of anger filled Claire's eyes. She ran after the captain and pulled on his arm. He turned aggressively, but seeing the look of horror on Claire's face he put up his hands. 'I'm sorry, I thought you were one of the guys. What do you want?'

'To ask you not to report the incident.' The frown on the Canadian captain's forehead deepened and his blue-grey eyes flashed with annoyance, but Claire carried on. 'You said you have no jurisdiction here, but you can still write it up.' Her heart pounded in her chest, but she was damned if she was going to let the RCAF captain intimidate her. 'I have a very important interview coming up. A black mark against my character would mean I won't be considered for the job I've been working towards since I joined the WAAF. I've been training for months, almost a year, so--'

'So you want me to forget what happened?'

'Yes! Please.'

The Canadian captain looked at her, his eyes as cold as steel. 'Okay,' he said after several seconds. 'But in future, if you want to protect your reputation, keep away from drunks.'

'I will,' Claire said, and the captain left. Fighting back the tears, Claire scanned the dance floor. Eddie was making her way through the crowd towards her.

'What the hell's going on? Oh my God, Claire, your nose is bleeding.'

'That's because I've just stopped a right hook.' Claire took a handkerchief from her handbag and held it on her nose. 'Bloody hurts,' she said. 'Come on, let's get out of here.'

Claire was so excited about the interview with her superior, Flight Officer Manders, and the RAF officers from the Advance Strike Force that she had hardly slept. When she did finally drop off, it was into a fitful sleep where she tossed and turned, waking every twenty minutes or so to check the alarm clock in case it hadn't gone off and she'd overslept.

The door to the FO's office opened and her secretary came out. 'Flight Officer Manders will see you now.'

Entering the office, Claire stood to attention and saluted her senior officer.

'At ease, Aircraftwoman First Class,' Flight Officer Manders said, reading Claire's file. She lifted her head. 'Congratulations on getting a distinction in French. It isn't often that an officer of your age gets a hundred percent pass, let alone a distinction.'

Aware that the man in the room was watching her, Claire held her head high, kept her back straight. She stifled a yawn.

Flight Officer Manders looked up and smiled approvingly. 'This is Colonel Smith,' she said, motioning with her hand to the man on her left. Claire saluted.

'I have some disappointing news for you, Aircraftwoman Dudley.' Claire's heart sank. She was sure she'd been called into the FO's office for an interview with the RAF Advance Air Strike Force. Her mind went into overdrive. What had she done, or not done, that had put an end to her dream? She couldn't think of anything. She had passed the French literacy, fluency and oral exams with top marks. She had even learned *La Marseillaise*, thinking it might come in handy when she was in France. And she had spent every minute of her spare time practising the German she knew and learning new words and phrases – including the difficult grammar. Damn! She stood firm, praying that the boiling frustration she felt didn't show in her face, or the tension in her shoulders show in her stance. She mentally checked herself and relaxed a little. 'The RAF Advance Air Strike Force, as we know it, is disbanding,' FO Manders said. 'Therefore it no longer requires British French speakers--'

The telephone on the FO's desk burst into life with a shrill ring. Claire felt her nerve ends flinch. The FO glared at it, before lifting the receiver to her ear. 'I said no calls!' she barked into the mouthpiece. A second later she said, 'That's different. Send him in. Captain Mitchell,' the FO said to the colonel. 'We'll proceed when he's here.' The colonel nodded.

There was a knock on the door. 'Captain Mitchell,' the FO's secretary said. She stood back to let the new arrival enter, saluted and left.

The FO stood up to greet the captain, who was dressed in civvies. She shook his hand. 'You know Colonel Smith?' The colonel stood up and also shook the captain's hand. 'And this is Aircraftwoman First Class Dudley.'

Claire turned to the captain and her knees turned to jelly. 'Sir!' she said, saluting the bad-tempered Canadian who, only a few days ago, had told her if she knew what was good for her she would stay out of his way.

'ACW First Class!' he said, returning the salute before giving Claire a disapproving look and sitting down in a chair next to the FO.

Claire kept her eyes front. This was meant to be the best day of her career. It was rapidly turning into the worst day of her life.

'Captain Mitchell is with the Royal Canadian Air Force,' the FO informed Claire, as if Claire didn't know. 'Colonel Smith is from the Special Operations Executive, which is why I called you in. Colonel Smith, if you'd like to take it from here?'

'Please sit, Miss Dudley,' the Colonel said.

Claire looked at the FO. She nodded.

'Thank you, sir.' Avoiding the Canadian captain's gaze, she sat on the chair in front of the FO's desk.

'You have an exemplary record, Miss Dudley,' the Colonel said. Claire heard the Canadian captain clear his throat. She stiffened slightly, but tried to ignore him and concentrate on what the colonel was saying. It wasn't easy. 'Fluent in French and proficient in German. And I see you have been trained in armed combat. Is that usual?' he asked, directing the question to Claire's senior officer.

'No, Colonel, but when Aircraftwoman Dudley and another French-speaking WAAF expressed a wish to work with the RAF in France, they were sent for training.'

'It's all helpful. One never knows when armed combat will be necessary.' Colonel Smith turned to Claire. 'With your knowledge of the French culture and way of life, being fluent in the language, as well as speaking and understanding German, you would be an asset to the Special Operations Executive, Miss Dudley.' Claire felt her pulse quicken. 'I should like you to consider leaving the WAAF for a period of time to work with us.' He leaned forward and picked up a folder. 'I recruit operatives for the French Office. We will eventually be conducting espionage, sabotage and reconnaissance in occupied Europe, as well as assisting the local Resistance movements.' Claire's heart leapt with excitement. 'What we need at this stage, however, are young women who are willing to go into the occupied zones and report back on German troop movements. It's dangerous work. There is no guarantee you'll return in one piece, if at all. I know that sounds harsh – and it is – but I want you to understand the risk you'll be taking if you accept the post.' The colonel paused, leaned forward and looked firmly into Claire's eyes. He's hoping to unnerve me, she thought, but that isn't going to happen. She held her reserve, determined that she would not show the slightest sign of fear or doubt. 'You must be absolutely certain that the kind of work we do at the SOE is for you.'

'Sir!' Claire gave a firm nod that she understood.

Colonel Smith's face relaxed. 'This is for your eyes only,' he said, handing Claire a file. 'Is that clear?'

'Yes sir.'

'The work we do is top secret. If you join the SOE you cannot tell anyone. If you are given an assignment you must not tell anyone what it is, or where you're going to carry it out. As far as friends and family are concerned, you are here at Coltishall. Do you understand?'

'Yes sir.'

'Everything you need to know about the SOE and the Secret Service Act is in there. Read it thoroughly and let Flight Officer Manders know your decision.'

'Thank you, colonel,' the FO said. 'Do you have anything to add, Captain Mitchell? The Canadian shook his head. 'Then that is all, ACW Dudley. Dismissed.'

Claire stood, saluted her superior officer, and turned towards the door. On her way out she glanced at the Canadian captain. He nodded.

Relieved that he hadn't taken the affray in the mess hall further, she left the room.

Clutching the buff folder, she marched along the corridor to the main exit. Once outside, she leant against the wall and inhaled until her lungs were full to capacity. Then, exhaling slowly, she walked across the square to her billet.

CHAPTER FOUR

Claire ran upstairs to the bedroom she shared with Eddie and slid the folder between the thin mattress and wooden base of her bed.

'Still in one piece then?' Eddie called from the bathroom. 'Did the Canuck beefcake shop you?'

Claire crossed the room and stood in the doorway. 'No, it was nothing to do with him,' she said. So why was he there, she wondered? Thinking about it, neither the FO nor the colonel had said anything about his part in the SOE – if indeed he played a part at all. Strange, that.

'What did Minty Manders want then?' Eddie asked, leaving the bathroom and walking past Claire, who was deep in thought. She followed Eddie into their bedroom. 'Must have been bad, you're frowning.'

'I was just thinking.' Claire needed to tell Eddie something; if she didn't, her friend would keep asking. Besides, Eddie might well be considered for the same work. Then she had a flash of inspiration. Tell Eddie the truth, or at least part of it. 'It wasn't good news. The RAF's Advance Air Strike Task Force is not recruiting French speakers anymore.'

'Damn! No canoodling with suave Frenchmen then?'

'Unfortunately not.' Claire hated lying to Eddie. 'Fancy going to the flicks?' she asked, changing the subject. 'We could see the new Clarke Gable picture.'

'Sorry darling, I promised Larry I'd see it with him.' Claire opened her mouth to ask who Larry was, but Eddie carried on. 'Must dash, he's picking me up in two minutes. We'll see something next week,' she shouted, running down the stairs.

'Thank you Larry, whoever you are!' Claire said aloud. 'Now I don't have to lie to my best friend, and I can read the information Colonel Smith gave me.' She took the folder from beneath the mattress, kicked off her shoes and sat on the bed. Drawing her knees up, she leant back onto her pillow and opened the folder. She heard a couple of girls come upstairs and go to their rooms. Judging by their conversation they had just come off duty and were changing to go out for the evening. As they passed Claire's door they waved, but didn't speak. Her housemates were used to seeing her with her nose stuck in a folder or a book.

Claire read on, losing all track of time. After a couple of hours she rubbed her eyes and, reaching out, took the alarm clock from the cupboard at the side of her bed. She held it up and squinted. It was half past nine. No wonder she was having difficulty reading; it was almost dark. The girls she shared the house with would be back soon, so she read to the end of the paragraph, ripped a strip of paper out of her notebook, placed it in the folder and closed it. She had read enough for one day. Yawning, she put the folder back under the mattress and sat on the bed. She wanted desperately to tell Eddie that she had been asked to consider working overseas with the SOE, but she couldn't. She closed her eyes to rest them and the next minute, or so it seemed, Eddie and a couple of WAAFs arrived, hushing and shushing each other. Giggling, Eddie ran to the bedroom window and closed the blackout curtains before putting on the light. The other girls shouted goodnight and stumbled into their bedroom, on the opposite side of the landing.

While Eddie talked animatedly about her date with Larry – how handsome he was, how tall and, my goodness what a good kisser – Claire took her wash bag and towel from the bedside cupboard and went to the bathroom. Eddie followed. Claire washed her face and brushed her teeth – and Eddie was still talking. Returning to the bedroom, Claire pulled back the bedclothes and climbed into bed.

'I'll tell you all about the film when I get back,' Eddie said, grabbing her wash bag and toothbrush. 'Shan't be long.' Claire was asleep in seconds.

'Looking forward to training with the Canuck today?' Eddie asked, as she and Claire took off their uniforms. Claire shrugged. 'He's quite yummy, if you like the beefcake type.'

'Can't say I've noticed,' Claire said. 'Rude yes, but *yummy*?'

'Blackouts have to be the least flattering drawers in the world,' Eddie said, looking down at her baggy knickers, which were almost down to her knees. 'Passion killers, that's what they are.'

'Oh I don't know,' Claire said, rolling the legs of hers up to her thighs and high-kicking.

Eddie laughed and did the same. 'Ouch! The bally elastic's tight,' she said, pushing the legs down again.

Claire looked from Eddie's thick woollen knickers to her own, and pulled a face. 'You'd think they'd give us shorts, as we're being trained by a man. Why are we being trained by a man?'

'We're guinea pigs. One of the girls said the Canuck has been in intelligence, and is going to put us through endurance tests as well as physical training.'

'It'll be an endurance test having to look at his miserable face every day. Come on, knees up, Mountjoy!' Claire shouted, running on the spot until Eddie joined her. Together they sprinted out of the house and across to the barrack square. Captain Mitchell stood with his hands on his hips while a dozen WAAFs milled around, chatting to each other.

'Good of you to join us, Aircraftwomen Dudley and Mountjoy.' The other women giggled. 'Okay!' he shouted. 'Let's warm up. Run on the spot, and at the sound of the whistle, six laps of the square. Let's go!'

'I like a masterful man,' Eddie whispered, as they began the first lap.

'Shush, Ed. If he catches you talking you'll be for it.'

'Would you like to share what it is that's more interesting than your training, ACW Dudley?'

Claire spun round, eyes wide with surprise that he had singled her out. 'No sir! Sorry sir!' she said, glaring at Eddie. She felt the colour creeping up her neck to her cheeks. She didn't like the Canadian captain. He was a bully.

'What a misery he is,' Eddie said, when they were in the showers. 'I'm sorry he ticked you off. It should have been me. I can tell him if you like, explain you were only talking because you were telling me to be quiet.'

'No! He'll see it as an excuse and it'll make

things worse. Forget about it and let's hope he does too.'

Later, when they were on their own, Claire told Eddie that she was being considered for a translating assignment. 'Whether I get it or not depends on Miserable Mitchell. The thing is, Ed, he doesn't like me. He probably doesn't think I'm up to the job, so I've got to show him that I am. I really want this, Ed, so be a pal and don't muck about when he's around. I need to work so hard that he forgets the ticking off he's already given me.'

'I need to work hard too. I wasn't going to tell you until I'd heard back from Minty Manders, but I've put in to take the French exam again.' Claire's face relaxed into a smile. 'I shall take it seriously this time. I want to do more than drive the brass about. I want to make a difference. So thanks for reminding me,' Eddie said. 'Pals?'

'Pals!'

'You wanted to see me, Aircraftwoman Dudley?'

'Yes, Flight.'

'Well?'

'Well--' Claire wasn't sure where to begin. She wasn't a complainer. She prided herself on getting on with the job, however difficult.

Leaning her elbows on the desk, Flight Officer Manders put her hands together and made a steeple of her fingers. 'I haven't got all day, Dudley.'

Claire took a breath. 'Captain Mitchell is unnecessarily hard on me, Flight. He works me longer and pushes me harder than he does any of the other women in my group. He has me jumping through hoops, literally. He barks orders at me,

51

makes me the scapegoat when anything goes wrong, and keeps me behind when everyone else has been dismissed.'

'Has he told you why he pushes you, or singles you out?'

'He says my arms are weak. He keeps me behind to do exercises, which he says will make them stronger.'

'And have they strengthened?'

'Yes,' Claire admitted, reluctantly, 'but--'

'Then my advice is keep doing what the captain tells you. He has your best interests at heart.' Claire stared into the mid-distance. She didn't think the Canadian captain had a heart. The FO picked up a file. 'This is your report.' Claire felt the nerves on the top of her stomach tighten. Expecting it to be full of critical and derogatory comments, she held her breath. 'Captain Mitchell has passed you fit, and recommended you to the SOE. You have an interview in the New Year. The bully you talk of is so confident that the SOE will want you that he has enrolled you in a parachute training course at Ringway airport, near Manchester.' Claire's eyes widened in astonishment. 'I take it you do still want to work with the SOE?'

'Yes, Flight.'

'Good. Then it was worth putting up with the captain's bad temper?'

Claire couldn't help but smile. 'Yes, Flight.'

'Then I suggest you start packing. Ringway are expecting you on Monday at 0:900 hours. You'll be staying at Dunham House, in Cheshire – it's all in here.' She handed Claire the file.

'Thank you, Flight.'

The FO chuckled. 'Reserve your thanks until you've read this lot,' she said, handing Claire two files that looked similar to the first. 'From Colonel Smith. Needless to say, they are for your eyes only.' Claire nodded. 'And I think it best if we keep this conversation between ourselves. There are a lot of *hoops to jump through* before the SOE posting is definite!'

'Understood!'

'Dismissed, Aircraftwoman First Class – and well done.'

'Thank you, Flight Officer Manders.' Claire felt like jumping for joy. Instead she saluted, turned on the spot, and marched out of the FO's office.

'This is worse than being at school,' Claire said. Rubbing her tired eyes, she closed the last of the folders that FO Manders had passed on to her from Colonel Smith.

'What is?' Eddie asked.

'This lot.' Claire put the folders face down on top of the cupboard. Eddie had been lying on her bed reading a magazine, but was now sitting up eagerly awaiting an explanation about Claire's reading matter. Claire ached to share her good news with her best friend. She knew she couldn't tell her everything, but since she was off on a parachute training course in a couple of days, she needed to tell her something. 'Minty Manders has organised a couple of courses for me,' she said. 'And if I get through them, she says she'll suggest me for a translating job.'

'That's great, Dudley,' Eddie said, smiling. 'The RAF are always looking for German speakers to interpret what Luftwaffe pilots are saying to each other, and what they say to their command centre.' Eddie's smile slowly faded. 'You'll be based on the south coast then?'

'I suppose I will.'

'How long will you be away?'

'Well, there's a couple of training courses, so it could be as long as six weeks, perhaps longer.'

Eddie stuck out her bottom lip. 'I shall miss you.'

'I'll miss you too, Ed, but it's too good an opportunity to turn down. Oh, and I've been given forty-eight hours leave. So if I get through the first course in time, I can go home for Christmas before I go south.' Claire looked away. She hated lying to Eddie. She hated lying full stop, which was why she rarely did it. She could remember anything she put her mind to, but she had a hard time remembering lies. She satisfied her conscience by telling herself that she *would* be going south, eventually. Now the Canadian captain had passed her physically and mentally fit, she would be going to London to meet officers of the Special Operations Executive, after she'd been to Manchester and learned how to jump out of aeroplanes. Bubbles of excitement fizzed in her stomach.

CHAPTER FIVE

Claire jumped out of the taxi, paid the driver and, taking her suitcase from the back seat, ran across the drive to the front door of Dunham House. The brief said to be there at six o'clock for tea and introductions. Dinner was at seven. She looked at her watch; it was five to six. She inhaled and exhaled slowly to calm her nerves. It didn't work. 'Here goes,' she said under her breath and, approaching the door, she lifted her hand to the bell.

'Hello?' Claire heard someone shout. She turned to see a young woman getting out of a car on the far side of the drive. 'Hang on, will you?' she shouted. Claire watched the girl pay the driver, grab the handle of her suitcase and drag it across the drive. 'I'm Ellen,' she said. Taking off a glove, she offered Claire her hand.

'Claire. How do you do?' Claire said, shaking Ellen's hand.

'Thanks for waiting for me. I was dreading going in on my own.'

'Me too.' Claire lifted her hand again and, with her forefinger poised before the bell, said, 'Shall we?'

Ellen hunched up her shoulders and, with her lips pressed tightly together, nodded.

No sooner had Claire pushed the brass button than the door opened. 'Welcome to Dunham House,' said a tall, grey-haired man in a black suit. He looked from Claire to Ellen. 'Miss Dudley and Miss Southall?'

'I'm Claire Dudley.'

'And I'm Ellen Southall.'

'If you'd like to follow me,' the man said, taking both suitcases. 'Two of the gentlemen on the training course have already arrived and are in the sitting room.' As they walked through the entrance hall the man dropped the cases at the side of a wide stairway. 'They will be taken to your room,' he said, opening the door opposite.

Claire followed Ellen into the sitting room. With matching settees and chairs, thick rugs on a parquet floor and tapestry-style drapes tied back with gold tasselled plaits, the room reminded her of the sitting room at Foxden Hall. In the hearth a fire blazed. 'Come and warm yourselves, ladies. I'm Johnny Tremaine and this is Nick Wood,' the taller of the two men said.

'Claire Dudley.' Claire shook Johnny's hand, and then Nick's.

'And I'm Ellen Southall.' Johnny took Ellen's hand, holding it for so long that Nick waved his hello over Johnny's shoulder. While the boys made a fuss of Ellen, Claire wandered over to one of the tall sash windows. The view reminded her of Foxden, before the war. The fields and meadows appeared to roll on forever and the drive leading to the house was lined with trees.

'Nice, isn't it?' Nick said, suddenly at Claire's side.

'Yes, it reminds me of where I was brought up.'

'Oh? Should I touch my forelock when I speak to you?'

Claire laughed. 'I don't think people do that these days. But no, my dad was head groom on a country estate and we lived in a tied cottage. The lord and his family were good people, but the only thing estate workers' kids shared with them was the view.'

Claire and Nick turned as the door opened and a waitress brought in tea. 'Come on,' Nick said, 'or Johnny will eat all the biscuits.'

'I'll be mum,' Ellen said, pouring the tea. Sitting round the table, they talked about the training and what they hoped to get from it. The others didn't say why they were on the course, so Claire didn't either.

At half past six, the RAF training instructor, Martin Richards, from Ringway's Parachute Training Squadron arrived. After introducing himself he spoke briefly. 'There are dozens of trainees like yourselves at Ringway. And, like you, they have been split into groups of four. Stay close and get to know each other until you can trust each other completely. Watch each other's backs, as you would do in the field. You are Group A, the first of my trainees to jump.' Martin moved between them handing out timetables and briefing notes. Claire glanced at the others. Their faces showed nervous eagerness and excitement, as she suspected her own did. 'Study the briefing notes until you are able to recite them backwards. Before you go up, you will know your chute and equipment as well as you know your own bodies. If you don't, you won't be going up. It's as simple as that. Get an early night – you've got a big day tomorrow.'

The four trainees stood to attention and saluted. Martin returned the salute and left.

Claire and Ellen went up to their room to change, meeting the lads twenty minutes later for dinner. When they had finished eating, Johnny tried to persuade them to go to his and Nick's room for drinks. Claire said she wanted to study the briefing notes and Ellen, blushing, said perhaps another night. Johnny pretended to be hurt, but Nick put his arm around his neck and strong-armed him out of the dining room.

In their bedroom Ellen confessed to Claire that she thought Johnny was nice looking and if he asked her to walk out with him she might. 'What about you? Do you like Nick?' she asked.

'He seems very nice. I like him, but that's all. Besides, he likes you.'

'Me?' Ellen said, sounding surprised. 'Why do you think that?'

'He goes doe-eyed when he looks at you, and when you speak he hangs on your every word.' Ellen sat on her bed and picked up her notes, but made no attempt to read them. 'I'm here to learn how to jump out of an aeroplane,' Claire said, 'not to find a sweetheart. It's important to me that I become proficient in parachuting. So no boys for me.'

The car arrived the following morning soon after breakfast. It left with its cargo of trainees at 08:30 hours, arriving at RAF Ringway shortly afterwards. Although she was nervous Claire entered the main building first and followed the signs to the lecture hall, or school room, as Martin Richards called it. On the door was a hand-written note that said IF YOU DO NOT WANT TO LEARN, DO NOT ENTER THIS ROOM. 'Better behave myself then,' Johnny said, as the four of them trooped in.

'I intend to,' Claire said. If things went wrong it would mean at best a broken leg, at worst a broken neck. Claire committed to memory everything she was told about the parachute, the transportation of equipment, how to fasten and unfasten the harness – and how to drop it if she landed in a tree or a river and needed to get rid of the release box, straps and buckles. By lunchtime she was exhausted. The afternoon session was about the full moon and the eight nights around it when a pilot would risk flying his plane without lights. And the wind, how the body oscillates while it descends, and how difficult it is to judge the swing when all you can see is the ground rushing towards you. Martin also talked about what to expect if a cord snapped or the chute didn't open. Claire looked at Ellen. Her face was as pale as Claire suspected her own was.

The following day, hardly able to contain her nerves, Claire scrambled onto what looked like a cradle attached to the underbelly of a balloon. She followed the instructor, who shouted, 'First trainee to board will be first to jump.' Again she tried breathing deeply to calm her nerves. Again it didn't work. Nick boarded behind her, followed by Ellen, and Johnny climbed in last.

The motorised winch juddered and the balloon began to rise, but Claire's stomach stayed on the ground. It soon caught up. All of a sudden the engine cut out and the winch jolted to a halt. Claire peered through the opening in the centre of the cradle at the fields below and wished she hadn't. Her heart was beating like a drum and her legs began to shake. Was she frightened of heights? She didn't think she was. In class, Martin said the balloon would be anchored at a thousand feet, which meant they were stuck at around five hundred.

'A small hitch,' Martin shouted above the

labouring engine and blustery wind. 'We'll be on the move soon.' And they were. It felt like an hour but could only have been a couple of minutes before Claire heard a dull cranking sound and the balloon began to rise again. She smiled nervously at Ellen who grinned back, her lips a tight line.

The winch stopped and Martin pointed at her. 'First,' he shouted, 'second, third and fourth,' he said to Nick, Ellen and Johnny. Keeping her eyes on him, Claire moved closer to the hole in the middle of the cradle. 'Prepare to jump,' he shouted. She nodded. 'And go!'

The next second Claire was plummeting to the ground. A squeezing sensation gripped the pit of her stomach and she squealed. Air rushed into her mouth and up her nose as she dropped like a stone. Worried that something had gone wrong, she looked up. At that moment the chute opened its dome and ballooned like a huge mushroom. She felt exhilarated, excited, and squealed again as she was swept up and dropped. Suddenly the ground was coming up to meet her. She began to panic and, misreading the swing of her body, landed badly. Propelled by a strong ground wind she was dragged along at a speed almost faster than her legs could cope with. She feared she would fall. Before she did, the wind lessened and she was able to slow down until she was sprinting and finally walking. Struggling for breath, she pulled the guide lines of the harness, controlled the parachute, and managed to collapse it.

She watched the others as they came down. All but the instructor and Johnny had a problem controlling the chute in the wind. Johnny, Claire thought, had probably controlled everything in his life, all of his life.

'Well done, everyone,' Martin said, as they walked back to the hanger. 'We'll go up in the balloon again in the morning, and in the afternoon I think you'll be ready for the real thing. Go to the canteen, get yourself something to eat, and do something relaxing for the rest of day. You've got a big day tomorrow. See you in the morning at 09:00 sharp,' he shouted, heading towards the next group of trainees.

In the canteen they joined a queue of flyers and ground staff. The choice of main course was meat and potato pie and gravy, or fish and chips with mushy peas. Claire loved fish and chips, but after looking at the greasy batter and thin chips she decided on the pie. She was ravenous – as, it seemed, were Ellen, Johnny and Nick. The four trainees, who Johnny referred to as the A team, had become firm friends after their shared experience. They talked excitedly about the jump, how much they'd enjoyed it, and how they were looking forward to the real thing the next day. When they had finished eating they decided to take the instructor's advice and relax by going to the flicks in Manchester.

The film showing at the Carlton was *Gone With The Wind*. Ellen swooned over Clark Gable as Rhett Butler. Claire, using Eddie's pet name for Captain Mitchell, said, 'He's all right if you like beefcakes. I prefer Leslie Howard.' The boys said they liked Vivien Leigh and Olivia de Havilland equally, so the girls chose Leigh for Nick and de Havilland for Johnny. They were still discussing which of the actresses was the most beautiful when the lights began to fade. A woman in front of them tutted loudly and Ellen giggled.

Johnny bought popcorn and tipped it accidentally, or so he said, down the neck of the tutting woman, which made Ellen giggle even more. Johnny and Nick smoked cigarettes and at the interval bought the girls ice cream.

During the second half of the film, Johnny put his arm around Ellen, catching Claire's shoulder. She looked at Ellen, who was smiling like the cat that had got the cream. Johnny whispered into Ellen's ear and she giggled again, causing the woman in front to turn and glare at her. She said, 'Shush' several times, but Ellen couldn't stop giggling.

When the flick ended they jumped into a taxi. There had been an air raid earlier in the day and the main route out of Manchester was blocked. By the time they got back to Dunham House there was no one in the dining room.

'The kitchen's closed,' the waitress said, as they entered. 'I can make you some sandwiches and there's apple cake left, if you'd like some?'

'That will be lovely,' Claire said. 'Could we also have some tea, please?'

'Yes,' the waitress said. 'If you'd like to go into the sitting room, I'll bring it in as soon as I've cleared the tables in here.' When she and the other waitress arrived with their supper, Johnny made a fuss of helping them, causing them to blush.

The lunch they'd had at Ringway was so filling that the girls weren't hungry. The boys were and devoured the sandwiches, insisting the girls shared the apple cake, which they did. It was a perfect end to an exciting day. When they finished supper they went up to their rooms. Johnny again tried to persuade Ellen to join him for a nightcap, but she wasn't having any of it.

'Nice of you to ask, Johnny, but I think we should all get some sleep. We've got an early start tomorrow. Night night,' she said, going into the bathroom as Claire came out.

Claire had just undressed, put on her pyjamas, and was sitting in bed reading the parachuting instructions when there was a knock on the door. 'Who is it?'

'Nick. Can I come in?'

Claire jumped out of bed and grabbed her dressing gown. Pulling it on, she opened the door. 'What's the matter?'

'Johnny has locked me out of our room. Ellen's in there with him. I can hear them talking.'

'I thought she'd been a long time. You don't think he'll take advantage of her, do you?'

'No. At least I don't think he will. He has done in the past. He sweeps girls off their feet with his charming ways, and a few days later he tires of them and leaves them, breaking their hearts.'

At that moment Ellen came skipping into the bedroom in her towelling robe, with her wash bag in her hand and a towel over her arm. 'Hello, been swapping notes? If you need to know anything, Claire's the girl to ask. There are a couple of things I need to pick her brain about, so if you don't mind,' she said, holding the door open and smiling at Nick.

Claire burst out laughing. 'Sorry, Nick, I think you've had your leg well and truly pulled.'

'I think I have.' Blushing with embarrassment or anger, Claire wasn't sure which, Nick said goodnight and left the girls' room.

'I'm going to sleep, unless you want to talk about tomorrow?' Claire said, taking off her dressing gown and getting into bed again.

'No. I only said that to get rid of Nick.'

'If you're sure?' Ellen nodded. 'Put the light out then, will you?' Claire turned over, pulled her pillow down so it nestled between her chin and her neck and was asleep in seconds.

At breakfast the next day the atmosphere between the boys was frosty. It didn't last long. By the time the car came for them they were talking, and by the time they arrived at the hanger, they were chatting as normal.

The windsock on the control tower had been horizontal the day before, but today it was drooping, which meant it wasn't as windy. Without a gusting ground wind the second jump from the balloon went well for all of them. Afterwards they were taken to another hanger and shown an old fuselage with a hole in the middle.

'This is the size of opening you'll be jumping through, ladies and gentlemen. Do you have any questions?'

'The hole doesn't look big enough for someone wearing a parachute to get through,' Claire said.

'Deceiving, isn't it? But I assure you it is. OK, take a break, eat something, and be back here at two o'clock.

Again they discussed the training over lunch. None of them ate much; they were all too nervous. Claire decided on a sandwich – it would be less to lose if there was turbulence. When they had finished eating they returned to the hanger, put on their parachutes, piled into a light utility truck called a Tilly, and were driven to an outlying runway where they boarded a twin-engine Whitley III.

As the Whitley took off, Claire's stomach churned. A few seconds later she went deaf. She swallowed hard and yawned. Neither action made any difference. Eventually the plane levelled and her ears popped, but all she could hear was the roar of the plane's engines.

Martin beckoned her with his thumb. She put two thumbs up to let him know she was ready. Staggering to the hole at the centre of the fuselage, she took a deep breath – and on Martin's count of three, Claire fell from the plane. Without a strong wind the drop was more enjoyable. Her tummy tightened, as she expected it to, and air whooshed into her mouth and up her nose. She was lifted and dropped, as she had been when she jumped out of the balloon, and the parachute opened. Swinging and falling, she looked down and prepared to land. When she landed it was at a speed she was comfortable with. Without a ground wind to hinder her, she gathered up the chute quickly. The next three practice falls were progressively better. The last, Martin said, was perfect. By the end of the course, Claire was confident that she was good enough to parachute into France. She hoped she was good enough to get the job with the SOE.

'Good work, all of you,' Martin said, when they were back in the hanger.

'I think I speak for all of us when I say we've had a marvellous time, sir,' Johnny said.

Claire nodded. 'We've learned so much. Thank you, sir.'

'Thank you, all of you. Working with young people like yourselves makes my job not only worthwhile, but pleasurable,' he said, shaking each of their hands. 'Now go home and...' They waited for the usual instruction which was *Go to bed, you've got a big day tomorrow*, but instead their instructor said, 'put on your best bibs and tuckers and go out dancing, or whatever it is young people do these days. You've worked hard and deserve some fun.'

They left the hanger chatting and laughing. Claire felt a pang of sadness collecting her hat and coat from her locker. It had been an extraordinary week – and she had enjoyed every minute of it.

'You ready, Claire?' Ellen shouted from the doorway.

'Coming!' she shouted back, as she put on her coat. Pulling on her hat, Claire joined the others at RAF Ringway's main gate. The car was waiting and no sooner had they jumped in than they were speeding though the Cheshire countryside. When they arrived at Dunham they went to the sitting room for tea. No one spoke for some time. It was Johnny who broke the silence.

'Hands up all those who think we should celebrate our last night at a dance in Manchester!'

Claire, pretending her hand was too heavy to lift, said, 'I'm game after dinner.'

'And me, but I'm going to have a bath first,' Ellen said, jumping up.

Claire followed her out. 'See you at dinner, lads.'

Ellen was first in the bathroom, but wasn't long, saying steam made her hair frizzy, so Claire allowed herself to lie back and relax for ten minutes. By the time she had dried herself and returned to the bedroom, Ellen was dressed and brushing her hair into curls that framed her face. At the back she had twiddled her hair into curly-rolls and pinned them in the nape of her neck. She looked pretty.

'Do you want me to do your hair for you, Claire?'

'That would be lovely, Ellen. I'm not much good with hair.'

'Sit here,' Ellen said, taking a brush and comb from the dressing table.

Claire sat on the stool and looked in the mirror. 'I'm useless, but my sister Ena has a real knack with hair. She does everyone's hair in the factory where she works.'

'She isn't a hairdresser then?'

'No, she'd have liked to have been, but mum and dad couldn't afford to buy all the equipment that's needed, or keep her while she did an apprenticeship, so she became a nanny.'

Ellen turned her nose up. 'Rather be a hairdresser than a nanny. Right,' she said, 'we've got to wait for the Amami lotion to dry. Get dressed and I'll brush it out just before we go down.'

Claire had only brought two dresses, which she had intended to save until she got to London, but this was a special occasion. She took her blue dress with a full skirt from a hanger in the wardrobe and put it on. Buckling the belt at her waist reminded her of Eddie and she wished she was there. Claire stepped into her navy shoes and took the matching handbag and her white gloves from the drawer.

'Let's see if your hair's set,' Ellen said, standing behind the stool. Claire sat down and watched Ellen take out rows of Kirby grips. She took the comb and lightly combed through Claire's hair, loosening the waves and pushing them back into place. Then she wound the length round her fingers and pinned it into a long roll that ended behind her ears. 'How's that?'

Looking in the mirror, Claire turned her head from left to right. She leaned forward. 'It's the best it has ever looked,' she said, jumping up and hugging Ellen.

The two new friends stood side by side and looked in the mirror. Ellen wore a pink and green floral frock with white shoes, handbag and gloves, and Claire wore blue with white and navy accessories. 'Come on, Claire, we'll knock 'em dead looking like this,' Ellen said, and arm in arm they went down to dinner.

Johnny and Nick stood up as they entered the dining room. 'Excuse me, ladies,' Johnny said. 'My friend and I are waiting for two girls. You don't happen to have seen them anywhere?' Ellen slapped him playfully on the shoulder and sat down. The others followed.

It was noticeable during the meal that Johnny was sweet on Ellen, because he directed everything he said to her. And Ellen clearly liked him, because she batted her eyelashes and looked serious, or amused, by everything he said. Their mutual attraction didn't abate when they were in the taxi on the way to Manchester, or in the dance hall.

'Would you do me the honour of this dance,

miss?' Johnny said, bowing with a flourish at Ellen's side. She took his arm and, as he led her to the dance floor, looked over her shoulder and giggled at Claire.

Clearly unimpressed by his friend's flamboyant gestures, Nick raised his eyes to the heavens. 'Would you like to dance, Claire?'

'I'd love to,' she said, and took Nick's arm.

On the dance floor it was obvious to Claire that Ellen had drawn the short straw. Nick was by far the better dancer of the two men.

'Johnny had his heart set on Ellen the second he saw her,' Nick said, as they danced.

'Are you sure it was his heart?' Claire said.

'No I'm not, that's the trouble. But what Johnny wants Johnny gets.' There was a bitter edge to Nick's voice.

'You should have asked Ellen to dance before Johnny did. She'd have said yes.'

'Would she? I wonder,' he sighed. 'Claire, I am sorry. Dancing with one beautiful woman and talking about another is impolite. What must you think?'

'That you like my friend?'

'Is it that obvious?'

'Yes. It wasn't when the four of us first met, but it is now.'

'Still, I've got the better dancer,' Nick said.

Looking across the room at Johnny and Ellen, Claire said, 'That's exactly what I thought. About you, I mean.' They both laughed. 'I appreciate the compliment, but when this dance ends we're going to go back to the table. Then, when Johnny and Ellen have finished dancing, you're going to ask

Ellen to dance.'

Nick's forehead wrinkled in an exaggerated frown. 'I feel awful now. Are you sure you don't mind?'

'Why should I? We're all friends.' The music came to an end, and the band leader announced the band was taking a fifteen minute break. 'Blow!' Claire said. 'We'll have to go with plan B.' Nick looked puzzled. 'You must be first to buy the drinks. That way Johnny won't get the chance to show off by flashing his money about. Then, when the band strikes up again, ask Ellen to dance before Johnny gets the chance.'

'What about you?'

'Don't worry about me. I won't sit at the table like a wallflower. Johnny is bound to ask me to dance. If he doesn't I'll ask him.'

'And you're not offended?'

'Just get the drinks,' Claire said, linking her arm through Nick's and jokingly dragging him back to the table. 'Gin and orange, thanks Nick,' she said, as soon as Johnny and Ellen were near enough to hear.

'Yes, of course. Ellen? Johnny?'

'Gin and orange for me too, please,' Ellen said.

'I'll come with you, old chap, help you carry them,' Johnny said. Putting his arm round Nick's shoulder, he looked back at Ellen and winked.

The dancing plot succeeded. Nick and Ellen danced the first couple of dances in the second set and Claire danced with Johnny. Johnny got the next round of drinks and they chatted while they drank. They danced some more and talked some more – and by the end of the night they were all pleasantly merry and danced off their feet.

Back at Dunham House Ellen and Claire gave in and went to Johnny and Nick's room for a nightcap. They discussed Paratroopers' Wings, and admitted to each other that they would love to wear them. They talked about spending Christmas with their families, and Nick said perhaps they could meet up in the New Year. Claire didn't say so – she didn't want to put a damper on their last night together – but it would be impossible for her to see anyone from Dunham again until the war was over – and perhaps not then. The SOE manual stipulated that, even if agents bumped into one another in the street, they must walk on without acknowledging each other.

The atmosphere was subdued at breakfast. Even Johnny was quiet. It was sad saying goodbye. They hadn't known each other long, but working together so intensely, they had become close. Claire looked at each of her friends and hoped that, wherever they were destined to go, they would be safe.

At Manchester's Piccadilly station, Ellen gave Claire her address. 'Drop me a line sometime,' she said. Claire lowered her eyes. She wished she could give Ellen her address, but… 'I won't ask for yours. I'd probably lose it anyway,' she said. Claire hugged her friend goodbye. 'Let me know you're safe, if you can,' Ellen whispered.

Claire's train was first to come into the station, so after hugging each of her friends she picked up her suitcase and said goodbye.

'Keep an eye on my bag, Johnny. I'll carry Claire's case for her,' Nick said, taking the case out of Claire's hand.

'That's very chivalrous of you, Nick.'

'I have an ulterior motive, I'm afraid. I was wondering if we could write to each other?'

'I can't, Nick, I'm sorry.'

'What, not even as pen-pals?' Claire shook her head. 'Take my address anyway and perhaps when the war's over we could go dancing again, just you and me?'

'This is my train,' Claire said, and began to walk faster. Nick put the case in the train and helped her up the steps. 'Thank you, Nick,' she said, and as she bent down to kiss him on the cheek, he turned his face and their lips met. Claire heard a whistle blow somewhere in the distance, the train clunked and started to move, and she broke away from him. 'I think you'd better go if you don't want to end up in Rugby.'

'If that's where you're going I shouldn't mind,' he said. Slamming the door on the moving train, Nick ran along the platform until the train picked up speed. The last Claire saw of him, he was waving in a cloud of steam.

Claire closed the window and found a seat a couple of carriages along. After putting her case on the overhead rack, she sat down and thought about Nick's kiss. She could have sworn he was sweet on Ellen. He was when they first met, but the kiss he'd just given her said something quite different. She hadn't thought about Nick in a romantic way until now. A smile played on her lips.

CHAPTER SIX

'Anyone home?'

'Claire? What on earth? Thomas, our Claire's here. Why didn't you let us know you were coming?' Claire's mother said. Wiping her hands on her pinafore, she crossed the kitchen with outstretched arms. 'Bess would have fetched you from the station.'

'Bess has enough to do up at the Hall. Besides, it was a last minute thing.' Claire dropped her suitcase and hugged her mother. 'A few of us were given forty-eight hours leave for good behaviour,' she joked, 'so I thought I'd surprise you.'

'You've certainly done that,' Claire's father said. 'Come here girl, let's have a look at you.'

Claire threw her arms around her father. 'Oooooo I've missed you, Dad. And you, Mam.'

'We've missed you too,' her mother said. 'Go through to the front room, it's warmer in there. Top the fire up, Thomas, the girl must be perished,' she called. 'Tea's almost ready. I'll bring it in shortly.'

'Thanks, Mam.' Claire followed her father through to the small sitting room with its familiar dark wood table and sideboard and comfortable old settee and armchairs. 'It's lovely to be home,' she said to her father.

'It's good to have you home, love. Your sisters will be pleased to see you. Ena's up at Foxden Hall helping Bess,' he said, adding a log to the fire. 'She'll be back for her tea, I expect. If not we'll go up there, see Bess at the same time. But first I want to hear about you. From your letters you seem to be enjoying the WAAF. Are you still learning French?'

'Yes, German too.' A frown replaced the look of interest on her father's face. 'They need German speakers to translate what Luftwaffe pilots say to each other, and what they say to their control room in Germany.'

Smiling again, her father shook his head and lit a cigarette. 'Who'd have thought when you were teaching young Franek English and he was teaching you Polish that you'd end up being able to speak foreign languages well enough to translate them.'

'I haven't got the posting yet. I might not be good enough.' Claire didn't want to lie to her father, which she would have to do if she didn't change the subject. 'Do you see anything of the Polish lads that were billeted in the village?'

'No, they're on the aerodrome now. There's all sorts up there; Australians, New Zealanders, Jamaicans, Canadians--'

'Tea's ready,' Claire's mum called, bringing in a tray. She put the teapot, milk jug, cups and saucers and a plate of tinned salmon sandwiches on the table. 'We'll start without Ena, she won't mind. She often has her tea up at the Hall with Bess and the land girls,' she said. 'Tuck in, Claire. You look as if you need feeding up, girl.'

'It's all the training we do, Mam.'

While they ate their tea, Claire's mother told her how hard her sister Bess was working. 'It's a big job, turning the estate into arable land.'

'She's not doing it single-handed,' her father said, laughing.

Claire's mother tutted. 'Course not. There's a lot of land girls work with her. Bess is in charge, of course. We thought she'd miss teaching, regret coming back, didn't we Thomas?' Claire's father nodded. 'But we needn't have worried.'

'With the farm work and turning a wing of Foxden Hall into rooms for recuperating servicemen, she's too busy to miss her old life in London,' Thomas Dudley said.

'Bess wrote to me, told me Tom came home after Dunkirk.'

'He wasn't well,' her father said, 'but Bess had him helping up at the Hall and it did him a power of good. He's gone back now.'

'Probably to France.' Lily Dudley drained her cup and stood up. 'I'll make more tea,' she said, reaching into the middle of the table and snatching the teapot as if it offended her.

'With Tom overseas and Margaret in London, you're just the tonic your mum needs,' Claire's father said, when her mother was safely out of earshot. 'How long can you stay?'

'Forty-eight hours.' Claire saw the disappointment in her father's eyes. 'Sorry it isn't longer, Dad.'

'Oh well… Forty-eight hours is better than nothing.'

'What's better than nothing?' Ena shouted from the hall.

'Come in and see,' her father called back to her.

Ena opened the living room door and squealed. Leaping up, Claire met her youngest sister in the middle of the room. They hugged each other and danced round in a circle. 'What are you doing here?'

'I've come home to see you, skinny,' Claire said, tickling her sister.

*

That evening, Claire told Ena about RAF Morecambe and Coltishall, her best friend Eddie, and about training with the Canadian captain. She told her how she had hated him when they first met, but liked him better after he'd given her a good report.

Ena told Claire that she was doing work for the government. 'What I do is called *sensitive* work,' she whispered. 'I had to sign to say I wouldn't talk about it.'

Claire laughed. 'I thought you worked in the factory?'

'I do!' Ena said, indignantly. 'But what I do is secret!' Red-faced, Ena stormed out of the room and ran upstairs. Claire heard the bedroom door slam.

Claire ran up after her. 'I'm sorry, Ena. I wasn't laughing at you, or at your job. It was the way you said it. I thought you were joking.' She tried the doorknob, but the door didn't open. 'Let me in, Ena!' Damn, she had only been home a few hours and already she and her sister had fallen out. 'Ena?' She tapped on the door. 'Please let me in, so I can say I'm sorry.' She put her ear to the door and heard Ena blow her nose. 'I might not be able to get home for a long time. Please don't let's fall out.'

She heard the key turn in the lock. 'I'm sorry,' Claire said, as she entered, 'I really am.'

Ena sniffed and pushed her hanky up her sleeve. 'What do you mean you might not get home for a long time?'

'I've got an interview coming up and if I get through it, I'll be doing sensitive work. I understand why you can't talk about what you're doing, because I can't either.' Ena rolled her eyes. 'I know what you think – that I'm only saying it – but it's true. I'm going to be listening to what German pilots say to each other and translating it to English,' which wasn't far from the truth – and was what she'd told her father.

'Mine isn't that important. I just make thin wires. I solder the ends into a tiny box that fits into a big machine. The boss and his assistant take my box of wires down south to where the machine is – and fit them on site. None of the other girls can do the job. It's ever so fiddly.'

'If it's labelled sensitive,' Claire said, 'it's important war work.'

'I suppose.' Ena shrugged, smiling. 'But we're not at work now. It's Christmas!' she shouted. 'Come on, let's go down, it's cold up here.'

'Friends?' Claire said, holding out her hand.

'Friends,' Ena said. Taking Claire's hand, Ena let her older sister lead her from the bedroom.

Christmas morning after church, Claire, Ena and their mother and father walked up to Foxden Hall. The Dudley women went to the kitchen to help Mrs Hartley, Foxden's house keeper and cook, to prepare Christmas lunch for the land girls and evacuated children.

An hour later Mrs Hartley and Claire's mother carried two large chickens into the main hall – and Claire and Ena brought in the vegetables. After lunch the little girls played with dolls that Father Christmas had brought them and the boys, wrapped up in winter coats, hats and gloves, went outside to build a snowman.

Not long after they had gone, they came crashing back through the front door. An Army lorry had ditched at the bottom of Shaft Hill on the Lowarth to Woodcote Road.

Bess and one of the land girls dashed off on foot, while Claire's father and Mr Porter, who was Foxden's estate manager before the war, followed on a tractor. Claire and Ena cleared the tables while their mother boiled water to make tea and Mrs Hartley began buttering bread for sandwiches.

The soldiers arrived as Mrs Hartley and Claire's mother were laying the table with chicken and ham sandwiches, fruitcake and Christmas puddings. Ena and Claire brought in pots of tea, cups and saucers, and giggled when the soldiers flirted with them.

While the soldiers ate their meal the children sang a selection of Christmas carols, recited poems and nursery rhymes, and danced jigs. The entertainment ended with everyone on their feet singing "Give A Little Whistle", followed by "Hands, Knees and Boomps-a-Daisy". The soldiers, clapping their hands when they should have been slapping their knees, made the children laugh. Coincidentally they conquered the moves at exactly the same time and everyone cheered. Then, after taking theatrical bows, all but one of the soldiers returned to their seats.

The sergeant stood at the top of the table and looked around the room until there was hush. 'On behalf of myself and the lads, I would like to thank you all. It's been a long time since any of us have sat down with friends to eat. And, because we're going overseas in the New Year, it may be a long time until we do it again. I think I speak for every soldier here when I say we will never forget what you did for us today. The next time we sit down with friends, wherever it is and whenever it is, we will remember today and every one of you.' He looked at his fellow soldiers. 'Look sharp, lads, it's time we were on our way.'

The soldiers pushed back their chairs and stood to attention. As they made their way to the door they shook the hands of the children nearest to them and saluted those who were too far away. At the door they turned as one and saluted Bess and the women of the land army, who were gathered around the piano.

'Time we made a move too,' Claire's father said when the soldiers had gone.

The Dudley family – except Bess, who lived at Foxden Hall – said goodbye and put on their coats. The walk home was pleasant. Claire and Ena, arm in arm, followed their parents along the lane leaving their footprints in the newly laid snow.

The following morning Claire was packing when Bess arrived. 'Knock, knock,' she said, opening the bedroom door. 'I've come to take you to the station.' Claire spun round in surprise. 'What time's your train?'

'Twelve o'clock, I think. The man in the Enquiries Office couldn't say for sure, with it being Boxing Day. He said they were expecting troop trains, so at least the trains are running.'

'Good.' Bess looked at her watch. 'We've got plenty of time then.'

'But I've booked Mr Crane's taxi to take me to the station.'

'I telephoned from the Hall and cancelled it. I

think he was pleased not to have to turn out in this weather. Besides, I want to pay you back for helping yesterday. One good turn deserves another. And I want to take you. We can have a chin-wag on the way and you can tell me all about this trainer chap you're sweet on. I'll take your case down, shall I?' Bess left the room without waiting for a reply.

Ena must have told Bess about Mitch. What made her think she was sweet on him, Claire wondered? By the time Claire arrived downstairs Bess had stowed her suitcase in the boot of Lady Foxden's Rover and Ena and her parents were waiting by the front door. 'Your coat,' her father said, taking it from the hook in the hall and helping Claire into it. 'Let me take your bag for you. Goodness, it's heavy,' he said. 'What have you got in here, Lady Foxden's jewels?'

'Only books, I'm afraid.'

'You're as bad as our Bess with your books.' He put Claire's satchel on the back seat of the car. 'Come home and see us soon, love,' her father said, opening the passenger door.

'I will.' Putting her arms round her father, Claire held him tightly and kissed his cheek. Then she kissed her mother, promising to write soon, and hugged her younger sister. 'Keep up the "sensitive" work,' she whispered. 'I'm proud of you, our Ena.'

'Be careful,' Ena said.

Claire winked. 'I always am,' she said, dropping onto the passenger seat. Bess put the car into gear and drove into the lane. Claire waved out of the window until they turned onto the main Lowarth road.

It started to snow as they pulled up at the

entrance to Rugby Station. Taking her bag from the car, Claire said, 'There's no need for you to come up to the platform with me. You get back while the snow isn't too heavy. I can manage both bags.' She put out her hand to take her suitcase, which Bess had fetched from the boot.

'It's no trouble.' Looking up, Bess said, 'The snow won't get heavier – there's too much blue sky. Besides, I want to wave you off.' She headed off along the tunnel leading to the platforms. 'Come on.'

'Bess – hang on, will you?'

'What is it?'

'I might as well tell you. You'll know anyway, when I buy my ticket.'

'Tell me what?'

'I'm not going back to Coltishall. I'm going to London.'

'London? Why?'

'I can't say. It's a bit hush-hush.'

'Is it to do with the RAF Task Force, or whatever it's called, in France? Is that why you've learnt French?'

'Not exactly. The Advanced Strike Force has disbanded, changed--'

'What then? Claire, you're worrying me. What have you got yourself into?'

'I haven't got myself into anything. Why do you always-- Sorry.' She thought carefully about how much she could tell Bess without causing her to worry even more. Worse still, go home and tell her father. 'I told Dad I was going to work as a translator, which is true. The thing is, translating is only a small part of the job.'

Frown lines appeared on Bess's forehead. 'What does the bigger part of the job entail?'

'If I tell you, you must give me your word that you won't tell anyone.'

Bess thought for a long minute. 'You have my word.'

'It's top secret. I shouldn't be talking about it, but if I'm not able to write home for a while, and Mam and Dad start fretting, I was hoping you'd cover for me if you understood how important the job is. Well?'

'Of course I will.'

Claire bit her bottom lip. She shouldn't be telling her sister, but she'd said too much now to go back. 'Some people to do with the government came up to Coltishall and interviewed me because I speak French.'

'So you are going to France?'

'No! I don't know. I've been asked to go for an interview.'

'In London?'

'Yes. And if they like me, if they think I'd be suitable, I'm in with a chance. But there's a rigorous training programme to get through first, and endless intelligence tests, which I probably won't pass. But,' Claire said, 'if I get through it all and they ask me to go to France, I will.' Bess smiled, but Claire could see worry in her sister's eyes. She put her hand on Bess's arm. 'You do understand, don't you?'

'If you've thought it through, and you're aware of the dangers of the job… You are, aren't you?' Claire took a deep breath and nodded. 'Then I understand.'

'Thank you,' Claire whispered.

'So come on then,' Bess said, 'you don't want miss your train, do you?'

'I didn't want to lie to Dad,' Claire said, as they reached the platform. 'He knows I'm going to be translating German military conversations. I just didn't tell him it might be in France. You won't tell him, will you?'

'Good God, no! He's worried enough about Tom going back to France and Margaret living in London. I don't intend to add to his worries. It doesn't stop me from worrying though.'

'But there's no need.' Claire threw her arms around her sister. 'If I go – and it's a big if – I shall only be observing and reporting back, so there's nothing to worry about. Anyway, I haven't got the job yet. I might not pass the tests.'

The train came into the station billowing steam. 'Well, this is it! I mean, for the time being,' Bess said, moving to the edge of the platform.

'Yes, for the time being.' Claire put down her case, took her handkerchief from her pocket and wiped her eyes. 'I'll write to you from London.'

'The train will leave without you if you don't get on. Here,' Bess opened the door and Claire threw her case in. 'Whatever happens, you'll let me know?'

'I will,' she shouted, boarding. The platform attendant blew his whistle and Claire waved goodbye to her oldest sister.

Suitcase in one hand and bag in the other, Claire struggled past dozens of servicemen standing in the crowded corridor smoking. She looked in each compartment. Every seat was taken, so in a fog of cigarette smoke she dropped her suitcase and sat on it. Looking over the ledge of the window, she gazed out. The snow-covered fields of Warwickshire, and then Northamptonshire, disappeared from view as quickly as they appeared. The rhythm of the train was comforting and Claire closed her eyes.

'Excuse me?' Claire sat up with a start when someone tapped her on the shoulder. 'Would you like my seat?' a middle-aged man in a smart suit asked.

Stumbling to her feet, Claire looked around to get her bearings. 'If you're sure?' she said, by which time the man was hauling her suitcase onto the overhead rack of the nearest compartment.

'I need to stretch my legs. Besides, I shall be leaving the train soon,' he said, picking up his briefcase.

Grateful to the man, Claire wriggled down in the seat, put her head on the backrest and closed her eyes. She woke when she was tapped on the shoulder again, this time by a porter at Euston.

CHAPTER SEVEN

Pushing though crowds of people clamouring to board the train that she had just left, Claire inched her way along the platform. She sighed, overwhelmed by the size of Euston Station and the number of people. She passed a couple of girls talking loudly about their sweethearts going off to their regiments. One of them burst into tears and her friend tried to console her: 'He promised to come back and marry you, Maisie. Don't cry now. Upsetting yourself like this isn't good for the baby.' Maisie looked at her friend, her eyes wide with incredulity, and howled. Claire looked briefly at the girl's stomach. If he's coming back to marry her before the child's born, he'd better only be going away for the weekend, she thought.

A train came in and Claire was almost knocked over by women of all ages running across the platform. She turned to see servicemen waving out of the windows and doors. There were more tears, this time of joy. On a platform further along, girls were dancing round excitedly as another train came in. Claire turned away and, weaving this way and that, finally left the platform.

The concourse was no less crowded. In a sea of Navy, Air Force blue and Army brown, it looked as if half the armed forces were coming to, or leaving, London. Claire looked around and spotted the sign for the Underground. Moving against the tide, she pushed her way across the concourse. She suddenly felt very lonely and wondered when she would next see Eddie. They had been together since the first day at Morecambe. If Eddie had passed her French oral exam the SOE might have recruited her. She would have loved to have told Eddie about the SOE; her father too. She had never kept anything from her dad before. None of the Dudley sisters did. He was easy to talk to. He understood things, where her mother often didn't. She wanted to tell him that all her hard work had paid off, make him proud of her, but she couldn't. Claire bit her bottom lip. She shouldn't have told Bess, but she knew that while Bess wouldn't tell anyone, she would say the right things to put their parents' minds at rest if she wasn't able to write home. Claire smiled. Bess had always been there for her and her sisters. Always thinking and caring about other people. Claire wished her older sister could find someone to care for her, love her. If anyone deserved to be loved, Bess did. But she couldn't think about Bess now, or anyone else. Leaning against the wall near the escalator, Claire took the Underground map from her pocket. Reminding herself that she needed to change at Leicester Square for Baker Street, she returned the map and stepped onto the moving stairs.

After travelling south through four stations, Claire left the train and followed the signs for the Bakerloo line. She jumped on the first train to arrive at the platform, checking first that it had Hammersmith on the front. The first stop was Piccadilly Circus, the second Baker Street.

Alighting at Baker Street, Claire felt the nerves on the top of her stomach flapping like a thousand butterflies. She quickly found number 64. It was an imposing five-storey building with rows of windows, one above the other. She focused her mind on the business in hand and, head held high, walked to the door. Lifting the brass knocker, she rapped twice.

The door was opened by a tall slim woman with dark hair that was loosely waved at the front with a small neat bun in the neck. She fingered her spectacles, which were attached to a gold chain around her neck. 'Miss Dudley?' Claire nodded. 'The colonel is expecting you. If you'd like to follow me?'

Colonel Smith's office was on the fourth floor at the end of a long corridor. The woman – his secretary, Claire thought – opened the door without knocking. 'Miss Dudley is here, sir,' she said, and stood back to let Claire pass.

The room was big and square – and cold. It wasn't as smartly decorated as Claire had imagined it would be. Nor was it furnished adequately for someone of a colonel's rank.

'Sit down, Miss Dudley.'

'Thank you, sir.' Claire put her suitcase down by the door, walked across bare floorboards to the colonel's desk, and sat in the only other chair in the room.

'I hope you're not cold. We moved into the building in October,' he said. 'You'd think the basics would have been sorted out by now.' He was clearly annoyed that they hadn't been.

Claire had noticed how cold it was as soon as she entered the room, but said, 'I'm fine, sir.'

'Good.' The colonel looked down briefly at a sheet of paper on his desk, lifted his head and smiled. He seemed different, more relaxed than when she had met him at Coltishall. 'Tell me about yourself, Miss Dudley – about your childhood, your family, where you were born and brought up.'

'My father served with the Royal Mounted Engineers in the last war,' Claire began. 'His regiment built bridges, on horseback. He had five horses killed under him. The last was in 1918, three months before the end of the war. A bullet went through his knee and into his horse's heart. The horse was killed and Dad was invalided out.' The colonel said nothing, so Claire carried on. 'Dad was a wonderful horseman. When his leg healed he got a job as a groom on a country estate called Foxden. I was born there, in an estate worker's cottage.'

'Tell me where you went to school,' the colonel said.

'I went to Woodcote Infant and Junior School in the village down the road from the estate until I was eleven. I passed the Eleven Plus, but my parents couldn't afford to buy the grammar school uniform, so I went to the Central School in Lowarth. That's the nearest town to Foxden.'

'Was it at the Central School that you learned to speak foreign languages?'

A smile threatened. 'No, sir. The Central School only taught English. I learned Polish from a pilot who escaped from Poland and crashed in France. He and his comrades were brought to England by officers of the RAF Advanced Air Strike Force. They had to crash land too, and brought the plane down in a field on the Foxden estate.'

'I can see why that would make you want to join the AASF, but how did you know the Polish pilot?'

'Foxden is a couple of miles from two

Commonwealth aerodromes, Bitteswell and Bruntingthorpe.' The colonel nodded as if he knew both places. 'Franek – that's the name of the pilot who taught me Polish – was billeted with us while they built living quarters at Bitteswell. I taught him English and he taught me Polish – and some German.'

'And French?'

'I didn't start learning French until I joined the WAAF and went to RAF Morecambe. When I was proficient in the language, I was sent to stay with a French family in the North East, before going to RAF Coltishall and taking my oral examination.'

The colonel nodded again and picked up Claire's file. 'Except for joining the WAAF, your life could have been lived in France.' Claire tilted her head and looked at the colonel enquiringly. 'All you need to do is change the name of the country estate, village, town and school, and you have a ready-made French history. We find if operatives base their French covers on their own experiences it's easier to remember. Then, if you are interrogated, it will ring true. But that's for another day.' Colonel Smith stood up and walked to the door. Claire followed. 'Miss Halliday, my personal assistant, will take you to your apartment. If there is anything you need she will be happy to help you.' The colonel opened the door, proffered his hand and, leaning forward, looked into Claire's eyes. 'China Blue.'

'Pardon?'

'Your code name is China Blue.'

'Thank you, sir.' Claire shook his hand, picked up her case, and left with Miss Halliday.

Dusk fell and the wind blowing across Portman Square whipped the last of the winter leaves from the trees. Claire closed the blackout curtains and switched on the light. She sat on the settee and cast her eyes over the small neatly furnished sitting room. She had never lived on her own before and found the silence disconcerting. At home, in the cottage on the Foxden estate, she'd had her parents, brother and sisters – until last year when her second oldest sister Margaret married Bill and went to live in Coventry with his parents, before following him to London. Her younger sister Ena had been in service as a nanny but came back when war was declared and her older brother Tom, who she and her sisters looked up to, joined the Army. And when she joined the WAAF, and was stationed at Morecambe, she shared a room with Eddie; in Coltishall too. Now, for the first time in her life, she was living on her own.

Claire wandered into the kitchen and explored the cupboards. First on the left was home to the iron and ironing board, carpet sweeper and small brush and pan. In the cupboard opposite there were two tins of Danish ham, a tin of spam, and a packet of dried egg. To the left, crockery and the teapot, and to the right, a bowl with four real eggs, a loaf of bread, a bottle of coffee, quarter of tea, and small bag of sugar. The cupboard beneath the sink held pots and pans, and the cold store next to it, a pint of milk and half a pound of butter. Claire was hungry, but didn't fancy tinned meat. She put a little water in a saucepan, put it on the stove and lit the gas. She turned the gas down when the water began to boil, and cracked two eggs into it. Poached eggs on toast would be enough. She filled the kettle, put it on the stove, and while it boiled cut a couple of slices of bread and put them under the grill. While the eggs simmered she turned the bread and made a pot of tea. Then she took the toast from the grill and buttered it, before spooning the eggs onto the plate. Putting her supper on a tray, she returned to the sitting room.

When she had finished eating, Claire took the dishes into the kitchen. Instead of washing them up she was distracted by classical music. She ran to the door, opened it, and stepped out into the hall. The music, louder now, was coming from the floor above.

The door of the flat opposite opened and a girl wearing a bathrobe came out. 'RAF,' she said, tutting. 'Plays that awful noise every night.' The girl ran up the stairs and banged on the door. 'Turn that racket down!' she shouted. She stood with her arms folded. She was about to knock again when the music quietened until it was hardly audible. 'There,' she said, running down to join Claire. 'Now I can hear myself think. I'm Milly,' she said. 'I don't usually mind, but I've got a test tomorrow.' Milly put her hand to the side of her mouth and whispered, 'If I pass I'll be translating Luftwaffe pilots' *gespräche* on the south coast.'

Claire was about to say something congratulatory in German, but thought better of it. 'I'm sure you'll sail through it.'

'Thanks. I'll let you know when I get back in a couple of days.'

'Please do. Good luck,' Claire called after her,

as she disappeared into her flat.

Claire stood for a moment and listened to the sound of the muffled music. She liked it. She liked Milly too, and hoped she would call on her with good news.

The next day Claire strolled down to Oxford Street. Some stores still had Christmas decorations in the windows, others were preparing for the January sales, and a couple were bravely advertising New Season and Spring Fashions. She shivered. It was still winter, much too cold to be thinking about spring jackets and short sleeved dresses. She went into Selfridges to get out of the cold. In the main entrance was a huge framed photograph of the famous signature window that was smashed when the store was hit by a high explosive bomb and several incendiaries in September 1940. The damage to Selfridges was substantial. John Lewis, further along Oxford Street, had been completely destroyed.

On the way home she bought more eggs, half a pound of cheese, and a jar of pickle. She fancied a cheese and pickle sandwich for lunch and an omelette with a few chips for supper. As potatoes weren't rationed she bought two pounds.

Back at the apartment Claire made a cup of tea, took a sheet of paper and a pencil from a drawer in the sideboard, and settled down to work on her French cover story, which she had begun in Cullercoats when she stayed with the Marron family. At the top of the page she wrote her code name, China Blue. Several young men had remarked on her blue eyes, but fancy Colonel Smith noticing. I bet he was a charmer in his day, Claire thought, and she chuckled. Underneath she wrote Claire, and then LeBlanc – White was her mother's maiden name. She added the names of her parents: Thomas and Lily; her father's job: groom; and the names and ages of two sisters: Élisabeth, thirteen and Marguèrite, twelve. If they were still at school she didn't have to invent jobs for them.

She was born and brought up on a farm just outside Tours and went to school in Tours itself. She added the names Mélanie Rolland and her brother Éric as friends. Reading through what she had written, she realised it wasn't enough, but it was a start. She left the piece of paper on the table to come back to later and stood up. A chill rippled down her back and she shivered. Stretching, she went over to the window and looked across Portman Square. It was getting dark; taxis and buses already had their sidelights on. Pulling the blackout curtains, she felt her way along the wall to the modern standard lamp and flicked it on. It shed a soft light.

She shook out her shoulders and, feeling cold, fetched a box of Swan Vesta matches from the kitchen, struck one and put it to the paper and sticks at the base of the laid fire in the small grate. Her stomach rumbled and she glanced at the clock. It had gone four and she hadn't eaten since breakfast. While the fire took hold she sliced and buttered a couple of pieces of bread and put them on a place with a wedge of cheddar and a spoonful of pickle.

She had just begun to eat her belated lunch when the telephone rang. It was the first time anyone had telephoned her and she looked at the thing for several seconds before answering it. 'Hello? Yes, this is Claire. Hello, Miss Halliday. Yes, I'm fine. I went for a walk along Oxford Street earlier and bought a few things on the way back. I hope it was all right to go out?' Claire held her breath... 'Oh good,' she said, relieved. She listened carefully to what Colonel Smith's P.A. told her and when she'd finished said, 'Nine o'clock tomorrow morning. I'll be ready. Goodbye.' Claire put the telephone's receiver back on its cradle and took a sip of her tea. It was cold. 'Oh my God!' Somewhere between wanting to scream with excitement and feeling more nervous than she had ever felt before, she went to the kitchen and made another pot of tea. On her way back she took the folder the SOE had given her from the drawer, sat down and read through the file labelled "Intelligence Training". On the first page in capital letters it said: *DO NOT TELL ANYONE WHERE YOU ARE GOING.*

CHAPTER EIGHT

Claire was waiting on the steps of the apartment building when the car taking her to Beaulieu pulled up. The driver took her suitcase and opened the nearside rear door. While he stowed her case in the boot, Claire threw her handbag and gas mask into the car and dropped onto the back seat. 'Argh!' she squealed. 'Captain Mitchell? I'm – I'm sorry, sir,' she stuttered. Her cheeks crimson with embarrassment, Claire gazed at her belongings wedged between the seat and the captain's right thigh. 'I didn't--'

'No damage done, Miss Dudley, though it might be worth remembering I'm not the enemy,' Captain Mitchell said, laughing. He took hold of Claire's gas mask as she made a grab for it, and let go of it at the same time as she did. 'Stalemate!' Captain Mitchell said. They both laughed. 'After you.'

Claire carefully moved her belongings from the captain's legs.

'Did you enjoy the parachute training, Miss Dudley?' Captain Mitchell asked, as they began their journey through London.

Claire thought it odd that he didn't address her by her rank, but then she wasn't with the WAAF now. 'I did. I was nervous in the beginning, but after the first jump I enjoyed it.' Remembering the feeling of excitement, she said, 'If I'm honest, I loved it, Captain Mitchell.'

'I knew you would, Miss Dudley.' Claire sat back in her seat, surprised and delighted that the captain had that much faith in her. 'Would it be okay if I call you Claire?'

'Yes, sir.' She felt her cheeks colour again.

'And I'm Alain, but my friends call me Mitch.'

'Alain? You pronounced it the French way.'

'C'est la façon dont ma mère se prononce. Je suis Canadien Français. Mes grands-parents maternels sont Français.'

The captain is testing me, she thought. Right, you clever... "'That is the way my mother pronounces it. I am French Canadian. My maternal grandparents are French?'"

'Well done, Claire. A perfect translation.'

'Your pronunciation and accent were perfect, so it wasn't difficult.'

'Don't be so modest. Are you as proficient in German?'

'No. I'd never be able to convince a German national that I was German, because of the grammar, but I'd be able to understand everything he or she said. The German language is easy to learn, but the grammar is difficult. If you don't get the sentence structure right, a German would know you weren't a citizen immediately.' Captain Mitchell nodded that he understood. 'What about your father? Is he Canadian?'

No, my father's parents are Scort'ish, from Glassgee.'

Claire laughed. 'Your French accent is better than your Scottish, sir.'

'Mitch.'

'Mitch. It feels odd calling you by your nickname, with you being a captain.'

'Until we get to Hampshire, I'm just plain old Mitch.'

Not plain, or old, Claire thought. Now he wasn't barking orders his voice sounded rich and smooth and his eyes were a soft blue-grey, not slate as she had first thought. She felt her cheeks redden and she looked out of the window at the River Thames. They were crossing Hammersmith Bridge.

'Excuse me, sir?' the driver said, some time later. 'We're almost at the halfway point. Would you like to stretch your legs?'

'Good idea, Tim. Pull over at the next pub, will you? Claire, would you like a cup of tea or coffee, use the ladies' bathroom, perhaps?'

'I'd love a cup of tea.'

'The Highwayman, sir,' Tim said, pulling up outside an old roadside inn. He jumped out of the driver's seat and opened Claire's door while Mitch let himself out. 'They do a good pint of mild, sir, if you don't fancy coffee.' With a wry smile, Tim closed Claire's door.

'Sounds good. You're welcome to join us, Tim.'

'Thank you, sir, but my mate is the chef here. I thought I'd go round to the kitchen and see him. I'll be back at the car before you're ready to leave.'

'Okay.' Mitch opened the door of the Highwayman for Claire to enter and followed her in. 'Wow!' He ducked, missing the carved lintel above the door by half an inch. 'I guess your British highwaymen weren't very tall.' In the porch of the old inn, Mitch's eyes widened in surprise at the uneven walls and low knotty wooden beams. 'So this is what they call oldie worldie, huh?'

'It is. My dad and brother's local, in the village near to where we live, has beams like this – although they're not as low and the pub isn't as smart.' Admiring the heavy oak furniture, Claire made her way to a table by the window overlooking a stream. 'Shall we sit here?'

'Sure. I'll get the drinks. What would you like?' Mitch asked, already on his way to the bar.

'Just tea, please.'

When he returned it was with a pint of dark beer. The waitress followed with the tea and two menus, giving one to Claire and leaving one on the table for Mitch. 'I thought you might like something to eat.' Looking at his menu, Mitch took a long drink of his beer. 'I like the sound of the ploughman's lunch. How about you?'

'It looks good. I'd like it too.'

Mitch looked over to the bar where the waitress stood talking to the barmaid. He put his hand up and the waitress came at once. 'Two ploughman's lunches, and could we get some meat with them?'

'We have ham on the menu, sir. I'm sure chef will add a couple of slices to your lunch.'

'Thank you, miss. Ham on the side for two,' Mitch said.

Claire looked out of the window at the small stream. It was so clear she could see the pebbles on the riverbed. 'I was surprised when Miss Halliday said a car was picking me up. It isn't usual for military personnel of my rank to be driven. We usually do the driving.'

'I guess it isn't. I don't always go down by car, because of the petrol. I jump on a train, but Tim had to go down to pick up some of the top brass and take them back to London, so I bummed a ride. And as I live round the corner from you on Portman Square, I mentioned to Vera Halliday that we had worked together at Coltishall, and suggested I offered you a lift.' Mitch smiled. 'I thought it might make up for pushing you so hard during your training.'

'It has, I assure you.'

They ate in relative silence and when they had finished, Mitch went to the bar to pay the bill and Claire went to the ladies'. When she arrived at the car, Tim was sitting in the driver's seat reading the newspaper. As soon as he saw Claire he folded the paper, dropped it on the passenger seat and put on his cap. 'Nice lunch?' he asked, jumping out and opening Claire's door.

She nodded. 'Lovely, thank you. Did you have anything to eat?'

Tim raised his eyebrows. 'Fresh bread – still warm, it was – and a couple of thick slices of ham,' he whispered conspiratorially.

Mitch came out of the pub and jumped into the car. Okay, let's go! Next stop *the school*.' He took a handful of folders from his briefcase and for the next hour read a variety of documents and a couple of letters. When he had finished reading he sat back in his seat and looked out of the window. 'We're getting close, Tim, aren't we?'

'Yes, sir, another ten minutes.'

From the second she got in the car Claire had been itching to ask Mitch about the training. She'd been with him for three hours and hadn't mentioned it. If she didn't ask him now, it would be too late. 'Can I ask you about the intelligence training, Mitch?'

'You can ask,' he said, his eyes sparkling, 'but I can't tell you.'

'I understand,' Claire said, wishing she hadn't

said anything. As the car pulled up outside the house, Tim leapt out and took the cases from the boot. 'Thank you, Tim.'

'My pleasure, miss.'

Claire turned to Alain Mitchell. 'Well, this is it,' she said, grinning nervously. 'Thank you for the lift, Captain Mitchell.'

'My pleasure, Miss Dudley.' They both laughed.

Picking up her case, Claire walked towards the front door. 'Miss Dudley?' She turned to see Alain Mitchell at her side. 'As an English WAAF, you speak and understand German, but as a French girl you only speak and understand French. Remember that. That you understand German will work to your advantage. But if anyone speaks to you in German while you are here, no way must you let them know you understand what they are saying. Right?'

'Right! Thank you, sir!' She daren't watch the captain walk away. She was too excited, too nervous. She needed time to compose herself, so she focussed her attention on the beautiful gardens. The lawns were short and neat – what her dad would call manicured – and beyond them she could see the River Beaulieu sparkling in the sun. She would explore the grounds and the river when she had time, but now she needed to sign in at the SOE Finishing School.

On her first morning, Claire was taken to meet Olivia the makeup artist. Olivia showed her ways of changing her appearance. She gave her a pair of reading glasses and a scarf. 'The glasses aren't a strong prescription, so they won't hurt your eyes, but if anyone puts them on to check they're authentic, they'll know they are.' Claire slipped them on. 'Now put the scarf on over your hair and tie it at the nape of your neck instead of under your chin,' Olivia said. 'You'll be surprised how different you look.' Claire did as she was instructed. 'Now let's add lipstick. What colour do you usually wear?'

'Dusky rose, sometimes a deeper pink.'

'Good.' Olivia took a lipstick from her makeup case. 'Look up. We'll see what this looks like.' Claire lifted her face, made her lips taut, and Olivia applied a maroon-coloured lipstick. 'What do you think?' she said, holding a mirror up so Claire could look at herself.

'Good Lord. I wouldn't have believed that by making a few changes I could look so different.' She looked to the left, and then the right. 'I don't wear glasses, so that's an obvious change, but with the scarf worn this way I look quite sophisticated.'

Olivia untied the scarf at the back and tied it at the front. 'And now?'

Claire laughed. 'Wearing the scarf like this, with the dark lipstick, I look much older.'

'It's amazing what a hat, or a different hairstyle, can do to change your appearance. Hats are provided by London, but if you need any help with your hair come and see me again before you leave,' Olivia said. 'I'll show you how to dress your hair in a couple of styles that you can do quickly yourself.' Before Claire had time to ask Olivia more on the subject of her hair, she heard the door open.

'And a change of character will make an even bigger difference,' a man trilled, as he entered the room.

'Claire, this is Billy. He's an actor and he's here to help you change your voice.'

'Voice is only part of it, my dear, as well you know,' he said, rolling his eyes good-naturedly at Olivia. 'A change of voice is not sustainable without a personality to go with it.' He pursed his lips. 'How good is your memory, Claire?'

'Pretty good,' she said modestly.

'Excellent, darling. Now…' Billy drummed the fingers of his right hand on his chin and looked to the heavens for inspiration. 'I want you to think of a situation, something that happened recently, that made you feel young and carefree.' Claire thought for a moment, and then nodded. 'Right! Tell me your name and tell me something mundane that you have to do. Then tell me what you would rather be doing – and it must be with a young and carefree air.'

'My name is Claire LeBlanc, monsieur. I am going to the market to buy vegetables.' Claire took an imaginary piece of paper from her pocket and read it. 'Cabbage!' She shuddered. 'I would rather be going to the boutique to buy a new dress, monsieur,' she said, wrinkling her nose playfully.

'Good.' Billy gave a little clap. 'Did you notice how your voice changed when you allowed yourself to be young and carefree?'

Claire did. She noticed her voice was different with several other personality changes too. When she thought of her older sister Bess, how sensible she was and how well she dealt with difficult situations, her voice took on a serious, understanding and caring tone. When she thought of her sister Margaret, she became chatty and cheeky.

And when she remembered how she felt when she received the news that she'd passed the Eleven Plus, even though her parents couldn't afford the uniform so she didn't go to the grammar school, her voice was confident and assertive.

'Thank you so much,' she said to Billy and Olivia when they had done with her. 'It's a relief to know I won't have to carry wigs and padding about.'

'That would be a real show stopper if you were searched by Uncle Gerry.' Billy pursed his lips. 'You'd end up playing the lead role in a high security venue, darling!'

In the days that followed, Claire was asked about her French parents and siblings. She was asked where she was born, brought up, went to school – and about her extended family. She was given instructions about code names and cover names. An agent's code name was their signature, and should only be used when communicating by wireless. The name on their identity papers, their cover name, must be used at all other times. When working with a partner you must only use his cover name. You must only speak French when you are in France. Speak it until you think in it. It must come naturally to you. One slip could cost you your life.

There were also staged interrogations. Endless questions about what she was doing. Why was she on the street? Where had she come from and where was she going? Towards the end of her training Claire was taken to a small room and left. Six hours later a member of staff playing an SS officer grilled her about her friends. Did she know any English men? Did she know any English women? Had she met any foreigners recently? Did she believe in a free France? Did she admire Charles de Gaulle? Had she heard of the Resistance movement? At the end of the day she was congratulated and asked to return the following morning.

'Good morning, Claire. Come in,' one of the two men in the room said in perfect German. 'Please, take a seat.' Claire felt the pulse in her temples start to throb and her heart began to race, but she didn't move. 'It says here that Claire speaks German,' the first man said to the second.

'Won't you sit down?' the second man said. Mitch's words came into her head. *You understand German, which will work to your advantage, but you must not show it.*

'My apologies, sirs,' she said in French, and turned and closed the door.

'So she apparently does not speak German.' Both men looked at her file. Claire's mouth was dry. She wanted to lick her lips; instead she swallowed. It didn't help. 'English girls are not taught other languages at school, so where did you learn French?' the first man asked. Frowning quizzically, Claire lifted her shoulders and, looking worried, let them drop.

'Are you taking us for fools?' the second man shouted. 'Well?' He slammed his fist down on the desk and Claire jumped. Without taking his eyes off her, he slowly walked towards her until his nose was almost touching hers. Claire held her nerve. She looked at him, tilted her head innocently as if she didn't understand, and said nothing. 'So,' he said, circling her, 'you have a brother in the British Army.' Claire felt perspiration run down her back.

Her breath threatened to burst from her lungs, but she quickly controlled it and it remained steady. 'His name is Tom. Is that correct? *Is that correct?*' he shouted into her ear.

Claire turned to him, her eyes pleading. 'I do not know what it is you want from me, sir,' she said in French.

'I want you to tell me about your brother Tom in the British Army.' He spoke French now, but with a German accent.

'I do not have a brother, sir. I have two sisters younger than myself. They are still at school and live with my parents.'

'Good! Well done, Claire,' the man said in English.

'Gerry is not going to get anything out of you if you're questioned,' the second man said. Pointing to the chair on the other side of his desk, he said again, 'Sit down, will you?' Claire didn't move. They were still testing her, trying to fox her with friendly and complimentary words. She knew they were SOE intelligence officers. Even so, she was not going to do anything they asked until they spoke to her in French. She remained standing.

'Please take a seat,' the second man said in French, sitting down in the chair behind the desk. The first man stood at his side and Claire sat in the chair in front of them. 'It has been a pleasure meeting you,' he continued in French. 'I feel sure that anyone lucky enough to partner you will be in safe hands.' The man standing nodded and smiled at her.

'Thank you,' Claire said, taking both men in.

The first man looked at the second. 'I think

that's it, don't you?'

'Yes, sir,' the second man said. 'Thank you, Miss...' He looked at the file. 'Le Blanc. You are free to go.'

Claire stood up, thanked both men, and left.

Shaking like a leaf, Claire ran up to her room. She flew to the wash basin, filled the glass holding her toothbrush with water and took a couple of sips. She felt no better and ran to the bathroom. Locking the door, she fell to her knees, began to retch, and was sick. Trembling, she returned to her room, threw herself onto the bed and closed her eyes. For the first time since she began training for the SOE she doubted herself. Was she doing the right thing? Was she tough enough for the job? She was eager and dedicated, but was she mentally strong enough? Would she be able to keep her resolve under real interrogation? Or would she capitulate, give up her fellow operatives? Tears squeezed through her eyelids. She turned over, held her aching stomach and slept.

The next day, lectures on traitors and what to look for, the importance of giving and receiving the correct passwords and patterns of words, controlling your fears and not showing your nerves, helped to put Claire back on the right path. She realised that she had done exactly what was required and expected of her during the interrogation. She now understood that what she thought was emotion was in fact adrenalin. Adrenalin pumped round your body when you were under duress and it kept you alert.

On the train back to London, Claire went through everything she had learned at Beaulieu. She had understood and enjoyed the change of voice and character work. She had passed the interrogation test, and all the other tests, but she had no certificate to frame, or promotion to show for her efforts. As far as the world was concerned the SOE training school at Beaulieu didn't exist. Therefore she had never been there. When she was leaving, the commandant shook her hand, congratulated her, and wished her luck. That was enough. She had no qualms about going overseas and no doubts about her strength, physical or mental. She had successfully completed every step of a secret agent's training and looked forward to her first mission into occupied France.

Claire hauled her case across the entrance hall to her ground floor apartment. She dove into her handbag, couldn't find her key, and began to panic. She dropped the case with a dull thud, knelt down and tipped the contents of her handbag onto the floor. 'Phew!' she gasped. The key was stuck in the lining. While she was throwing her belongings back into her bag, Milly opened her apartment door and leapt out.

'You're back!' she shouted, dashing across to Claire. 'You look all in. When you've unpacked come over to mine. I've got some eggs from a pal who hates them. I'll do fried eggs and chips.'

'Thanks, Milly, I'd love to. I didn't have time to eat anything before I left, and I was too tired to go to the shops when I got back to London.' Claire opened the door and threw in her suitcase and gas mask. 'My feet are killing me,' she said, kicking off her shoes.

'By the time you've sorted yourself out supper will be ready.' Milly handed Claire her handbag. 'I'll leave the door on the latch,' she said, disappearing into her apartment.

Entering the sitting room, Claire shivered. The flat was so cold, bordering on damp. She decided to unpack later and set about building a fire. It took hold quickly and after putting the fireguard in front of it, she went to the bathroom and had a quick wash. Pushing her feet into her slippers, she grabbed her keys and crossed the hall to Milly's flat. 'Hellooo?'

'Come in!' Milly shouted from the kitchen. 'Supper's almost ready. There are a couple of bottles of beer in the sideboard cupboard. Open them, will you?'

'Are you sure you don't want to save them for a special occasion?'

'This *is* a special occasion. Open them, woman!' Milly ordered, bringing in bread and butter and a bowl of chips. 'One minute and the eggs will be done,' she said, disappearing back into the kitchen.

Claire opened a bottle of beer, shared it between the two glasses, and put the other bottle on the table. She had just sat down when Milly returned carrying two plates, with an egg on each. After passing Claire hers she spooned half the chips onto Claire's plate and emptied the rest onto her own. 'Help yourself to bread and butter,' Milly said, taking a slice and dipping it in the yoke of her egg.

When they had finished eating, Milly lifted her glass of beer. 'I got the job as a translator.'

'Congratulations. I'm pleased for you,' Claire said, lifting her glass and clinking Milly's.

'It's been so long since the interview, I'd almost given up. I only got the letter today, in the last post. You're the first person I've told. I'll go to the phone box in the morning and ring my mum. She'll be so pleased, dad too.' Milly chattered on, hardly taking a breath. 'I'm not sure which they'll be more pleased about – that I got the job, or that I won't be going overseas.'

For a moment Claire thought about her own mum and dad, wondered how they would feel if they knew she might soon be going to France. She tried to shake the thought from her mind, but she was tired and felt emotional thinking about them. 'There's no need to wait until tomorrow.'

'For what?'

'To speak to your mum and dad. Use my telephone. Ring them now.'

'I didn't know you had a telephone.'

'It was in the flat when I moved in.'

'Thank you – if you're sure? I'll pay you for the call.'

'Don't be silly. It's the least I can do after you cooked me this lovely meal.'

While Milly telephoned her mother, Claire washed the dishes. Afterwards the two girls sat with the second bottle of beer and listened to the wireless.

Claire turned off the light and looked out of the window. There was a full moon. Four nights left of the eight where pilots would risk flying into France by moonlight. But with no French identity papers, clothes and accessories, Claire knew she wouldn't be going to France this month. She dropped the blackout curtains back into place, felt her way across her small sitting room and switched the light back on. Itching for something to do, she flopped onto the settee and picked up a magazine. She had already read it.

She was out of her mind with boredom. She spoke to Eddie and her sister Bess on the telephone often, so when it rang she jumped up, ran to it, and sang, 'Hello?'

'Claire? It's Vera Halliday here.'

'Hello, Miss Halliday,' Claire said, her heart beating with expectation.

'Your French identity papers and clothes are here. Would you come into the office tomorrow at ten o'clock and collect them?'

'Yes.' Claire could barely control the excitement in her voice.

'I'll see you at ten. Make sure the clothes fit and the paperwork is in order. The colonel will brief you at eleven.'

'Do I need to bring anything?' Claire asked.

'No, everything you need is here. See you tomorrow. Goodbye.'

'Goodbye.' Claire put down the telephone and squealed with excitement. At last things were moving.

CHAPTER NINE

'What do you want to do, Captain?' the pilot shouted.

'Have we got enough gas to circle again?'

'Once, but that's it!'

'We'll have to go in blind,' Mitch shouted into Claire's ear. The cabin was so noisy Claire didn't attempt to reply and nodded that she understood. There was a muffled banging on the side of the fuselage and the Halifax lifted and dropped. 'It's getting windy out there.'

Getting? The contents of Claire's stomach rose to her throat with every gust – and had done since leaving England. It was windy crossing the Channel, and getting progressively worse over the coastal towns and villages of France. The plane rose and fell again, and Claire looked at the brown paper bag she'd been given in case she was sick.

'Whoa!' The plane plunged and Claire swallowed hard. 'Wasn't like this in training, was it, China?' Not daring to speak, Claire forced a smile between tight lips, while keeping an eye on the brown paper bag.

'OK! I've got the River Loire in my sights. Prepare to jump if you're going to, Captain,' the pilot shouted. 'We're over Blois. I can see the island in the middle of the river. Now I can see lights,' he whooped, a few seconds later.

'Okay. Let's do it. We've got a reception committee, China. You ready?' Mitch shouted.

Claire put both thumbs up. 'See you in France, Alain.' She moved to the door and looked down.

Lights were twinkling below. They reminded her of the sparklers Lord Foxden gave her and her sisters on Guy Fawkes Night. She could hear the rumble of thunder and feel the wind buffeting the plane. If she didn't jump soon she was sure she'd be sick.

'Go!' Mitch shouted and she let herself fall out of the plane into the night. Freezing rain numbed her face. She pulled on the parachute cord and held her breath until she felt the tug and whoosh as it began to open. Against the natural force of gravity, she was dragged upwards. The parachute opened fully and she breathed again. She pulled on a riser and the great mushroom that loomed above her tilted slightly. She pulled again, and this time it was angled enough to keep the icy wind and rain from blinding her. For a second she enjoyed the feeling of floating. Then she bent her knees before her feet touched the ground and landed well.

She began to run, but soon slowed and the parachute wafted around. She unfastened her harness and looked up. A slice of moon peeped through the storm clouds giving enough light for her to see Mitch was down and folding his parachute. Claire flattened hers and began to fold it.

'You okay here on your own?' Mitch shouted. 'We've been blown off course. I'm going to look for the drop.'

'Don't go yet. Look!' Claire pointed to half a dozen men walking across the field. Mitch ran to meet them and Claire followed.

'Hello, sir. Miss,' one of the men said, shaking Mitch's hand and then Claire's. The British SOE operatives and French Resistance members stood and looked at each other. They would go no further until coded questions had been asked and answered, Claire thought. She smiled at them.

'I am Alain, and this is Claire.'

'André,' the Frenchman said. 'Why are you here?'

'To visit an old friend in the town of Gisoir. You might know him. He is a flamboyant fellow. He loves to bake.'

The Frenchman shrugged his shoulders. 'Bake what?'

'Cakes. Is he baking tonight?'

'No, sir, he does not have the ingredients.'

'Then I shall visit him tomorrow at twelve. No.' Alain put his hand up. 'At twelve-ten. And I shall give him the ingredients.'

'Welcome to France, Alain,' André said, shaking Alain's hand. 'Claire, welcome.' After introducing them to his brother Frédéric, friends Pierre and Marcel Ruban, and the rest of the Resistance cell, he instructed the men to fetch the crates and packages from the drop and take them to the barn.

He beckoned Alain and Claire with a wave of his arm. 'My mother has made food and prepared rooms.' Once through a small wood, Claire saw a farmhouse, the outline of a barn and a row of outbuildings. André lead the way to the house, where an attractive middle-aged woman was laying the table. 'My mother,' he said, 'Édith Belland. Mama, this is Alain and Claire. Excuse me while I see to the drop.' He turned and left.

'Welcome,' Édith Belland said, with a warm smile. 'Let me take your coats. You are soaked to the skin, both of you.' Claire and Alain struggled out of their wet outer clothes and Madame Belland laid them over a large fireguard in front of an iron range. 'Sit down, please. You must be hungry.' She pointed to a large oblong scrubbed oak table surrounded by six chairs.

'Can I do anything to help you, Madame?' Claire asked.

'Thank you, but no,' Édith Belland said, taking a large earthenware pot from the oven next to the fire and placing it in the middle of the table. At that moment André returned with his brother Frédéric. 'Wash your hands, boys,' their mother said, ruffling her youngest son's hair. 'Dinner is ready.'

Dinner was meat and spicy dumplings in an aromatic gravy, with carrots and green beans. There was a large crusty loaf in the middle of the table that the Belland brothers pulled apart with their hands. André poured them each a small glass of red wine, raised his glass in a welcoming gesture and drank to Alain and Claire – the others around the table followed. Claire took a sip. The dry and slightly sharp taste made her want to smack her lips. She resisted and sipped again. This time as she swallowed the taste was crisp and fruity. In England she only drank beer, but she could get used to drinking wine, she thought, and raised her glass in thanks.

'Let us go through to the front room,' Madame Belland said, when they had finished eating. 'There is a fire, it is warmer. André, bring another bottle of wine.'

Spring sunshine played across Claire's face. She opened her eyes. The wooden shutters at the window, closed when she went to bed the night before, stood half open. She stretched her legs until her feet touched a wooden box at the end of the single bed, and then slipped from between the coarse cotton sheets. She crossed barefoot to the window, pushed it open, and caught her breath. On the horizon she saw fields of purple flowers. Lavender, or perhaps flowering broccoli? She knew lavender was grown mostly in the south of France, but maybe it was grown in the middle regions too. She stuck her head out of the window, inhaled deeply, and coughed as the smell of cow dung filled her nostrils. She didn't care and flung the window open wide. She was in France at last.

There was a knock at the door. 'Claire? I have brought you water,' Édith Belland called from the landing. 'I shall leave it outside your room. Breakfast is ready when you are.'

'Thank you, Madame.' Claire skipped to the door and opened it, but Édith Belland had gone. Claire threw the towel over her shoulder and lifted the bowl. Placing it on the tiled washstand at the side of the window, she washed and dried her face. She dressed quickly, brushed her hair and ran downstairs.

As she entered the kitchen, Claire was greeted by four smiling faces. 'Good morning, China.' Mitch looked at his wristwatch. 'Or is it afternoon?'

'French, Alain! While we are here, we must only speak French. *Bonjour*, Alain.'

André smiled. 'Claire is right, Alain. What is it that you say in England? The walls, they have ears? They have ears in France also.'

'I stand corrected,' Alain said in perfect French.

Madame Belland pulled out a chair. 'Sit, please,' she said, pouring Claire a small cup of coffee.

'Thank you, Madame.' Claire took a sip. It was too strong. She added milk to the dark brown liquid until the cup was full to the brim. Lifting it carefully, she drank again. It tasted better. It was still potent, with a slightly burnt aftertaste, but it was preferable to Camp coffee, which didn't taste like coffee at all. She didn't take sugar, but a little might take the edge off. She looked at the condiments on the table. Two small glass bowls – one with salt, the other pepper – a dish with butter and several bottles of different coloured oils, but no sugar. Oh well... when in Rome, she thought, and, drinking the coffee, she tucked into croissants and bread spread with soft cheese.

When they had finished eating, Édith Belland cleared the dishes, leaving the cups. Placing a refreshed pot of coffee in the middle of the table, she sat down. 'Now,' she said, 'if you are the children of my brothers,' she looked at Claire and Alain, 'you will have known me all your lives – and so you would not address me as Madame, you would call me Aunt Édith. Of course now you are grown up, you might have dropped the title aunt and just call me Édith, but you would not call me Madame.'

'Édith it is,' agreed Alain.

'I shall call you *Aunt* Édith,' Claire said, squeezing Édith Belland's hand and smiling at Alain.

'May I have another cup of coffee, Édith?' Alain said.

'Of course you may.' Édith Belland laughed and

filled Alain's cup, before pouring coffee for everyone else.

When they had finished their coffee, Frédéric left the table. Taking his work overalls from the back of the door, he began to step into them. 'Can I see the animals?' Claire asked.

'Of course,' Frédéric said.

'Frédéric will show you round the farm, while Alain and I go to the barn. We must check that the package for Jacques is in one piece.'

'What time will we be taking it to Jacques, Alain?' Claire asked.

It was André who answered. 'I think the first time Jacques meets new agents it should be with me, someone he already knows and trusts. He is passionate about a free France and a loyal Resistance member, but he is suspicious of people he doesn't know. There will be plenty of time to meet Jacques in the future.'

'Coming, Claire?' Frédéric called, before Claire had time to argue about being left behind. She thanked Édith for breakfast and ran out to join Frédéric, who was sitting on the wall of the well smoking a cigarette. Skipping across the cobbled yard, she sat next to him.

'You'll need these,' he said, handing her a pair of wellingtons. 'It can get muddy in the cowshed.

Claire took off her shoes and put on the wellingtons. 'It's a big well,' she said, jumping down and picking up her shoes. She took them to the house and dropped them at the side of the kitchen door. On her return she picked up a pebble and dropped it into the well. She heard a hollow plop as it hit the water, but not another sound. 'It must be very deep,' she said, leaning over and peering into the dark water.

'So you had better be careful. If you fall in you might disappear forever,' Frédéric said, pretending to push Claire while holding the top of her arms securely. She squealed and Frédéric lessened his grip to allow her to move away. 'Come on,' he said, turning the handle at the side of the well's ornate roof until the bucket disappeared into the water. Hauling up a full bucket, he said, 'One more to fill. Will you pass it, please?' Claire turned and saw a metal pail on the ground. She lifted it as Frédéric swung the well's bucket over the wall. After filling the pail he lowered the bucket back into the well until it was a couple of feet below the top. 'Come on,' he said, 'we have work to do in the cowshed.'

'Are we going to milk the cows?'

'We?' Frédéric hooted. 'You've milked cows before, have you?'

'Not exactly, but I was brought up on a country estate.' Frédéric raised his eyebrows. 'And one of the estate farms had a herd of cows.' Claire could see Frédéric was trying not to laugh. 'I have seen cows being milked, many times,' she lied, 'and I'm a quick learner.'

'Sorry to disappoint you, Claire, but we are going to wash the floor of the cowshed, not milk the cows. The cowman and I did that at six o'clock this morning, while you were sleeping. But then, with your vast knowledge of dairy farming, you will know that by this time of day the milking has been done.'

Claire pushed Frédéric playfully and he spilt water on his feet. 'Sorry,' she said, running ahead of him to the first of the wooden structures.

'The next building,' Frédéric shouted, 'and pick up a bucket of water before you go in.' Frédéric took his large pail inside and, holding the rim at the top with one hand, he gripped the bottom of the pail with the other. Claire watched as he swung the pail back before hurling it forward, forcing the water out of it and across the floor. Dropping her bucket, Claire jumped out of the way as cow dung and straw went swimming past her and out of the door. Frédéric followed the water with a wide brush on a long handle. 'Mind your feet,' he shouted as he almost swept her out of the cowshed.

Claire picked up another bucket and copied Frédéric. He stood to one side and leant on the brush, nodding. When they finished in the cowshed they brushed the yard, making sure the waste from the shed was in a drainage ditch away from the well.

'I'll teach you how to milk the cows if you want,' Frédéric said, as they put the pails and brushes in the smallest of the sheds.

'All right,' Claire said, half-heartedly. 'I suppose if I'm staying with my aunt and cousins on their farm, I ought to know something about farming – and *cows.*' She screwed up her face.

'And horses? We have two plough horses.' Claire followed Frédéric past the barn to the stables. 'Working horses with no work to do,' Frédéric sighed, opening the stable door. 'Come on, girls.' He clicked his tongue and the horses plodded out of the dark stalls into the sunshine. 'In the winter I take them to the field for exercise – and to eat, as fodder is hard to come by – and bring them back before it is dark. Now spring is here the fields are their home for four, maybe five, months.'

The horses clip-clopped across the cobbles to a field bordering the farmyard. Whinnying and shaking their manes, when Frédéric opened the five-bar gate they skittered through. He closed the gate after them and, with Claire standing on the bottom rung, watched as the horses trotted down to the small brook.

'Why aren't you working them?' Claire asked.

'The Germans have forbidden us to till the land. They informed us after last year's harvest; after the corn fires. They took our produce, saying the land belonged to them, therefore what it yields also belongs to them.'

They walked back to the house in silence. Frédéric looked about her age, she thought, his older brother André a similar age to Alain. 'André wears a ring on his wedding finger. Is he married?' Claire asked.

'Yes, to Thérèse. She is good for André, keeps his feet in the earth. Being the oldest brother, he can be…'

'Bossy?' Claire offered.

'You could say that. Since my father died, André takes being the head of the family very seriously.'

'But he doesn't live here, does he?'

'No, he and Thérèse live with her parents. They have a farm north of Gisoir, the nearest town to them, and to us,' Frédéric said. 'They are old and depend on Thérèse to help in the house.'

'And André works the farm?'

'No, André spends his days here. They employ labourers to do the farm work. You met some of

120

them last night. They were part of the reception committee.' Claire recalled each one of them. 'They work as farm labourers, but they are engineers, architects and electricians.'

'Why do they work as labourers when they have professions and trades?'

'To continue working with the Resistance. The Germans send qualified men to work for the Fatherland. They think farm labourers are stupid, so they ignore them.' Frédéric laughed bitterly. 'These so-called labourers are brave fighters, and saboteurs.'

At the back door Claire took off her wellingtons and put on her shoes. 'I'll wash the mud off these when I do mine,' Frédéric said. 'Tell Mama I'll be in for coffee shortly.'

The smell of fresh coffee and newly baked bread met Claire as she entered the kitchen. Édith Belland was at the stove. She turned as Claire entered. 'Can I do anything to help, Édith?'

'No, my dear, it was only a stir of the soup that was needed.' Édith took the coffee pot from the stove. 'André and Alain are in the front room. They will be through in a minute, or perhaps you would like to join them?'

'I'm fine. It's nice and warm in here. It's homely too,' Claire observed, 'for such a big kitchen.'

'The kitchen is where friends meet and drink coffee – and gossip,' Édith whispered. 'In the evenings we sit and listen to the wireless, and drink a glass of wine by the fire in the front room – and always formal occasions take place in there – but the kitchen is, as you say, homely.'

CHAPTER TEN

Claire, playing the part of visiting younger cousin, trailed behind André and Alain as they strolled into Gisoir. 'I'll meet you back here at one o'clock,' Alain said to Claire when they arrived in the town square. He looked around. 'In Café La Ronde,' he said, pointing to a double-fronted café a few shops along from where they were standing.

Claire nodded. 'Aunt Édith has given me a shopping list. There isn't much on it, so I shouldn't be long,' she said, taking in her surroundings and making a mental note of everything she saw. The cafés and bars around the square were teeming with Gestapo. 'It is turning into a very grey day. Greyer than we were led to expect, don't you think?'

'Much greyer,' Alain agreed.

'Be careful what you say, cousins, in case any of them speak French,' André warned. They walked along the pavement past dozens of German officers sitting outside bistros and cafés. Lounging arrogantly in their chairs, legs outstretched, ignoring anyone who wanted to pass, they told jokes and laughed loudly – and threw cigarette butts in the path of passers-by.

'There are a hell of a lot more than I thought there would be,' Alain said, when they were out of earshot.

'That's what's worrying me,' André said. 'There's easily twice as many Gestapo here this week than there was last.'

'The influx must be recent, or London would have said something.'

'While you buy provisions, Claire, Alain and I will call on Jacques, see if there are any messages. Afterwards, I shall go home to Thérèse. What will you do, Alain?'

'Buy a newspaper and sit outside one of the bars. I'll have a beer, watch the world go by, and listen to a few conversations. Frenchmen are still allowed to frequent the cafés and bars, I hope?'

'Yes, but I needn't tell you to keep a low profile. You too, Claire, try not to attract attention,' André said, before walking on slowly.

'Not easy with legs like yours,' Alain whispered.

Claire felt the colour rise in her cheeks. 'See you in Café La Ronde at one,' she said, looking back at the café so Alain couldn't see her blush.

They parted company on the west side of the square. Alain followed André, and Claire crossed the road and walked along the north side until she came to a parade of shops. There was as little in the shops of Gisoir as there had been in Morecambe and London. She stepped into the doorway of a grocery shop as someone was coming out. When he drew level, Claire saw it was a Gestapo officer. He smiled and her stomach lurched. She smiled briefly and walked to the meat counter.

'Hello, Miss. What can I do for you?'

Looking down and concentrating on the meagre slices of pale meat alongside a dozen sausages, Claire heard the door close. She hadn't realised she'd been holding her breath and exhaled noisily. The shop owner nodded.

'He took most of my produce,' he said. 'This is all I have left.'

'I'll take five slices of meat. And can you spare five sausages?'

'Yes. When the food is gone, it is gone!' he said in a tired and resigned voice.

Claire smiled sympathetically. She took out several food tickets and put them on the counter. She knew the Gestapo didn't pay for their goods and wished she could buy more. She walked over to the patisserie counter and gazed at a couple of sticky fruit buns. Her mouth watered, but she didn't have enough coupons for cakes. She had money, but she didn't want to draw attention to herself so she thanked the shopkeeper and made for the door.

'Miss?' he called after her. As she turned she saw he was bending down. He stood up with a bounce and beckoned her conspiratorially. Claire walked back to the counter and the baker held up a sultana loaf with a sweet glaze on the top. 'My wife made it. Try it and tell me what you think.' He put the loaf on the counter, sliced off a chunk, and handed it to her. 'Well?' he said when she had taken a bite.

'It is wonderful,' Claire mumbled with her mouth full. 'I haven't tasted anything like it since before--' The shopkeeper nodded that he understood and shrugged his shoulders. When she had eaten the delicious bread she licked her fingers.

The shopkeeper cut off another slice, wrapped it in greaseproof paper and said, 'Put it in the bottom of your shopping basket.' He wagged his podgy forefinger. 'Do not let anyone see.'

Claire stood, open-mouthed. Dare she offer him money? He appeared to dislike the German officer who had just left his shop, but it wasn't wise to trust anyone. Deciding against it she said, 'I'm sorry I can't pay you.'

The rosy-cheeked retailer shook his head and leaned forward. 'Enjoy.'

Claire looked into the man's kind eyes. The French were proud people. He would probably be insulted if she gave him money now. She bit her lip. Professor Marron had told her when she was in Cullercoats that such generosity had once been commonplace in small market towns like Gisoir. He said people used to greet you in the street, pass the time of day, and smile when they served you in shops and cafés. Now there were so many Germans in France that people didn't speak unless they were spoken to – and who could blame them? 'Thank you very much,' Claire said. Smiling her gratitude, she stowed the treat under her shopping, put her purse on top, and left.

Café La Ronde, like all the other cafés on the square, was packed with Germans, mostly officers. Claire greeted the manager with a smile when she entered, and he nodded towards the back of the café where Alain sat in a booth.

'It's busy in here today,' Alain said, as she sat down.

'Too busy for comfort. Learned anything?'

'Yes! I'll tell you later. You?'

Claire patted her shopping basket. 'I'll show you later,' she laughed. 'Damn!'

'What?'

'Three stripes at ten o'clock. Must have followed me from the shop. He was coming out as I was going in. Sorry, I shouldn't have laughed so loud.'

'Don't worry about him. He's a man doing what men do.' The frown lines on Claire's forehead deepened and she tutted. 'What's a guy supposed to do when a pretty girl catches his eye, look the other way?' Alain beckoned the waiter for Claire's coffee. 'He's bound to look, it's only natural.'

'Even so--'

'You worry too much.'

'Apologies for the delay, Miss.' The waiter wiped the table before putting the coffee down. 'This week we have suddenly become very busy.' He flashed a sideways glance to the table nearest the door, where half a dozen Gestapo officers sat drinking beer and talking loudly. 'The Hun on the left has been watching you,' he whispered. Then in his normal voice he said, 'Enjoy your coffee.' Smiling, he collected the dirty crockery from the table next to theirs and made his way back to the counter.

'So the influx of Boche happened a week ago?'

'By the number of vehicles parked outside the hotels, they've taken them over. I'm going to check the back of the café, see if there's an escape route,' he whispered. 'Will you be okay if I go to the toilet, China?'

Claire tutted. 'Of course I will, but stop calling me China,' she whispered. 'I am Claire! Are you listening?' She elbowed Alain in the ribs and he nodded. 'If you're overheard-- Well, it doesn't bear thinking about.'

'I know. I'm sorry. So excuse me, *Claire*, I am going for a pee.'

As Alain got up from the table, Claire saw a movement out of the corner of her eye. A second later the German officer who had been watching her stood up and walked across to her table. Pretending she hadn't seen him, she took a book from her shopping bag and began to read.

'Interesting reading?' the German asked. Claire had to stop herself from showing surprise, his French was so good.

The nerves on the top of her stomach began to tighten. She looked up into a pair of cold, ice-blue eyes. 'Er, yes … it is.'

The German moved to her side and looked down at the book, now on the table. '*Delphine*?'

'Yes, Madame de Staël was my mother's favourite novelist.'

'Was your mother interested in politics?'

Claire forced herself to smile. 'No, she just enjoyed reading historical novels. She wasn't formally educated and said reading was a good way to learn.'

'Do you know the book *De l'Allemagne*?'

'No. I'm afraid I only read fiction.'

'That is a shame. Madame de Staël's book was a great influence on German literature. And your sweetheart? Does he read to you?' the German asked suddenly, tilting his head in the direction of the toilets.

'My sweetheart? Do you mean--' Claire wrinkled her nose in disgust. 'He is my cousin.'

'Is she talking your head off?' Alain asked, walking briskly to the table where the German officer was leaning uncomfortably close to Claire.

The German straightened as Alain sat down. 'No. We were discussing literature.' Clicking his heels, he bowed his head. 'Goodbye,' he said, and left. The men who had been sitting with him jumped up and followed him out of the café.

'Learn anything?'

'What? For goodness' sake, give me a second to gather my wits. My heart's pounding.'

Claire inhaled deeply, closed her eyes, and slowly let the air out of her lungs.

'He was that good, eh?'

'He was actually. He asked me a lot of questions in a very short time.'

'I think he's sweet on you.'

'You could be right, or making up to me could have been a smokescreen. I'll tell you what he said on the way back to the farm. Let's get out of here, I need some air.'

'OK, but go to the toilet first. Give me a chance to have a look out front. Don't rush,' Alain added. 'I'll wait for you outside.'

Claire went to the back of the café and opened the toilet door. Instead of going in, she watched Alain stroll across the café to the counter and pay. Outside he lit a cigarette, shifted his weight from one leg to the other and looked at his watch several times. When she thought he had waited for long enough, she left.

As she stepped through the café's front door, Alain blew out a cloud of smoke. He flicked the cigarette butt to the ground and stamped on it as if he was angry having to wait for her. In a raised voice he complained that she always kept him waiting. Claire argued back saying the toilet wasn't vacant and she had to wait for ages, because someone was in there. Alain threw his hands up in the air and marched off. Claire ran after him.

On the road to the farm they discussed and dissected the conversation. The conclusion Alain came to was that the German officer was attracted to her. 'He questioned you about me to see if you were available. You did well,' he said, 'especially using the novel. Well done, China.'

Claire tutted and smiled. For once she didn't tell Alain off for using her code name, or at least half of it.

'Shush! I can hear vehicles.' Claire heard them too. 'Drop back a few paces and stay behind me until they pass. You're still annoyed with me for shouting at you, right?'

'Right!' Swinging her basket in one hand, Claire put the other on her hip in a defiant gesture. She kicked the grass verge in anger. Realising that she had scuffed her shoes, she stopped to look at them for a second. As the German vehicles got closer Claire pretended to hear them and looked back along the road, before running to catch up with Alain. She hadn't reached him by the time the convoy drove by. In the short time it took the vehicles to turn the bend in the road, Claire had counted how many lorries of soldiers there were, and how many covered trucks carrying equipment and artillery.

When the last truck disappeared out of sight, Alain stopped and Claire caught up with him. 'We're not going down the lane to Belland Farm. We'll carry on as far as the bridge at the back of the house. You fill the water bottle in the river and I'll go into the trees opening my flies, as if I'm going to have a pee. I'll be able to see if Gerry's at the farm from the far side of the copse.'

'What will we do if they are there?'

'Walk on. And we won't stop until we are far enough away that any suspicions the Germans might have about us won't be linked to the Belland family.'

Claire filled the water bottle, scrambled up the riverbank and sat on the bridge. She dangled her legs over the edge and began to count the windows on the back of the farmhouse. Suddenly the window of her bedroom flew open, followed by the rug from the side of her bed and Édith's head. After shaking the thin pegged mat and filling the air with dust, Édith waved. Claire daren't wave back in case she was being watched.

'No German vehicles in the farmyard, or on the lane leading to it,' Alain said. 'It's clear.'

'Good. Can we go in then?'

'Yes, but not into the house in case the Germans come back. We'll stay in the barn tonight. Come on,' he said, 'let's go!'

They scrambled up the bank to the road, ran across it and rolled down the other side. As they neared the lane Édith was coming out of the kitchen door. Alain motioned that he and Claire were going into the barn. She nodded that she understood.

'What has happened?' Édith asked, joining them ten minutes later.

'A Boche officer sweet-talked Claire and asked her questions,' Alain said. Édith took Claire's hand. 'She didn't say anything of course, except about the book she was reading and her bore of an older cousin, but they passed us on the road a mile back, so I think it best if we stay in here tonight, in case they decide to pay you a visit.'

'Good idea. Get what you need from your rooms, and I'll bring you some food. It will be cold, I'm afraid. The smell of cooked food would be noticed.'

'Of course. Anything will do. Thank you, Édith.'

Claire ran upstairs and pulled on a thick woollen jumper. On her way out she grabbed her coat. Returning to the barn, Alain took a ladder from behind bales of hay and held it while Claire climbed up. 'At the far end there's a trap door,' he said. 'Open it and grab a couple of pillows and however many blankets there are.'

By the time Claire had made up two makeshift beds at the back of the loft, Édith was back with their supper.

'I shall spread your clothes and toiletries between my room and the room Thérèse and André sleep in when they stay here. And yours, Alain, will be among Frédéric's things in his room,' she said, handing Alain the tray of food. 'I'll see you both in the morning.'

Alain gave the tray to Claire while he pulled up the ladder. They ate in silence. When they'd finished they discussed what had happened during the day in whispers and sign language. By the time they had analysed and every detail, it was almost dark.

Alain slipped the bolt from the door to the hay pulley, in case they needed to use it as an escape route during the night. Then they settled down on the straw fully dressed.

Claire lay and watched Alain as he slept. He turned over. His face was inches from hers; she could hear the rhythm of his breathing, feel his breath on her cheek. She felt a stirring in the pit of her stomach and closed her eyes.

The following morning, Édith Belland called them to the house for breakfast. 'Did you sleep well?' Alain asked Claire as they put away the blankets.

'Yes,' she lied. 'Did you?'

'Like a log,' he said, shinning down the ladder. He lifted his arms and stretched. 'Come on, China, shake a leg. I'm starving,' he said, holding the ladder for her. As soon as she was on the ground he jogged to the kitchen ahead of her.

CHAPTER ELEVEN

'China?' Claire looked up to see Mitch walking along Baker Street towards her. 'I thought I might see you today. Have you been to see the colonel for your debrief?'

'Yes. Is that where you're going?'

'Yes and no. I'm going to see him but I was debriefed yesterday,' he whispered. 'Let's grab a coffee. Here,' Mitch said, opening the door of a restaurant a couple of doors along from Baker Street underground station. Claire followed him in. 'Are you hungry?'

'No. Just coffee for me, please.' The butterflies in her stomach that had begun to calm after being debriefed whirled like dervishes the second she saw Mitch.

Mitch beckoned the waitress and asked for two cups of coffee. They didn't have to wait long. 'How was the DB?' he asked, when the waitress left.

'Fine.' She hoped she didn't sound over-confident and said, 'The colonel wanted to know about troop movements, obviously, the different regiments in Gisoir, and the ranks of the German officers – whether there were fewer high ranking officers around now or more. And more specifically, if I had noticed any very young or much older soldiers.

'And were you specific?'

'Of course. You know, some of the youngest soldiers we saw were only boys. They should have had pens in their hands, not guns. And the older soldiers had probably fought in the Great War.'

Claire thought for a moment. 'Why do you ask? Do you doubt my accuracy?'

Mitch laughed. 'I wouldn't dare, China.'

'Stop it,' Claire said, 'I'm being serious.' She sipped her coffee. 'There was one thing I might not have been as specific about as the colonel hoped. Don't get me wrong, I was positive about everything I reported, but he asked me over and over again about--' Claire stopped speaking and looked around to make sure she couldn't be overheard, 'Panzer Divisions. He said it was of the utmost importance that he knew whether there had been an increase or a decrease in armoured vehicles, specifically in Panzer Divisions. I told him there had been a decrease, that the only armoured tanks, motorised infantry, rifle battalions or artillery regiments I'd seen in the last month were on main roads going north. He seemed relieved.'

'He would be. The Germans are hitting the Soviets with everything they've got. The last intelligence received from the Eastern Front reported Panzer Divisions a hundred miles from Moscow. They're gearing up in the north and south to take the capital. The only thing that will stop them now is the weather. It's thirty degrees below zero over there, and it'll get colder as winter sets in. The Soviet Army is used to severe weather conditions and will dress accordingly, but the Germans aren't. If the Germans don't take Moscow soon there's a good chance their army will freeze to death.'

'So the briefing was to make sure the intelligence was correct?'

'And it appears it is.' Mitch finished his coffee.

'You did well,' he said, putting his hand on hers. Claire was about to thank him when he looked at his wristwatch. 'Hell, I have to go,' he said, getting to his feet. 'The colonel doesn't like to be kept waiting.' Claire's heart sank. 'See you soon, China.' He leaned across the table and kissed her on the cheek.

The note Claire received took her by surprise. "Hi China. Are you free to meet for coffee tomorrow? I'll be in Lyons Corner House, Piccadilly, at twelve. Hope you can make it. Mitch."

Unable to sleep, Claire rose early, bathed, and took extra care styling her hair and applying her makeup. She slipped into a close-fitting navy blue two-piece with a white collar and put on the hat she'd dashed out and bought after receiving Mitch's note.

A last quick look in the hall mirror showed that the jaunty angle at which she wore the hat looked quite chic. A girlish giggle escaped her lips. Unlocking the door, she grabbed her coat, gas mask and handbag, and left the flat. She crossed Oxford Street to a passageway with steps that eventually took her to Soho Square. She stopped for a second to enjoy the warm dappled sunshine. It had been a long winter and even though spring was round the corner, the sun wasn't high enough in the sky to shine on the narrow streets leading from Soho to Piccadilly. She looked up. Smoke clung to the roofs of tall buildings and the stench of burnt wood and oil from incendiary bombs hung in the air.

Entering the Corner House in Piccadilly, Claire joined the queue of people at the shiny steel and glass counter. Nerves like jumping beans played havoc in her stomach. She hadn't seen Mitch since the weekend they were debriefed. She had hoped he would telephone – and dreamed that he would come to Coltishall to see her. He hadn't done either. But why would he? She let her mind wander to the night they lay next to each other in the hayloft in France. He had slept soundly while she, unable to sleep, laid and watched him. She felt a stirring in the pit of her stomach and inhaled slowly.

'Can I help you, madam?'

'Excuse me?' Claire felt someone tap her on the shoulder. 'It's your turn.'

'Oh, I'm so sorry,' Claire blushed. 'I was thinking, deciding, what to have.' She was thinking how wonderful it would be to be made love to by Alain Mitchell.

The girl behind the counter sighed. 'Have you thought yet, madam?'

'A pot of tea and…'

'And?' the girl snapped.

'A pot of coffee, please.' Claire watched as the girl poured boiling water into the tea and coffee pots. She put both on a tray with cups and saucers, milk jug and a dish with two sugar cubes and put it down in front of Claire with a clatter. 'And two tea cakes please. Sorry,' Claire said politely to the woman standing behind her, who rolled her eyes and pouted pinched pencil-thin lips. Blushing with embarrassment, Claire looked along the queue. It had grown. 'Don't worry about the teacakes, if--'

'I've taken them from the cake stand now!' Wishing she was invisible, Claire paid and found a table with a clear view of the door. Today it wasn't because she needed to watch for Germans, or because she might have to leave in a hurry, it was because she wanted to see the man who had woken so many feelings in her; feelings she hadn't been aware of until that night in the barn. She poured a cup of tea and cut one of the teacakes in half. She was too nervous to eat but, keeping her eyes on the door, she sipped her tea.

The door opened and her heart soared – then crashed. A small child ran in, followed by a large lady. Claire looked at the man behind them, expecting to see the child's father. Instead she saw Mitch. She stood up and waved. He saw her and, smiling broadly, weaved his way through the tables until he was standing next to her. She expected – hoped – he would kiss her on each cheek. Instead he put his arms around her and kissed her full on the lips. 'Boy, have I missed you, China!' he said and, keeping his arms round her, hugged her to him.

Claire laughed. She didn't have to remind him not to call her China in London. 'I've missed you too,' she said.

Mitch let her go and held her at arm's length. He looked into her eyes for what felt to Claire like minutes. She searched his face, sure that he wanted to say something. Instead he looked down at the table. 'This coffee for me?'

'Yes. It isn't a patch on the coffee Édith makes, I'm afraid.'

'I'm not here for the coffee, China,' he said, dropping his shoulder bag and gas mask on the floor and sitting down.

Her heart began to pound with excitement, and she felt her cheeks flush. It had been three months since they were in France together and she had thought of him every day; wondered where he was, how he was. She sat down and picked up her cup. The tea was cold; she didn't care. 'What have you been up to since we got back?' she asked.

'I've been putting young British women through their paces down in Hampshire. You?'

Claire felt a stab of jealousy. 'I spent a couple of weeks in the north east with my French professor friend and his family. I promised his son, again, if I was ever in Paris I'd look his mother up.' Claire saw Mitch tense. 'Don't worry, he's just a boy who is missing his mum. He has no idea what I do.' Claire wasn't sure that was true. Although they had never spoken about her work, the professor probably knew – and Éric was a bright boy. She decided she had said enough about the professor and his son. 'But for most of the time, I've been mentoring new recruits at Coltishall. I went to a couple of dances with Eddie. And I didn't get into any fights.' They both laughed. 'Eddie has finally cracked French grammar. She is hoping to take the fluency exam soon, so we had to speak French whenever we were alone. It was good for me, too, in case the colonel wants me to go back into the field,' she whispered.

Mitch leaned towards her. 'What do you want to do, China?'

'Go back to France, of course. I'm hoping that's why I've been called back to London.'

'In the meantime,' Mitch said, 'let's see some of this wonderful city while there is some of it left to see.'

Claire picked up her bag and gas mask and followed Mitch out into the fading sunshine. After buttoning her coat she caught hold of his outstretched hand and together they strolled through Piccadilly, past the theatres on the Haymarket and down to Trafalgar Square, where Mitch bought some stale bread from a shabbily-dressed boy of about twelve who was leaning on a sign that said Do Not Feed the Pigeons.

'My baby sister, Aimée, made me promise to do two things while I was in London. One was feed the birds in Trafalgar Square, and the other was send her a photograph of me doing it. Come on,' Mitch said, taking Claire by the hand and running across the square to a lion. As if she was a feather, Mitch lifted her onto the plinth. 'Stand close to the lion. I want to get you both in the picture.' Claire leant into the lion and looked over her shoulder. 'Perfect. Now turn and face me. Keep still and… smile! Okay! Now you take one of me.' As he lifted her down, Mitch held her close. She felt his warm breath on her face when he said, 'Did I tell you I've missed you, China?'

'Yes. But I don't mind you telling me again,' Claire purred.

Mitch kissed her. 'Okay, my turn.' He took the camera from around his neck and gave it to Claire. He leapt onto the plinth and again onto the back of the lion. 'It's a great view from up here,' he shouted, surveying the square.

'Sit still or the photograph will be blurred.' Mitch put his hand up to his brow, as if he was Admiral Nelson looking out to sea. He held the pose and Claire took the photograph.

'Boy, it's cold when the sun goes in,' he said, jumping down. 'When does the British summer begin?' He didn't wait for an answer. 'Let's go.' They ran through Trafalgar Square, scattering the pigeons. Claire let go of Mitch's hand and, as he turned, she took a snap. 'Aimée will love that,' he said, 'with all the pigeons flying around.'

Leaving the lions and pigeons behind, Mitch and Claire crossed the road to the National Gallery, walked for a few minutes, and turned onto the Strand. Near the top, a little before the Aldwych, they came to the Prince Albert Theatre. Either the windows were boarded up to protect them from bomb damage, or they had already been damaged, Claire couldn't tell. 'My sister works here,' she said. 'She started as an usherette, learned the songs and dances and when there was an opening, got a part in the chorus. I'd love to see her on stage, but...'

'But what?'

'She took over from a girl whose boyfriend was a Nazi sympathiser. He'd been a member of the BUF, or something, so...'

'So it's a scenario the colonel wouldn't want you to be involved in?'

'Something like that.'

Mitch put his arm round her shoulder. 'Tell you what, China. When this damn war's over, I'll take you to see your sister in the show.'

'Promise?'

'Promise! Hey, you're shivering.' Mitch pulled her closer. 'Are you hungry, China?'

'A little.'

'Okay,' Mitch beamed, 'I've got eggs and ham and bread, beer and-- All sorts of stuff at my place. Let's go back and have a feast. I'll make you my special omelette.' He put his fingers up to his lips and kissed the air. 'Or we could go to a restaurant if you'd rather?'

'No.' Claire laughed. 'I'd rather sample your culinary delights.'

Leaving the Strand, Mitch and Claire walked through Covent Garden to St Giles Circus, on to Tottenham Court Road and along Oxford Street towards Marble Arch. 'Is you're apartment actually in Portman Square?' Claire asked, as they turned into Orchard Street.

'Corner of Portland and Baker Street. Come on, China, we're nearly there,' Mitch said, walking faster until they were almost running. They arrived out of breath and laughing. Mitch took the key to the outside door from his pocket and raced up the steps and Claire followed. 'On the right,' he said, stopping to open a grey letterbox – the first in a row of several that was fixed to the wall just inside the door. 'A letter from Colonel Smith, but it can wait,' Mitch whispered, unlocking the door to flat number one.

'It's lovely,' Claire said, entering and turning full circle. 'It's so big. My flat isn't half the size of this.'

'I hadn't thought about it. I guess it's because it's my home in England. I can hardly pop over to Canada when I get forty-eight hours leave.' Mitch took Claire's coat and hung it up in the hall.

'Thank you. Can I use the bathroom?'

'Sure.' Mitch opened a door on the left.

In the bathroom Claire took Mitch's after shave lotion from the shelf. It was French. She took out the cork stopper and lifted the bottle to her nose. She closed her eyes, remembering the night they slept in the hayloft. She put the bottle back, turned the key in the lock and used the toilet. While she washed her hands she looked in the mirror. She looked a mess, which wasn't surprising; she had been running. She put the comb through her hair, applied a little lipstick and left.

'I thought we'd get warmed up before we eat.' Mitch handed Claire a cup of coffee and sat with his own.

'Were you here last night?' Claire asked.

'Yes, looking over some papers that the colonel sent over.' Mitch got up and crossed the room to the gramophone. 'What kind of music do you like, China?'

'I like swing, and jazz – all sorts really.'

'You'll like Billie Holiday then. "I've got my love to keep me warm…"' Mitch sang. A second later there was a crackle, followed by Billie Holiday's distinctive New York American accent. Sad and reflective one minute, strident and forceful the next, the jazz singer's unique voice filled the room. Mitch took a bottle of cognac from the cupboard beneath the gramophone, put it on the occasional table, and went into the kitchen. Waltzing back with two glasses, he put them next to the bottle and sat down on the settee by Claire. 'A drop of this will warm you up, China,' he said, pouring equal measures of the amber liquid into both glasses. He handed one glass to Claire and picked up the other.

Claire took a sip and a burning sensation hit the back of her throat. It took her breath away. She took a second sip and what tasted at first like a sharp spirit seemed to have mellowed to warm caramel.

Rich and smooth, it slipped down her throat. She emptied the glass, put it on the table and laid her head on the back of the settee. Humming along to another Billie Holiday song, Claire closed her eyes.

She had no idea how long she'd been sitting there, but when Billie Holiday stopped singing, she opened her eyes. She looked around. It took her a second to gather her wits. Then she saw Mitch sitting at the dining table with a stack of files in front of him. One file lay open and he was reading a large sheet of paper by the light of a standard lamp, the only light in the room.

'Hi, China. Had a good sleep?'

'I haven't been asleep,' Claire laughed. 'I closed my eyes to enjoy the music. What's the time?'

Mitch got up from the table and looked at his wristwatch. 'Ten-fifteen,' he said, dropping onto the settee next to her.

'What? Oh my God, I have been asleep. How embarrassing,' she said, burying her face in her hands.

'I've made coffee. Do you want some?'

'I ought to go and let you get on with…'

'What?'

Claire looked over to the table. 'Whatever it was you were reading.'

'Oh that. It's not important. It's only the date for the drop in France, and a list of what we're taking.'

Claire squealed. 'Are you teasing me? If you are, I swear I shall never forgive you,' she said, pretending to beat his chest.

Mitch took hold of her wrists and drew her to him until her lips were almost touching his. 'They are our instructions, but it's too late to go through them now. We'll look at them tomorrow, together.'

'Okay.'

'Do you want me to take you home, China?'

'No,' she whispered. 'I want to stay here with you tonight.'

Mitch picked her up and carried her to the bedroom. He laid her on the bed and looked into her eyes. 'Are you sure, China? Sure you want this?'

Claire put her arms around his neck and, arching her back, lifted her face until her lips met his. 'Yes, I'm sure,' she said, and kissed him.

Mitch took off her blouse and kissed her breasts. She tugged at his jumper. He pushed himself up until he was kneeling, pulled the jumper over his head, and threw it on the floor. He was soon kissing her again – on her lips, her ears, her neck. Claire became aroused and beneath his weight unbuttoned his shirt. Still kissing her, Mitch took off his trousers and pushed up her skirt. In a jumble of clothes and bed linen they found each other and made love.

Claire turned over and opened her eyes. Disappointed that Mitch wasn't lying next to her, she wiggled out of bed and wrapped a sheet around her. She could smell coffee and hear jazz music coming from the sitting room. Mitch was sitting at the table in boxer shorts reading the documents he had abandoned the night before. 'Good morning,' she said, putting her arms around his neck and kissing his bare shoulder. 'What are you reading?'

'Good morning, China. I'll tell you later,' he said, turning to face her. Pushing his chair back, he pulled her to him and kissed her. The butterflies in the pit of her stomach took flight. She let go of the sheet and it fell to the floor. She lifted her leg over his and lowered herself into a sitting position. Aroused, Mitch lifted her up and laid her on the settee. Without taking his eyes off her naked body, he took off his shorts and made love to her.

'You awake, China?' Mitch asked when Claire stirred.

She snuggled up to him and said, 'No.'

'You don't want to go back to France then?'

'What?' She opened her eyes. 'Of course I want to go back to France. Why?'

'I've got to see the colonel,' he said, pushing himself off the settee and putting his shorts back on. 'I bet you an English pound you'll be summoned in to see him later today.'

Suddenly wide awake, Claire sat up. 'I'd better go back to my flat,' she said, 'in case Vera Halliday rings.'

'Not before you've had a cup of coffee and some eggs,' Mitch said.

Claire was so excited she didn't think she'd be able to eat anything, but she ate two eggs on toast. 'That was lovely,' she said. When she'd finished eating, she took the dishes into the kitchen.

Mitch followed her in. 'China, we can't let anyone know you stayed here last night.' The sparkle in Claire's eyes faded. 'If Colonel Smith finds out we're seeing each other, we won't be able to work together.'

'I know,' she sighed. 'It isn't fair!'

Mitch put his finger up to her lips. 'It may not be fair, China, but it's a rule and it's one the colonel feels strongly about. He thinks if partners are lovers and one of them is caught in a dangerous situation, the other wouldn't act rationally – and if they didn't they would put their comrades in danger and compromise the Resistance cell.'

Claire thought for a second before looking up at Mitch and nodding. 'I can see how that could happen. So,' she stood on her tiptoes and kissed him on the cheek, 'I'll see you when I see you, partner.'

'We won't have to wait long, China. There's a full moon next week. Then,' he said, putting his arms around her and holding her close, 'when the tour's done--'

'I know.' They kissed passionately, but didn't speak again.

Mitch walked Claire to the door and when she opened her mouth to say goodbye he kissed her. As she walked down the steps of his apartment building, she sensed his eyes on her. She was still glowing from their lovemaking and excited because they were going back to France. Before crossing the road, she looked back. He was no longer at the door but watching from the window. She put her fingers to her lips and blew him a kiss. Smiling, Mitch saluted.

CHAPTER TWELVE

Holding onto the safety line, Claire beckoned Mitch. 'I can't see any lights,' she shouted above the noise of the Halifax's engines.

'With the wireless out of action, André might not have received confirmation of the drop,' Mitch shouted back.

'What if it's a trap? Jacques wouldn't have been able to let London know if the drop, or even the Resistance cell, had been compromised.'

Mitch shook his head vigorously. 'He'd have gone to another cell, another wireless operator.' He tapped the shoulder of the engineer, who was on his knees looking out of the door. Claire moved closer to hear what they were saying. 'The clouds are clearing. We've got eighty percent visual.'

Mitch turned to Claire. 'We're near the end of the full moon this month. If we don't get the wireless crystals to Jacques this drop, the Resistance will be out of contact for three, maybe four weeks. We're going in.' Claire nodded that she agreed.

The Halifax made a broad sweep of the area and came in at a thousand feet. The engineer bellowed, 'If you're going, captain, this is it!' He looked first at Mitch who nodded, and then at Claire who gave him the thumbs up.

'Ready?'

Claire stood beside the gaping aperture and waited. Her stomach lurched. She always thought she'd be sick before she jumped. She never was. She swallowed hard. The engineer brought his arm down like a whip and she jumped.

Clearing the plane, Claire began to glide. A second later Mitch was at her side and a second after that she pulled the ripcord. She felt the straps tighten and after being jerked up a little to the left she levelled. Mitch was below her. He had stayed in free-fall longer. Claire saw his parachute billowing on the ground. As her feet touched down a gust of wind took hold of her chute and she began to run. Bending her knees she regained control, and a second later her bottom cushioned the fall.

Quickly she gathered up her chute. She looked up as several parachutes floated down, the moon reflecting off their silky blooms. She ran across the field. Her fingers nimbly unbuckled the harness and she took out her overcoat. After putting it on she took out Mitch's coat and helped him into it. She next took her suitcase, basket and handbag from the container while Mitch put in their harnesses and parachutes.

There had always been a reception committee with the Belland brothers, to help carry the drop and hide it, but tonight there was only Claire and Mitch. She looked around. 'It's very quiet, Mitch. Are you worried?'

'No. We were late telling them there was a drop.' Claire wasn't convinced that was the reason. She didn't think Mitch was either, but she didn't question him; he had more experience than she did. 'Come on, Claire, put your back into it,' he said, lifting the end of a large cylinder-shaped container. Claire put her hands under the other end and hauled it to her knees. Jostling it until it was level and its weight distributed equally, she followed Mitch into woods near the farm.

Between them they carried every container into the densest part of the wood. 'Cover them with anything you can find,' Mitch said. 'I'm going to have a look around.'

Claire wanted to tell him to be careful; instead she said, 'Will do.' She piled sods of earth, brambles, broken branches and sticks onto the containers and when they were concealed, she looked for Mitch. She found him crouching at the edge of the wood watching the farmhouse.

The house was in darkness, which after curfew shouldn't have bothered Claire, but it did. The absence of the reception committee weighed heavily on her mind. She touched Mitch's arm and he stood up. When he turned to face her she stood on tiptoe and whispered in his ear, 'Something is wrong.' Mitch nodded that he thought so too. He began to move forward and suddenly stopped. Claire, close behind, almost walked into his back. He turned to her, put his forefinger to his lips, and shook his head. She nodded. The moon appeared hazily through a break in the clouds, giving enough light for Claire to see that the curtains at the windows of the farmhouse were not drawn, confirming something was wrong. She shivered with cold and fear.

Mitch tapped her again. He pointed to his eyes, and then the barn. Without making a sound he stepped from the wood to the cobbled farmyard, but returned almost immediately. 'Back!' he hissed. 'Get down!'

Claire hit the ground as a vehicle, its engine at full throttle, roared through the open doors at the back of the barn. As it sped through the barn's tall front doors, skidding into the farmyard, its half-shaded headlights swept across Claire's back. She held her breath and prayed she hadn't been seen. The vehicle came to a screeching halt at the front of the farmhouse. On her stomach, using her elbows and knees, Claire slowly edged her way a little further into the wood. Her heart pounded in her chest as she lay face down in the damp earth and listened. From what she could make out the Germans were part of a field patrol that had been sent to check on unoccupied farms in the area.

'No one here,' she heard one of them say.

'Shame. I'd have enjoyed a bit of target practice tonight,' another said, and fired into the wood.

Claire bit her clenched fist as a bullet whizzed past her head before burying itself in the ground inches from where she lay.

'Coming out here every night is a waste of time,' the first German said. 'We could be in the brothel, eating French tart,' he laughed.

'You'll catch something in that place.'

'Come on, let's go. We have better things to do than idle about here.'

'One minute, Hans, I'm having a piss,' a different voice shouted.

Hans muttered something in response that Claire didn't understand. She lifted her head just enough to see the one called Hans take a packet of cigarettes from his pocket. He put one in his mouth and lit it before passing the pack to the other men. Having overheard the banter, the soldier who had relieved himself against the farmhouse wall swaggered over to the well clutching his crotch crudely and making obscene remarks. His speech was slurred and

150

peppered with expletives. He was laughing, which made it difficult for Claire to understand what he was saying. She caught *bomb* and *window*, but the gist of his crude remarks was that he had found a virgin at the farm after he'd burned the farmer out and had given her what she wanted. She had begged him to stop, but he laughed in her face saying, "*No comprendre le Français*" and took her again. Claire turned her head in the direction of the braggart's voice. Illuminated by a match as he lit his cigarette, his broad plate-like face, stone-cold eyes and pug nose above a drunken slobbering mouth was one she would not forget.

A few minutes later they clambered into a Kübelwagen, the German military's version of the US Army's four wheel drive, and, laughing and cheering, roared out of the yard the way they had come. Claire couldn't make out everything they had said, but she understood enough to know that their next port of call was a brothel on the way to Bloir.

'Psst!' Mitch tapped her on the shoulder. She pushed herself up until she was on her knees. He pointed to a small gap between two bushes, and again to his eyes. When he moved, Claire followed. Crouching, she crept stealthily towards the opening. She felt his hand on her shoulder again, her cue to stop. The clouds had cleared and the moon's eerie yellow light shone down onto the kitchen window. There was no reflection. There was no glass in it.

Claire watched Mitch run across the yard to the barn and disappear inside. A second later he reappeared and, with his back flat against the wall of the farmhouse, he waved at her to come. As Mitch had, Claire kept low and ran like a hare until she was standing next to him. Panting with fear and exertion, but not daring to make a sound, she flattened her body against the wall. Mitch touched his nose and whispered, 'Fire.' Claire sniffed and nodded. She could smell it now; gasoline and burnt wood. She tapped Mitch on the shoulder and pointed to the kitchen window ledge on which she had been leaning. He ran the palm of his hand along it and charred paint chipped off. 'Come on, let's have a look.'

Inside, the smell of gasoline wasn't as strong. Carefully, cupping it in his hand, Mitch struck a match. Its pale glow was enough to show the damage the fire had done. Someone had put the fire out, or the rain had got in, because the floor was wet. Mitch blew out the flame, spat on his finger, and held the match between finger and thumb before putting it into his pocket. He rubbed the stone floor with his other hand and sniffed. 'Water,' he said with relief. He led the way along the plastered wall of the passage to Édith Belland's front room and lit another match. 'Not as much fire damage in here,' he said. 'Odd that this room has hardly been touched when the kitchen is half gutted. The kitchen window ledge outside is so blistered, you'd think…'

'The fire was started outside, by one of the thugs who were here earlier.'

'How do you know?'

'I heard him bragging about it to the others. He threw a bomb through the window.' Claire felt tears threaten. Édith's front room, her best room, stank of smoke and the settee was rotting with damp. She followed Mitch upstairs. The fire hadn't touched the first floor, but the German soldiers had. The beds were a jumble of ripped and stained sheets and blankets. Empty beer bottles and half-eaten scraps of food littered the floors. 'I'm tired,' Claire said, yawning. 'Would it hurt if we had a rest? We could take it in turns to keep watch.'

'No, it wouldn't hurt. We should get some sleep, but not in the house. I wouldn't put it past those horny jackasses to pick up a couple of girls and bring them back here. Come on. Let's get out.'

Claire followed Mitch downstairs and after checking that there was no one outside, he led the way to the barn. Claire stopped as soon as they were inside. 'You said you wouldn't put it past them to come back tonight. Won't they drive through here as they did earlier?'

'Yes, but they won't know we're here, because we'll be up there.' Mitch pointed to the store loft. 'We'll have the advantage because we'll be able to see and hear them.'

'What if they set fire to the place again?'

'Why would they? What would be the point?' He took the ladder from behind a stack of hay and leant it against the floor of the loft. Claire climbed up. 'Get the bedding from the secret store while I fetch the bags.'

'At least it's dry up here,' she said, when Mitch returned.

After passing up the cases and Claire's basket and handbag, Mitch took the ladder two rungs at a time, and then pulled it up. Claire made up two makeshift beds while Mitch unbolted the door to the rope-pulley. He pushed it open a few inches. 'In case we have to leave in a hurry.' Claire smelled the pillows and grimaced. 'You can't afford to be fussy,

China,' Mitch said, taking the pillows and placing them next to each other. 'We might not be warm, but we will be safe. No one will suspect we're up here.' He lay down. 'Let's get some shut-eye. I'll wake you in a couple of hours. We need to be on the road before dawn.'

Claire lay uneasily between the itchy blankets. She looked across the loft, through the ill-fitting pulley door, and out into the night. The clouds had cleared. She could see stars glinting in the sapphire sky. She sighed.

'Can't you sleep?' Mitch whispered.

'No.' Claire turned over and Mitch put his arms around her.

'Try, China. Tomorrow is going to be a long one.'

Claire lifted her face and looked into Mitch's eyes. He kissed her and she became aroused. 'Make love to me, Mitch. Make love to me and make me forget the horridness of all this.'

Claire opened her eyes. Mitch was watching her. 'What time is it?'

'Almost four-thirty.'

'I could just drink a lovely cup of coffee,' she said, yawning.

Mitch laughed. 'You hate French coffee. You said it tastes like tar.'

'That was a lifetime ago. I'm used to it now.'

'Well, the sooner you're up and dressed, the sooner we can find you a café and buy you some. So jump to it.'

'I need to use the toilet and have a wash,' she said shyly.

'You can use the outside toilet, but you can't wash in the kitchen. We need to leave it as the Germans left it. Wash in the river at the back of the house. Go upstream a way, you won't be seen.' Mitch kissed her on the cheek. He then kissed her on the lips. Sighing, he kissed her again and Claire pushed him away playfully. 'Okay, let's make this place look as it did when we arrived. The Germans are bound to come back.'

Claire folded the blankets and dropped them into the hiding place, lowered the trap-door and covered it with straw. While she gathered her belongings, Mitch bolted the rope-pulley door and roughed up the straw where they had lain. With all evidence that they had been there eradicated, Claire climbed down, leaving Mitch to bring down the bags and hide the ladder.

'Why can't we use the well?' Claire called. Kneeling beside it, she picked up a shiny object.

'It isn't clean,' Mitch shouted, running across the yard to her.

'What's this?' Claire held up a pretty silver hair slide. 'These little stones look like real diamonds and sapphires,' she said, running her finger along the spine of the slide. 'I wonder who it belongs to?' She turned, put the hair slide on the low wall surrounding the well, and froze.

Mitch grabbed her by her upper arms and roughly swung her round until she was facing him. 'I said the water isn't clean,' he hollered. 'Wash in the river. That's an order!'

'Mitch, stop!' Claire shouted, twisting free of his grip. 'It's too late. I've seen her. I've seen the girl in the well.'

Mitch closed his eyes and lowered his head. 'I saw her earlier, but I didn't want you to--'

'I know.' Claire turned back to the girl. 'She looks like marble. And her head... Do you think she's the girl the German soldier was talking about?'

Mitch nodded. 'Looks as if one of them broke the poor kid's neck.'

'What? We need to report it to the authorities.'

'We don't. We're fighting a war. We need to walk away and forget what we've seen.'

'How can we? Killing that girl wasn't war. It was murder.'

'We don't know that. It could have been an accident. She might have been running in the dark, slipped and fell.'

'But you said--'

'Whatever happened to her, we can't report it. We'll be putting ourselves, the Belland family, the Resistance group and everyone who has ever helped us in danger. No, Claire, we walk away. We'll tell Édith when we find her. She'll know what to do.'

'*If* we find her.'

'We will find her. But until then, we forget what we've seen.' Mitch put his hand under Claire's chin and lifted her face to his. 'Do you understand?'

'I understand.' After using the toilet Claire went back to the well. She took the hair slide from the wall and put it in her coat pocket. Then she closed her eyes and said a prayer.

It only took her a few seconds to walk to the back of the house. She heard the splash and tumble of the river falling like a waterfall over the rocks beneath the bridge as soon as she turned the corner.

Running to the river's edge, she fell to her knees, plunged her hands into the water and rubbed them vigorously. Then she cupped a handful and splashed it on her face. She gasped. It was so cold it took her breath away. It was May, almost summer, but the water coming from the hills was icy. She braced herself and washed as much of her body as she was able, without undressing.

'Are you ready, China?' Mitch shouted.

'Yes, I'm coming.' Mitch acknowledged her reply with a wave and walked on. Taking a small towel from her case, Claire began to dry herself. She lifted her arms. Her skin was white and mottled from the cold, like the girl in the well. She shook her head in an attempt to shake away the image of the dead girl, and returned the towel to her case. It was wet, but there was nothing she could do about it. She rolled it up and placed it as far away from her second set of clothes as she could. It would eventually make them damp. She looked up at the sky, at the dark and gloomy clouds; she would probably be as wet as the towel before she arrived in Gisoir. She quickly closed the case and got to her feet. Running along the lane, she caught up with Mitch. 'From now on, I don't think you should call me China,' she said.

'*Désolé, mademoiselle,*' he said, with a twinkle in his eye. 'Are you all right?'

Claire sighed. 'As I'll ever be.' She was used to being called mademoiselle. She liked it, especially when Mitch said it. She liked her code name too, China Blue. When she told Mitch someone had said her eyes were the colour of Wedgwood, he'd said, "Yeah? Who's Wedgwood?" Being a Canadian, she wasn't surprised that Mitch didn't know Wedgwood was the name of a maker of fine china, but she was disappointed that he hadn't noticed her blue eyes. Everybody did, even Colonel Smith. She sighed.

'Come on, dreamer, we need to get going,' he said, taking her case and walking away.

'Yes. Sorry.' Claire fell into step at his side. 'Give me something to carry.'

'Take your shopping basket. I'll give you your suitcase when we get to Gisoir, in case we get split up.'

Claire shuddered at the thought and put the notion out of her mind. She had been trained to compartmentalise things. Though a compartment where she could put the girl in the well, she was yet to find out. With Mitch carrying her case, Claire was able to walk faster. 'From now on, we should only speak French. You must only call me Claire, and I shall only call you Alain. Are you listening, Alain?'

'What?'

'French! We should--'

'OK, China,' Mitch winked.

'I'm serious, Alain. I am your cousin,' Claire said, in French.

'What? My kissing cousin?'

'Hey!' She clipped him across the shoulder. 'Less of the sauce.'

Side by side they walked along, chatting French. The heavy drizzle turned into rain – and with the rain came a feeling of uncertainty. On the outskirts of Gisoir, they stopped to discuss what they were going to do once they were in the town.

'You pick up some food from the market while I

deliver the wireless crystals to Jacques. I'll ask him about the fire at the farm and where the Belland family are living.'

'Will you tell him about the girl?'

'No. I shall only mention the fire – say we were passing and noticed it. He's bound to know something. If he doesn't I'll ask around.'

'Is that wise? You never know who you're talking to these days.' She stopped speaking and checked herself. Alain was not a novice; he would be discreet. 'Right! Where shall we meet?'

'I'll see you in Café La Ronde at twelve. Don't worry if I'm a bit late. If I get an address for Édith, and it's near, I might call on her.' Alain looked at his wristwatch. 'It's almost eleven. That gives you enough time to buy food, doesn't it?'

'Yes, plenty.' Claire shivered. She pulled her coat around her and buttoned it up to the neck. 'I've got coins for the market, but only enough tokens for a loaf and some cheese.'

'Keep an eye on the road,' Alain said, taking off his right shoe. He took several notes from it and handed them to Claire. 'Get a decent bottle of wine and some cakes, if you can. On second thoughts, take the lot.' He took off his other shoe. 'It's what the colonel gave us for weapons and bribes and stuff.' Claire's mouth fell open. 'Men are stopped more often than women – and if I'm stopped with this amount of money on me, I'll be arrested. You, on the other hand, can bat your eyelashes and say it's your parents' life savings that they have given you to take to your grandparents in Paris. Keep a couple of notes in your purse for food and wine and put a wad in the compartment in the bottom of your shopping basket, the rest in your shoes.' Claire looked questioningly at Alain. 'If you're searched they'll find it in your basket, and won't check your shoes.' When Claire had done as Alain instructed she put her shoes back on, taking care not to scrunch up the notes, buckled them and stood up. 'You'd better take your case too, in case we get separated.'

Claire hated the thought of them being separated, but took the case. 'I suppose if I was going all the way to Paris to visit *Granny*, I'd have a change of clothes with me.' She looked into Alain's eyes and fought back the tears.

'Don't worry, China, it's only to be on the safe side. Yes?'

'Yes,' she said, reluctantly.

'Good. And remember, if one of us gets stopped by the Gestapo, or any member of their puppet show, the other one keeps walking. We walk and we don't look back for anything. Claire? Is that clear?' Alain put his hand under her chin and lifted her face. She looked up. 'Is that clear?'

'Yes!' she snapped. 'Of course it is!'

'Good. Come on then, little cousin, I'll buy you something nice to eat at lunchtime, if you're a good girl,' he laughed.

CHAPTER THIRTEEN

Claire sauntered along pretending to be uninterested in her surroundings while taking everything in. A convoy of Field cars and black Mercedes, the car of choice for German officers, passed them on the road going into Gisoir. By the time she arrived in the town centre the vehicles were parked along the main boulevard. Soldiers stood around smoking cigarettes and talking loudly. As she approached them they lowered their voices. As she drew level they whispered. Claire could feel their eyes on her, watching her as she walked past.

There was a sudden burst of laughter and one of them shouted, 'Here pussy, pussy!'

'Stupid French bitch,' another said. 'She's got a fat arse.'

'Good to hang onto when giving it a shag.' They all laughed.

Claire stopped dead. She recognised two of the voices from the farm the night before. The braggart wasn't one of them. Even so, she wanted to round on them, tell them what filthy murdering pigs they were – but she didn't react. She lifted her head, confident in the knowledge that they didn't know she could understand what they were saying, and walked on. At the bakery, she caught her reflection in the window and pretended to check her appearance. Instead she checked theirs. She committed to memory every strand of hair, every skin tone, eye colour, lip and nose shape. Claire hadn't always appreciated the photographic memory that she'd had since childhood, but she did now. She slipped her hand into her coat pocket and fingered the small silver hair slide she had found by the well. If she ever saw the brute who raped and probably killed the girl, she hoped it would be on a dark night when she had Alain and the Belland brothers with her.

She browsed the produce in the window of the bakery and opened the door. Loud laughter and more rude comments followed her in. She closed the door firmly and asked the baker for a loaf and a couple of buns. 'I promised my cousin I would try to find something sweet for him,' she explained. The door opened and Claire could tell by the sudden look of fear in the baker's eyes that it wasn't a paying customer. Claire could feel the German soldier's eyes boring into her. She straightened and watched the baker take a loaf from the shelf behind. Turning back to the counter, he almost dropped it. Claire smiled, trying to reassure him.

The baker took two iced buns from beneath the counter. He wrapped them in a sheet of white paper, did the same to the loaf, and handed them to her.

'Thank you,' she said, giving him the food tickets. Putting the white parcels in her basket, Claire turned to leave. 'Excuse me,' she said to the soldier, but he didn't move. 'Please...' she said politely, looking into his face. While he stood like an arrogant stuffed shirt, she took in every whisker and blemish on his face. In a few seconds she had committed to memory everything he saw in his shaving mirror. It was him. The drunken soldier from the farm – the bastard who, if he hadn't killed the girl in the well, had raped her – was barring her way. Eventually he moved. 'Thank you,' she said, in

162

a voice much higher than usual. She walked out of the shop and into the sunshine, hoping he hadn't noticed how frightened she was.

Letting the door swing shut behind her, Claire turned towards the town square. Her heart was thumping against her ribs and her legs felt like jelly. If she could make it as far as the market she'd hide among the stalls. At the entrance she looked back and let out a long sigh. The soldier who had followed her into the bakery was nowhere to be seen. Relieved, she walked into the covered market. She bought a small camembert and wedge of brie. She also bought a couple of apples and three tomatoes from an old woman selling produce from a wooden tray. She had tied rope to either end of the tray and hung it round her neck. The rope bit into the old woman's wrinkled skin. She gave Claire a tired smile, displaying brown teeth from smoking strong tobacco, and offered her a stick of celery.

'Thank you, Madame.'

'You are welcome, Miss,' she said, and shuffled on.

Claire put the food in her basket and set off across the square to the Café La Ronde to meet Alain. As she entered the bell attached to the top of the door jingled. She looked around. Alain wasn't there. The clock above the counter said five minutes to twelve. She was hungry, but decided to wait until Alain arrived before ordering lunch. She asked for a cup of coffee and found a table for two that had a good view of the door. She would see Alain when he came in – the German too, if he had followed her. She lifted her shopping basket onto the seat of the vacant chair to give the impression it was taken.

The café was always busy at lunchtime and Claire didn't want to risk someone taking the chair before Alain claimed it.

The waiter arrived and placed a cup of coffee and a small dish in front of her. Claire dropped a couple of coins into the dish and lifted the cup without taking her eyes off the door. She looked at the clock again. Ten minutes past twelve. Alain was late, but then he was going to find out where Édith and the family had moved to. Speculating on where they might be, Claire sipped her coffee. Thérèse's parents lived north of the town; they would know. Alain had probably gone to see them, or to one of the Resistance men's homes. Suddenly several customers jumped up, left their seats, and ran to the window. Claire took her basket and joined them. Half a dozen German soldiers had surrounded someone, a man, demanding to know who he was. Although his back was to her, Claire recognised the soldier who had followed her. 'Damn bully,' she said under her breath. A staff car screeched to a halt in front of the café, blocking the view.

Several men cursed and a couple went outside to see more clearly what was going on. Claire followed. She looked up at each one as he spoke, pretending she was with them. A soldier ran to the car and opened the back door. A tall hard-faced captain with skeletal features and small piercing eyes, wearing the dark field green uniform of the Waffen SS – the death mask on his peaked hat highly polished – stepped from it and strode across to the pack of grey uniforms. A corporal broke the circle to let the SS officer in, and Claire gasped. The recipient of the German soldier's victimization was

164

Alain.

'Halt!' the SS officer shouted.

The soldiers did as ordered and moved away. With a sardonic lopsided smirk, the SS officer ordered Alain to produce his identity papers. Alain put his hand inside his jacket and the officer drew his gun. Alain put the offending hand in the air and held his jacket open with the other. The officer nodded sharply to one of the soldiers, who snatched Alain's papers roughly. The soldier handed the folded document to his superior.

'I'm afraid,' Alain said, 'there has been a mistake. I'm--'

'Silence!' the captain shouted. Alain stopped speaking immediately and bowed his head. The SS officer circled him, hitting the palm of his black leather-gloved hand with his truncheon. 'English pig!'

'No.' Alain straightened. 'I'm--'

'I said silence!' Snarling, the officer raised the truncheon and brought it down on Alain's left shoulder. The force of the blow sent Alain sprawling to his knees. 'Get up!' the German shouted. Alain stumbled to his feet and the officer brought the truncheon down again, this time sideways across his face. Alain's cheek split open on impact and Claire saw him wince as he fell to the ground. Blood gushed from the wound, but the brave Canadian said nothing.

The officer flicked his hand at two soldiers. 'Take him to headquarters.'

Both clicked their heels. '*Hauptsturmführer*!' they said as one, and hauled Alain to his feet.

The commotion had brought people out of their

houses and shops. Inquisitive at first, they stayed to watch the sport. Elbowing her way to the front of the crowd, Claire caught Alain's eye. The lines on his forehead deepened when he saw her and he shook his head. Tears filled her eyes as she pushed her way towards him.

'No!' he shouted. Struggling, he continued, 'Leave me! Go!'

Claire stopped in her tracks. Alain was shouting to her, telling her to leave. But because he was being dragged away by German soldiers they assumed he was shouting at them and punched him in the stomach. He doubled over, but remained on his feet. Claire screamed. She had caused her brave lover to be hurt again.

Carried along by a crowd that had grown from a few dozen to what looked like a hundred people, Claire had no choice but to keep moving forward. Suddenly a huge man pushed her out of the way and she found herself with room to turn and look back. Standing on tiptoe, she could see the SS officer's black Mercedes. If she could only get to him, explain. She pushed through the oncoming tide of people and there he was, getting into his car. She needed to move quickly. She broke through the crowd and raised her arm. But before she had time to attract his attention, someone grabbed her from behind and pulled her back into the throng. She struggled to free herself, twisting and kicking. 'Now now, my little tiger of a wife!' she heard a familiar voice say. 'Why so passionate about a stranger? Save your passion for me in our bed.'

Several men, having heard the dialogue, burst into laughter. But the SS officer, unaware or uninterested, got into his car and a second later was driven away. Claire glared at them, but they continued to joke crudely. 'Ouch! Very well, *husband*,' she shouted. 'Not so tight, you're hurting me.'

Frédéric Belland relaxed his grip. 'Be quiet, Claire,' he whispered. 'Do not attract attention. It is too late. You can do nothing to help Alain now.' Emotionally drained, with tears streaming down her face, Claire let Frédéric lead her away. At the end of the road she looked back. Alain and the Germans were gone. The crowd had dispersed. The square was empty.

'Is there something between you and Alain, Claire? Something perhaps that has developed since you were last in France?'

'I don't know what you mean. Mitch – Alain – is my partner. I look on him as a brother.'

'In the square you looked on him as a lover. You cannot fool me. I know love.' Claire tutted and ran on ahead. Frédéric caught up with her. 'Since you were last here I too have found love. The way you looked at Alain is the way my beautiful Monique looks at me.'

'I'm pleased you've found love, Frédéric, and I'm sure Monique is beautiful, but stop this nonsense about Alain and me and tell me what happened at the farm.'

Walking through the cobbled streets of the old town, Frédéric told Claire that the first farmhouse to be burned was Thérèse's parents' home. 'Thérèse was visiting them when German soldiers arrived. They beat up her father and turned Thérèse and her mother out of the house. Then they set fire to it.'

'What about the animals?'

'They loaded them into trucks and took them away. They didn't set fire to the barn, but they took the machinery. Theirs was the first farm, but it was not the last.'

Claire put her hand on Frédéric's arm. 'When did you lose your farm?'

'One week later. We had moved Mother out by then. She did not want to leave, but André is very persuasive. Being the oldest son, she does what he says. She doesn't even ask me. A know-it-all, that is André. But,' Frédéric admitted, 'on this occasion he was right.'

Ever since Claire had known the Belland brothers there had been friction between them. Their relationship reminded her of hers with her sister Ena. When they were children they argued about anything and everything; it almost became a game. She thought of her younger sister now with love, pleased that she had chosen a safe way to help the war effort by working in a factory, instead of joining the armed forces. She brought her focus back to Frédéric. 'Your brother is just looking after you.'

'Huh!' Frédéric grunted.

'I don't know how your mother puts up with you two,' Claire said, smiling up at Frédéric. When she and Alain first stayed with Édith and her sons, Claire was sure Frédéric had a crush on her. He would blush when she spoke to him and look shyly at her from under long black eyelashes. She looked at him now. He didn't blush. 'So tell me about your new sweetheart. Are you serious about each other?'

'Yes. We are engaged. I haven't bought her a ring yet, but I asked her to marry me and she has said yes.'

'The ring isn't important. It's the commitment that matters,' Claire said. Why hadn't she told Mitch how she felt about him in London, or even last night, when she had the chance?

'Are you thinking about Alain?' Frédéric asked.

'Alain? No! Well yes, of course, but at that moment I was thinking about your mother,' she lied. 'Wondering how she is managing away from the farm.'

'You will find out in one minute. We are almost there.'

Leaving the wide road behind them, they turned into a narrow avenue and Claire saw Édith Belland waving from a door in a wall at the back of a terraced house. She ran to her. 'Édith!' she cried, falling into her friend's arms.

'What is it, my dear? Why the tears?' Édith Belland wrapped her arms around Claire tightly. Then she held her at arm's length and searched her face. 'Come,' she said, looking left and right before leading Claire through the door and across a small yard with outhouses on the right. 'Where is Alain?' she asked, once they were in the house.

'The Germans stopped and questioned him and--'

'They've taken him to headquarters, Mama.'

'When? How? What time was this? Did he see Jacques, before…?'

'Yes,' Claire said. 'We arranged to meet in the café on the square after he'd been to Jacques. We were going to look for you when we'd had lunch. Alain said if Jacques didn't know where you were, he was going to ask around.'

'We haven't told Jacques. We haven't told anyone. We thought if no one knew no one could be forced to tell. Oh Claire…' Édith Belland put her head in her hands. 'The silly boy should have known we would have found you.' She looked up at Frédéric. 'Go to your brother. Tell him Claire is here and she is safe. Then tell him what has happened to Alain. And be careful!' she shouted as Frédéric left.

'I am so sorry you've lost the farm, Édith,' Claire said when they were alone.

'The farm? It was the dream of my late husband. Once he had gone and the children were grown…' She threw her hands in the air and shrugged. 'Besides, it is still there. The Germans had no intention of destroying it. They could have burned it to the ground, but no!' she said, shaking her head vehemently. 'The pathetic incendiary device they threw through the kitchen window was a warning. When they realised we had already left, they put the fire out immediately.'

'How do you know?'

'André and Frédéric were watching from the woods. They went back after moving me here, to make sure we hadn't left anything behind that would lead the Germans to suspect we were part of the Resistance. They have burnt out other farmers, and always put the fires out as soon as they've left. It is bully-boy tactics only. They want to keep the farms intact to farm the land themselves when they have brought France to its knees. Ha!' Édith guffawed and pretended to spit. 'They have no intention of destroying our property. It is our morale they wish to destroy, but that will never happen. You must be hungry, child,' she said, pulling Claire's coat from her back and hanging it up on a hook on the back of the kitchen door. 'I shall make something to eat.'

Claire handed her the shopping basket. 'There isn't much, I'm afraid – just bread and cheese, a little fruit and a couple of buns. But there is this,' she said, taking the false bottom out of her shopping basket.

Édith's mouth fell open. 'How much is here?'

Claire handed Édith 100,000 francs. 'And there is 25,000 in each of my shoes,' she said taking them off.

'Good God, child, how did you manage to walk on all this?'

'It wasn't easy. It was very uncomfortable,' Claire said, rubbing her feet, 'but Alain wanted me to carry it in case he--' Tears fell from her eyes.

'Come now, child, don't upset yourself. The Gestapo stop people all the time, keep them overnight for questioning, and release them the following day.' Édith looked at the money again and shook her head. 'We must hide this,' she said, taking a brick from the side of the hearth. She rolled up the cash and put it into the hole, replacing the brick and brushing dust up against it. She stood back and looked at the hiding place, then put her arms around Claire. 'Thank you, child. Money buys many things, including information. If Alain has not been released by this time tomorrow, we will use some of it to find out why. But now you must eat. And when the boys get here, after they have eaten, they will fetch the drop.'

Claire couldn't get the girl in the well out of her mind. She looked across the room at Édith, already busy boiling pans of water and chopping vegetables. Claire had no idea where André was, or how long it would take Frédéric to find him. What she did know was that she needed to speak to Édith now, because her sons could be back any minute. 'Édith, will you sit down? I need to tell you something.' Édith carried on chopping carrots, smiled and looked up questioningly. 'Please,' Claire said, 'it is important.' Claire waited for the older woman to sit.

'What is it, child? Out with it. You're worrying me.'

Claire cleared her throat. 'There's a young woman at the farm--'

'What? Living there?'

'No. She was dead.'

'But why would a young woman be at a deserted farm? Where did she come from? How did she--' Suddenly a look of horror crossed Édith's face.

'What is it, Édith?'

She closed her eyes and put her hands together in prayer. 'No, no, no. Please God,' she howled, 'do not let it be Monique.'

'Monique? Frédéric's fiancée?' Claire put her arms round her friend. 'Hush now. I'm sure the girl isn't local. When we arrived we heard Germans soldiers bragging that they pick up girls from the town and bring them to the farm. It is more likely to be one of them. A local girl would be missed. Monique would be missed.'

Shaking her head, Édith lifted the skirt of her pinafore and wiped her tear-stained face. 'The day after we left the farm Monique was going to visit her grandmother in--' She waved her hand in the air as if to say the name of the place didn't matter. It didn't. 'She promised to call to say goodbye on the way to the station. Frédéric went to the farm, but Monique wasn't there. He went to her house and her mother said she had left, that they must have missed each other. Frédéric was disappointed that he didn't get to see her, but with transport unreliable these days we assumed she had caught an earlier or an unscheduled train, and didn't have time to stop by.'

'Has no one been back to the farm since?'

'Yes. The boys went over a day, maybe two, before the drop and it was clear then that German soldiers were using the house as a brothel. They wanted to send a message to London, to arrange another field for the drop, but as you know Jacques' wireless wasn't working, which is why Alain brought the crystals...' Édith Belland's face was suddenly as white as flour. She put her hands to the crucifix that hung from her neck. 'You don't think the Germans…?'

'I don't know… No. Alain said it looked like an accident.'

'An accident? Where was she? If you saw her, why didn't the boys see her? You must tell me, Claire. If it is Monique, I need to prepare Frédéric.'

'The girl we found – and I'm sure it is not Monique – was in the well.'

Édith Belland began to tremble. 'We will say nothing, Claire. We must not speak of this to Frédéric, or André, not until we know whether or not the girl is Monique. Yes?'

'Yes,' Claire agreed. 'But how will we--?' Édith pulled her coat from a hook on the back of the kitchen door. 'You're going to the farm, aren't you?' Édith looked at Claire. She didn't need to speak. 'I'm coming with you.' Claire grabbed her coat and followed Édith out of the house.

Édith opened the door of a small shed next to the toilet in the cobbled back yard. 'Thérèse's bicycle,' she said, hauling her daughter-in-law's bike towards Claire. 'Mine is here, against the wall. Come, we have little time. We must be back before curfew.'

Ten minutes later they had left Gisoir behind and were cycling along the road to the farm. There was no traffic. Claire was sick with worry about Mitch, but there was nothing she could do to find out why he had been taken to Gestapo headquarters, or how long they intended to keep him, until tomorrow. Her legs were tired and she felt lightheaded with hunger. It had been almost twenty-four hours since she had eaten, but that wasn't important. It was important to find out if the girl in the well was Frédéric's fiancée, so she pushed down on the bike's pedals and followed Édith. When the farm came into view, Édith slowed down and, taking her feet off the pedals, coasted until she was able to put them on the ground. Claire pulled on the brakes and stopped beside her. 'We must hide the bicycles and go the rest of the way on foot,' Édith whispered. She wheeled her bike down a slope and into a small wood. 'Here,' she hissed, beckoning Claire, 'behind these trees.' Claire followed and once the bikes were hidden, she and Édith weaved their way through the trees to the farm.

From the edge of the wood the two women waited and watched. It was eerily quiet. Not even a rustle of leaves as the wind blew. The sun, a fading orange ball in a darkening sky, had begun to slip down behind the hills in the west. 'It will soon be dusk, Édith. We should hurry,' Claire said.

'Yes, if we are going to get back before dark we must move.' Quickly and quietly Édith made her way across the farmyard to the well, looked in, and fell to her knees. 'Monique,' she cried, making the sign of the cross. She leaned forward and took the girl's hand.

'Édith,' Claire said softly, 'we must go if we're going to get home before curfew.' Claire put her arm on Édith's shoulder; the woman was praying. Claire didn't want to be disrespectful but to be found here by the Germans would mean capture at the very least. And if they suspected that either she or Édith knew the dead girl, they would probably be killed too. 'Édith?'

'Yes, I am coming. But first we must take Monique from the well. Frédéric must not find her here. We will lay her by the river. We'll make it look as if she was taking a short cut to the station and fell from the bridge.'

There was no arguing with her. Édith took one of Monique's arms and motioned Claire to take the other. As they pulled the girl's white marbled body from the well there was a sickening crack, as if her body was breaking, and a foul smell. Claire thought she would be sick and held her breath. Monique's legs came free of the bucket easily and between them Claire and Édith carried her to the river and laid her at the water's edge.

'Look.' Édith pointed to a large round stone under the bridge. 'Move her so her head is lying on it like a pillow.'

They positioned Monique's thin body to look as if she had fallen from the narrow bridge. 'An

accident!' Édith shook her head. 'A tragic accident!
Now you are safe, and you are decent,' she said,
pulling on Monique's bloodstained skirt.
'Goodnight, child. Tomorrow Frédéric will find you
and bring you home.'

They cycled back in silence. It wasn't a long
journey but Claire felt more tired with every bend in
the road. In the small enclosed back yard Claire
returned Thérèse's bicycle to the shed, and after
bolting the door to the yard, Édith propped her
bicycle against the wall. Claire stood at the side of
the kitchen door, waiting for Édith to enter first. As
she passed, Édith took Claire's hand. 'Thank you,
my dear. We will talk later, but for the time being
we will say nothing. We must be brave for
Frédéric's sake, yes?'

Claire nodded and gave Édith's hand a
reassuring squeeze. She took a deep breath and
heard Édith do the same.

CHAPTER FOURTEEN

Édith Belland opened the back door and entered the kitchen to two pairs of questioning eyes. Claire followed her in. 'Mother? We've been out of our minds with worry. Where the hell have you been?' André demanded.

'Trying to find out why the Gestapo took Alain, where do you think?'

'And did you find out?' he asked.

'No. Claire will go into the town tomorrow and speak to Jacques. He may know something.' She went to the stove. 'Being out of your mind with worry didn't affect your appetite, I see.' She steadied herself against the range and looked into a large saucepan. 'I am sorry, son. Thank you for making supper and for leaving some for Claire and me.' Édith took two dishes from the shelf and spooned a helping of vegetables into each. 'Frédéric, put a log on the fire in the sitting room. Claire and I will join you when we have eaten.' When her sons had left the kitchen, Édith put the two dishes of food on the table. Claire heaved as the bitter taste of bile rose from her stomach to her throat. She closed her eyes. To eat after what she had just seen and done wouldn't be easy, but she felt dizzy from lack of sustenance and her head was pounding with dehydration. Calling on every ounce of willpower she possessed, Claire did what she had been trained to do, put what had happened during the day to the back of her mind and turned to her meal. The two women ate without speaking. When they had finished they joined André and Frédéric in the sitting room.

Sitting by the fire, they drank red wine and listened to the wireless. The atmosphere was subdued. André left after half an hour saying he would be back in the morning to discuss how they were going to get Alain out of German headquarters, after he had organised the distribution of the drop. Shortly after his brother had gone, Frédéric left saying he was going to his room to write a letter to Monique at her grandmother's house.

In a strained voice, Édith called goodnight to her son, but Claire, in fear of breaking down, dropped to her knees and attended to the fire. Looking into the flames, she heard Frédéric's step on the stairs. He was humming a tune. As he reached his bedroom door she heard it click open – and a second later it clicked shut. 'Édith, you can't let Frédéric find Monique tomorrow,' she said, leaping up and sitting beside her friend. 'Losing his fiancée will break his heart, but finding her dead in the river will destroy him. If you tell him she fell from the bridge, he is sure to think she was on her way to see him, and will blame himself for her death.'

Édith Belland thought for some minutes before draining her glass. 'You are right. Finding Monique – seeing her as she looks now – will be too much for the boy. At dawn tomorrow I will go to see Father Albert and ask him to take me to Monique in his car. We will bring her back to the church. I shall take off her soiled dress and put her in one of mine.'

'We have money, Édith. Could we not buy a new dress?'

Édith smiled. 'The dress I am thinking of is

cream and made of silk. It was part of my trousseau. It is beautiful, as Monique is beautiful. And I shall brush her hair. Did you find her handbag?' Claire shook her head. 'Then I shall take my powder and lipstick – and rouge for her cheeks. I shall make her look lovely again. Then Father Albert and I will lay her in the chapel.'

Suddenly remembering the hair slide, Claire said, 'I won't be a moment.' She ran to the kitchen and took the silver slide from her coat pocket. 'I found this,' she said, on her return.

Édith took the slide and clutched it to her breast. Large pear-shaped tears fell from her eyes and she wiped them away with the flat of her hand. 'It is one of a pair. They belonged to my mother. She wore them on her wedding day, and I wore them on mine. I gave one to Thérèse when she and André got engaged and this one I gave to Monique when she and Frédéric announced... Thank you. I shall put it in the child's hair tomorrow.'

'And you won't tell Frédéric that Monique died at the farm?'

'No. And I won't tell him that you and Alain found her.' Claire was relieved. Frédéric would want to know where and how; details that Claire didn't want him to know. 'I shall suggest to Father Albert, strongly, that he tells Frédéric that Monique was found by the railway station. So he will not blame himself for her death. It is sometimes necessary, to save those we love from heartache, not to tell them the truth.' Édith Belland looked at Claire through tired eyes. 'I am not sure how happy Father Albert will be about lying, but I do the cleaning at the church, and wash and iron the altar linen as well as his robes. I don't think he'll want to lose my services, do you?' The question was rhetorical. 'If he wants to debate the moral rights and wrongs of what I ask of him, I shall tell him firmly that Monique and Frédéric are innocent victims. It is German soldiers who are guilty.' She put her hands up to her mouth and took a sharp breath.

'What is it, Édith?'

'Frédéric must never know that Monique's death was anything to do with the Germans.'

'But surely he'll find out eventually. Won't the authorities want to talk to him--?'

'Why should they? If we don't tell them they won't need to talk to him. No! We will not tell anyone. What happened to Monique will stay between you, Alain, and me.'

'That means the soldiers who killed her will get away with murder.'

'People are killed all the time, in many different ways, in war.'

'Killing Monique, having their way with her before they killed her, wasn't war. It was rape and murder, Édith. They should be punished,' Claire said.

'Of course they should, but it will not bring Monique back and it will devastate Frédéric.' Claire saw fear in Édith's eyes. 'He would blame himself, because his fiancée went to the farm and he wasn't there, and then he would go looking for the German soldiers and... Either way it would destroy him. He is passionate, some would say hot-headed. He acts before he thinks. If he even suspected there had been foul play, he would go after the German soldiers who go to the farm with girls – and he would get himself killed.' Édith made two fists and crossed her arms over her chest. 'I beg you, my dear, do not tell him.'

'Shush…' Claire put her arms round her friend. 'If you don't want me to tell him I won't.'

'Promise me that it will be our secret, that you will never tell Frédéric, or anyone.'

'I promise. Now,' Claire said, 'I'll clear up down here, and you go up to bed. You look exhausted.' She took Édith's glass and put it on the shelf above the fire.

'Tomorrow,' Édith said, flicking the air as if it irritated her. 'We will wash up tomorrow.' On the landing outside her bedroom Édith hugged Claire. 'I shall never forget what you did for Monique and Frédéric,' she whispered.

Claire kissed her friend goodnight and went into her room. Too tired to wash, she kicked off her shoes and fell onto the bed.

Claire woke to what sounded like a howling animal caught in a trap. She took her wristwatch from the side of the bed. It was almost twelve o'clock. She had overslept. She pulled on a skirt and jumper and ran downstairs to the kitchen. Father Albert was standing in the doorway. Édith was on her knees with her arms around her distraught son, who was on the floor. 'Frédéric has had some tragic news, Claire,' Édith said, looking up at Claire, her voice hoarse with pain for her son. 'His fiancée Monique has had an accident. Father Albert found her this morning.'

'She is dead!' Frédéric sobbed. 'My beautiful

Monique is dead!' Suddenly he lifted his head from his mother's arms and turned to the priest. 'Perhaps you have made a mistake, Father. Yes, that is it, Mama. Father Albert has made a mistake.' Frédéric scrambled to his knees and, gripping the table, pulled himself to his feet. 'Monique is at her grandmother's house. I write to her every day,' he cried. 'Tell him, Mama. Tell Father Albert he has made a mistake.'

The priest crossed the room to Édith; she closed her eyes. He put his hand on Frédéric's shoulder. 'Frédéric, perhaps I did make a mistake.' Édith shot the priest a look of apprehension. 'So,' he said pointedly, 'when you are ready, we will go to the church together and you can tell me if the young lady who lies in the chapel is Monique, or another unfortunate young woman.' Claire saw Édith's shoulders drop.

'Now!' Frédéric said. 'We must go now!' Édith stood up and began to take off her pinafore. 'No, Mama, I will go alone with Father Albert,' he said. Édith looked pleadingly at the priest.

'He will be fine with me, Madame,' the priest said, opening the door to allow the broken-hearted Frédéric to leave first. Before closing the door the priest said, 'Do not worry, Madame, I will take good care of him.'

'Thank you, Father,' Édith whispered. She turned to Claire. 'I have always tried to shield Frédéric, but this is out of my hands. I feel so… useless.'

'Not useless, Édith. You've saved him much pain by moving Monique to the river. Did you tell Father Albert where she was killed and that it was

Alain and I who found her?'

'No! He is a priest. I could not expect him to know that, and then tell an outright lie. He found it difficult enough to say it was him who found her. He only told Frédéric that she was on her way to the station because I told him she was. I begged him not to say she was found near the farm. He agreed that there was no reason to tell Frédéric more than he needed to know. That way he did not have to lie. No.' Édith Belland sighed and shook her head. 'Let the sin of lying be mine.'

CHAPTER FIFTEEN

Wandering along in the warm May sunshine as if she didn't have a care in the world, Claire spotted a vacant bench and sat down. Casually she took in her surroundings. The statue of Napoleon that had dwarfed the main square in Gisoir had gone. From the look of the jagged stone around the top of the plinth the statue had been knocked down, not taken down. That noted, she lifted her face to the sun and closed her eyes. No sooner had she settled than she was surrounded by pigeons pecking the ground at her feet. 'Sorry,' she said, standing up, 'but I don't have any food.' Clicking her tongue, she zigzagged her way through the birds, talking to them as she went. She strolled along with no obvious purpose to anyone watching other than to take the air. The last thing she wanted, with Jacques' money in her shoes, was to attract attention.

Claire had never met Jacques. She wished now that she had, but it was always Alain who delivered wireless parts, or sent messages to London. Was it a coincidence that Alain had been to see Jacques less than an hour before the Gestapo took him for questioning? Could it have been the wireless operator who betrayed Alain yesterday? If so, might he betray her today? Édith Belland was sure it was not. She said Jacques was one of the most dedicated of the Resistance and would give his life for France. Even so, she hadn't told him where she and her sons were living. Claire decided that, if Jacques asked her, she wouldn't tell him either. She brushed thoughts of betrayal from her mind and concentrated on the job she was there to do – a small part in the scheme of the war, but necessary if the Resistance was to carry out its work against the Germans in Gisoir and the surrounding area. She also needed to offload the money she was carrying. She hadn't brought her travel permit, so if she was stopped with twenty thousand francs on her, she would have some explaining to do. More importantly, she had to get a message to London to let the colonel know the Gestapo had taken Alain.

The owner of Café La Ronde, setting up tables and chairs on the pavement beneath the café's striped awning, shouted hello. Claire waved. 'Will you be joining us for coffee today?' he called.

'Yes. When I've been to the market.'

'I look forward to it, Miss.'

Claire walked on to the covered market. She bought cheese, beans and onions, and left by the stall-holders' entrance. Looking around her, Claire realised she had lost her bearings. Then, just when she thought she would have to go back to the public entrance at the front of the market and risk being seen, she spotted Avenue Gambon to her right. She walked along the avenue until she came to a three-storey brick villa with white shutters opposite the third streetlight. Jacques' house was exactly as Édith had described it, right down to the terracotta tiled steps and blue planter of red geraniums by the front door. She crossed the road and ran up the steps.

In a state of heightened tension, Claire cleared her throat. Be vigilant and keep the meeting simple, she told herself. No chit-chat – just hand over the money and give the man the message for Colonel Smith. Ask him to repeat it verbatim and if he gets it right, leave. It couldn't be simpler. She approached the door, and stopped. Damn! Her hands were shaking. They often did when she was nervous. She took a deep breath and, feeling calmer, knocked on the door. There was no reply. She knocked again, this time louder. 'Yes?' a man called from inside the house.

'Are you Jacques?'

'Who wants to know?'

'A friend. I am looking for a baker who bakes cakes. I'd like him to bake tonight.' The wireless operator didn't speak. Claire felt the drum of panic begin to beat on the top of her stomach. She looked down and, pretending to admire the geraniums, scanned the avenue. There was no one about. 'I have something for you,' she said, in a loud whisper, 'but if I can't give it to you…' She turned and walked down the steps.

'Miss LeBlanc?' Claire stopped at the sound of her name. 'Quickly,' Jacques hissed, summoning her, while his eyes darted left and right frantically. 'I was expecting a male friend,' he said, ushering Claire into the house. Once inside, he closed the door and locked it. Bobbles of perspiration stood out on his brow, there were circles of damp under his arms and he reeked of sweet cologne. He took a red silk handkerchief from his pocket and dabbed at his chubby face, before waving it at her. 'You are sure you are alone? As I said, I was expecting to see my male friend again today,' he said, pulling back what looked like a velvet blackout curtain at a small window overlooking the avenue.

'I am sorry to tell you that your friend has been taken for questioning by the Gestapo.' Jacques spun round and fell against the door frame. He put his hand up to his mouth and gasped. 'Another friend, Édith, suggested I bring you this.' Claire kicked off her shoes and handed Jacques a wad of notes. His shocked expression turned into a grateful smile. Slipping her feet back into the shoes, she said, 'Tonight, when you speak to the people who share your love of cake, you must tell them that your friend, The French Can, has been unavoidably detained, but China Blue is safe.'

'The Can, unavoidably detained, China Blue safe,' Jacques repeated, nodding. 'My poor friend,' he said, stuffing the money into the pockets of a white linen jacket that hung on the end of the stair rail. He mopped his brow again.

'I must go,' Claire said, bending down and buckling her shoes. Jacques looked relieved and offered his hand. It was warm and damp – and as she shook it the acrid scent of sweat, mingled with his cologne, filled her nostrils. She wondered if it was guilt or fear that made him perspire so profusely. She decided it was fear. 'I shall take coffee in the Café La Ronde tomorrow morning at eleven,' she said, opening the door and stepping out into the warm sunshine. 'Would you meet me there? Let me know you were able to pass on the message about your friend?'

'Unavoidably detained, Miss?'

'Sorry, I didn't mean to doubt you. Until tomorrow then?' she said, turning and leaving. Before she reached the bottom of the steps she heard the door shut and the key turn in the lock. The bolt slid into place with a clunk.

Now Jacques' money had been delivered,

Claire's time was her own. She went into the patisserie, bought a pastry, and asked the owner if he had heard anything about the man who had been taken to German headquarters the day before. He had not, and said the Germans were always taking people in for no reason. He told her how some people had been taken to a prison in Paris. Claire's stomach took a dive. 'Chains around their ankles and herded onto trains like animals. Like the Jews,' he said. Before he could elaborate further, Claire thanked him and left.

She walked briskly to German headquarters. The four-storey municipal building had once housed Gisoir's town councillors. Now the German eagle, with Hitler's swastika in its claws, adorned the main entrance, and flags with swastikas hung from the ornate iron balconies.

The clock above the entrance door said five o'clock. Claire looked up at the windows on the first, second and third floors. She didn't know what she hoped to see. Yes she did, but there was no way Alain would be looking out of the window. Claire wondered if he was still there, or-- A couple of office workers hurried past her, interrupting her thoughts. They were talking about catching their train home. The baker had said Alain might be taken to Paris by train. Claire fell into step behind them. While they stood on the platform, she asked the man in the ticket office about trains to Paris.

'No trains to Paris tonight,' he said sharply. 'Trains to Paris are at 9am and 3pm.' He took a timetable from beneath the counter and ran a shaky finger down it. He's nervous, Claire thought. 'The nine o'clock train stops at--' A man standing directly behind her stamped his foot and sighed loudly.

'There is no need to explain further,' Claire said politely, and, without looking at the man, stomped out. At the door she looked back and her pulse quickened. The man was a Wehrmacht officer – and he and the ticket attendant were laughing. You didn't know who was a German sympathiser these days. The French railwaymen – many of whom were communists – were some of the bravest of the Resistance, sabotaging tracks, derailing carriages, and sending German troop trains miles out of their way. Gisoir station's ticket collector did not look like one of them. She would tell Édith about him when she got home.

Walking through the park, she began to tremble. She sat on the bench she'd sat on earlier and took the pastry from its wrapping. Her stomach turned at the sight of it. She was hungry, but feared she wouldn't keep even simple pastry down. Shredding it, she fed the pigeons before going to the Café La Ronde and ordering coffee.

She sat at the back of the room and when the waiter brought her coffee she asked him if he'd heard anything about the man the Germans took to their headquarters the day before. He hadn't, but said he didn't expect he'd be there long.

'If he is French they will release him soon. But if he is English...' the proprietor tutted.

'He is not English,' Claire said, 'he is my cousin. I swear to you, on my life, he is not English.' The waiter nodded sympathetically and began to wipe the table. 'But if the Germans think he is English,' she whispered, 'what will happen to him?'

The proprietor shrugged. 'They will put him in prison, or…'

'Or what? Please?' Claire fought back the tears and asked him again. 'Or what?'

The proprietor put his hand up and shushed her. 'Take him to Germany,' he hissed.

'Where in Germany?'

'I don't know… A camp. A prisoner of war camp, or a work camp. Please, we should not be speaking of such things. There are too many uniforms.' The door opened and German voices boomed in. The waiter spun round. 'Enjoy your coffee, Miss,' he said over his shoulder, and dashed to attend to three German officers.

Claire looked at her watch. It was after six and the café was getting busy. It had become increasingly popular with the Germans, which was why she and Alain went there. Today it was uncomfortably overpopulated. She looked over the rim of her coffee cup but didn't recognise any of them. She hoped they didn't recognise her. If they did they might remember that she and Alain were regular visitors to the café. She got up to leave. Keeping her head down, she walked unhurriedly to the door.

'No book today?' she heard someone say.

She looked to her left and saw the Gestapo officer who had asked her about the book she was reading on her first tour to France walking towards her. Did he remember on that occasion she had told him Alain was her cousin? If he did, did he know Alain had been taken to headquarters for questioning? 'No. No book today.'

He lifted the checked cloth on the top of her basket and looked inside. 'No book and,' he turned up his nose, 'hardly enough food to feed a bird. In that case,' he said, dropping the cloth, 'I shall take you to dinner tonight.'

Claire smiled, not with pleasure but with relief, because the German had looked in her basket after she had paid Jacques and not before. 'I'm afraid I cannot tonight. Maybe another time?'

'I look forward to it.' The German opened the door and Claire smiled her thanks as she went out. Dinner with him, however unpalatable, might be a way of finding out if Alain was still at headquarters, and if he was how long they were likely to keep him. But not today. He had caught her off guard. She didn't trust herself not to say something stupid and give herself away.

At the end of the road she looked back to where Alain had been beaten up the day before and saw the German officer coming out of the café. Pretending she was looking at him, she waved goodbye and turned the corner.

Damn! She had broken the first two rules. Walk with purpose, especially if it is getting dark, the security instructor had told her, and don't look back, it looks suspicious. She ran through the rules in her head. If anyone speaks to you nod, don't let them involve you in conversation. If they persist, politely make your excuses and walk on. If it is cold, use it. Shiver and say you think you have a cold, or influenza. Or say you'll be in trouble if you are late home for dinner. If they suggest they walk with you, say your father is very strict and would be angry if he saw you with a man. If you are followed into a restaurant or café, order something to drink. When the waiter brings it, take a couple of sips before casually getting up and going to the toilet. There will be a back door you can slip out of, or a window you can climb through. If there is neither, go back to your drink, finish it and leave as if you haven't a care in the world. Walk without attracting attention, and don't look back. Whatever you do you must not let the man or woman following you know you're aware of them.

Claire walked briskly and at last arrived at the tree-lined avenue where Édith and Frédéric lived. A few yards more and she would be safe. She stopped, put her foot up on a low wall, and took off her shoe. Wielding it in the air as if it had taken in a stone and she was shaking it out, Claire glanced along the avenue. Her heart sank. For a second she saw the back of a man wearing a military hat disappear into a doorway. She looked ahead. The Belland house was close, too close. She blew out her cheeks in frustration and walked on. As she passed the alley that ran along the side of the house she saw a shadowy figure, followed by the dim glow of a lighted cigarette. She pulled on the collar of her coat and crossed the road.

There was a café opposite the church where the Belland family worshipped. It was getting dark, so the café may have closed by now, but she would go there anyway. She had to go somewhere – and the further away from the Belland house the safer they would be. She turned the corner and exhaled with relief. A narrow shaft of light escaped into the street as the café's door opened. A young man and woman left and Claire slipped in.

Inside she waved to the man behind the counter as if she knew him. He put up his hand in a tired but welcoming gesture. She spotted a vacant table and made her way to it. As she sat down, she heard the door open. The waiter sauntered over with his notebook in one hand, taking his pencil from his waistcoat pocket with the other.

'I won't be eating tonight,' Claire said, glancing sideways at the lunch board above the counter. 'Lunch was wonderful, but so filling, I don't think I'll need to eat again until breakfast,' she laughed. 'Just a cup of your delicious coffee, please.' The café owner puffed out his chest and nodded. When he brought her coffee, Claire continued to chat in a familiar way. 'You look tired. Have you had another busy day?' Before the café owner had time to reply, Claire took a sip of her coffee. 'Mmm, she crooned, closing her eyes, 'lovely.' The café owner smiled his thanks through a yawn.

Claire sipped her coffee and watched as customers finished their meals, paid and left. Of the half dozen Germans still lounging about drinking, she wondered which of them had followed her. She couldn't be sure he had even come into the café. She heard the door open just after she entered, but it could have been anyone. The coffee was good; she would come here again. She picked up a newspaper from the table next to hers and began to read. She must act normally. Soon she would go to the ladies', and see if there was a back door, or window she could climb out of. She absentmindedly took a sip of her coffee. It was hot. She put the cup down and got up, taking her handbag with her, but leaving her basket, so it looked like she was coming back. She walked to the back of the café. There was a sign above an alcove saying Toilet, and an arrow pointing to the left. She followed the arrow, but instead of turning into the toilet, she walked on to a door marked Exit. She pushed on it, but it was locked. She turned and opened the toilet door. There was no window. So much for making her escape, she thought. She pulled the piece of string that doubled for a chain and returned to her seat.

The café owner met her as she sat down. 'I will be closing in ten minutes. Would like another cup of the coffee you love so much, before you leave?'

'Thank you, that's very kind.' As he poured the coffee, Claire looked up at him, wondering if he had guessed she was being followed.

'I will also have another cup before you close,' Claire heard someone with a German accent say.

'Certainly, sir,' the owner sighed.

She was watching him pour the German officer's coffee when the door burst open. Claire's jaw dropped at the sight of a woman she recognised from a photograph on Édith's mantle as André Belland's wife, Thérèse. Bustling into the café and expounding how sorry she was to have kept her best friend waiting, Thérèse said, 'I had to make Father's dinner. You know mother and the little ones have the chicken pox? Covered in weeping sores, they are.' Thérèse shivered. Trying to hide her surprise, Claire nodded vigorously. 'Well, because it's so contagious Father won't allow them downstairs when he is home, in case he catches it. Did I say it was contagious? Oh yes. Well, it isn't fair, I have to do all the housework and look after Mother and the children.' Waving to the café owner, Thérèse pulled

Claire to her feet. 'I feel itchy myself,' she said, scratching her head and the top of her arm, before opening the door.

The two women hurried off in the direction of the town. 'How did you know where to find me?' Claire whispered.

'Frédéric saw you in the avenue. When you kept walking after he'd given the all clear signal, he knew something was wrong and he followed you. When he came back, Mother-in-law said I was to come to the café and get you out.'

'That was brave of you, Thérèse, thank you.'

'Not really. Frédéric and André were behind me. They were waiting outside the café to make sure we weren't followed when we left.' When they had walked along several streets, Thérèse looked back. 'All the talk about chicken pox has put your stalker off,' she laughed. Linking her arm though Claire's, she said, 'I think it's safe to go home now.'

'After the day I've had, I can't think of anything better.'

Thérèse laughed. 'I'm not sure you'll feel that way after you've seen Mother-in-law. She is furious with you for going off without telling anyone.'

Claire knew she had broken the rules. She had put herself and Thérèse in danger, Frédéric and André too. They walked in silence until they arrived at the alley that ran alongside the short row of houses. A cigarette glowed and brightened. Thérèse opened the door in the wall and Claire followed her into the yard. 'I'm sorry I put you in danger, Thérèse. I just needed to check out a few things in town on my own.'

'Save it for Édith. I appreciate how worried you

are. Mother-in-law is not as understanding.'

Claire followed Thérèse into the house. The kitchen table was set for two. Thérèse went to the cooker, looked in the oven and wrinkled her nose. 'Mmmm… Garlic sausage and potatoes.' The potatoes were dry and looked like cardboard. The sausages were brown and the skins more wrinkled than Édith's neighbour Madame Oran's face. 'We are going to have to eat this,' Thérèse said.

'I haven't eaten anything since breakfast. I'll have yours if you don't want it,' Claire said. Thérèse laughed and dished up two helpings. With gravy, it was edible.

When they had finished eating and were washing the dishes, André and Édith entered the kitchen. 'Thank you, Édith,' Claire said over her shoulder, 'the food was lovely.' She dried the plates and hung the tea towel on the rack at the side of the fire.

André held Thérèse's coat. She put it on and thanked Édith for the food, kissing her on both cheeks. 'I'll see you tomorrow, Claire. And don't worry about Alain. I'm sure he will be back with us soon.' Claire kissed Thérèse and André goodbye, and watched them leave.

Édith sat in the chair that Thérèse had vacated. Claire could feel Édith watching her. She turned with the coffee pot, placed it on the table and took two cups and saucers from the dresser. After fetching the jug of milk from the larder she poured coffee for both of them and added a little milk. 'I'm sorry, Édith,' she said. 'I shouldn't have been in the streets after curfew. I don't know what I'd have done if Thérèse hadn't come into the café.'

'Were you aware that you were followed from the railway station?'

Claire gasped. 'How do you know I went to the station?'

'The ticket attendant is one of the leaders of the railwaymen; a member of *Resistance Fer*. But that doesn't matter. What matters is going off on your own, asking questions about Alain the day after he was taken to Gestapo headquarters for questioning.'

Claire hadn't mentioned Alain to the ticket attendant, but she had to the baker and the proprietor of Café La Ronde. Édith had ears all over Gisoir. 'I wanted to find out if he was still here. They take political prisoners, or those they think are communists or spies, to a jail near Paris. I wanted to know if they had taken Alain there.'

'The name of the prison is Périgueux. And no, he is not there, he is still at Gestapo headquarters.'

'How do you know?'

'The men and women of the Resistance live locally, work locally, and travel in and out of the town regularly. Some work in shops and cafés, others at the railway station!' Claire could hear exasperation in Édith's voice, and she looked down. 'You know how it works, Claire. When locals enquire about trains to Paris, or talk between themselves about why the Germans took a man in for questioning, it is not thought unusual. The Germans just see local people wondering, as any inquisitive citizen would. But when they hear a stranger ask – a young woman at that – it raises questions. Who is she? Where has she come from? Does she know the man the Germans took away?'

'I am so sorry, Édith. I was worried and didn't

think.'

'Then we'll say no more about it.' Pushing the coffee pot out of the way, Édith took a bottle of red wine and two glasses from the work surface next to the sink. She poured wine for them both. 'I understand you and Jacques are meeting in the Café La Ronde tomorrow?' Édith placed a glass in front of Claire.

'I want him to confirm he's sent the message about Alain to London.'

'Good idea. We shall go together. If that is all right with you?'

'Of course. I am sorry I put everyone at risk today. Will the Resistance ever forgive me?'

'They don't know. I didn't think it was worth worrying them, since no one has been compromised.'

Claire put her hand on top of Édith's. 'Thank you.'

CHAPTER SIXTEEN

Claire watched Jacques shuffle through the door of the Café La Ronde, shopping bag in one hand and umbrella in the other. She nudged Édith. 'He's carrying an umbrella – in this heat.'

'He uses it as a stick,' Édith whispered, 'and a parasol.'

Except for the white fedora that made his linen coat look even shabbier than Claire remembered, the multi-coloured cravat at his throat and the brown and white wingtip dance shoes, Jacques was wearing the same clothes that he wore the day before. Unable to help herself, Claire began to giggle. She put her hand up to her mouth. 'I'm sorry, Édith, but he looks so--'

'Flamboyant?' Édith laughed with her.

'I thought we were meant to keep a low profile.'

'It's best to, yes, but not if it means a sudden change of character. Jacques was a famous impresario in the 1920s. He married a beautiful and very talented dancer – and took dance troupes out on grand tours. He was devastated when she died. Shhh, he will hear us.'

'Madame Belland,' Jacques said, bowing theatrically before proffering his podgy white hand. 'How are you, my dear lady?' Squeezing his bulk into the seat next to Édith, he bumped the table with his knee, sending Édith and Claire's coffee spilling into their saucers. 'A million apologies, Madame. Waiter?' he called. 'A cloth, if you please?'

Jacques ordered coffee and a pastry with cream, and while the waiter wiped the table he apologised again to Édith and Claire. 'To business,' he whispered when the waiter left. 'You know I have a friend at German headquarters.' Édith nodded. 'Well,' Jacques leaned forward, 'he told me earlier that the Gestapo took seven men to the station this morning, and your friend may have been among them. Of course he cannot say for sure. Shush,' he said, as the waiter returned with his coffee and a cake. 'Thank you, Robert,' he sang.

'Does your friend know where the men were taken?' Édith asked when the waiter was out of earshot.

'To Périgueux, of course.' Claire felt numb. Jacques took a bite of his cake, leaving a white sugary substance on the narrow slug of hair above his top lip, and turned his attention to Claire. 'The message you asked me to send was given as you instructed, Miss,' he said, with his mouth full. 'There was no reply to *that* message, but there is to be a--' Jacques looked at the door, wiped his hand across his mouth and mumbled, 'drop!'

'When?'

'Monday. One package is to go to Orléans and one to Paris.'

'I shall deliver the package to Paris. Tell *them* tonight when you bake, Jacques, that China Blue will deliver to Paris,' Claire said.

'Claire dear, there's almost a week before the drop. I think Jacques should wait until we've discussed it with André, don't you?'

Claire rolled her eyes and blew out her cheeks. 'Very well, but I shall go to Paris next week anyway. Whether I take anything with me is up to André, but since I don't have any work over the next few weeks, I would like to visit the wife of a friend who had to stay in Paris with her parents when her husband and their children escaped to England.' Édith lifted her empty coffee cup and pretended to drink. She wasn't convinced, Claire thought. 'It doesn't make sense to take someone away from important work to make a delivery when I am free and can do it.'

Jacques finished his coffee and wiped a serviette across his face. 'I shall say goodbye. I look forward to seeing you when you have made a decision,' he said, lifting his chair and placing it carefully under the table. Then he put his hand in his pocket and gasped. 'Madame,' he whispered, putting his other hand up to his mouth, 'I have forgotten my wallet.'

Édith smiled. 'It will be my pleasure to buy your coffee, my friend.'

'And the pastry,' he giggled. Jacques put on his fedora, picked up his umbrella and after bowing to both women, he left.

André paced the kitchen floor. 'I don't like the idea of you delivering money to this new *Maquis* group calling themselves the *Paris Centre* on your own,' he told Claire.

'And your reasoning?'

'You don't know these men. You don't know Paris.'

'I know people in Paris that I can stay with. They don't know about the work I do and I have no intention of telling them, unless I think their house will be a good safe house.'

André looked to his mother for support. Édith shrugged and André threw his hands in the air. 'All right! You can go to Paris if you give me your word you will not go to Périgueux.' Claire nodded. 'You must deliver the money to the leader of Paris Centre first. Only then can you visit your friend. Agreed?' Claire nodded again.

Claire had never been part of a reception committee and found waiting for the aircraft as frustrating as waiting to jump out of it. She looked up at the sky. There were only a few puff-ball clouds, and the moon was almost full. A torch flashed at the bottom of the field, followed by a second and a third. Small, round, and bright enough for an aircraft to see at a thousand feet, the torches formed a straight line. Almost immediately Claire heard the familiar grumbling of a Halifax engine. She looked to the east and her tummy fluttered with excitement. She thought of Mitch and wished it was him landing. She swallowed hard. If he was in Périgueux prison in Paris, at least he was still in France, not in a work camp in Poland or Germany. Or in a concentration camp – she shivered – where Jewish people were taken and never heard of again.

The plane, silhouetted against the clear sky, came into view and Claire watched the parachutes fall. She ran with the others to claim them. The speed of the operation was paramount. Collapse the chutes, fold them as small as possible and bury them. With Frédéric, she began to dig the damp mossy ground on the edge of the wood bordering a field that had once had wheat standing tall waiting to be harvested. Now it was overgrown and the crop, strangled by weeds, was dried and dead.

Half an hour after the drop, the crates were

buried. 'Money,' André said, handing Claire two small leather wallets. She placed them in her shoulder bag, buckled it and set off home.

The following day after breakfast, Claire sat down with André, Frédéric, Édith and Pierre Ruban to discuss getting the money to Paris. All modes of travel were dangerous, but travelling by train was more so, because of the numerous identity paper checks. The Germans were paranoid. Every city and town a train went through brought out the local gendarmes who took delight in stopping and boarding the train to check its passengers' papers. They often travelled on the trains. On those occasions there were fewer delays. Claire hoped that would be the case. It only took one over-zealous young gendarme wanting to impress his Gestapo masters to hinder, sometimes end, a passenger's journey. Claire took out the Metro underground map that Professor Marron's son Éric had given her. 'I would like to visit someone in the 8th Arrondissement,' she said. 'I understand it is unusual to take time out when delivering, but ...'

'But what?' Pierre asked.

What she was about to say sounded sentimental in such circumstances, but she was not going to hide anything from the brave men she worked with. 'I promised the son of a French professor I stayed with while I was training that I would visit his mother in Paris if I got the chance.' No one spoke. 'And I thought another safe house in Paris, which the house may well become, would be useful. We have lost so many.'

'You are right – but you will deliver the money first?' André asked.

'Of course. Once I've handed it over, I'll spend a couple of hours looking for Madame Marron's house. If I find it and I think it's safe to introduce myself, I will. If I don't find it, or find it and don't think it's safe, I'll come straight back. '

'What's your cover story?'

'If I'm stopped on the train I shall say my grandmother lives in Paris. My parents are worried about her, so they have sent me to look after her. I'll say the same at the Marron house, but if I get a hostile reception, I'll apologise and say I have the wrong address.'

'And what if you're stopped by the Gestapo, or the gendarmerie, and they find the money?'

I shall keep a third of it in my own purse. If they search me and find it I'll tell them the same story, but add that the money is for my grandmother. I will of course give them a false address.'

'You'll be carrying money for *Paris Centre* too?'

Claire nodded. 'Granny's francs will be in my bag – easy to find – and the money for the Maquis will be in my shoes. Hopefully if I am stopped they'll be satisfied that they've found some money and won't search me for any more.'

Everyone agreed with the plan. Before he left, Pierre shook Claire's hand and wished her luck. 'I'll see you on my return from Paris,' she said, kissing him on both cheeks.

'I look forward to it,' he said, and after shaking hands with André and Frédéric, he kissed Édith goodbye and left.

'Phew!' Claire blew out her cheeks. 'I'm really going to Paris!'

'You are, but it is not a holiday,' Édith warned. 'Remember, it is dangerous to travel to the capital these days. It is dangerous too, in the streets of the capital. You must not trust anyone. Before you hand over the money you must be certain it is to the right person.'

'Keep the money in the wallet,' André said. 'Loose notes are not easy to pass to someone without being seen.' Claire nodded that she understood. 'Buy a newspaper – most Parisians get a paper on their way to work. Then if the contact's held up, or isn't able to approach you for some reason, you will have something to do. This is the rendezvous address.' André handed her a small piece of paper. Claire read it and gave it him back. 'There is one more thing,' André said. 'These are the questions you will be asked and the answers you will give. If one word is different from what is on that paper, you are to get the hell out. Do you understand?' Claire started reading the questions and answers and committing them to memory. 'Claire?' She looked up. 'If the questions you are asked by Thomas Durand, the leader of Paris Centre, deviate in any way--'

'Don't worry, I will learn them verbatim and if there's the slightest difference to what is on this piece of paper, I shall suddenly notice the time, excuse myself and high-tail it to Granny's.'

André explained to Claire again, as they drove to the railway station at Orléans in Father Albert's old car, how important it was to be vigilant. If she felt in danger, or compromised in any way, she was to return home immediately.

Claire thought André was fussing, but didn't say

so. She felt comforted that André, Frédéric, and Édith, who Claire had become very fond of, cared for her; cared for her safety. She assured him that she would do as he said.

There was a bomb crater where Orléans station's car park had once been, so, because it was almost time for the 9.05 train to Paris to leave, Claire jumped out of the car and ran into the station. With only minutes to spare she bought her ticket, ran across the concourse to Platform Three and boarded the train. She found a carriage with one vacant seat and quickly claimed it. Closing the door, she threw her holdall onto the overhead rack and sat down. Almost immediately the door opened and a young gendarme entered. With pale green eyes, shorter than fashionable blond hair, and a sharply ironed uniform, he looked more like a member of the Hitler Youth movement than the French gendarmerie.

People fidgeted in their seats. Some took their papers from their pockets, and others, like Claire, took them from bags and cases on the overhead rack. Returning to her seat, Claire held her identity papers as casually as she was able. Her heart was beating so loud she thought the young policeman would hear it and think she was concealing a ticking bomb.

He went first to an elderly woman, the only one in the carriage who hadn't found her identity papers. 'Papers!' he said, as she searched in her handbag. He tapped his foot on the floor impatiently and shouted, 'Papers!'

'Ah,' the old lady said, trembling. 'Here they are. I am sorry,' she said, as the policeman snatched them out of her hand. He looked at her with contempt, before glancing at her papers. He returned them to her with an unnecessary flick of the wrist that made her jump. She nervously muttered thank you, but was so frightened she could hardly formulate the words.

The gendarme moved from one person to another, looking at their identity papers and nodding, until he came to Claire. She handed him her papers as everyone else had done, but instead of looking at them and moving on to the next passenger in the carriage he said, 'Why are you going to Paris?'

'I am going to visit my grandmother, sir,' she said, calmly.

He scrutinised her papers, then stared at her for what seemed an age. She began to panic. Was there something wrong with her documents? How could there be? The paper was authentic and the creases, where they had been opened and folded so many times, were as worn as André's or Frédéric's. She smiled up at him. Did he know her from Gisoir? Had he seen her perhaps in the market or shops? She hadn't seen him before; if she had she would have remembered. She half smiled and looked at her papers in his hand, willing him to give them back to her.

'What's in your bag?'

Claire instinctively looked up at the holdall. 'Clothes, some food, and a little money for my grandmother. She has not been well and--'

Ignoring her explanation he said, 'Get it down.'

Standing on tiptoe, she reached up for the bag, but before she could lift it down there was a commotion in the corridor. 'Assistance!

Assistance!' a man was shouting.

The gendarme flashed an angry look at Claire, as if she had somehow engineered the disturbance, and ran out of the carriage. Claire, already on her feet, followed him to the door. Sideways on, to make herself small, she peered out. Half a dozen policemen were chasing a man along the platform, while in the corridor a policeman had been floored by a man twice his size. The young policeman from Claire's carriage jumped on the back of the big man, who swung him over his shoulder onto the first policeman. Leaving them in a heap on the floor, the man leapt out of the carriage and in seconds had disappeared. The last Claire saw of the gendarmes who had chased the first man, they were pushing their way through the crowds empty-handed.

Claire returned to her seat and sat down. She allowed herself a breath of relief before joining in the general conversation as to who the two men were and what they had done. Claire wondered if they were part of a Resistance group and hoped if they were they had got away.

Claire arrived at Paris's Gare d'Austerlitz railway station nervous and excited. Since her first French lesson she had dreamed of visiting Paris. She had seen photographs and read articles in English and French magazines about the most romantic city in Europe, where artists sat in cafés on the Left Bank and talked about painting, poetry and the theatre – and where lovers, hand in hand, strolled along the banks of the River Seine. Claire checked the time on the station clock. The journey from Orléans to Paris, even with all the stopping and starting, had only taken a couple of hours. She had an hour before she needed to meet Thomas Durand at Le Park Café on the Avenue de Champs Élysées. After that she would be free to find Professor Marron's wife at her parents' house. Claire left the station and walked along the Quai d'Austerlitz.

She felt hungry. She didn't want to eat at the rendezvous, so she ran across the busy street to a café. She ordered coffee and an open cheese sandwich and found a table. While she waited she took from her bag the copy of the Métro directory that Éric Marron had given her. The small book gave the names of Paris' underground stations and times of the trains. It also had a comprehensive street map of the city folded neatly in the back. Claire laid the directory on the table and carefully opened the map square by square until the whole of Paris lay before her. The paper was thin. It felt like tissue paper. She worried that it would tear before she was able to find the street where Madame Marron's parents lived. She scanned the maze of streets and avenues. Éric had said it was central, quite near the Champs Élysées, which Claire found almost immediately. She closed her eyes to remember what else Éric had said, what he had shown her on his father's map. *Six*. Yes, there was a six. Her photographic memory could be a nightmare, literally, but now if she could only bring the information the boy had given her to the front of her mind it would be a godsend. Sixty. The SOE offices are number sixty-four, Éric's grandmother's address is sixty-five! That was it, 65 Avenue St. Julien. Claire looked again. Just a few stops further on the Métro from the Champs Élysées. Not quite the centre of Paris, as Éric had said, but not far away either. Claire memorised the route, folded the map and put it back in her bag. Her refreshments arrived. She thanked the waiter and bit into her sandwich hungrily. She had woken feeling nervous, which built into a feeling of nausea, so she had given breakfast a miss, saying she didn't have time. The truth was she felt overwhelmed by the thought of travelling to Paris and having to find her way about on her own. She didn't tell Édith how she felt or she'd have insisted André or Frédéric accompany her. She looked out of the window at the busy Parisian thoroughfare and laughed. Travelling from Orléans to Paris had been no more difficult than travelling from Rugby to London, but it was a great deal more exciting. She washed her sandwich down with coffee, put a franc on the table and left.

Claire walked along the Rue d'Austerlitz in the summer sunshine and crossed the River Seine by the Austerlitz Bridge. The Resistance had taken down some of the street names to confuse the Germans. Claire didn't know about the Germans, but the lack of information certainly confused her. She turned right after the bridge and right again into the Boulevard de la Bastille. A few minutes later she was stopped in her tracks by the splendour that was L'Opéra. With its large arcades and tall pillars behind marble figurines, the opera house was the most beautiful building she had ever seen. She looked at the upper levels. Tall double columns framed huge windows and above that, breath-taking, thrilling decoration. She wished she had time to look inside. 'One day,' she said to herself.

After walking for half an hour, Claire sat on a

bench overlooking a small fountain and took out the Métro map. She was in the Marais district, bordering the 3rd and 4th arrondissements, so she was heading in the right direction. She continued along the Rue Saint-Antoine to the Place de la Concorde. She marvelled at the vastness of the squares, the lifelike statues, the tiered fountain that reminded her of a cake stand, and what had to be the tallest obelisk in the world. From there she walked west along the Avenue des Champs-Élysées, passing palaces, monuments, and a theatre. She came to a parade of shops by a small park, and slowed her pace. According to the directions she had memorised, she was close to the rendezvous. There were several cafés with tables and chairs outside on the pavement. She looked at the names above the different coloured striped awnings. The third in the row was Le Park Café.

She checked her wristwatch. She had time to buy a newspaper from the shop next to the café. With the *Paris-Soir* under her arm she sat down at the table furthest away from the café's entrance. She read the paper and when the waiter came, ordered coffee.

She sipped her coffee, occasionally looking across the avenue at the people passing by, as anyone who was new to the city would. She took the Métro map from her bag and laid it on the table. The directory was the first clue as to who she was. She then took her wallet out to pay for her coffee.

As the café became busy the three chairs around each table were moved about. A middle-aged man asked if he could take a chair from Claire's table. Smiling, she said, 'Please do.' If someone asked for

211

the remaining chair she would have to let them take it. Then where would Thomas Durand sit when he arrived? If he arrived…

'Excuse me, Miss. Is anyone sitting here?'

Claire jumped. Deep in thought, the sound of a man's voice took her by surprise. She looked up. 'Please do,' she said, politely. The man, tall, in his mid-twenties, with black hair curling over the collar of his shirt, pulled out the chair and sat down. Claire resumed reading her newspaper.

The waiter brought the man a cup of coffee. 'Your usual,' he said, putting the coffee on the table.

'Thank you, Armand,' the man said.

By the way the waiter spoke to him, and because the man knew the waiter's name, he was obviously a regular customer. Claire felt disappointment and gratitude at the same time. Disappointed because the man sitting opposite her wasn't who she was expecting and grateful for the same reason. She wondered if Thomas Durand was wandering about waiting for his chance. Or maybe he was sitting at another table, ready to join her when the regular customer left. She put the paper down and looked across the avenue. Then she casually brought her focus to the men at the other tables.

'I see you have a copy of the Métro. Are you a visitor to Paris?'

Claire's heart almost stopped. It was him! The man sitting at her table was Thomas Durand! 'Not exactly. I am in Paris to visit my grandmother, but thought I'd take in the sights while I am here. Are you a visitor?'

'No, I'm here to meet a friend, but she appears to be late.'

That was Claire's cue to leave. She stood up, put the money for her coffee on the table, and put the Métro back in her bag. 'Goodbye. I hope your friend arrives soon,' she said and left.

On the far side of the avenue she looked back at the café. Thomas Durand was reading *Paris-Soir*. Her eyes dropped to the table. The wallet had gone. She walked away, confident that the money she had delivered would buy much needed guns and ammunition for the Paris Centre Maquis group.

She turned towards the Arc de Triomphe and shortly afterwards arrived at the Champs Élysées. Stopped in her tracks, Claire gasped at the sight of the bomb damage. The underground newspaper reports had shown devastating photographs of German tanks thundering down the Champs Élysées, stormtroopers strutting through the streets of Paris. The German machine – convoys of armoured cars, trucks, and tanks – crushing everything in their way.

Seeing the destruction in person saddened her, reminding her how the Luftwaffe had bombed Coventry, Liverpool, Newcastle and many other British cities. And how they had blitzed London's East End. Night after night throughout September and October of 1940 hundreds of German bombers, escorted by fighter planes, dropped their bombs on huge areas of East and South East London until many of the boroughs had been turned to rubble. The damage Claire was seeing now had been done by Britain and her allies as well as the Germans.

She looked along the street at burned-out and smoke-stained buildings that had every other window blown out of its frame. Windows that had survived the allied bombing were thick with dust and grime, their shutters dangling from tall sash windows in large square bays. Gates were hanging off their hinges and doors blown in. She turned away in tears.

Three stops on the Métro, a short walk, and she would have a safe place to stay tonight. Maybe tomorrow and over the weekend too, if Madame Marron was as generous as her husband.

CHAPTER SEVENTEEN

Claire left the Métro at Les Sablons. Rue de Lesseps was wide and tree-lined. She took the first left, which Éric had told her was where his grandparents lived. She had to look for a tall arched window at the front. Most of the houses were three-storey and built of white stone. The upper windows had ornate black balconies; the lower and ground floor windows didn't. On closer inspection Claire could see that most of them had once had balconies on the first and ground floor, but they had been removed. The further down the street she walked the more run down the houses became. Some had smashed windows, doors standing open, and the shutters of some were hanging off, exposing ragged curtains.

Claire stopped in front of the only house with an arched window and climbed the steps to a paint-chipped olive green door. She knocked, but there was no reply. After some minutes she knocked again. She was about to leave when the door opened.

'Can I help you?'

'Yes. My name is Claire LeBlanc. I am an associate of Madame Marron's husband. I was fortunate enough to meet the Professor at the university where he works.' A slight deviation from the truth, but *I lived with her husband* – under whatever circumstances – probably wouldn't get her invited in to meet Madame Marron. She smiled and waited for the girl to decide whether she was going to ask her in or not. She was sure she'd said enough. If she hadn't it was too bad. She wasn't prepared to say anything else until she was sure she hadn't knocked on the door of Nazi sympathisers.

'Come in. I will see if Madame Marron is at home.'

The bare floorboards of the entrance hall creaked as Claire entered. Shooting Claire a sideways glance, the girl scurried across the unpolished floor and disappeared through a door on the right. Stairs leading from the centre of the hall rose steeply before branching left and right to landings with four doors on each side. The ceiling was high, with a circular pendant in the centre. It had once been a grand residence.

A minute or so later the girl returned. 'Madame will see you. If you would like to wait in the salon,' she said. Claire followed her into the room. 'May I take your coat?' It was sunny and warm outside, but the house felt damp and cold. Claire thought about keeping it on, but the girl was clearly suspicious of her, so she shrugged it off and smiled reassuringly. 'Take a seat. Madame will be with you shortly.' The maid did a little bob and left.

Claire perched on the edge of the nearest armchair and looked around. The shutters were almost closed but there was enough light to see that although the Turkish carpet was stained and threadbare in places, it would have cost a fortune in its day. The curtains, now frayed and hanging off their fittings, were thick velvet, and the tapestry-covered settee next to the chair she was sitting on was the best quality, or had been. A shame to let the place go like this, Claire thought. They might have lost everything in the Depression; many Parisians had. She looked along the wall of empty bookcases to a set of double doors and wondered where they led. Perhaps to more comfortable and better furnished rooms. She was pondering what lay beyond the doors when they opened.

'Miss LeBlanc?'

Claire jumped up. 'Yes, how do you do, Madame?' She offered Madame Marron her hand, which the older woman shook with a guarded smile.

'I understand you work with my husband?'

'Yes.' For the time being she would let Professor Marron's wife think she worked at the university. To tell her the truth about how she knew her husband was unnecessary – and potentially dangerous. She would tell her the whys and wherefores if she got to know her better. She might even tell her about the work she was doing in France and that safe houses were needed in Paris, if she believed in a free France. With a husband like Professor Marron, it was hard to think she could believe in anything else.

'Did you meet my children, Miss LeBlanc? Are they well?'

'The children are very well. Éric is a charming young man. He likes his school. He excels at most of his studies and, as I'm sure you know, hopes to go to university.'

'And my daughter?'

'Mélanie is an amazing young woman. She is bright and pretty. She is very clever and has a mind of her own.' Madame Marron nodded in agreement and laughed. 'She misses you, of course, but she is a positive girl. She is certain that you will all be together when the war is over, if not before.'

Madame Marron took a handkerchief from her

pocket and dabbed her eyes.

'And how is my husband?' she whispered.

'He works all the time. He is respected and liked at the university, by his colleagues and his students. We didn't speak intimately, but his face changed from *The Professor* to loving father and husband when he spoke of you and the children.'

Madame Marron inhaled and closed her eyes. When she opened them she smiled. 'Thank you, Miss LeBlanc.'

'Please call me Claire.'

'And I am Antoinette. I am pleased to meet you, and pleased to hear about Auguste and the children. I miss them so much. I came to Paris to pack up my parents' house. We were going to follow my husband to England, but the German High Command stopped Jewish people from travelling, unless it was to work in labour camps for the good of the Fatherland. Many Jewish people have been sent to Germany, or Poland. Repatriation, they call it. They break down our doors and take us from our homes by force.'

'But they have not taken you, thank goodness,' Claire said.

'I have my husband's name. Marron is a very old French name. My parents do not have the same name, obviously.' Antoinette Marron's almond-shaped, brown eyes filled with tears again. 'The Germans are transporting whole families to these so-called *work* camps.' Frowning, she searched Claire's face. 'Some say they are--' She threw her head back and shook it as if she couldn't bring herself to say the word.

'Prison camps,' Claire whispered.

Antoinette Marron nodded. 'Many of them are never heard of again.'

Claire shivered and pulled her cardigan around her middle. 'You are cold,' Antoinette said, 'Let us go through to the back of the house where we dare open the blinds and let in the light. The rooms at the front of the house are always cold because we have to keep the shutters closed.'

Claire looked at the shutters at the large windows. Narrow shafts of light squeezed through gaps where they didn't meet in the middle. There was some light, but not enough to give even the smallest amount of warmth. 'Do you have to keep them closed?'

'Yes. Many houses in this street and in neighbouring streets have been gutted. Families who had lived here for generations were evicted in the first few months of the German occupation. Whole families were turned out of their homes. They were only allowed to take one bag of clothes each. If they were seen taking more all their possessions were confiscated.' Antoinette stopped speaking and took a deep breath. Claire put her hand on her arm, and she nodded. 'I'm fine,' she said, and carried on. 'If they were found with valuables, or money, it was taken from them and they were given a beating. It seemed the world had gone mad. French citizens, who had lived and worked in Paris all their lives, were not only thrown out of their homes, but they were denied travel permits, so they could not go to family or friends who lived in unoccupied France.' Antoinette Marron laughed bitterly. 'The irony is, it is against the law to be homeless, so the same people who put the Jewish families out of their homes rounded them up like stray dogs and took them away in cattle wagons to God knows where.'

Claire wondered why Antoinette and her parents hadn't been evicted. By the way she spoke, Antoinette was clearly not a sympathiser. No one who agreed remotely with the Germans would shed tears as she had done. 'Please don't think me rude, Antoinette, but why have the Germans left you and your parents alone?'

'After the first wave of evictions it went quiet, so my neighbour and I threw bricks through our own front windows. We ripped most of the curtains and stained what remained, so it looked from the outside as if the damage had been done for some time. We wrenched the balconies from the downstairs windows, and used axes to damage the wooden blinds, even pulling some of them off their hinges. To all intents and purposes our homes were no longer habitable. From the outside it looked as if the Germans had looted our houses along with the rest of the street. So, like my neighbour, my parents and I live in rooms at the back of the house. Come,' she said, 'now I am sure you are not a German spy I will take you through.'

'And now I know you are not, I am happy to come through,' Claire laughed. It was clear to her, as she followed Antoinette Marron through a succession of rooms, that this Parisian townhouse had been beautiful in its day. For obvious reasons, the rooms at the front of the house were sparsely furnished with smashed light fittings and broken furniture, but as they walked deeper into the house the rooms were furnished comfortably. The furniture was old-fashioned, but even in the dim light Claire could see it was excellent quality. The ceilings were high with ornate floral cornices. Doors on either side of a bare hall led to a sitting room, dining room, breakfast room, study and library. Some of the furniture – large settees and chairs, corner seats, huge mirrors – were covered with dust sheets. Walking through the rooms now and seeing all the furniture covered like this, Claire realised how close Antoinette had been to getting her parents out of Paris. That she hadn't saddened Claire.

'My father was a banker in the city. He is retired now, I am pleased to say. My mother was a volunteer worker with an organisation that helped the poor.' Antoinette turned to Claire. 'They are good, honest people who enjoyed going to the theatre and the opera with their friends. Now they are too frightened to go out of the house.'

'And their friends?'

'Gone. Hopefully they got out of Paris, but...' Antoinette shook her head. 'No one knows.'

Sorry was an inadequate response, so Claire didn't say anything.

In the back sitting room Antoinette's mother sat at a large oblong table surrounded by pieces of a half-completed jigsaw puzzle. Her father was writing at a bureau.

'Mama, Papa, this is Claire. She is a friend of Auguste's, and has come all the way from--' Antoinette Marron faltered.

'Gisoir, near Orléans,' Claire said. Antoinette's parents looked up from their respective activities and eyed Claire in much the same way that the maid had done – with suspicion.

It was Antoinette's mother who greeted Claire

first. 'How do you do?' she said, smiling tentatively. Her father followed his wife's lead, nodding and smiling.

'We usually have something to eat at this time of day,' Antoinette said. 'Yvonne, our maid, went to the shops earlier – not that there is much in them these days, but she is a clever girl. She can make a meal out of very little. I'll ask her to set another place at the table.'

CHAPTER EIGHTEEN

Claire knelt beside the river and splashed water onto her face. Sitting on her heels with her hands in the small of her back, she stretched and looked up. Rays of sunlight streaked through the trees warming her face. After a hot and humid August, September was warm and sunny with a refreshing early morning breeze. She unbuttoned her shirt and, leaning forward, dipped her hands into the cool river. Bringing them up to her throat, she allowed the water to trickle through her fingers onto her breasts. She closed her eyes and with slow circular movements gently rubbed her temples. She rolled her shoulders and with the tips of her fingers massaged the nape of her neck and down her back as far as she was able to reach.

André had arrived that morning on his way back to Gisoir after delivering money to a Resistance group near Fontainebleau. Claire asked him if he had news of Alain. He hadn't. Pierre put his arm around her, as her father might do, and asked her if it was time she came to terms with possibly never seeing Alain again. Claire had reacted badly. She shouted at Pierre and had to be calmed by his wife, Yvette, who dug her husband in the ribs, saying no news meant good news. Yvette probably didn't believe it, but it was all Claire had. It wasn't all, but…

'Who's there?' Sure that she had heard someone, or something, moving in the wood, Claire opened her eyes. Clumsily she got to her feet, stood perfectly still, and listened. She was getting jumpy.

'What the--?'

'Shush,' a man said, behind her. She began to turn round, but wasn't quick enough. The man put one hand over her mouth and the other round her waist.

Instinctively, she brought her free arm forward and in a flash of anger jerked it back, jabbing her elbow into the man's ribs. He loosened his grip for a second, giving Claire time to lift her right foot. She brought it down on his shin, scraping the heel of her boot along the bone. The man fell to the ground cursing. Claire took a gun from her pocket and aimed. 'Frédéric? What the hell were you doing, grabbing me like that? I could have shot you.'

Holding his hands up, Frédéric stumbled to his feet. 'I'm sorry. I didn't know you were--'

'What's going on?' Pierre shouted, coming out of the woods.

'If you say anything about-- I *will* bloody shoot you,' Claire hissed.

Pierre looked from Frédéric to Claire. He took Claire's gun and turned to Frédéric. 'You idiot,' he said. 'What were you doing here while Claire was washing?

'I wanted to say I was sorry that there has been no news of Alain. I didn't know she was-- I thought she was drinking from the river.'

'Get out of my sight. Go home. You are finished here.'

Claire quickly buttoned her shirt. 'Frédéric was being mischievous, Pierre. He didn't mean to insult me. I wouldn't have used it,' she said, when the Resistance leader gave the gun back to her, 'not on Frédéric.'

'Creeping up on you like that, how could you know it was him? And what if it had been a German soldier, his aim to cut your throat? Would you wait to see if he was a friend or foe before shooting? I hope not.' Pierre shook his head.

'I know Frédéric didn't think,' Claire said, 'but he will from now on.' Ticking Frédéric off reminded Claire it was dangerous to be on her own in the woods with so many German patrols about. She needed to be more careful. 'I shouldn't have come to the woods on my own either. It won't happen again, Pierre.' Claire picked up her jacket and slipped her arms down the sleeves. She looked at Pierre. 'Was there something else?'

'I came to speak to you about Alain,' Pierre said. 'I am sorry for being insensitive. Alain is a strong man, a brave man. He will not give us away.' Claire wasn't sure this was what she wanted to hear. Giving resisters away meant torture, but that was not what Pierre meant. She smiled to let him know she accepted his apology. 'So we are friends again?' Claire nodded. 'Good. Shall we go?'

'Of course, but first-- Sending Frédéric home will mean one of the other men will have to blow up the German troop train tonight.' As the leader of this Resistance group, Pierre was well aware of what sending Frédéric home would mean. 'What I'm trying to say is none of the other men have had the experience that Frédéric has. They don't understand explosives the way he does. Only Marcel knows how to set a detonator and he is not here. So I wondered if you would consider reinstating him.'

'I don't want to send him home but his behaviour was reckless.' Pierre's brow furrowed.

'What he did was stupid and dangerous. He's a hot-head who acts before he thinks. I'm worried that he'll get himself killed one of these days.'

'I don't think he cares about his own life. He hasn't done since his fiancée was found dead.' Claire paused, realising she'd said too much. 'But he cares about the group. He would never do anything to put his comrades in danger. His energy level is a little high now – it always is before a big sabotage job – but tonight he will be calm, focused, and precise setting the detonators. You know he always is.'

'You are right. I shall go and find him.' Before he got to the wood, Pierre turned back. 'You are an attractive woman, Claire. I overheard the men talking. They have great respect for you, but some are young and--'

'Don't worry, I can look after myself.'

'I noticed.' Claire could see relief on Pierre's face. 'I admit that, as angry as I was with Frédéric, I didn't know what I was going to do without him. I will speak to him immediately. I don't expect he'll have left yet anyway. He'll have invented a dozen excuses for what he did by the time we get back to the safe house. Are you coming?'

'Give me a minute. I'll catch you up.' When she was sure Pierre would not return, Claire crossed her arms protectively over her stomach. She looked down. Until now she had managed to hide her expanding waistline. Not for much longer, she thought, tucking her shirt into the waistband of her trousers. The belt she used to use to hold up her trousers had been in her kitbag for more than a month.

'Frédéric has something to say to you, Claire,' Pierre said, as she stepped out of the wood and into the clearing. 'I'll see you at the house.'

'Thank you for talking Pierre into keeping me in the group,' Frédéric said when they were on their own. 'After frightening you like that I don't deserve your kindness.'

'It wasn't kindness, Frédéric. The group needs you.' Frédéric looked down. 'I'm sure the whole thing at the river was a misunderstanding. I will forget it, if you do, okay?'

'Okay. I will not say anything,' he said, looking at her stomach.

'You won't have to say anything if you keep looking at me like that, Frédéric. Forget what you saw and concentrate on what you have to do tonight. We are all relying on you. Come on,' she said, walking towards the safe house. Frédéric limped along beside her.

'Food, Claire? Frédéric?' Pierre's wife, Yvette, said when they arrived. 'Sit down and eat.'

Claire sat between two of her comrades and watched Yvette dish up a watery stew that had small chunks of rabbit in it, but was mostly vegetables. The lads tucked in and Claire followed. She didn't want the food, but she didn't want to give anyone reason to wonder why she wasn't eating either. She joined in the discussion on tonight's sortie and tomorrow's. She thought about what Pierre had said to Frédéric. He was not a liability, but she might be. She wasn't able to move as quickly, let alone run, which wasn't fair on the rest of the group. Nor was it fair on the baby she was carrying. Suddenly the baby kicked and she put her hand on her stomach. She smiled inwardly, and wanted to laugh. She wanted to tell everyone that she and Alain had made something beautiful. Instead, she caressed her tummy beneath the table.

She had grown too big for her single cot at the safe house, and wasn't able to sleep, so she volunteered to do another watch, two hours on and two hours off. She looked around the table. She loved the people she was sharing the meal with. They were like family. She trusted them with her life, and they trusted her with theirs. With that thought foremost in her mind, Claire decided to tell Pierre she would be leaving the group at the end of the week. Tomorrow would be soon enough. For now she was part of this amazingly brave Resistance group and, although she felt like curling up in her comfortable bed at Édith's house in Gisoir, she sat and ate and laughed with her comrades.

CHAPTER NINETEEN

'Claire? Welcome home, my dear.' Édith Belland, her face lighting up with surprise, jumped up and dashed across the room. 'Come in, come in,' she said, leading Claire to the table and pulling out a chair. 'Sit down, you look exhausted.' Édith helped Claire out of her coat and hung it up. 'Is Frédéric with you, or André?'

'Here, Mother,' André called from the kitchen door. Édith turned, ran to her son and put her arms round him. He picked her up and swung her around.

'Put me down!' Édith giggled like a young girl. 'Stop now. I'm dizzy as if on a merry-go-round.' André put his mother down and held her until she got her balance. Still laughing, she pulled her pinafore down and patted her hair. 'Where is Frédéric?'

'He sends his love. He and Pierre have stayed to take some telephone lines down.' Claire saw disappointment in Édith's eyes.

'Sit down and I'll make coffee.' She put her hands to her face. 'I don't have any hot food for you. I wasn't expecting you until tomorrow, so I didn't cook. There is cheese and cold meat, and bread.' Édith dropped onto the chair next to Claire and began to weep.

'Mama, don't cry. Frédéric will be here tomorrow, the next day at the latest. Come on now.'

'I know. I'm being silly. I have been worried, imagining all sorts of things, here on my own. I want my children home and safe,' she said, squeezing André's hand and then Claire's.

Holding onto the table, Claire pulled herself up. 'I'll pour the coffee.' She reached up and took cups from the dresser, before going over to the range.

'Not for me, Claire. I want to see Thérèse. I have *missed* my wife,' André laughed. Édith tutted shyly and shook her head. 'See you tomorrow, Mama,' he said, kissing his mother. 'You too, Claire. Sleep well in your comfortable warm bed.'

'I can't wait,' Claire said, bringing the coffee pot to the table and taking her seat.

While Claire drank her coffee, Édith went to the larder, returning with the promised cold fare. 'You must be ravenous, child. When did you last eat?' she asked, placing the food on the table.

'At lunchtime. We sat and ate together – all of us – before going our separate ways. The others are meeting back at the safe house in three days. Frédéric reckons that's how long it will take the Germans to replace the tracks we sabotaged with tracks from the sidings.'

Édith sat down. 'Eat, child.'

Claire helped herself to bread and cheese, and Édith forked a slice of white meat – chicken or pork, Claire couldn't tell, nor did she care – onto her plate. 'Thank you, I am hungry,' she said, tucking into her supper.

Édith poured them both another cup of coffee, sat down and nibbled at a small piece of cheese. 'You said the others are meeting at the safe house in three days. Does that mean you won't be going back?'

'Not for a while.' Claire looked at Édith for a long minute. Finally she plucked up the courage to say, 'I am expecting a baby.'

Édith's face lit up. 'I know!'

'How? Has Frédéric written to you? I told him not to tell anyone.'

'Frédéric? No. He may sometimes speak before he thinks, but he is an honourable boy. If you tell him a secret, he will keep it.'

Claire laughed. 'I didn't tell him, exactly. He grabbed me from behind when I was at the river. He put his arm round my waist – well, where my waist used to be. It was a joke, to surprise me, and it did.' Claire decided not to tell Édith that she had pulled a gun on her son. They carried on eating. 'How long have you known?'

'Since you came back from Paris.'

'Why didn't you say something?'

'I hoped you would tell me. I was worried when you went with André and Frédéric to work with Pierre Ruban's group. But I told myself you are a strong woman and you would not risk your life, or the lives of the men and women you were working with.'

'I think Pierre guessed. He gave me safe jobs, made sure I was always close to base. In the last couple of weeks I took over from Yvette as housekeeper. I complained that I was bored once and he said someone had to do it and it was my turn. But I knew he was looking after me. I'd have told him if I thought for a second I was putting anyone in danger. I don't run as fast these days.'

'Did Alain know?'

'No.' Claire caressed Alain's unborn child, and yawned.

'I know what you need,' Édith said, leaping out of her chair. She opened the walk-in cupboard next to the scullery and disappeared inside. A few seconds later she appeared again, dragging the bath into the room. 'A long soak and to bed.' She placed the bath in the middle of the room and went over to the sink. She filled two large saucepans with water, placing one on the hook above the fire and the other in the oven. While the water boiled Édith took the clothes horse and opened it up, draping old curtains round it, for privacy. When the water in the saucepan above the fire began to boil she took it from the hook and poured it into the bath. She did the same with the saucepan in the oven. 'It's too hot,' she said, dipping her hand in it. 'It needs a little cold water.' She filled the empty saucepan with cold water, poured some in and tested it again. 'Perfect.'

'Thank you, Édith,' Claire said. 'Oh!' she gasped.

'Is everything all right, child?' Édith asked, rushing to Claire's side.

'Yes, fine. I think I have a footballer in my tummy.'

Édith laughed. 'Thank goodness! I thought something was wrong.'

'Oh, and again.' Claire took Édith's hand and placed it palm down on the right side of her stomach, below her bellybutton. 'There. Did you feel it, Édith? Did you feel my baby kick?'

Édith looked at Claire with tears in her eyes. 'Yes, child, I felt your baby. It is the most beautiful thing in the world.'

'It is, isn't it?' Claire put her arms round Édith and cried tears of happiness and exhaustion.

'Come on now,' Édith said, wiping Claire's face

with her pinafore. 'The bath water is the right temperature. If you don't bathe soon, I shall have to start boiling pans again.'

Claire began to undress. She took off her ill-fitting shirt and trousers, socks and underwear and stepped into the bath. Édith picked up her clothes and took them to the scullery. 'We will wash these tomorrow.'

'There's no rush. I'm not going back until after the baby is born.' Claire heard a pause in Édith's footsteps.

'I will wrap a hot brick in clean rags and put it into your bed. Shall I bring your night clothes when I come down?'

'Yes please. Bring my pyjama jacket and my dressing gown, I don't think I'll get into my nightdress. Don't be too long, you may have to help me out of here,' Claire said, laughing. Leaning her head on the back of the bath she closed her eyes. 'Mmmmmm, this is lovely.'

André and Thérèse arrived after breakfast. Thérèse ran in to greet Claire. She threw her arms around her when she stood up from behind the table – and jumped back. 'Oh,' she said, looking down at Claire's stomach, her eyes wide with astonishment.

'This is becoming a habit,' Claire laughed. 'Yes, I am expecting and no, Alain doesn't know, I'm pleased to say. He will have enough on his mind without worrying about us.' Claire smiled. It felt good to talk openly about the baby. 'Come on, Thérèse, let's go into town and I'll tell you all about it. Well not quite all,' she laughed.

'Have a pastry, if there are any,' André said,

handing Thérèse some money.

'Wait! I would like you to wear this,' Édith said, taking off her wedding ring.

'Are you ashamed of me, Édith? Of my baby and my love for Alain?'

'No, my darling, of course not! It is in case you are stopped by the Germans. If you're not wearing a wedding ring it will be a reason for them to treat you with disrespect.'

'But it's the ring your husband gave you--'

'No. It is not. The ring Henri put on my finger the day we were married is next to my bed. It became too tight and dug into my finger, so I had it cut off. This is a cheap replica. It was only ever meant to be temporary, until I had my wedding band repaired, but somehow I didn't get round to it. I shall now. We shall take it to the jeweller next time we go into town together.'

'Thank you, I will take care of it,' Claire said, allowing Édith to slip the ring onto her wedding finger. She held her hand at arm's length. 'One day,' she said, 'when I find Alain, I shall have one just like this.' Thérèse and Claire kissed Édith and André goodbye and trooped out of the back door giggling.

Trips into Gisoir had become a weekly treat. The centre was still overrun by officers of the Wehrmacht and Waffen SS who lounged about barking orders for drinks and food in every café, bar, and hotel in town. With autumn having rapidly turned into winter the weather had become inclement, and tables on the pavements of the cafés were vacated for those inside, making it impossible for Thérèse and Claire to find a seat in their favourite café.

'Let's go home, it's packed in there,' Thérèse said, peering through the window of Café La Ronde.

'I would, if I could, but I don't think I can take another step until I've been to the toilet.' Claire took a deep breath. 'I can't wait, Thérèse,' she said, pushing open the café's door and waddling between the tables to the back of the room.

Thérèse followed at the same pace, apologising as she snaked her way past one officer coming towards from the left, and another from the right. 'Are you all right, Claire?' Thérèse asked from outside the toilet door.

'Yes. I'm sorry,' Claire said, coming out a couple of minutes later, 'but my back aches and my feet are killing me. I need to sit down.' She looked round the café. 'Not one vacant table,' she tutted. 'Come on, let's go home.'

They took the walk home slowly and by the time they arrived, the pain in Claire's back had eased. 'Phew! Thank goodness for that,' she said, 'we're home. I need to go to the toilet again. You go in. I'll be with you in a minute.'

'Claire? It's Édith, are you all right?'

'Yes, apart from not making it to the lavatory in time.'

'Can you open the door, dear?'

Claire struggled from the seat and pushed back the bolt. Édith entered and when she saw the puddle of water on the floor, she shook her head.

'I'm sorry about the mess, Édith. I'll mop it up when I get out of here.'

'It is not important. Can you walk?'

'I think so.' As Claire shuffled out of the toilet, Édith shouted for Thérèse. 'I didn't make it,' Claire said to her friend.

'Thérèse, can you take Claire's other arm? I think the baby is coming.'

'It can't come yet, it's too soon. It's only November. It is only eight months since Alain and I...'

Édith laughed. 'Babies come when they are ready; they do not count the months. Your waters have broken. That means the baby is on the way.' Between them, Édith and Thérèse managed to get Claire into the kitchen.

'But nothing is ready-- Argh! What the--? Argh!' Claire shouted again. 'What the hell?' She lunged forward and, breathing heavily, gripped the table.

Édith and Thérèse, either side of her, waited. When the pains had subsided Édith said, 'Can you walk?' Panting, Claire nodded. 'Then I suggest we go into the front room.'

Thérèse and Édith pulled gently on Claire's arms and she allowed them to lead her. In the sitting room Claire fell to her knees and buried her head in the cushion on the settee. 'Whoever said giving birth was beautiful is a bloody liar,' she said, lifting her head. 'It's the most-- Argh!'

Kneeling beside Claire, Thérèse and Édith supported her by her elbows. 'Claire, will you let us help you onto the settee? I think you should lie down,' Édith said. Claire nodded. 'Thérèse? One two three, and up.' Claire stood, but doubled over. 'Now gently turn round. And sit down,' she said, when Claire had her back to the settee. 'Good girl. Now lean back. That's it. A little further until you are lying down. Good. Go and put the kettle on, Thérèse, and while it boils fetch some towels from the chest in my bedroom.' Thérèse left and Édith wiped Claire's face with a tea towel that was tucked into the top of her pinafore. 'There. Does that feel better?'

'No!' Claire spat. 'It feels bloody awful. What the hell is happening?' She cried out at the top of her lungs. Thérèse came rushing in with a damp cloth. 'André is here. He is watching the kettle. He won't come in, but asks if there is anything he can do.'

'Yes, tell him to fetch the doctor. And tell him to hurry. If André gets there before surgery finishes, the doctor should still be sober.' Édith looked at the clock on the mantle shelf. 'Tell André to tell the doctor that Claire's contractions are coming every ten minutes. Tell him it is urgent, and he must come as soon as possible.' Claire lifted her head, called out again, and Édith dabbed her forehead with the damp cloth. 'And Thérèse?' Édith shouted. 'When the kettle boils fill the white bowl. It's under a sterilised cloth in the pantry. And fetch those damn towels.' Édith wiped Claire's forehead again and she fell back onto the settee.

'Argh! You must be mad to have gone through this twice, Édith. Never, never, never, again. Argh!'

'Claire, put your knees up,' Édith said, trying to lift Claire's legs.

'No!' Claire panted. 'Where the hell's that doctor?' Thérèse came in with the bowl of boiling water, put it on the table, and then ran upstairs for the towels. On her return she dropped the towels onto the armchair and knelt beside Claire. Between them, Édith and Thérèse took off Claire's underwear and lifted her knees. Then, while Thérèse held Claire's hand, Édith went to the bottom of the settee. 'The baby is coming, Claire. Breathe slowly. In and out, in and out – now push!'

Claire pushed and screamed and pushed again. 'Only push once, Claire. Breathe again for me. In and out – and now, push!' Claire growled and pushed with all her strength. 'I can see the baby's head,' Édith cried. Claire collapsed exhausted. 'Don't stop, Claire, you must breathe. Again now, in and out, and... push! Push, Claire. Just a little more.'

'I can't. I'm too bloody tired,' Claire shouted, closing her eyes.

'No! Don't close your eyes. Your baby is almost here. I can see its head. You mustn't stop now. Thérèse, talk to her while I see what's going on.' Édith opened Claire's legs wider. 'Claire? Listen to me. One more push and your child will be here. Come on now, Claire,' Édith said, sternly. 'Breathe and push!' Claire pushed as hard as she was able. Her face was distorted and crimson, her hair soaked in sweat, and she grunted and screamed.

'Keep pushing, my darling child, keep pushing. Your baby is almost here. Yes, yes!' Édith shouted. 'She is here!' Édith laughed as the tiny premature baby cried at the top of her lungs. 'Hello, little one,' Édith cooed. 'That's right. You tell the world you have arrived.' Édith looked at Thérèse and they both laughed at the racket Claire's baby was making.

Worn out, Claire sank into the settee. 'A towel, Thérèse,' Édith whispered. And when her daughter-in-law passed her a small white hand towel, Édith wrapped the tiny mite in it. Then she laid the child in Claire's arms. 'Say hello to your daughter, my darling.'

Claire looked down and smiled. 'Hello baby,' she whispered, and closed her eyes.

'Stay with her, Thérèse. I am going to wash my hands and fetch a blanket. Then,' she said, 'You and I have earned a glass of wine.'

As Édith left the sitting room the doctor arrived. 'Boil some water, Madame. How many minutes between contractions?' He took off his coat, threw it across a chair and began rolling up his sleeves.

'The baby is here,' she said, pouring hot water into the bowl in the sink for the doctor to wash his hands. 'Use this, I will boil some more.' The doctor scrubbed his hands and lower arms. 'My niece is in the sitting room, with my daughter-in-law. If you'd like to go through, I shall bring in the water.'

CHAPTER TWENTY

'Wish your Aunt Édith a happy Christmas, Baby,' Claire said, as Édith entered the kitchen. Kissing her daughter on the top of her head, she handed her to Édith. 'I'll make the coffee.'

'Hello, beautiful baby. Yes, you are beautiful, aren't you? Yes you are.... You can't keep calling her Baby,' Édith said, rocking the contented child, who suddenly jerked her head towards her. 'You see, she agrees with her old aunt, don't you my darling? Yes you do.'

Claire put the coffee pot on the table and sat down. 'I wish...' She looked at her daughter and broke down in tears. 'I wish Alain was here,' she sobbed.

Putting the baby in her Moses basket, Édith held Claire until she had exhausted herself crying. 'Is Alain alive, Édith? I keep telling myself he is, but if only I knew for certain. If only I knew I would see him again, that he would one day know his daughter. I keep dreaming that he's… No! I will not say the word,' Claire said, and sobbed again. Édith held her and rocked her gently. 'Aimée,' Claire said suddenly. 'I shall call her Aimée, after Alain's sister. And her middle names will be Edwina, after my best friend in England, and Édith, after my wonderful friend and aunt in France.'

'And her aunt will take care of her, and you, until Alain returns. And he will return, you know,' Édith said, wiping Claire's face.

'Will he?' Claire whispered. 'My head says he is dead, but my heart says he is alive.' Claire looked pleadingly into Édith's eyes. 'I would know, wouldn't I? Feel it, if he was dead?' She inhaled deeply and blew out a shuddering breath. 'I'm sorry for being weak, Édith. I'm just tired.'

'You are not weak, child, you are strong. You have been very strong since Aimée's birth. Sometimes it can take months for a woman to settle down after she has a baby.' Édith pushed a stray curl of hair from Claire's face. 'At times like Christmas your emotions are bound to be on the surface. I know mine are. But,' she said, smiling, 'we must be positive and try to enjoy the holiday. First we enjoy our coffee, yes?' Claire nodded. 'Then we prepare the food. André and Thérèse are coming over, Frédéric will be here of course, and you, me, and *Aimée.*' Smiling, Claire looked at her sleeping daughter. 'That's better,' Édith said. 'All will be well, you'll see.'

André and Thérèse arrived mid-morning with gifts. 'They are mostly for Baby,' Thérèse said, looking in the cradle and cooing.

Claire went over to her friends and welcomed them. 'I have decided on a name. Aimée Edwina Édith, meet your Aunt Thérèse and Uncle André,' Claire said, lifting Aimée out of the basket and handing her to Thérèse.

'What beautiful names. We love the name Aimée, don't we, André?'

'If you say so, my love,' André said, looking at Claire and shrugging his shoulders as if to say he had no recollection of having discussed names.

Édith had said it wasn't good to keep picking Aimée up, but Claire was not going to stop Thérèse from doing so. She and André had been trying for a

241

baby for as long as they had been married. Thérèse blamed herself for not conceiving, but she couldn't know. Édith said it would happen when they least expected it, and that it was just a matter of time. Watching Thérèse with Aimée now, Claire knew she'd make a good mother.

'As soon as Aimée has been fed and Frédéric is down, we will go to church. Shout up to your brother, André. Tell him if he isn't downstairs in five minutes, he will be going to church without any breakfast.' André left the room, muttering under his breath.

Taking Aimée from Thérèse, Claire followed André. 'I'll take Aimée up and feed her.'

'I'll bring you up a cup of coffee, shall I, Claire?'

'No, I won't drink coffee while I'm feeding her.' Thérèse looked disappointed. 'But come up and keep me company. Aimée isn't much of a conversationalist yet.'

When she'd had enough to eat, Aimée fell asleep. Claire laid her on a towel and Thérèse changed her nappy, while Claire dressed in a warm woollen skirt and thick jumper. Sitting at the dressing table mirror, Claire watched how loving and gentle her friend was with Aimée and hoped with all her heart that she would have a child of her own soon. 'I'm going down. See you two in a minute,' she said, putting out Aimée's clothes and leaving Thérèse to dress her.

When Frédéric came down, the Belland family left for church. The two brothers, tall and handsome in their best winter coats and trilby hats, led the way. Thérèse followed, pushing Aimée, who was hidden beneath warm blankets, in the pram she had bought in preparation for when she had her own child. Claire and Édith, arm in arm, trailed behind.

Walking to church after a recent snowfall reminded Claire of Foxden. She breathed the cold winter air. 'The last Christmas I was home it was just like this,' she said to Édith. 'Snow for as far as you could see.'

'Have you written to your family lately?'

'Yes, I wrote to my oldest sister. I also wrote to my friend in the WAAF. I enclosed a letter for my parents and asked her to post it on to them, so it would have an English postmark. My parents can't know I'm here, but if I didn't get in touch at this time of year they would worry.'

'Did you tell your sister about Aimée?'

'No. Do you think I should have?'

'No. I just wondered.'

The two women walked the rest of the way to the church in silence. The sound of the organ playing a slow and rather sad tune, and the scents of musky spice and vanilla, met them as they entered. The church was full except for the pew at the front, where the Belland family sat. Édith stopped to speak to one of her neighbours and ended up sitting nearest the aisle and the pram. Claire was next to her and Thérèse sat between her husband and her brother-in-law.

The priest walked down the aisle swinging the incense bowl, and when he'd lit the altar candles the service began. Kneeling in a Catholic church with her French family, Claire prayed for their safety and for the safety of her brave comrades of the Resistance. She prayed too for her parents, her friend Eddie in the WAAF, her brother Tom in the Army, and her sisters Bess, Margaret and Ena. And she prayed for Mitch. She prayed that he would come home to her and his daughter. She looked along the pew. Édith was rocking the pram gently.

When the service ended, Claire took the pram and joined the worshippers standing in line to thank the priest. When it came to her turn, she put out her hand to shake his, and he said, 'When will you be having your child christened?'

Shocked, Claire replied, 'When my husband comes home.'

'I look forward to that day, Madame,' he said, shaking Claire's hand. Bending over and smiling at Aimée, he said, 'God bless you my child.'

'That was nice of Father Albert to offer to christen Aimée,' Thérèse said, 'especially as he doesn't really know you.'

'I've been to a few services where he has officiated,' Claire said.

'Of course.' Thérèse rested her hand on the handle of the pram and walked at Claire's side. 'And you met him at mother-in-law's house when he came to tell us that poor Monique was dead.' Claire looked at Édith. She hadn't told André and Thérèse how Monique had died, or that it was Claire and Alain who had found her. That was a secret shared only by Édith, Father Albert and herself.

CHAPTER TWENTY-ONE

Claire unpacked the shopping and put it in the larder. Leaving a tin of baby milk and a small bottle with a rubber teat on the table, she made coffee. Pleased that she had found the baby formula she sat down, sipped her coffee, and read the back of the tin. Baby's first formula, six to twelve months, and instructions on how to make it. She took the teat from the bottle and rinsed it under the tap. Then she filled the kettle, put it on the cooker and lit the gas. As soon as it boiled, Claire poured the water into Édith's white jug and while it cooled she went into the yard to get the washing in.

The garments that were dry she folded and took into the laundry room. She checked the water again. It was cooler, so she spooned two teaspoons of the formula into the bottle, added the water, and after shaking the bottle, tested it on her wrist. It felt like the correct temperature.

'Hey... Baby,' she said to Aimée, who had woken and was kicking her legs contentedly. She lifted Aimée out of the pram and, sitting on the wooden bench by the back door, teased her with the warm teat on the bottle. Aimée's mouth opened, but before Claire had time to place the teat between her lips she closed her mouth and turned her head away. Claire lowered the bottle. 'If you don't like it, darling, you don't have to drink it,' she said, and unbuttoned her blouse. She offered Aimée her breast, but as she did to the bottle, she turned away. 'Not hungry?' She put Aimée back into her pram and buttoned her blouse. Rocking the pram with her foot, she picked up the bottle of formula and put it to her own lips. It was sweet, a bit thick and powdery-tasting, but it had all the goodness required. Aimée began a grizzly hungry cry, so Claire took her from her pram and put the bottle to her lips again. She sucked and pulled a face. Then she closed her eyes and sucked contentedly. By the time the bottle was empty, Aimée was almost asleep. 'Good girl,' Claire said, lifting her daughter and putting her over her shoulder. She rubbed Aimée's back until she was winded, and then put her down for her afternoon nap in the warm June sunshine.

Édith entered the yard and went straight over to Aimée. 'So you are home from your walk, my lovely,' she cooed to the sleeping child. 'It is a beautiful day, but too hot for your aunt.' She turned the pram a little so the sun was not directly on it. 'Any news?'

'Jacques said more men were taken from German headquarters to Périgueux prison today. He didn't know if Alain was among them.' Claire shook her head. 'His friend who works there is trying to find out, but as always I don't expect he'll come up with anything.'

Édith touched Claire affectionately on the shoulder. 'I must take off these shoes,' she said, entering the kitchen.

'There's coffee in the pot,' Claire called after her.

'What is this?' Édith returned almost immediately holding the baby formula at arm's length.

Claire knew Édith wouldn't approve. 'I thought

I'd try her on it in case I was ever held up somewhere. Then you could give her a feed. I mean, if you don't mind?'

'Mind? Of course I don't mind.' She clicked her tongue, looked into the pram, and cooed again the way doting aunts do.

'This message is to go to London as soon as possible, Jacques.' Claire gave the wireless operator the hand-written message.

'Hot dogs in abundance. Uncle Sam looking for his children. Might hitch a lift. But need seaside togs and papers. Any news of The French Can? China Blue,' Jacques read. 'At this time of day I expect a reply. If you would like to wait?' he said, showing Claire into his sitting room. Ten minutes later Jacques joined her. 'It is done. And the reply,' he said, 'Paris is nice at this time of year.'

'Thank you, Jacques. London has given me permission to go to Paris.' Claire put her arms round the flamboyant man, who when they first met she had not trusted, and hugged him to her.

'You are welcome,' he said, when Claire released him.

Claire had grown fond of Jacques. His jubilant personality and extravagant clothes, a cover for the heartbreak he felt over the loss of his wife, was as much a part of him now as his fedora and umbrella.

Claire left Jacques at seven and strolled along the avenue. It was a sultry evening, a perfect evening for lovers. She began to walk faster. God willing she would one day, in the not too distant future, see her lover again. But now it was her daughter that she longed to see.

247

As she entered the yard and approached the kitchen, Claire heard Aimée laughing. She put her hand on the doorknob, but didn't turn it. It was a joy to hear her daughter happy. When she left that morning Aimée was grizzling. Her cheeks were bright red. She'd made a fist of her small hand and was trying to put it in her mouth. Édith said she was teething and had rubbed something on her gums to soothe them. It had obviously worked; it appeared to be working still.

'Hello?' Claire called, opening the door. Entering the kitchen she saw Aimée, held safely in Édith's strong hands, sitting astride a wooden rocking horse. When she saw her mother the little girl squealed.

'Just in time for dinner,' Édith said. Claire put her hands out to lift Aimée from the horse, but the little girl held on to the horse's mane and kicked out, making the horse quiver beneath her small frame. Édith and Claire laughed, and Aimée squealed again. 'I may have made a mistake borrowing the horse,' Édith said. 'Put your hands over your ears. I don't think this little miss will be happy when I lift her off.' With a swoop, she took Aimée in her arms and swung her round. Aimée began to wail and Édith began to sing. Claire moved the rocking horse into the passage and by the time Édith had stopped singing, Aimée had stopped crying. A few minutes later, Aimée rubbed her eyes with the back of her small hands and reached for her mother. Claire bounced her sleepy daughter on her knee while Édith filled two large bowls and one small one with stew. When they were sitting with their food in front of them, Édith added a cold potato that she had taken from the stew earlier. She chopped it up into small pieces and mashed it into Aimée's meal.

Claire fed her daughter while her own food cooled. At first Aimée ate greedily, wanting another spoonful as soon as she had swallowed the first. Then she turned her head away and yawned. Claire wiped gravy from her mouth and chin, lifted her up, and held her against her chest. Supporting the sleepy child with her left hand, Claire ate her supper with her right. By the time she'd finished, Aimée was asleep. 'I'll take her up,' she said.

When she returned, Édith had cleared the kitchen and was in the sitting room listening to the wireless. 'You look worried, Claire. What is it?'

'I've asked England to send my WAAF uniform and papers.' Édith's eyes widened with surprise. 'The Americans and Canadians are setting up a task force to investigate prisoner of war camps and prisons. With Périgueux being in Paris, I'm going to ask them if they'll help me find Alain. Before I approach them, I need my papers and permission from my commanding officer. I'm not technically in the WAAF now, so she'll have to send them to London, and they'll add them to the next drop. But,' Claire said, 'I can only go to Paris if you'll look after Aimée?'

'Of course, but--'

'And perhaps Frédéric would bring the papers to me when they come?'

CHAPTER TWENTY-TWO

Claire spent the morning waiting for Frédéric, watching for him to arrive from behind the broken shutters of Antoinette Marron's front windows. She smiled, remembering the look of astonishment on Frédéric's face when he put his arms round her and realised she was having a baby. Because he was the first in the Belland family to find out she was pregnant he was very protective of her – of Aimée too. He doted on her almost as much as his mother did. Claire sighed. She had never missed anyone, with the exception of Alain, as much as she missed her daughter. She promised herself that when she found him she would never let him, or Aimée, out of her sight again.

She looked along the street. Frédéric was nowhere to be seen. If she didn't have her WAAF papers by Sunday night she would have to cancel the meeting with the US-Canadian task force. She paced the floor. The Americans weren't as particular, but the Canadians were sticklers for protocol. They wouldn't let her go with them to look for Mitch without the correct military documents, because she wouldn't be protected by the Geneva Convention.

'You're restless, Claire,' Antoinette said, joining her.

'I think I'll take a walk to the post office,' Claire said. 'There might be a message for me.'

'You must do what you think best, but if there has been a change to the scheduled drop they would have let you know.'

'You're right, of course, but I need to be sure.' Claire went to the hall and put on her jacket. 'Do you need anything while I'm out?' Antoinette shook her head. 'Then I shall see you in an hour.'

Antoinette followed Claire to the front door. 'Be careful,' she said, opening it and scanning the street. 'What a lovely day. It is more like mid-summer than late spring,' she said, to give herself time to study the empty houses opposite before letting Claire pass. 'See you later, my dear.'

Claire nodded. 'I won't be long,' she whispered, kissing Antoinette on both cheeks. 'Yes, see you later,' she called, running down the steps and through the gate.

She took a long breath. It felt good to be out of the house. She walked towards Boulevard Victor Hugo, sitting for a second on the base of the nineteenth century statue of the Duke of Orléans on his horse. She pondered going back in case Frédéric arrived. Instead she walked on. On either side of a narrow road that cut through the tree-lined avenue where the post office was situated were boarded-up flats. She stopped and looked through the railings of a two-storey block of what had once been elegant apartments. They reminded her of a dolls' house with its front open, except the front of this building had been blown off. She could see into the halls and sitting rooms, bathrooms and bedrooms where people had once lived. As she turned to leave she saw a speck of blue out of the corner of her eye. She knelt down. A single bluebell had forced its way through the broken concrete façade. She felt the backs of her eyes tingle. She was more tired than she thought.

At the post office Claire asked for two stamps and while the postmistress took them from the post-book she sighed and said in a flat disappointed tone, 'I was expecting a letter from my brother, but it seems he has forgotten my birthday.'

The postmistress looked over her shoulder at the large round clock that hung on the wall. 'It's still early,' she said. 'I expect it's on its way.' Claire handed her a franc in payment for the stamps. 'It may have been a little delayed because of the trains. Another was blown up last night,' she said, tutting. Claire saw a twinkle in her eyes, and knew it was a German troop train and not a passenger train. If Frédéric had made the train, he was safe. She gave a little cough to hide her relief. The postmistress gave Claire her change, pressing it into the palm of her hand for a second longer than necessary. 'If I was you I would go home. By now the postman should have delivered to your house.'

Wishing the postmistress a good day, Claire stepped away from the counter to allow the next customer to take her place. She put the stamps safely in her purse, walked to the door and out onto the pavement. So Frédéric was in Paris and on his way to Antoinette's. She walked quickly, stopping momentarily at the apartments where she had seen the bluebell. She thought about picking it, but decided it looked better where it was, however broken and sorry the surroundings.

As she mounted the steps to the house the door opened. 'Eddie?'

'Come in quickly,' she whispered, 'in case I was followed.'

A momentary glance as she closed the door showed Claire they were safe. Unable to contain her excitement, Claire threw her arms round her friend. 'What are you doing here?'

'I've brought you something.' Taking off her coat, Eddie picked at the loose stitching of its lining until there was enough space to slip her thumb and finger inside. Grinning, she said, 'Ta dah!' and handed Claire a manila envelope.

Thrilled at last to have her WAAF papers, Claire tore open the envelope and pulled out the letter. 'What?'

'Congratulations, Leading Aircraftwoman Dudley.'

Claire's heart sank. 'Promotion, and I'm not even there,' she said, attempting a joke to cover her disappointment. 'Manders is getting soft in her old age.' She returned the letter to its envelope. 'Where are my papers? And where's Frédéric?'

'Frédéric couldn't get away. Some last minute Resistance thing came up', Eddie said, 'but he sent this.'

Claire unfolded a second sheet of paper to reveal a pencil sketch of Aimée. 'My daughter,' she said, moving closer to Eddie so she could see the sketch.

'I know. I met her. André and Thérèse were part of my reception committee. They took me to Édith's – who, by the way, sends her love. Aimée is beautiful, Claire, like her mummy.'

'I don't know about that, but she is beautiful,' Claire said, her voice cracking with emotion. She cleared her throat. 'Now, tell me about you?'

'Well, I came top of the class in combat and firearms.'

'Firearms?'

'Yes,' Eddie laughed. 'I'm aristocracy darling, remember. I could shoot with the best of Daddy's cronies before I went up to Oxford.'

'And how long have you been working for the colonel?'

'Since the autumn of forty-three, but this is my first drop. I've been sitting by the telephone, watching the full moon come and go for months. I was back at Coltishall when you requested your papers, so the FO suggested I took them down to London. The day I arrived I was briefed on the drop, and a couple of days later I was parachuted into France.'

Claire looked at Eddie expectantly. 'So where are they? Obviously you couldn't risk travelling with the uniform, but you've brought my papers, haven't you?'

Eddie shook her head. 'Sorry, Dudley, the colonel has them. My orders are to take you back to London for a debriefing.'

'But the colonel said Paris was nice at this time of year, which meant he'd given me permission to look for Mitch.'

'You still can, when you come back. Sorry, Dudley, but you don't have a choice. Colonel Smith is miffed with you for not keeping in touch, so you'd better not ruffle his feathers further by sending me home on my own.'

'Oh well,' Claire said, overwhelmed by a feeling of defeat, 'without my WAAF uniform and papers the Americans won't take me anyway.'

'The Americans? Take you where?'

'To find Mitch. The Americans and Canadians

are gearing up to go into prisons and POW camps to get their citizens out. I had an appointment with them next week, but without my papers to prove I was – am – with the WAAF they wouldn't take me. Since forty-two, when Hitler ordered all Allied commandos, agents, the Resistance – anyone who was not wearing a full uniform – to be killed without trial, the military has become very strict.' Claire put her head in her hands.

At that moment Antoinette brought in a tray with a pot of coffee, cups, saucers, plates and a cake. She placed them on an elegant but unpolished and distressed occasional table between the settee and armchairs. 'Let me know if you need anything else.'

Claire thanked her and asked her to join them, but Antoinette said she would first prepare a bedroom for Edwina and would be back shortly. Claire poured the coffee, handed a cup to Eddie, and sliced the cake. Eddie's eyes lit up. 'I'm pleased you met Aimée. How is she?'

'She is darling and Édith is in her element looking after her.'

'Spoiling her, no doubt,' Claire said, fighting back her tears. 'And André and Thérèse? You said they were part of your reception committee. Are they well?'

'Yes. They are staying with Édith.'

'Staying with Édith? Why?'

'Oh … I don't know. It's a temporary thing, I think.' Eddie took a sip of her coffee.

'Eddie? I know when you're hiding something. What is it?'

'Nothing. They didn't say why they were

255

staying at Édith's. I mean, they wouldn't, would they? They don't know me--'

'I'm sorry to grill you. It's just that Édith has been like a mother to me – and Aimée adores her. André is like a big brother, and Frédéric...' Claire laughed. 'When I first met Frédéric I think he was sweet on me. Then he met a local girl, Monique, and fell head over heels in love. He talked about her all the time, wrote her endless letters-- Poor Frédéric. He thought – well, everyone did – that Monique was visiting her grandmother near Tours, but she never got there. Mitch and I found her at the farm, dead. She'd been killed by German soldiers.'

Eddie grimaced and shook her head slowly. 'Poor girl... And poor Frédéric.'

'He doesn't know how Monique died, thank goodness. It would kill him if he knew she'd been raped and murdered. I'm sorry,' Claire said, 'let's talk about something more cheerful.'

'No need to apologise. I know the Belland family mean a lot to you. You mean a lot to them too.' Eddie laughed. 'Aimée is a real little French mademoiselle.' Claire listened to what Eddie told her about her daughter, laughing one minute and crying the next. 'They are looking forward to you going home to Gisoir. When do you think that will be?' Eddie asked.

'I've nothing to stay for in Paris now, so the sooner the better. I'd rather spend the time I have left in France with Aimée.'

At that moment Antoinette popped her head round the door. 'Your room is ready, Edwina.'

'Thank you, Antoinette, I'll take Eddie up. She is lovely,' Claire said when Antoinette had gone.

'She's the wife of the professor I stayed with in Newcastle when we did our French family training.'

'That's why London has lost track of you. This address isn't on the safe house list, is it?'

'It will be soon. I don't know what I'd have done without Antoinette. A dozen or more agents and goodness knows how many Resistance members have been taken prisoner over the last six months – and many of them after staying in Paris. The Gestapo and the SS have got intelligence of some kind. It's almost as if they know our movements. Anyway, I didn't know who to trust, so I asked Antoinette if I could stay here. She said yes immediately and asked if there was anything else she could do to help the Resistance. I broached the subject of a safe house and she jumped at the chance to help. She had to ask her parents of course, as it's their home – and they said yes immediately. So this address will be on the safe house register as soon as I get to a wireless.'

CHAPTER TWENTY-THREE

It was early afternoon by the time Claire and Eddie arrived in Gisoir. The train from Paris to Orléans had stopped at every station, or so it seemed, and at every station the Gestapo and half a dozen gendarmes boarded to check passengers' identity papers. Claire and Eddie, who travelled in the same carriage but didn't sit next to each other, kept their identity papers and travel permits on their laps, as did most of the passengers. Halfway through the journey an over-zealous young gendarme ordered everyone to open their cases. Eddie and Claire only carried handbags, which he searched first. Tipping the contents of Eddie's bag into her lap and finding only a powder compact, comb and lipstick, the gendarme turned to Claire. She glanced at Eddie, saw a look of horror in her eyes, and blinked twice, which was the code for all is well. She had burned the letter from Flight Officer Manders promoting her before leaving Antoinette's. Finding nothing suspicious, the gendarme ripped open the lining of Claire's bag before upending it onto her lap.

When the train pulled into Gisoir station, Claire looked out of the window expecting to see Frédéric. He hadn't made it to Paris, but she felt sure he would be at the station to meet her. He wasn't. Leaving the train, it crossed her mind that being so near to Jacques' house she could call on him, introduce Eddie, and ask him if he had any news of Alain. But if she did that, Eddie would ask Jacques to send a message to the colonel and her time in Gisoir with Aimée would be one day less, so she decided against it. If Jacques had heard anything he would have told André or Frédéric. She would know soon enough.

Claire was doubly disappointed that Frédéric wasn't in the alley at the back of the house to greet them. She looked up at his bedroom window. Eddie followed her gaze. 'What is it?'

'The curtains in Frédéric's room are drawn. That's why he wasn't at the station to meet us. The lazy devil's still in bed. We'll have to go round the front,' Claire said, already on the move.

Claire knocked at the front door and waited. There was no reply. She knocked again, this time louder. Still no one answered. She stepped carefully through the flower bed under the front window and peered inside. 'It doesn't look as if anyone's home.'

'Madame LeBlanc?' Claire turned to see Édith's neighbour, Madame Oran, at her front door. 'You are back. Édith will be pleased to have you home.'

'We're pleased to be home,' Claire said, including Eddie with a gesture of her hand. 'Do you know where Édith is, Madame?'

'Yes. She has gone to see Father Albert. She left the key with me, to let Thérèse and Aimée in when they returned from visiting Thérèse's mother. As you have arrived first, I will get it.' Knots of love and emotion tightened in Claire's stomach at the thought of seeing her daughter. Madame Oran gave her Édith's key and said, 'Welcome home.'

Claire unlocked the door, stood back to let Eddie enter, and followed her in closing the door behind her. After taking off her coat, she hung it up and went through to the kitchen. A chill washed over her and she shivered. The fire in the range, which Édith never allowed to go out, had died down to a few embers. Claire filled the kettle and put it on the stove. 'Find a match and light the gas, Eddie, while I get the fire going.' She took a few dry sticks from the wood pile, laid them carefully on what was left of the fire and fanned them with a newspaper. When the kindling took hold she added a couple of logs. Then she went into the sitting room and did the same to the fire in there.

While Eddie made the tea Claire went upstairs. Édith's bed was unmade, which was unusual, and Frédéric's hadn't been slept in. She looked into André's old room and saw Thérèse's nightdress folded neatly on one side of the bed and André's pyjamas on the other. Her room was much as she had left it. She went downstairs and joined Eddie in the kitchen. 'I'm going to the church.'

'I'll come with you,' Eddie said.

'Do you mind staying, Ed? Someone needs to be here when Thérèse and Aimée get back. I wouldn't ask, but I'm worried about Édith. It isn't unusual for Thérèse to take Aimée out, but it is that Édith isn't here when they are due home. And going out when she knew we were expected is completely out of character.' Claire looked around the kitchen. 'She hasn't even left a note. Something is wrong, Eddie, I can feel it.'

'Wouldn't you rather be here when Aimée gets back?' Eddie asked.

'Of course, but you don't know where the church is and I do.' At the front door, putting on her coat, Claire turned to Eddie. 'Add a log to the fires will you, Ed, make sure they don't go out. I'll be back before you know it.'

She walked quickly. It wasn't far to the church, but the sooner she got there the sooner she would see Édith and the sooner they could go home. As she neared the beautiful old building she could see the door leading into the church was ajar. Entering the vestibule, she pushed on the door and stepped into the nave. She saw Édith immediately, kneeling before the altar. Holding onto the end of a pew, Claire bobbed down and made the sign of the cross, as Édith always did, before slipping silently onto the nearest seat.

After some time, when Édith hadn't moved, Claire stood up and walked down the aisle. Passing under the dome of the crossing she entered the chancel, knelt down beside Édith and took hold of her hand. Édith lifted her head, and though Claire could see relief in her eyes, Édith collapsed and began to sob.

Claire held her friend, rocking her as she would a child until the wrenching sobs that came from somewhere deep inside her subsided. When she had worn herself out Claire said, 'It is cold for you sitting on the stone floor. Shall we sit in the choir stalls?'

Without argument Édith allowed Claire to help her to her feet and together they slowly walked across the apse to where the choir normally sat. Édith flopped down in the first seat and cried silently.

For Édith to be so heartbroken, so despairing, something terrible must have happened. 'What is it?' Claire whispered. 'Won't you tell me?'

Édith looked up, her red and swollen eyes looking into Claire's. 'My beautiful boy, my courageous Frédéric is dead,' she wailed. Burying her head in her hands, she began to rock backwards and forwards.

Claire's mouth fell open in disbelief. Her temples throbbed and her head pounded as if a rod of pain was being driven through her skull. 'How?' she whispered. 'When?' Claire put her hand on Édith's arm. 'Édith, stop! Please,' she begged, 'you'll hurt yourself.

Édith stopped rocking and said again, 'Frédéric is dead.'

Tears fell from Claire's eyes. She couldn't keep her feelings in check any longer. 'I'm sorry,' she heard a small voice that sounded similar to her own say. Sorry seemed inadequate, *was* inadequate. She felt Édith's arms around her. Now it was Claire's turn to be comforted.

'He was a good boy, a clever boy,' Édith said. 'He did much for the Resistance. André said he did well while they were away.' Claire nodded through her tears. Frédéric had done more than well. He had done jobs no one else was capable of doing, or wanted to do. 'And when they came home they spent time together. As children, young men even, they were never close. But after the sabotage of Flurand station, André showed Frédéric respect and it seemed at last they loved each other as brothers should.' Édith turned back to the altar. Standing next to it was a statue of the Madonna and Child. She smiled. Then her eyes filled with tears again. 'Father Albert said he bought flowers for Monique.' She took a shuddering breath and shook her head, too bereft to speak.

'Take your time.' Claire held Édith's trembling

hands in hers.

'Father Albert told me that he heard the confession of a German soldier earlier and was entering the confessional again to hear someone else's confession when he saw Frédéric. As soon as he was able, Father Albert went to look for Frédéric. He found him at Monique's grave. The German soldier was also there, begging for forgiveness. Frédéric pulled the soldier up by his coat collar and pushed him away. He then laid the flowers he had brought for Monique at the head of the grave. The German stumbled back, crushing the flowers. "Get away from her," Frédéric shouted, but the soldier ignored him.

'Father Albert heard Frédéric ask the German what the hell he thought he was doing, and the soldier told Frédéric that he had killed the girl in the grave at the Belland Farm, and the priest told him to pray for forgiveness. Staggering about drunk, the soldier put his hands together and fell to his knees, begging Monique to forgive him.

'"Did you hear me? Frédéric shouted again. Get out of here, or I'll kill you." The soldier, suddenly full of bravado, took his gun from its holster and waved it in Frédéric's face. Frédéric lunged at the soldier and wrestled him to the ground – and the gun went off. The two boys, for that was all they were, stood perfectly still and looked at each other as if they were in shock, Father Albert said. Then Frédéric fell to the ground. The German soldier bellowed, "No! God forgive me." Then he laid down beside Frédéric, put the gun to his head and pulled the trigger.'

Claire sat and stared, seeing nothing, and then

said, 'I saw a bunch of flowers on a pew when I walked down to you. Are they for Frédéric?' Édith nodded. 'May I come with you to put them on his grave?' Édith nodded again.

Together they walked back to the nave and picked up the flowers. 'They are for Monique too,' Édith said. 'They are together now. Together,' she sighed.

They left for the churchyard by the side door. It was almost dark. 'Aimée and Thérèse will be home now,' Édith said. 'You wait until you see your daughter, Claire. She is so beautiful.' Édith began to cry softly.

There was no gravestone when Claire last visited Monique's grave. There was now. Frédéric's name was above that of his fiancée. Édith took off the old flowers and put on the new. The two women stood either side of the grave in silence. Claire wanted to be strong for Édith and forced herself not to cry. Édith prayed. When she had finished she looked around, spotted a grave without flowers and put Frédéric and Monique's old flowers on it. They looked fresh. Claire suspected they were and that Édith came to Frédéric's grave every day. 'Shall we go home?' she said. 'It's getting cold and your coat is thin.' Édith put her arm through Claire's and they walked slowly home.

As they entered the house, the difference in temperature from when Claire and Eddie first arrived was pleasantly noticeable. Claire helped Édith out of her coat and Eddie greeted her by putting her arms around her and kissing her. She raised her eyebrows over Édith's shoulder and Claire shook her head, as if to say don't ask. 'I have made coffee,' Eddie said, 'and when you're ready I will make us a meal.' She went to the stove, brought back the coffee pot and filled three cups. She pushed the milk jug towards Édith, who ignored it, so Claire added milk to all three cups.

When Édith finished her coffee she excused herself, saying she was going upstairs to have a lie down. Claire stood up when Édith did, ready to go with her if she asked. She didn't. 'I'll see you at dinner?' Édith shook her head. 'I'll pop in anyway. If you're awake you may be hungry.' Édith left the room, closing the door quietly behind her.

Eddie poured herself and Claire more coffee. 'You've been gone ages. What happened?'

Claire told Eddie how Frédéric had found the German soldier who had killed Monique at her grave. How they had fought and how Frédéric had been killed. 'I think it was an accident. I didn't say so to Édith, but I really think the German wanted Frédéric to shoot him. When he didn't, or when the soldier realised he'd killed Frédéric – we'll never know – the soldier shot himself.'

'Three years, four, since Frédéric joined the Resistance and he hasn't had a scratch – and then he is killed at his fiancée's grave.' Eddie hung her head. 'It makes no sense.'

Claire was about to agree when she heard a bump at the kitchen door. Eddie was nearest and stood up. 'I'll get it,' Claire said. 'It'll be Thérèse and Aimée.' She jumped up and put out the light as the door swung open.

Thérèse, with her back to Claire, lifted the handle of the pram and took several steps backwards into the kitchen until the pram's back wheels had cleared the step. She then pushed down on the handle to lift the front wheels over and brought the pram into the kitchen, kicking the door shut behind her. Claire flicked the light on and Thérèse turned a rosy face to her. 'My dear. How lovely to see you,' she said, taking a step back so Claire could see her daughter.

Claire looked into the pram and then at Thérèse. 'Can I?'

Thérèse laughed. 'Of course.' She moved to the fire as Claire lifted Aimée out of the pram. Sitting next to Eddie, she beamed at her daughter as she bounced her on her lap. 'Hello, my beautiful girl,' she said to the gurgling baby. 'In such a short time she has changed so much.'

'So have you, Claire, you are very thin. You have not been taking care of yourself,' Thérèse said. 'But I'm sure Édith will fatten you up now you are back.'

'I'm afraid I may not be here long enough. I have to go to England for a couple of weeks.'

Eddie raised her eyebrows. 'We don't know how long we'll be away, but we'll be leaving sooner rather than later.'

'It *will* only be for a couple of weeks,' Claire insisted. 'And we don't know when we'll be leaving. We'll see Jacques tomorrow. He'll let London know we're here, and they'll inform him when they're going to pick us up. I need to ask Jacques if he's heard anything about Alain, too.'

Édith didn't come down again that day, but she was up early the following morning and seemed more like her old self. After breakfast they all went into Gisoir. Thérèse left them to visit her parents

266

and Édith, pushing Aimée in a borrowed pushchair, went to the market leaving Claire and Eddie to see Jacques.

CHAPTER TWENTY-FOUR

On her hands and knees, Claire chased her daughter in crawling versions of catch me if you can and peep-o, surprising her with a knitted teddy bear and dolls with china faces that looked round curtains, or popped up unexpectedly from behind chairs. Aimée clapped and squealed every time, but the game she liked best was knocking down the wooden farm animals that André and Frédéric's father had crafted for them when they were Aimée's age. Time after time, before Claire had placed the last animal in position in the farmyard beside timber farm buildings – a boy's version of a dolls' house – Aimée knocked them down. Feigning surprise, Claire put her hands up to her face and gasped and Aimée laughed with mischievous satisfaction. Crawling away as fast as she was able, she hid behind the chair until Claire found her and tickled her, making her laugh even more.

'That looks like a fun game,' Édith said from the door. Aimée offered Édith a black and white horse, which Édith took and stroked. 'It is time, Claire.'

Claire scooped Aimée up in her arms and rocked her. 'I have to go to work now, darling, on a big aeroplane.' Aimée laid her head on Claire's chest. 'When I come back,' she whispered, 'I am going to find your daddy.' Aimée wriggled and put her thumb in her mouth. Claire looked down. Her daughter's eyes were heavy. Slowly, her eyelids lowered and closed. Then she jerked her head, opened them wide, looked up at Claire and smiled. A second later she closed her eyes and they stayed closed. Claire breathed in Aimée's scent: the warm subtle smell of baby, of orange blossom on her hair, the clean fresh smell of her clothes that Édith insisted on washing and ironing, and a hint of lavender from Thérèse's perfume. Claire was overwhelmed by the love she felt for her daughter – Mitch's daughter. She listened to Aimée's breathing, a little erratic at first, but soon becoming calm and rhythmical, and she wished with all her heart she didn't have to leave her. As tears fell from her eyes, the door opened again. It was Eddie. Claire nodded that she knew it was time to leave and pushed herself up. Aimée's eyes fluttered, but she didn't wake. She was fast asleep when Claire laid her in her pram.

Turning away from Aimée, Claire cried silently. Édith wrapped her arms around her. 'Dry your eyes, my dear. Come now,' she said, 'shush… Thérèse and I will look after Aimée for you.' Claire nodded, but her throat was so tight with emotion, she wasn't able to speak. 'You must go now, or you will miss the plane.' Claire wiped her eyes and turned to pick up her case. 'Pierre has taken it.'

'André is outside with the pushbikes, Dudley. We really should go,' Eddie said, holding the kitchen door open.

Claire kissed Thérèse and Édith goodbye, but still she wasn't able to speak. Eddie did the same, promising to look after Claire. She followed Claire out of the warm kitchen and into the cool evening air. André was waiting in the alley with the bicycles. Claire mounted Édith's bike and Eddie Thérèse's. They cycled through the backstreets of Gisoir as fast as they were able.

'You have two minutes once the plane has landed,' André said, when they arrived. 'Are you ready?' Claire and Eddie both nodded. 'It has been a pleasure knowing you,' he said to Eddie.

'For me too. Until the next time,' she said, kissing him goodbye.

While André said goodbye to Claire, Eddie shook hands and thanked the other resisters. 'Mother and Thérèse are devoted to Aimée, so do not worry, Claire. Your daughter will be looked after and loved – and waiting for your return.'

'I know,' Claire said, putting her arms around André and hugging him tightly. Then she took a step back and looked into his eyes. 'Promise me you won't stop looking for Alain,' she said. 'He is still alive, I know he is.' At that moment a Lysander came into view. It was low in the sky to avoid radar and looked as if it was going to land. It did. The engineer knelt by the open door and hauled Claire and Eddie in. André threw Claire's suitcase in after her. 'Promise me you'll keep looking for Alain, André,' Claire shouted.

'I promise,' André shouted back. A second later the door slid into position and locked, and the Lysander began to taxi along the field. After a couple of bumps and a rattle that sounded like marbles rolling around in a bath tub, the Lysander picked up speed and lifted off.

Claire hooked her belt onto a safety strap, leaned her head against the side of the aircraft and listened to it hum. She was on her way home to England, but she had left her heart in France.

*

'Going down!' the pilot shouted, and Claire and Eddie held onto the straps. The Lysander landed at RAF Hawkinge and taxied along the runway to the fuel point. As Claire and Eddie jumped out of the aircraft a couple of engineers ran to it with fuel hoses. The pilot slid back the cockpit and clambered out. 'When she's been refuelled, I'm taking her up to Coltishall.' He patted the plane's fuselage. 'If you want a ride, be back here at four.'

'Thanks, but we'll hitch a lift to the railway station as soon as it's light,' Eddie said.

Claire and Eddie followed the pilot across the tarmac and into a single-storey prefabricated building. 'I'm going to get my head down for an hour,' he said. 'Someone will be here to meet you soon.' A second later he had turned the corner and disappeared.

'We could get our heads down in one of these offices,' Eddie said, opening the first door along the corridor and poking her head in. 'This room will do, Dudley.' Claire yawned and followed her. 'Argh!' A rattle of bones caused Eddie to step back onto Claire's foot.

'Ouch!'

'Sorry, Dudley.' Eddie felt along the wall for the light switch, found it and flicked it on. 'A bloody skeleton!' she screamed. Claire laughed. 'It isn't funny, Dudley. The damn thing gave me a real fright.'

'It must be a medical training room.' Claire lifted a dummy, the kind clothes shops have in their windows, from a makeshift bed. As she sat down, the thin metal legs of the bed buckled and she almost fell off. 'Damn thing dips in the middle like a flaming hammock,' she said. 'Come on, Ed. There's another bed over there. Let's get some sleep.' Slowly she lifted her feet up and leaned back until she was lying down. Once her body weight was spread equally she buttoned her coat.

Eddie switched off the light and felt her way along the wall to the other bed. Claire heard her curse under her breath, and then she said, 'Night, Dudley. Sleep well, old thing.'

After what seemed like only a few minutes Claire snapped awake and fell off the bed. 'Thank goodness this damn contraption is only a few inches off the floor,' she mumbled. 'Eddie?' she hissed. 'Eddie?' She heard Eddie groan. 'There's activity in the corridor. I think it's time to make a move.'

'Right-ho!' Eddie pushed herself up and yawned. 'I'm ravenous,' she said, stumbling to her feet.

The smell of fried bacon met them as soon as they opened the door. 'Follow that delicious aroma,' Eddie said, already halfway down the corridor to the canteen. Breakfast was in full swing. Eddie joined the queue waiting to be served while Claire found a table. She put her case on one chair and her coat and scarf on another. When she joined Eddie, she was being served.

'Scrambled eggs and bacon, and a cup of tea, please,' Claire said.

The kitchen assistant scooped a portion of watery egg and slopped it onto Claire's plate. Then she forked a rasher of streaky bacon from among many, dropped it on top of the egg and threatened, 'Another?' Claire shook her head, moved to the end of the counter and poured a cup of tea from a large urn. 'Help yourself to bread,' the woman called. Claire turned, smiled half-heartedly, and took two rounds of bread and butter.

'Got any English money, Eddie?' Claire asked, as they ate their food. 'I don't think the local taxis will take francs. Nor will the railway station for that matter.'

'Allow me. You must be Aircraftwomen First Class Mountjoy and Dudley?' Both women stood up and saluted. 'At ease,' the officer said. 'Eat your breakfast or it will get cold. I looked for you last night, but when I couldn't find you I returned to my quarters.'

Claire felt her cheeks redden. 'I'm afraid we were a little tired, so--'

'So you were resourceful?' he laughed. 'I was told you might be.' Still smiling, he turned towards the door and motioned to another officer. 'Officer Warner will take you to Folkestone station, when you are ready. This is sufficient for your tickets to London,' he said, handing Claire several pound notes. 'There's a little extra for a drink and something to eat. No telling how long you'll have to wait for a train.'

Claire and Eddie thanked the officer and when he stood up to leave, they stood and saluted again. Eddie swooped down on the last piece of bread and butter before following Claire outside. Officer Warner was by the car reading his newspaper. He stood to attention when he saw them. By the time they had walked over, he had opened both back and front passenger doors. Claire slipped into the front seat and Eddie into the back with the case. After closing the doors, Officer Warner jumped into the driver's seat.

'Just heard that Folkestone railway station is closed again, but it doesn't take long to get to Dover,' the driver said, holding his pass against his windscreen at the main gate. The MP waved the car through and it cruised effortlessly onto the main road.

Arriving at Priory railway station, Dover, Claire and Eddie ran onto the platform as a train disappeared amidst a cloud of steam. At the ticket office Claire asked if that was the nine-twenty to London. It was. 'What time is the next train?'

'Eleven o'clock, Miss.'

'Two tickets then, please, one way.'

Eddie blew out her cheeks in frustration. 'Tea?'

'Tea!' Claire agreed.

Eddie bought the teas and took them over to Claire, who was seated and staring out of the window. 'Penny for them?'

As she turned to face Eddie, Claire fought back her tears. 'They're worth much more than that,' she whispered.

'I'm sorry, Dudley,' Eddie said, putting the teas on the table and sitting next to Claire. 'Damn silly thing to say. I can't begin to imagine how you're feeling.' Eddie put her hand on Claire's. 'She'll be fine, you know? Édith will make sure of that. She'll want for nothing.'

'Unless the Gestapo find out about the Resistance cell, which André and Frédéric --' Claire burst into tears. She took a handkerchief from her bag. 'You knew Frédéric was dead when you came to Paris, didn't you?' Eddie looked down and nodded. 'Did Édith tell you?'

'No. I only saw Édith for a couple of hours when I arrived and an hour in the morning. Thérèse cooked breakfast for André and me, while Édith fed Aimée. Then she took Aimée upstairs to wash and dress her. She was still up there when I left. It was André who told me his brother was dead, while we waited for the train at Gisoir station. He didn't say how he'd died, just that he had. When he gave me the drawing, he made me promise not to tell you, just to say Frédéric had sent it. I thought about telling you while we were at Antoinette's, but decided you had enough on your mind.'

Claire smiled through her tears. 'Thank you.'

When the eleven o'clock train to Charing Cross pulled into Dover's Priory station it was packed to the gunnels with servicemen. Claire and Eddie stood in the corridor, moving only occasionally to let someone pass. It was a short journey, thank goodness, which went quickly.

At Charing Cross station they were met by Vera Halliday. 'Welcome Edwina, Claire. My goodness, you have lost weight, Claire,' she said, taking Claire's case. 'I've got a cab waiting. I expect you're looking forward to getting home.'

'I'm looking forward to a long hot bath in a proper bathroom,' Claire said.

'And a lie-in in the morning,' Eddie added.

'Colonel Smith doesn't want to see either of you until tomorrow afternoon,' Vera Halliday said, 'so you have time to do all that.

'Is there any news of Captain Mitchell?' Claire asked.

'Not that I've heard.' Claire sighed. 'That

doesn't mean there hasn't been any news. It means I haven't been told of any. Colonel Smith will inform you of any developments tomorrow.' The cab came to a halt at the front of the small apartment block on Portman Square. 'There is food in your larders. Bread, milk, eggs, that sort of thing. I'll telephone you tomorrow morning with the times of your appointments.'

Eddie jumped out of the cab first and took the case from the front seat. 'You look worn out, Claire,' Vera Halliday said. 'Are you all right?'

'Yes, Miss Halliday. I'm a bit run down, but it's nothing a few early nights won't put right.'

'And a few good meals,' Vera said, concerned. 'Goodnight.'

'Night,' Claire waved, and ran up the steps to where Eddie was holding the entrance door to the apartments open.

CHAPTER TWENTY-FIVE

As she neared the top of the Strand, Claire wondered if the Prince Albert Theatre, where her sister Margaret was a dancer, had been repaired. The last time she passed by the windows were boarded up. In a letter at the time, Bess said Margaret had been delayed on the Strand, signing her autograph for a fan, and hadn't arrived at the stage door until after the bomb had exploded. Apparently, Margaret had turned into Maiden Lane as the upper floor of a building opposite collapsed, killing two of her friends. Margaret had suffered a nervous breakdown and spent time in hospital. Claire wished she had been able to visit her, or go up to Foxden when she was recuperating there, but it hadn't been possible. It wasn't now. She was pleased to see the glass had been replaced and there were large framed posters advertising future shows. Claire stopped in her tracks. 'Oh my…' she gasped. Bursting with pride she saw Margaret, or Margot as she was known in the theatre, in a beautiful gold evening dress, smiling out of a huge poster. Claire put her hand to her mouth to stop herself from shouting, 'That's my big sister!' Next to Margot's photograph was one of the company, with Margot in the centre at the front, and next to that a poster advertising the forthcoming show: Margot Dudley and the Prince Albert Theatre Company, opening soon in a revue of popular songs and sketches.

Claire opened the theatre's main door and took a peek inside. On the wall opposite was another photograph of Margot in a gilt frame. To hell with it, Claire thought. She opened the door and stepped into the foyer. Once inside, her eyes met a vista of maroon and gold. The wallpaper was Regency stripes. She walked over to a maroon-coloured seat that ran the length of the wall on the far side of the foyer and sat down. The curtains at the windows and doors were velvet, the same colour as the seat she was sitting on. She wanted so much to see her sister, but she didn't trust herself not to tell her about Mitch and Aimée.

With a heavy heart, Claire pushed herself off the plush velvet seat. She wandered casually around the semi-circular foyer looking at the photographs on the walls. When she got to the door she looked over at the box office. The round wall clock hanging above the glass window, with its porcelain face and Latin numerals, told her it was time to go. Claire turned, smiled up at the framed photograph of Margot hanging above the seat where she had been sitting, and left.

Once outside she turned into a narrow passageway at the side of the theatre. With her head down, she moved quickly. She didn't want to bump into Margot; she would be sure to want to know what she'd been doing for the last four years. She turned into Maiden Lane, then Southampton Street, and strode through Covent Garden. At the top of Macklin Street she went into a café, ordered a cup of tea and found a seat near the window. One day perhaps, when the war was over, she might be able to tell her family about her work in France, the brave men and women of the Resistance, and about her second family. Though according to the Official Secrets Act, that day might never come.

Claire arrived at the SOE and was shown into the colonel's office. After her last debrief she had bumped into Mitch on the way back to the station and they had gone to a café for coffee. She wished that would be the case today, but… She swallowed hard. She was anxious to know if the colonel had heard anything, negative or positive, about the man she loved. She would ask him as soon as her debrief was over.

'Miss Dudley!' The colonel stood up as Claire entered and gestured to the usual chair in front of his desk. 'It's been a while.'

'Yes, sir.'

The colonel began by congratulating her on the detailed intelligence she'd sent via wireless operators in Gisoir and Paris, until six months ago. He mentioned finding another safe house in Paris, the successful deliveries she had made to various Resistance groups, and the sabotage work she had done with the Gisoir Resistance cell.

The colonel looked down at a folder on his desk that was date-stamped in red, 1941. 'The last time you graced us with your presence it was forty-one.' Here comes the ticking off, Claire thought. 'The intelligence you gave us confirmed what we had been told by our operatives on the Eastern Front – and the winter did the rest. It was a close call.' Colonel Smith shook his head. 'So what's happening in France?'

'The sabotaging of German troop trains has been a success. The Germans are still transporting Jewish citizens to concentration camps. Some of the transport trains were sabotaged, but few people tried to escape. I'm afraid those who did were shot.'

Claire looked down and took a second to compose herself. 'The Germans cracked down on anyone who didn't visibly toe the party line, but it was more than that. Some Resistance groups were compromised earlier in the year; some disbanded temporarily and their members joined other groups. Some, mostly Maquis groups, went into hiding in the hills. At the same time several wireless operators were arrested; one in Bloir and two in Orleans. The Maquis in Paris Central, who I met when I first went to Paris, got a message through saying they had seen white surveillance vans trawling the avenues between five-thirty and seven at night – when people have arrived home from work. After that our wireless operator, Jacques, went quiet for a week. When he began transmitting again he varied the time, as you know.'

Colonel Smith nodded. 'Did you see any surveillance vans in Gisoir, or the surrounding area?'

'No. I'm sure if there had been, someone from the Resistance would have seen them. They're big and they have huge circular wireless detection aerials on the roof.'

'Not discreet then?'

'No. Such vehicles are rare and would be spotted easily in a small town like Gisoir.' Claire watched as the colonel closed several folders and stacked the remainder. She wondered why he hadn't mentioned Mitch. He'd had her report, but even so… She began to panic. *Any minute now he's going to stand up and shake my hand. And if that happens I shall have to leave without asking him if he has any news.* She needed to speak now, or it would be too late.

But before she had time, the colonel leaned forward, a puzzled look on his face.

'Why are you wearing a wedding ring?'

Thrown by the question, Claire lifted her hand dumbly and looked at Édith Belland's thin wedding band on her finger. 'It isn't mine,' she said. 'Madame Belland gave it to me after Captain Mitchell was taken in for questioning.'

'So you are not actually married?' he laughed.

'No, sir!' The nerves on the top of her stomach began to tighten, taking her breath away. She cleared her throat and forced herself to laugh with him. What was the colonel insinuating? Did he know about her relationship with Mitch? She hoped not, or he wouldn't let her go back to France. 'I'd forgotten I had it on.' Taking the ring off, she laid it on the desk. 'It was Édith Belland's idea. She said, after Captain Mitchell was taken by the Gestapo for questioning, that now I was on my own, and German soldiers had no respect for French women, I would attract less attention if I wore a wedding ring.'

'And if you were stopped and your papers checked?'

'I'd say it was my mother who gave me the ring because she thought as a young woman on my own I'd be safer travelling.' The colonel's brow furrowed. He didn't look convinced. 'Frédéric Belland's fiancée was raped and killed by a gang of drunken German soldiers. It was Captain Mitchell and I who found her body. It was after that that Édith gave me the ring.'

'Reason enough,' the colonel said.

'Yes, sir. And I shall wear it until Captain

Mitchell returns.' It was now or never, Claire thought. 'Have you had any news of Captain Mitchell, sir?'

The colonel took a folder from his desk, opened it, and took out a sheet of paper. He ran his eyes over the page and replaced it. 'Captain Mitchell was moved from Périgueux prison to a prison camp in Mauzac some months ago, along with--'

'Months ago? The Bellands and I have been out of our minds with worry. Why weren't we told he'd been moved at the time?'

'Because we didn't know until recently.' Claire nodded apologetically. 'Captain Mitchell and another Canadian airman, two RAF pilots, and two French resisters were moved to the camp in Mauzac at the same time. Shortly after arriving they escaped. The details are sketchy, but they made their way to the Pyrenees where they met up with an MI9 chap and a courier who took them over the mountain and across the border to Spain.'

'So Mitch – Captain Mitchell – is in Spain?' Claire wanted to jump up, run round to the other side of the desk and throw her arms around Colonel Smith, but she knew she had to control herself. So, although her heart was bursting with happiness, she said, 'Thank goodness,' as casually as she was able. 'When is he expected back?'

The colonel replaced the folder and a dark worried look crossed his face. 'I don't know.' Claire felt her pulse quicken. There was something wrong. Colonel Smith put his pipe to his mouth and held it between his teeth. Claire wanted to scream with impatience as he struck a match, put it up to the flakes of tobacco in the bowl and sucked several times, making a popping noise each time he drew in air. At last he said, 'Three men arrived in Barcelona. Captain Mitchell was not one of them.'

'What?' Claire began to tremble. 'You said six men escaped from Mauzac, so what happened to the others? Were they captured?' Colonel Smith didn't answer. 'Are they dead or alive? Sir?'

'We don't know. They were ambushed outside a small border town by German snipers. According to MI9, one RAF officer was shot in the head and, they assumed, died instantly. Two other men, both wearing civilian clothes, took body shots and went down. He didn't know if they were dead or only injured.'

Dread flooded Claire's mind and the colour drained from her face. She thought her heart would stop beating, but she had to ask the question: 'Was one of the men Captain Mitchell?'

The colonel's gaze fell on the document in front of him. 'I'm afraid so.' He looked up at Claire. 'Captain Mitchell was one of three men left behind.'

'MI9 left him?'

'They had to. They had no way of telling if he was dead or alive. By going back, the lives of the courier, the MI9 chap and the other escapees would have been at risk. You know the score, Miss Dudley.' The colonel stood up, pushed away his chair and walked round the desk. He offered Claire his hand and she took it shakily. He helped her out of her chair.

'Thank you,' she whispered. When they got to the door, Vera Halliday opened it. Shaking the colonel's hand again, Claire said, 'Would you let me know if you hear anything more about Captain

Mitchell – anything at all?'

'Of course.'

She rubbed the top of her thumb on the inside of her wedding finger, a habit she'd acquired to check the ring was still there. It had never been a tight fit, but since she'd lost weight it had become loose. It wasn't there. 'Excuse me, sir,' she said, running back to the desk. 'Édith Belland's wedding ring. I'll need it when I go back to France.' She followed Vera Halliday out of the office and along the corridor.

'You don't want to go back to France right away, do you, Claire?' Miss Halliday asked.

'I certainly do. And I shall keep going back until I find Captain Mitchell.'

As she opened the front door to the apartment block Claire saw Eddie going up the stairs. Eddie looked over her shoulder and stopped. 'How did the meeting go with you-know-who?'

'You-know-who,' was all Claire said before her legs gave way and she fell to the ground.

'What on earth?' Eddie flew down the stairs and dropped to her knees. 'What is it, Dudley?'

Claire hung onto Eddie and sobbed. 'Mitch has been shot.'

'Come on.' Eddie took Claire by her arms and slowly pulled her to her feet. Taking Claire's weight, she walked her across the foyer to her apartment. Inside, she pulled Claire's coat off and threw it across a chair. 'Sit down,' she said, leading Claire to the settee. 'Will you be all right for a second? I think it's time to open the medicinal brandy.' Claire nodded and Eddie ran upstairs to her flat.

On her return Eddie took two glasses from the sideboard and poured them both a large brandy. She put one glass into Claire's hand and the other on the small occasional table, before going over to the fire. It wasn't giving out much heat, so she added a couple of logs and a pan of coal, before joining Claire on the settee. She took a sip of her brandy. Claire took a swig and almost choked. 'Steady on, old thing. Best to sip it.' The wood crackled. The fire had taken hold and flames licked at the coal. It would soon be warm.

The two friends sipped their drinks and watched the flames flicker up the chimney. 'They left him for dead in the Pyrenees,' Claire said, suddenly. She took a shuddering breath. 'He had been shot and they left him,' she cried.

Eddie took Claire's glass and put it on the table with her own. She put her arms round her friend and Claire clung on to her, as a hurt child would, and sobbed. When she had worn herself out, Eddie slipped from the settee, put a cushion under Claire's head and lifted her feet up. She then took a blanket from Claire's bed and put it over her. Sitting on the rug by the fire, Eddie sipped her brandy and watched Claire as she slept.

Claire stirred. She was hot. She felt as if she was suffocating. She gulped air, threw off the blanket and struggled to sit up. For a moment she didn't remember the meeting with Colonel Smith, or that Mitch was…. She put her hand over her mouth to stifle a scream. She looked around. A fire blazed in the hearth and the blackout curtains were drawn. A beam of light shone into the sitting room from the kitchen. Claire put her feet to the floor and stood up. She crossed to the standard lamp and switched it on. Drowning in a sea of despair, she took her hand from her mouth and let out the pain in a howl.

'Dudley?' Eddie rushed in from the kitchen. She pulled out a chair at the dining table and guided Claire into it. Claire took the remains of her brandy and drank it down in one. 'I've made us some supper. Fried Spam, mash, and bread and butter. Is that all right?'

Claire nodded, but said, 'I'm not hungry.'

'Lift the drinks, will you?' Claire complied and Eddie threw a tablecloth across the table, before fetching the food from the kitchen. 'Damn, forgot the bread. Pour another drink, Dudley,' she said, going back to the kitchen and returning almost immediately with bread and butter. 'You may need a stiff drink before you sample my cooking.' Claire smiled thinly. 'That's better,' Eddie said. 'Now eat!'

Claire ate most of the mashed potato and felt better for it. When they had finished their meal they cleared the table together, leaving the dishes in the sink. Back in the sitting room, they refreshed their glasses and sat by the fire. Claire related the conversation she'd had with Colonel Smith and when she'd finished, Eddie said, 'With such scant information it's impossible to know what happened to Mitch.'

'He was shot, the colonel said. The men who escaped saw him go down. At best he's stuck on a mountain with snakes and mosquitoes in the day and temperatures below zero at night, and at worst, he's…' Claire couldn't bring herself to say the word.

'If they fought back, it's more than likely that they killed the German snipers. In which case,' Eddie said, 'Mitch could be found by a Maquis group, or a farmer.'

'Or not,' Claire said.

'Look, Dudley, you don't know that he's dead. He's injured, yes, but you don't know how badly. You need to be positive. Think about Aimée. Focus on her. And focus on getting fit, so the colonel sends you back to France.'

Claire thought of Aimée and smiled. 'You're right. Thank you, Eddie.'

'My advice, my friend,' Eddie said, sharing the last of the brandy between their glasses, 'is to wait for further intelligence before you write the Canuck beefcake off.' Claire laughed and wiped the back of her hands across her face. 'I'm serious, Dudley. There are a hundred things that could have happened.'

CHAPTER TWENTY-SIX

Claire rolled over and pulled her pillow down until she was hugging it. She thought about Mitch every day, sometimes every hour of every day, her daughter too. She ached to see Aimée and played every minute of the last day they had spent together over and over in her mind. The alarm clock emitted a loud invasive ring, interrupting her reflections. In a state of agitation she reached out and slammed her hand down on the bell. She closed her eyes, crossed her arms over her chest and hugged her shoulders. She had just begun to relive the last time she and Mitch made love when a frantic knocking brought her back to the present. She dragged the eiderdown over her head and buried her face in its quilted satin. 'Damn!'

With her dream of Mitch interrupted, Claire put her hands over her ears. She could still hear knocking, and moaned. Five minutes later the telephone rang. She jumped out of bed. 'Mitch,' she shouted, stumbling barefoot into the sitting room. Fearing the phone would stop ringing before she had time to answer it, she snatched up the receiver, overbalanced, and fell sideways into the armchair. 'Miss Halliday?' she said, out of breath.

'No, Dudley, it's me, Eddie. Answer your bloody door, will you?'

Claire sighed. 'Okay…'

'What the hell are you doing,' Eddie said, 'hiding yourself away like this?' She blustered into the flat carrying a large shopping bag and marched straight through to the kitchen. 'Put some clothes on while I make breakfast.' Claire groaned in protest. Eddie ignored her. 'Eggs, toast, and tea!' she said, putting lard into the frying pan and lighting the gas under it. 'It'll be ready by the time you've washed and dressed.' Claire flopped down on the settee, but Eddie wasn't having it. 'Get up, Dudley. You can't mooch about in your nightclothes all day,' she said, crossing to the settee and pulling Claire to her feet. 'Damn!' she said, sniffing. 'Something's burning.' As Eddie ran into the kitchen, Claire sauntered into the bedroom and dressed.

'Thank you, Eddie,' Claire said on her return.

'I'd reserve your thanks if I was you until you've tasted the delicately smoke-flavoured fried egg with the black specks, which is haute cuisine don't you know, and the half toasted bread,' she said, in an exaggerated French accent. She put two plates on the table, one in front of Claire. 'I'll get the tea.'

Claire laughed. It had been a while since she'd seen Eddie, longer since she had laughed. 'It looks good, really,' she said, taking a slice of toast and dipping the crust into the yolk of the egg. She could hardly remember the last time she'd cooked anything. For more than a week, while Eddie had been in Coltishall, she had lived in a dreamlike state, getting up only to go to the bathroom and make tea. She was glad Eddie was back.

When they had finished eating Eddie suggested Claire took a bath. 'Throw in a couple of rose-scented bath cubes and have a soak while I clear away the dishes. And if you want to talk?'

Feeling emotional, but determined not to cry, Claire stood up and left the table. 'Thanks, Ed. If you don't mind sticking around, I would like to talk.'

'Good. Now shoo!' Eddie said. 'Go and have your bath while I get this place ship-shape.'

By the time Eddie had put what remained of the food she'd bought away, washed the dishes and built a fire, Claire had bathed and washed her hair.

Sitting on the floor in front of the fire, Claire told Eddie again how she and Mitch had fallen in love in Gisoir, and how against SOE regulations she had stayed with him in his apartment in London. She told her how the Gestapo had stopped him and taken him to headquarters at the insistence of an SS officer, and about Aimée's premature birth. 'The worst of it,' she said, fighting back the tears, 'is Aimée will never know her daddy. I know she won't be the only one. So many children will grow up without fathers, some without mothers, but it doesn't make it any easier to bear.'

'Dudley, you don't know-- Mitch is a resourceful guy. Chances are he'll have escaped.'

Claire jumped up and went to the sideboard. She took a map from the drawer, opened it and spread it over the table, smoothing the creases where it had been folded with the flat of her hand. 'The Pyrenees!'

Eddie shot Claire a look of surprise. 'Where did you get this?'

'Vera Halliday. She brought it over while you were in Coltishall. I telephoned her so many times I think I beat her into submission, or she took pity on me.' Claire circled an area at the bottom of the mountains with a pencil. 'Miss Halliday said that according to MI9 this is where Mitch was ambushed.' Leaning forward, Eddie scrutinised the map. 'In that kind of terrain, with only one way back,' Claire ran her finger along the only visible route, 'how could a man who had been shot by a sniper – and was probably surrounded by snipers – escape?' Eddie didn't answer. 'He couldn't.'

'But you don't know that for certain.'

'And I won't know for certain until I get back to France.'

'You're in no fit state to go mountain climbing, Dudley.'

'I wouldn't dream of it. If the border guards caught me, I'd be jeopardising MI9's escape route. You can imagine what they'd do to me if I did that.'

'Put you in chains and throw away the key?'

'And if the Gestapo caught me? Well, we both know I'm not strong enough to withstand interrogation at the moment.' Claire shuddered. 'Besides, I have Aimée to consider now.' Claire folded the map. 'I'm not going to do anything to put myself at risk. Aimée may have lost her father; she is not going to lose her mother too.' Claire returned the map to the sideboard drawer, came back to the table and sat down. 'I've made a decision. I have been wallowing in self-pity, thinking only of myself, my loss, my pain. But I have a daughter in France who needs me – and a job that I have been trained to do, which I do well and which I hope to go back to. So I need to accept Mitch has gone, get myself fit again – mentally as well as physically – and go back to France to my daughter and my job.'

CHAPTER TWENTY-SEVEN

Claire arrived home soaked. 'The bloody British summer!' she mumbled, unlocking the door to the apartments. Dropping her shopping bag and gas mask on the floor of the entrance foyer, she wedged the door open with her foot and stuck her head out. Sheltering beneath the art deco portico, she collapsed the umbrella and shook off the excess rain. It had thrown it down for days, which had made trawling the empty shops for food even more miserable. As she stepped inside, letting the door swing shut behind her, she heard the discordant whine of the air raid siren. She turned and looked up at the sky. It was still light. The Luftwaffe had long since stopped waiting until it was dark to drop their bombs. The maxim now, it seemed, was anytime, anywhere. Grabbing her belongings, she ran across the foyer as the ack-ack of the anti-aircraft guns in Hyde Park began firing. Opening her apartment door, she put her shopping bag down and shrugged off her coat.

'Coming, Dudley?' Eddie shouted, as she and several tenants from flats on the upper floors ran past. Claire had no intention of going down to the shelter, but as she turned to close her door she saw Eddie leaning on the wall at the top of the basement stairs, swinging her gas mask nonchalantly.

'On my way,' Claire sighed. With her coat over her arm, she grabbed her own mask.

'You won't need your coat, darling, it's like a sauna down there with all the hot water pipes.'

'It's wet. It will dry quicker in the basement than

it will in my hall.'

Most people had taken a cup, a chair, and something to occupy themselves with – a book, board game or playing cards. Some had even left mattresses down there. The apartments' oldest tenant, Mr Smallman, who held everyone's spare keys, had appointed himself air raid warden. In charge of the tea and dried milk, he was already boiling the kettle.

Claire and Eddie sat down on a wooden bench with their backs to a panel of warm pipes. They were the only tenants who had not taken anything comfortable to sit on. Neither had been in residence for long enough at any one time to warrant it. There was a sudden muted rumble, followed by a deep boom, and instinctively they looked up. 'The bombs are close tonight,' someone said, to which Mr Smallman replied, 'We're safe enough down here.'

'So how did it go with the colonel?' Eddie whispered. Claire grimaced. 'That bad, eh?'

She shrugged. When the old man shouted, 'Tea up!' Claire went over to where he was handing out hot drinks. She waited in the short queue until he had filled every cup, thanked him, and took hers and Eddie's back to the bench.

'I can tell by your face it didn't go the way you'd hoped,' Eddie said.

'It didn't, but I can't tell you about it here. Come to mine when the raid's over.' Eddie nodded. When they had finished their drinks, Claire took their empty cups back to Mr Smallman who, after the first air raid, had taken on the job of washing the cups and keeping the basement tidy.

It was still early when the all-clear siren sounded

and the old man boomed, 'Air raid over!' Above the clatter of scraping chairs and people gathering their belongings, Eddie and Claire made their escape.

Claire unlocked the door of her flat and after hanging up her coat, which was now dry, she went into the sitting room and dropped into the chair. Eddie followed and perched on the chair's arm. 'I'm sorry, Dudley. Is there anything I can do?'

Claire shook her head. 'I'm afraid not, but thanks anyway, you're a pal. Have you eaten?'

'No, you?'

'No.' Claire pushed herself out of the chair and went to the kitchen. 'I'll make a sandwich. Tinned ham do?'

'You certainly know how to spoil a girl, Dudley.'

Claire laughed. 'I'll take that as a yes.' Pulling a silly face, Eddie pressed her lips together in a wide grin. 'I'll scrape the jelly stuff off and cover it with mustard and pickle – you'll hardly taste the ham.'

While they ate, Claire told Eddie about the meeting she'd had with Colonel Smith that day. 'The colonel has no objection to me going back to France. He said he needed me. Apparently, any day now, there's going to be a massive push to drive the Germans out of France. Its codename is Operation Overlord, and the colonel said it's going to be the biggest amphibious invasion since the war began. The Boche have been fed false intelligence,' Claire said, excitedly. 'They think the invasion is going to take place in Calais, but it's actually going to happen all along the Normandy coastline. If everything goes to plan, which the colonel is confident it will, Hitler and his Nazis will be pushed out of Western Europe all the way back to Berlin.'

'So what's the problem?'

'He made me see a psychiatrist who doesn't deem me mentally or physically fit enough to go back into the field. Though what my physical fitness has to do with him I should like to know. In his opinion – and I quote – "I would not be happy if Miss Dudley returned to the stresses and dangers of occupied France just yet."' Claire poured the tea. 'In my bloody opinion the only thing that would make the trick-cyclist happy is if women were confined to the house. Better still, if they were tied to the kitchen sink.'

'So what are you going to do?'

'I have no choice. Go up to Coltishall, stuff myself with canteen stodge, eat as much chocolate as I can get my hands on, do lots of square bashing and get plenty of sleep. I'll show the mealy-mouthed, beaky nosed, pathetic little weasel--'

'Cripes, Dudley, don't hold back on your opinion of the chap.' Claire began to add to the description of the psychiatrist, but Eddie put her hands up. 'Enough already!' she laughed. 'So, if you're going up to Coltishall, you'll need your uniform. Put it on, let's have you on parade. Chop-chop! And worry not. If it needs a nip and a tuck, I'm your gal.'

Claire's mouth fell open. 'You can't sew a button on, Mountjoy.'

'Who said anything about buttons?'

'I'll get the uniform,' Claire said, leaving the room laughing.

When she returned wearing her WAAF uniform, Eddie gulped. 'Good God, Dudley. Forget a nip and a tuck, that jacket needs major surgery before you go anywhere in it. It isn't damn fair. I put weight on just looking at a bar of Cadbury's. You eat it as if it isn't rationed and you're skinnier now than you were when you came back from France.' Eddie lifted the shoulders of Claire's jacket into place. 'Good Lord, Dudley, when did you last try this on?'

'When Noah was a lad.'

'That recently?'

Claire took the jacket off. 'I'll take it in to Vera Halliday tomorrow. She'll have it altered for me.' She pulled on the waistband of the skirt. 'It needs taking in, or the belt. I don't suppose you've borrowed it?'

Batting her eyes in surprised innocence, Eddie pretended she didn't know what Claire was talking about, but she couldn't keep it up. As a rosy blush began to bloom on her cheeks, Eddie started to giggle. 'I might have borrowed it. I do have one or two of your belts upstairs in my drawer,' she said, leaping up and running out of the room. 'Back in a jiff.'

'I'm going to give my sister Bess a quick call,' Claire shouted after her, 'so leave the door open.'

Claire picked up the telephone. She longed to see her mum and dad, sisters Ena and Bess, but she couldn't until she'd been to Coltishall. On her way back to London she would stop off as she had done before. In the meantime she would write. The operator came on the line. 'Number please, caller.'

'Lowarth 154, please.'

'Trying to connect you, caller,' the operator said after a few seconds.

Claire hoped it would be all right to telephone

Bess at Foxden Hall. Her parents didn't have a telephone. No one in the village did except Mr Clark, the local taxi driver, Mrs Moore at Woodcote's shop and post office, and of course the vicar. The vicarage was at Mysterton, which was close to Foxden, but when the vicar delivered a message it was usually one you didn't want to receive.

'You're connected, caller,' the operator said, and immediately Claire heard Bess's voice.

'Lowarth 154.'

'Hello Bess, it's Claire.'

'Claire? Oh my-- How lovely to hear from you. How are you? It's been so long.'

'Didn't you get my letters? My friend said she'd posted them.'

'Yes, I meant since we had spoken. It's wonderful to hear your voice – and to know you're alive,' Bess whispered. 'Are you going to get up to see us?'

'I'm going to RAF Coltishall. I'll try to call in on the way back.'

'Mam and Dad would love to see you, Ena too. She has been very quiet lately, almost withdrawn. I think she's really missing you.'

'I'm missing her, mum and dad too. I'd love to see them, but I can't promise anything. I don't know when I'll have to go back... to the south coast,' she added, in case anyone was listening in to the call. 'Do you think you could get Mam to go to the post office tomorrow for eleven, and I'll telephone her?'

'I'm sure I can. I'll have to tell her you're going to phone though, or she won't go. You know what she's like. Give me your telephone number in case we get cut off. The lines are terrible at the moment.'

'I can't do that, Bess.' There was a knock on the door. 'My friend Eddie's at the door. I'll speak to you tomorrow morning. Give Mam and Dad my love – and Ena.'

'I will – and Claire? I've missed you.'

'I've missed you too, Bess. Night!'

'Goodnight!' she heard her older sister say, and she placed the telephone on its cradle.

Grumbling, Claire ran to the door. She had told Eddie to leave it open. 'Miss Halliday!' A searing wave of panic shot through her body and her legs began to shake. Had Colonel Smith's secretary brought bad news?

'Captain Mitchell is alive,' Vera Halliday said immediately.

Claire gasped. Frozen to the spot, hardly daring to believe that the man she loved was alive, she whispered, 'Alive?' Miss Halliday was smiling. 'Mitch is alive,' she heard a small voice that sounded like her own say.

'Yes. Colonel Smith received word as I was leaving the office. He asked me to telephone you tomorrow, but I thought you'd like to know tonight.'

Claire couldn't take it in. For months, years, she had believed that the man she loved was alive. Then, for the sake of her sanity, when she was told he had been shot and left for dead in the mountains, she made herself face the fact that he could be dead, and had given up hope of ever seeing him again. Claire stared at Vera Halliday. Suddenly aware that her visitor was standing in the hall, she gathered her wits. 'Come in,' she said, showing Miss Halliday into the sitting room. As she turned to close the door she saw Eddie leaning over the banister outside her flat. 'Mitch is alive,' she said in a daze. Eddie whooped. 'Miss Halliday is here. Come down.'

Eddie shook her head. 'I don't think I should,' she whispered. 'You can tell me what she says later.' As she turned to go inside, Eddie hissed, 'Dudley? Daddy gave me a bottle of hooch last week. I'll bring it down when Miss H has gone and we'll celebrate.'

Claire put her thumbs up and returned to the apartment. She asked Miss Halliday to take a seat and offered her tea. Vera Halliday sat down, but politely refused the tea. 'Are you sure it is Mitch who is alive, Miss Halliday?' Claire asked, sitting next to her.

'I'm sure, my dear. I don't know the details, but the leader of a Maquis group that you helped in Paris got a message to the wireless operator in Gisoir via Antoinette Marron at the Paris safe house. Loosely translated, Captain Mitchell knew he wouldn't be able to make it across the Pyrenees and pretended to be dead so his fellow escapees would go on without him. And as you know they did. When night fell, the captain rolled into a ditch and covered himself with vegetation.'

Claire took a shivering breath. 'But the temperature at night… It's so cold.'

'Thankfully not as cold at that time of year – and not at the foot of the mountains.' Claire looked at Vera Halliday, her eyes pleading for more news. 'He was found by a retired doctor who, with the help of a couple of members of the Maquis, carried him to his house.'

'Carried him? How badly was he hurt?' Claire

forced herself to ask.

'We don't know. He was shot in the leg once, maybe twice, we can't be sure.' Claire put her hand up to her mouth and gasped. 'He couldn't climb the mountain, but that doesn't mean he was badly injured, just that he was brave and sensible and didn't want to put the lives of his comrades in danger.' Miss Halliday smiled and looked into Claire's eyes. 'I don't know many able-bodied men who could cross the Pyrenees. I must go,' she said, standing up. Claire stood up too, and in shock showed her guest to the door. 'Captain Mitchell is alive, Claire. Hang on to that,' Vera Halliday said.

Claire guided her across the dark entrance foyer to the main door. 'As soon as we have any news as to where Captain Mitchell is, I'll be in touch. In the meantime, get some sleep. You look exhausted.' Vera Halliday opened her handbag and, after fishing around for a couple of seconds, produced a handful of food tokens. 'Go to the shops. Buy some food. You won't be any good to Captain Mitchell if you're not well – which,' Miss Halliday said, 'by the look of you, you are not.'

Claire opened the street door. Vera Halliday hesitated. Claire sensed the colonel's secretary wanted to say something and looked questioningly at her. 'I shouldn't be telling you this, but I know you want to get back to France.' Claire nodded. 'There is an important drop coming up, but Colonel Smith is reluctant to send you. If you want to go back to France, you must get yourself fit.'

'Thank you,' Claire said, grateful for the information. 'And thank you for calling to tell me Captain Mitchell is alive.' Vera Halliday put her arms round Claire and hugged her. When she left, Claire watched her walk down the street and fade into the night. Then she turned and went back to her apartment. At the door the emotion she had suppressed throughout Miss Halliday's visit gushed from her like an open faucet. She cried with fear and laughed with happiness. When she calmed down, she wiped the back of her hand across her face, shook out her shoulders, and opened the door.

'Brandy?'

Claire jumped. Looking up, she saw Eddie making her way down the stairs. With a torch in one hand, pointing its slim yellow beam on the edge of each stair, and a bottle in the other, she arrived at Claire's door.

In the sitting room Claire went to the sideboard cupboard and took out two glasses. Emotionally drained, she put them on the table, dropped onto the settee and put her head in her hands.

'My God, Dudley, I thought Miss Halliday had brought good news. Here!' She handed Claire a glass of brandy. 'Get this down you. It'll make you feel better.'

With tears running down her face, Claire told her, 'She did bring good news, Ed. Mitch is alive. He was shot in the leg somewhere in the Pyrenees and survived.' Claire whooped, took a drink, and choked when the strong spirit hit the back of her throat.

Eddie knocked her brandy back, replenished both glasses and made a toast. 'To the beefcake Canuck.' They both drank.

'To *my* beefcake Canuck,' Claire said, and they emptied their glasses. She told Eddie what Miss

Halliday had told her.

'That's great news, Dudley,' Eddie said, putting her arms round Claire. Exhausted from emotion and alcohol, the two friends fell backwards onto the settee. 'And you gave her your uniform?'

Claire groaned. 'I forgot.'

'Oh Dudley!' The two friends looked at each other, lifted their empty glasses, and roared with laughter.

Knowing Colonel Smith wouldn't send her back to France until she was fully fit, Claire went up to RAF Coltishall. She was there on June 6, D-Day, until the end of the summer, when she was summoned back to London without leave, which meant she wasn't able to visit her parents and sisters at Foxden as she had promised.

The train was late getting into Euston. Claire looked at her wristwatch. It was twenty-past two. She was expected at three at the new SOE offices, St. Michael's House in Oxford Street. She didn't have time to go to the apartment to drop off her suitcase, so she arrived early and sat with Miss Halliday until the time of her appointment.

'We haven't received any news of Captain Mitchell,' Vera Halliday said. 'Because of the German wireless detecting equipment, the telegraphy operators are only sending urgent messages. They arrive at all hours of the day and night, so the Germans can't track them. Some operators have abandoned their equipment and moved away. Sadly some have been caught.' She spread her fingers on the top of the desk, a sorrowful expression on her face.

'I understand,' Claire said. 'He's alive, that's all that matters.' That she intended to find him as soon as she was able, she didn't share with Vera Halliday. After a couple of minutes Claire went up to the office of the psychiatrist for what she hoped would be her last assessment. The session went well, she thought. She didn't like the man, which he picked up on, turning her lack of "connection" with him into concern about her general happiness. Claire assured him that she was, and had always been, a happy and optimistic person, but there was a war on in which she should be doing her job. The only worry she had was whether he was going to sign her off as fit enough to do that job. The psychiatrist said he was reluctant, because in his opinion she had anger issues. Claire wanted to slap him and tell him he was talking rubbish. Instead she thanked him and asked him to consider recommending her return to France. With clenched fists, she left his office to keep her appointment with Colonel Smith.

The colonel was on the telephone when she entered, so Claire stood just inside the door and waited. Finally he put the telephone down and motioned to her to come over. 'That was the doctor,' he said. 'You are officially signed fit for duty and will be going back to France during the next full moon cycle – or the one after, depending on the weather.'

'We're in the middle of a full moon cycle now, sir,' Claire said. 'I thought you had brought me back to London to fly out this month. The sooner I start training the new Maquis groups in Paris--'

'Miss Mountjoy has replaced you on that.'

Claire felt panic beating in her chest. The Allies

hadn't liberated Paris yet. There was fighting in the streets. Hitler had given a general called von Choltitz power of life and death over anyone who lived in the city. That, coupled with the Resistance cells becoming more active and therefore their work becoming more dangerous, meant Paris was a hazardous place to be. 'It's a dangerous assignment, sir. It's one that needs an experienced agent and Miss Mountjoy isn't experienced.'

'You didn't have experience once, Miss Dudley.'

'No, sir.' Claire gritted her teeth. 'Excuse me for asking, but wasn't Miss Mountjoy assigned to go back to France next month?'

'She was, but Paris became urgent, and as you weren't here--'

'I was a train journey away, sir.'

'Well it's done now! Miss Mountjoy was happy to go to Paris. She said you had a closer relationship with the Resistance group at Gisoir--'

'Gisoir?'

'Yes, Gisoir. But it's academic in any event. Miss Mountjoy flew out last night.'

Claire was still angry when she got home. She wasn't angry with Eddie for taking her drop. She understood why she'd done it and, however foolish, she would have done the same if the situation had been reversed. She was angry with the colonel for letting Eddie persuade him to send her to Paris.

Arriving home, she picked up two unstamped pieces of post that had been pushed under the door. One was a badly printed leaflet reminding residents that they must use the shelter in the basement when there was an air raid and the other, when Claire pulled it out of the envelope, was a letter from Eddie. She took off her coat, went into the sitting room and read Eddie's letter.

Dearest D,

By now you'll know I am in F. Don't be angry with me for taking your place. I didn't actually ask for P, although if my plan hadn't worked I would have. No, I suggested to Miss H that if the handsome C was able to travel, it would be to G that he went – and she did the rest. She's a love, isn't she? I shall try to get up to G to see A and the B clan. Be a hoot if I can get there when you're there. I shall do my best, but if I don't see you in G, I'll see you back here when the game is won.

Until then, chin up, my friend. You'll soon be with A.

Look after yourself.

Love, E. x

P.S. Almost forgot. I sweet-talked Mr S to let me into your place. There's a bottle of brandy in the cupboard. Cheers!

Claire missed Aimée so much she thought her heart would break. She missed Eddie too, as much as she would have done any of her sisters. In October she counted the days around the full moon and listened to the BBC's nightly news broadcasts, which were becoming more and more disheartening.

'Although there have been many airborne successes,' the news reader said, 'the Allied advance to the German frontier is not sustainable and the Germans are regrouping. With winter approaching,' he concluded, 'it appears the Allied campaign is slowing down.'

Claire switched off the wireless, put out the light and went to bed.

CHAPTER TWENTY-EIGHT

The thrust as she was swept up took Claire by surprise, and she felt breathless until she dropped. Looking up, she watched the dome of the parachute open and bloom into the familiar mushroom. She felt it tilt and pulled on a riser until it levelled. As she floated down the old feeling of excitement and exhilaration flooded back. She landed well and began to run, but she stopped too soon and, with the wind at her back, folds of silk billowed up around her. She unbuckled the harness and batted the ballooning silk, finally controlling it. The excitement of the jump and the prospect of seeing her daughter had overwhelmed her – and she hadn't watched what she was doing.

She had almost finished folding the parachute when André and the men and women of the reception committee arrived. Each of them shook her hand, kissed her, and welcomed her warmly. Claire returned their greetings. 'Édith!' she exclaimed, delighted yet surprised to see her old friend. 'What are you doing here?' She threw her arms around her. 'Are you part of the reception committee now?'

'Only for tonight,' Édith laughed. 'And do not worry about the little one. Thérèse is at home in case she wakes.'

'I didn't think for a second that you would leave her on her own.' Claire took Édith's hand and together they trudged across the field to the Belland Farm. It was still uninhabited, but it was no longer being used as a whore house by drunken German soldiers. They were better employed trying to stop the Allies and the Resistance groups from kicking them out of France.

The bicycles were hidden in the small wood, as they had been on the night Édith and Claire cycled to the farm to move Monique's body from the well. So much had happened since that night. Édith tapped Claire on the arm. 'Sorry, I was thinking…'

'I thought of her too, and Frédéric, when I arrived.' In a voice cracking with pain and emotion, Édith said, 'Are you ready?'

Pushing her bicycle out of the wood, Claire followed Édith up the muddy bank to the road. As she mounted she wobbled and put her feet to the ground. She pushed off again and this time retained her balance. Side by side, Claire and Édith began the short journey to Gisoir.

Édith knocked on the kitchen door and waited to give Thérèse time to switch off the light. A minute later her daughter-in-law opened the door. Claire followed Édith into the familiar warm kitchen. 'My dearest Claire,' Thérèse cried, clicking the light on.

Seeing Thérèse wearing a maternity smock, Claire ran to her and held her at arm's length. 'Congratulations, my friend,' she said, looking down at her extended stomach. 'When is the baby due?'

'Not for months, but André and Mother have been feeding me up,' she laughed. 'Come and sit down, you must be tired. Would you like coffee?' Claire looked at the door leading to the hall and stairs.

'I think Claire would like to see Aimée,' Édith

whispered to her daughter-in-law. 'You go up, my dear, while Thérèse and I prepare some food. There's plenty of time for coffee.'

Claire looked from Édith to Thérèse. 'Would it be better if one of you came with me? If Aimée wakes she might be frightened if she sees me in her bedroom.'

Édith laughed. 'I do not think so. She talks to your picture every day.'

'My picture? But how…?'

'Your friend Edwina left a photograph of you next to Aimée's bed. It is of you both in uniform, but she folded it down the middle so only your face is seen. I found it just after you left, when I put Aimée down for her afternoon nap. You are the first person she sees in the morning and the last at night.'

'She sometimes puts your photograph in her bed with Dolly and Teddy,' Thérèse laughed. 'She has only been in bed a couple of hours. I do not think she will wake. She has worn herself out running to the door every five minutes, ready to open it when you arrived.'

Claire bit her lip and frowned. 'I have disappointed her already…'

'What nonsense,' Thérèse said, crossing to Claire and taking her by the hand. 'She is not disappointed. We told her when she wakes in the morning she will see her mummy.'

'It is just your daughter's impatient nature that has had her running around today. Go now, go up to her.'

Claire took the stairs slowly and at the top took a deep breath before opening the bedroom door. In a single cot at the side of Édith's bed she saw a mop of golden curls above a pink and white knitted blanket. She tiptoed into the room, knelt beside her daughter and watched her sleep. Aimée lay on her right side, one hand under the covers, the other on the pillow by her face. Claire bit back her tears. Her daughter had changed. She was bigger, longer – and the back of her hands had lost their dimples. Suddenly Aimée's eyelids flickered and her breathing changed from a calm rhythm to what sounded like a complaining sigh. Leaning away from the bed, Claire sat back on her heels, worried that if Aimée woke she would be frightened seeing someone leaning over her. A second later the child opened her small mouth and smacked her lips as she did when she was a baby and was hungry. Then her thumb found its way to her mouth and she became calm again. Steeling herself from touching her daughter in case she woke her, Claire whispered, 'Sleep well, my beautiful girl,' and quietly left the room.

Back in the kitchen Édith spooned thick aromatic soup into Claire's bowl. The nerves in her stomach were jumping, sending messages to her brain to say she wasn't hungry, but Claire knew she needed to keep her strength up for the long nights to come. The packages that were dropped with her contained materials to make explosives. She was capable of putting them together, but hadn't had experience. Since Frédéric's death it had become Pierre Ruban's brother Marcel's job – André's if Marcel wasn't there – and she was part of the lookout team.

Claire ate enthusiastically and when she had finished she took the loaf, broke off a sizeable chunk and mopped up the dish. 'Isn't André coming for supper?'

'No, he and two of the men are hiding the drop. They can't transport it in daylight and with the train due in just a few days, they must prepare early.'

'It is a dangerous mission,' Thérèse said, caressing her stomach.

Claire was only too aware of the danger and hoped it wasn't André who was going into the tunnel to place the explosives. He and Thérèse had been trying for a baby since before Aimée was born. Claire smiled at Thérèse. 'Try not to worry about André. He is experienced and professional. He will not take unnecessary risks.'

Édith took hold of Thérèse and Claire's hands and gently squeezed them. 'A glass of wine I think, to welcome you home.' She poured wine for herself and Claire, and milk for Thérèse, who pulled a face.

Claire sipped her wine in the warm kitchen, with its familiar smells of parsley, thyme and garlic. She felt at home in the Belland house – and although it was whcre Mitch had been stopped and taken to German headquarters, she felt safe in the streets and avenues of Gisoir – a lot safer than she did in Orléans or Paris.

'Claire?'

'Sorry, Édith, I was miles away.'

'Look at the door. It stands ajar and a little girl is peeping at you from behind her dolly. She really should be in bed. What do you think?'

Claire's heart leapt in her chest. Aimée half smiled, stepped back, and the gap between door and frame narrowed. 'I think we should invite her to join us? What do you think, Aunt Thérèse?'

'I think that would be lovely. Since she's awake, it cannot hurt.'

Édith raised her eyebrows. 'Aimée, would you like to come in and see your mummy?'

Aimée pushed the door with both hands, squashing her doll. Édith held it so it didn't swing shut while the little girl made up her mind. Claire smiled at her again. She wanted to run to her, pick her up and hold her tightly, but she didn't want to frighten her. It had been six months since Aimée had seen her, a very long time to a child.

'Mama?' Claire looked down. Aimée was at her knee. With big blue eyes, the little girl looked up and offered Claire her doll.

'For me?' Claire said. 'Thank you, Aimée. Oh but,' Claire put her hand to her mouth, 'what shall I call her?'

'Twicoté,' Aimée said. Then, craning her neck to look over the table at Édith, she lifted her arms. Claire wished it was her that Aimée wanted to go to, and swallowed. Édith picked Aimée up and sat her on her knee.

Claire did the same with the doll. 'Hello, Tricoté. What a lovely little one you are.' She couldn't help laughing because tricot meant knitted. 'What a lovely name.'

Without taking her eyes off Claire, Aimée put her hands out for the doll, and Claire gave it to her. She then gave it to Édith, put her hands up to Claire and said: 'Me.' Claire lifted her daughter out of Édith's arms, hugged her to her chest, and in no time Aimée was asleep.

Édith took hot bricks from the oven and wrapped them in clean rags. 'Do you want to take her up, dear?' Édith whispered. Claire nodded.

Édith put the hot bricks in Claire's bed while Claire put Aimée in her small cot. The little girl stirred but didn't wake. Claire stepped back and watched her daughter turn this way and that before settling down. After a sleepy sigh, Aimée put her thumb in her mouth. A second later she was fast asleep. Claire pulled the blankets up and tucked her in. Édith watched from the doorway and when Claire left the bedroom, she switched off the light. 'She is beautiful,' Claire said, taking a last quick look at her daughter before Édith closed the door.

'You are doing a wonderful job of bringing Aimée up, Édith,' Claire said, when she and Édith were back in the kitchen. 'She is a lovely little girl,' she continued, giving in to the tears that had threatened since she arrived in Gisoir.

'Shhhhhh child.' Thérèse passed Édith a clean handkerchief and she knelt before Claire and wiped her tears. 'She is a lovely child, yes. She takes after her mother.'

Thérèse agreed as she eased herself out of her chair. 'I cannot keep my eyes open. Forgive me, I am tired and should go to bed,' she said, holding her side with one hand and her stomach with the other. 'It is good to have you home,' she said, giving Claire's shoulder a squeeze as she passed her. 'Goodnight.'

'Goodnight, Thérèse.'

'Until the morning, daughter,' Édith said, as Thérèse left. She pushed a strand of hair from Claire's face. 'You look exhausted, child. I think you too should go to bed.' Édith looked at Claire questioningly. 'Would you like to sleep in my room tonight, to be near Aimée?'

Claire thought for a moment, then shook her head. 'No. I would love to, of course, but if she wakes in the night and sees a strange person-- I mean, someone other than you in your bed, it may upset her. In a couple of days I shall be leaving again and I don't know how long I'll be away. No,' Claire said again, 'to break her routine would be confusing for her. When I return I shall be working in the Gisoir area. Perhaps then, but not tonight. Besides, I wouldn't get any sleep. I'd lie awake and watch her all night.' Claire yawned and stood up. 'I'll see you in the morning, my dear friend.' She kissed Édith goodnight and went up to bed.

The next morning, after an erratic night's sleep, Claire felt something, or someone, leaning on her. She opened her eyes and saw Aimée sitting on the bed, watching her. 'Hello, Aimée.' The little girl walked her doll up Claire's arm and nuzzled her under the chin. 'And good morning, Tricoté.'

'Grandma say come,' Aimée said, sliding off the bed. Waving her dolly in the air, she ran out of the room. Claire sat up and watched her descend the stairs on her bottom, calling, 'Grandma? Grandma?'

Claire swung her legs out of bed, pushed her feet into her slippers and threw on her dressing gown. She went downstairs to fetch water to wash, but stayed there drinking coffee with Édith. 'Aimée called you Grandma,' she said.

Édith looked up, a worried expression on her face. 'Do you mind, my dear?'

'Of course not. It is who you are to her.'

'Thérèse calls me grandma when she speaks of the baby. I think Aimée has heard her and doesn't

314

want to be left out. She is a bright one, this beautiful child of yours,' Édith said, straightening Aimée's bibbed pinafore, before scooping a soft boiled egg out of its shell and mashing it up in Aimée's dish.

Claire watched Aimée as she dipped strips of buttered bread, which Claire's mother had called soldiers, into the yolk of her egg in the same way as she had when she was Aimée's age. When she had finished Aimée took the last soldier and put it up to her doll's mouth. 'Come on,' she cajoled, 'eat all up.' Then she dabbed the doll's mouth with her pinafore. 'Good girl.'

Claire wanted to laugh at her clever, funny little daughter. Aimée looked up at her with wide eyes, and Claire smiled. Aimée had changed so much while she had been away in England. She could say lots of words – and she could put them together and make sentences. 'Have you finished your breakfast, Aimée?' Édith asked.

'Yes, Grandma.' Aimée closed her mouth, pressed her lips together and held out her hands. Édith took a flannel from beside the sink and wiped egg and butter from her face and hands. When she had finished, Aimée held up her doll and Édith wiped her too.

'I think I'd better wash my face, before I go into town,' Claire said, taking the bowl from beneath the sink and filling it with water. 'I'll be back soon,' she said to Aimée, taking Édith in, as she left the kitchen.

Édith was making coffee and Thérèse, with Aimée on her knee, was looking at a story book with pictures of ladybirds and bees when Claire returned from Gisoir. 'Ah, you are back,' Édith said. She took the shopping basket out of Claire's hand and put it on the table at the side of the sink among a pile of half prepared vegetables. 'Take off your coat and sit down.' After pouring coffee, Édith produced a tin with the German flag on its lid.

Claire's eyes widened. 'What the--?' She looked at the side of the tin and read *Qualität schokolade kekse, Deutschland.* She opened it and laughed. 'Where on earth did you get German chocolate biscuits?'

'André. The last train he and Pierre sabotaged was being prepared to pick up some high ranking German officers in Blois and take them south. An SS guard, assuming André was an engineer because he was in work clothes, ordered him to get on with his job. And this is what he left the train with!' Édith laughed, holding up a packet of real coffee. 'And the chocolate biscuits.'

'A perk of the job,' André said, entering the kitchen from the hall.

'André.' Claire put her arms around her comrade. 'When do we leave?'

'Tonight, immediately after curfew.' André took a map from his jacket pocket and laid it on the table. With one hand he pointed to the area that they were heading for. With the other he drew an imaginary line parallel with the road, but through the fields and woods. 'We travel on foot as far as here.' He tapped the map. 'We stay away from the main roads because there are road blocks. But never mind for now. We'll discuss it later when Pierre and Marcel get here.'

'Come now, children, drink the coffee and eat the biscuits *Die Schicklgruber* gave you,' Édith said. Everyone laughed. Aimée squealed and clapped her small hands – which made them laugh more.

It had been years since Claire had tasted real coffee. If coffee could be found in the shops in London it was Camp, which left a sickly bitter-sweet aftertaste in your mouth. She closed her eyes, inhaled the aroma, and sipped the delicious beverage. When she opened her eyes she looked across the table to see Aimée watching her. She smiled at her daughter and put out her hands. Aimée wriggled down from Thérèse's lap and disappeared under the table.

'Aimée, no! Walk round the table, please,' Édith said. 'You will bump your head one of these days, and we know what will happen then, don't we?' Édith looked under the table.

Aimée arrived at Claire's side unscathed and held her arms out to be lifted up. Once on Claire's knee, Aimée put her hand on her head and said, 'No bang Grandma, no...'

Claire looked at Thérèse and they both laughed. 'Sorry, Édith,' Claire said. 'We shouldn't laugh when she does something you tell her not to do, but...'

'But she is funny. And she knows it too, don't you?' Aimée giggled. 'She knows exactly what she is doing. She is a little madam,' Édith said, wagging her finger playfully.

Aimée put her hands up and Édith bent down. When Édith's face was almost touching Aimée's she squealed and put her arms around Édith's neck. 'Grandma!' she said, making a show of kissing

Édith.

That night, after bathing her daughter, Claire put her in her nightgown, sat her on the stool in front of Édith's dressing table mirror and brushed her hair. 'Aimée?' Aimée looked up at Claire with big blue eyes, eager to hear what her mother had to say. Claire didn't know how to tell her daughter that she was going away again. She couldn't tell her she was going with Uncle André and Uncles Pierre and Marcel. Her small daughter spoke sentences now and chatted to anyone who would listen. If Édith or Thérèse took her into Gisoir shopping and they were stopped and questioned by the Gestapo – which happened all too often these days – Aimée, in her innocence, might say something to cause them to be suspicious. The Gestapo probably wouldn't take any notice of a child, but Claire couldn't take the risk; the consequences were too terrible to contemplate. 'I'm going away tomorrow, darling, but I'll be back very soon,' she said.

Aimée leaned forward, took the photograph of Claire from the dressing table, looked at it, and her bottom lip quivered. Claire thought her heart would break. She cleared her throat, put the hairbrush down and knelt beside Aimée. 'I'm sorry, darling. It will be the last time Mummy leaves you, I promise. All right?' she said, pushing a wisp of hair from Aimée's face. The little girl nodded. 'Good girl.' Forcing herself not to show how upset she was, Claire put her arms round her daughter and held her tight. 'And,' she said, 'while I'm away, I would like you to look after Grandma Édith and Aunt Thérèse. Will you do that for me?'

Brightening, Aimée nodded. Jumping down

from the stool, she put the photograph and her doll on the bed and clambered onto it. Taking the doll by the arm, she put her under the covers, leaving only her head showing. Then she took the photograph of Claire, kissed it and said, 'Night, night, Mummy.' Kneeling on her pillow, she put the photograph on the small table between her bed and Édith's. Without taking her eyes off the photograph, she wriggled down and pulled the bedclothes up to her chin.

'Aimée, have you got a kiss for Mummy?' Aimée looked up at the photograph. Claire realised that for a long time Mummy had been the photograph and her daughter was preparing herself for that again. Claire bit back her tears and sat on the edge of Aimée's bed. 'I promise--' She had no right to make her daughter promises that she might not be able to keep, but she did it anyway. 'I promise I will come back soon, and when I do, I will never go away again.' Aimée reached up, put her arms around Claire's neck, and hung on. Claire lowered her head until it was on the pillow. Her face was so close to her daughter's she could feel her warm breath on her cheek. She watched Aimée's eyes grow heavy and close.

Claire sensed someone at the door. It was time to go, but she didn't move. She didn't want to wake her daughter. When she was sure Aimée was asleep, Claire kissed her on the forehead and slowly shifted her weight from the bed. Kneeling beside her, Claire took Aimée's small hands, put them under the bedclothes and tucked her in.

Claire clamped her hand over her mouth to stop herself from crying out, left her daughter's bedroom and went into her own. Trying to put Aimée into a safe but unobtrusive place in her mind, she quickly took off her dress and put on thick socks, trousers, boots, shirt, and combat jacket. She went to the wardrobe and from the small space between the top and the ceiling she took a knife and truncheon. She wrapped them in a towel and hid them in the false bottom of her rucksack. She packed her wash bag, towel, and a spare set of clothes. When she was satisfied she had everything, she returned to the wardrobe and took down her gun. She checked it carefully and put it in the front right-hand pocket of her jacket. She was almost ready.

Claire looked in the long mirror at the side of the door and stood up straight. She had a job to do, which she would not be able to do unless she was fully committed to it. She picked up her rucksack, threw it over her shoulder and slipped her hand into her pocket. The hard cold metal that met her fingers reminded her why she had joined the SOE, and why she had chosen to work with the Resistance in France. Putting everything and everyone she loved into the furthest compartment of her mind, Claire affirmed her commitment to a free world and to ending fascism, whatever it took. She left her bedroom, mentally and physically ready to do that.

CHAPTER TWENTY-NINE

Moving quickly and quietly, Claire followed Pierre. André led the way and Marcel brought up the rear. They stayed close and moved swiftly through woods and copses that ran parallel with the country roads. It took them two hours to get to Meung-sur-Loire, three times longer than it would have taken them had they been able to travel by road, but they had seen spotter planes flying low over the Loire and doubling back above the roads, so they stuck to the woods.

Other Resistance groups that Claire had worked with were north of Gisoir, around Orléans, or in Paris. This terrain – dense woodland and ground cover so thick in brambles and briars it cut and stung your legs – was alien to her. It was hard going and Claire was relieved when André stopped in a small clearing. Taking the map and a torch from his jacket pocket he beckoned Pierre, who shaded the faint beam beneath his large hands. A second later André whispered, 'Devil's Bridge.' Folding the map and returning it to his pocket, he said, 'This is where we cross the river.' He took off his rucksack and handed it to Marcel. 'I shall see if it is safe.'

There was nowhere to sit, so they shook out their legs, rotating their ankles and rubbing their hands together. Claire thought it was the damp wood that made her clothes and hair wet, but looking in the direction of the bridge to where the wood was less dense, she saw fine rain. She hugged herself, shifted her weight from one leg to the other and saw a movement in the trees.

With his head down André ran into the clearing. 'There's a roadblock on this side of the bridge and I can see a dozen sentries posted on it. We will have to cross further down.'

'What about Beaugency?' Claire asked.

'It's more than seven kilometres away. It would take us an hour if we could travel by road, which we can't. No, we'll have to cross somewhere nearer.'

'I know somewhere,' Pierre said. 'It's a couple of kilometres down river.'

Pierre led the way. Eventually he stopped. 'We are here,' he whispered. 'The bridge is on the other side of the road.' Claire watched him, head down and body low, dash across the road and into the field. Once safely in the long grass he fell to the ground. André was next. Claire looked to Marcel. He nodded. Keeping as low as possible, they followed André. They lay in the grass for some time. When they were sure they had not been seen they each got to their knees and crawled to the riverbank.

Pierre pointed to a wooden footbridge with rope handrails. 'I'll try it, see if it holds.'

Claire looked up. The footbridge rose steeply above the swollen river to a high bank on the other side. The wind gusted and it began to swing. It looked unstable. 'Are you sure we shouldn't go on until we find a regular bridge?'

'The nearest is at Meung. It's too far,' Pierre said. 'Let me see if this one is strong enough to take our weight before we go on.'

Out of the corner of her eye, Claire saw dim lights. She turned and looked north. 'Germans!' she hissed. 'Pierre?' He turned. 'Get down!' They all slid down the river bank and lay in the reeds at the water's edge until the convoy of German vehicles had passed.

'Shit!' André said,' that was close. He looked at his watch. 'It's dangerous to hang about. I think we should cross here.' Pierre and Marcel agreed. 'You can swim, can't you, Claire?'

'Yes but I don't intend to, not carrying this lot,' she said, hitching up her rucksack.

'Okay, I'm the heaviest, I'll go first.' Pierre looked at André. 'If I get across without bringing the bridge down, you come after me. Claire next and you, Marcel, will cross last. The bridge will be at its weakest, but you are the strongest swimmer.'

Pierre pulled on the wooden slats of the makeshift bridge. He put his hand up, which meant it was strong enough to take him. Claire hoped it was. He then took hold of the ropes at the side and hauled himself up.

Standing in the mud at the water's edge, Claire watched Pierre inch his way along the bridge. When he arrived at the halfway point the bridge began to sway. With her heart in her mouth, Claire watched the big man freeze. Clinging to the ropes he stood motionless until the bridge was stable again. Then he walked slowly and firmly until he stepped off on the other side of the river. Claire looked at André and Marcel. She could see in their faces that, like her, they had been worried.

André took off his rucksack and took two packages from it. He gave them to Claire. 'This is the dynamite for the pylons. Pierre, Marcel, and I are carrying equal amounts for the tunnel. If anything happens to any of us, you must go on and sabotage the pylons.' Claire understood and put the packages in her rucksack.

André crossed the bridge in the same way that Pierre had done, waiting when it began to sway and moving again with even steps when it steadied. Finally, Pierre's strong hands grasped André's wrists and pulled him onto firm ground. As soon as André reached the other side, Claire began her journey. She placed a muddy boot on the first rung of the ladder, but it slipped off almost immediately. She stumbled, regained her balance and tried again. This time, gripping the rope handrail, she put her foot down more firmly and hauled herself up quickly, so both feet were level on the first rung. The ladder swayed with the sudden impact. It was raining hard and the wind seemed stronger. She could hear the river running fast beneath her and looked down. She wished she hadn't, wobbled, and immediately looked up again. Pierre and André were beckoning her, nodding encouragingly. Keeping her eyes on them, Claire planted her feet firmly on each slippery wooden slat and, gripping the rope-handles on either side to keep herself standing upright, she slowly walked on. After a short pause midway while she waited for the sagging rope ladder to stop swinging in the increasing wind, she arrived on the other side of the river and was hauled to safety by her comrades.

Still trembling, Claire watched Marcel pull himself onto the bridge. She put her hand up to shield her eyes from the rain. It was lashing down now and the wind had whipped up. After a few steps Marcel stopped. The bridge was swaying, not from his weight, but from the strong wind. Claire looked at André. His forehead was creased with worry. Rain dripped from the peak on his cap and he wiped his hand across his face. She looked back to Marcel. He was tentatively walking towards them. She sighed with relief. In the middle of the bridge he halted as the rest of them had done and waited for the sway to ease. When it did he walked on carefully and purposefully. As Marcel neared the end of the bridge and safety, Pierre put his hand out and his brother reached for it. Suddenly the handrail on the right snapped and fell into the swirling river, sending Marcel sliding sideways. Clinging to the left handrail, Marcel flung his right arm out and caught hold of a wooden rung. He looked up at his comrades and, as his body hung above the engorged river, began to swing his legs backwards and forwards. With every undulating movement the rope ladder weakened, but Marcel didn't stop. Finally he hooked the ladder with the toe of his boot and after several frantic jerks pulled it to him. Suspended in the air, with the rain driving down and the river raging beneath him, Marcel heaved himself up until he was lying on the ladder's slippery rungs. He lay face down for several minutes. Claire prayed for his safety harder than she had done since she'd prayed for Mitch. With the Loire threatening, Marcel inched his way along the ladder on his stomach. Claire and André held Pierre round the waist to stop him from sliding forwards in the mud and again, when Marcel was a few feet from him, Pierre put out his hand. Marcel looked up, let go of the left handrail and reached out to his brother. As their fingers met, the rope rail flew out of its fixing on the riverbank, struck Marcel across his back, and plunged into the river. Marcel hollered, grasped the ladder with both hands, and clung on.

'Marcel?' Pierre shouted. 'Marcel!' he called again. 'Give me your hand.' Claire followed Marcel's gaze as he stared down at the river. It seemed to be flowing faster now. Marcel looked up and slowly moved one foot up a rung of the ladder. He did the same with his other foot and then his hands until he was a few rungs away from his brother for the third time. Claire could see the fear on Marcel's face as he forced himself to reach up. Again, Pierre and Marcel's fingers touched. Claire and André shuffled forwards, so Pierre was nearer to grab Marcel's hand. He did. He grasped Marcel by the wrist. 'Let go of the ladder, Marcel, I've got you.' Claire could see indecision in Marcel's eyes. He was so near, why didn't he--? Suddenly he looked up at his brother, let go of the ladder, and thrust his hand in the air. Pierre pitched forward and caught it. 'I have you!' he shouted. Holding Marcel's hands in a vice-like grip, Pierre hauled his brother to safety.

Breathing heavily, Claire leant forward and put her hands on her knees to steady herself. The physical exertion of being Pierre's anchor, coupled with the fear that her comrade might fall into the Loire and be lost forever, had drained her. The four comrades fell to the ground, exhausted. Claire jumped up almost immediately. 'It's wet!' Her comrades laughed and she laughed with them.

'It is wet,' André said, 'and it will soon be light.' He lifted his arm and rotated his wrist until he was able to see the time. 'We have two hours until we need to be at the tunnel.'

Trekking south across the fields, they came to a derelict barn. André put out his arm and they stopped walking. He ran to the barn's door, opened it and looked in. Then he turned and summoned the others. 'We'll get out of the rain for half an hour and have something to eat.'

It was dry inside and smelled of hay, reminding Claire of the night she and Mitch had slept in the barn on the Belland farm. She quickly put the thought out of her mind and sat down on one of several logs that were dotted about the floor. The barn had clearly been used by someone other than the farmer. Lovers perhaps, Claire thought. André gave each of them thick cheese sandwiches that Édith had made. They ate hungrily.

CHAPTER THIRTY

The sabotage party arrived at the tunnel just before sunrise. Claire and André climbed the steep embankment, took binoculars from their rucksacks and lay on their stomachs. Their job was to look for German vehicles, snipers, or spotter planes that often accompanied important trains. The job of blowing up the tunnel and the train transporting German troops to Normandy to fight the Allies was Pierre and Marcel's. They walked quickly and cautiously to the centre of the tunnel and placed dynamite against the tracks and the walls. When they had finished, they replaced Claire and André on the embankment and waited for the train.

Keeping low, Claire and André ran to where the line curved fifty yards from the tunnel. Claire fell to the ground and lay in long meadow grass on the right side of the track; André did the same on the left. Claire lifted her head and, leaning on her elbows, put binoculars to her eyes. Apart from the slight bend, which allowed them to see but not be seen, the railway line was straight for miles.

Claire suddenly saw a black speck in the far distance. She blinked rapidly to moisten her eyes and rid them of field dust, and looked again. A second later the speck grew into a square and turned into the engine of a train with steam billowing from its funnel. She estimated it was two miles away and whistled sharply twice. André replied with identical blasts; he had seen the train at the same time. Running as fast as she was able, Claire joined Pierre and Marcel above the entrance of the tunnel on the north side. 'It's coming!' she shouted. 'A mile and a half away by now.' Having crossed the tracks, André joined them.

'Go!' Pierre handed Claire her rucksack and his own. 'See you at the safe house.'

'Aren't you coming?'

'No, I'll stay here with Marcel.' He took a hand grenade from his pocket. 'The dynamite was damp. It may need a little help to detonate.'

'I'll stay too. Two hand grenades are--'

'No you won't,' André said. 'It's too dangerous. Besides, you're carrying the dynamite for the pylons.' Claire hugged Pierre and Marcel. 'Be careful,' she said to Marcel. He nodded and kissed her on both cheeks. Having almost lost him to the river, Claire felt protective towards him and wanted to stay. But André was right. With a rucksack full of dynamite it was too dangerous. Pierre gave André the two remaining rucksacks. 'The train will only be a mile away now, probably less. We must go!'

'One more thing,' Claire said, looking from Pierre to Marcel. 'When you have detonated, you leave straight away. Whatever happens, you must both get out immediately, right?'

'That's an order!' André added. The four comrades shook hands, wished each other luck, and went their separate ways – Pierre into the meadow grass, Marcel to the south entrance of the tunnel, and André and Claire across the fields.

Claire and André heard the explosion as they entered a wood on the outskirts of a small hamlet. Claire stopped and turned. Tears filled her eyes. 'All those men!'

André dropped Marcel's bag and put his arms

around her. 'Killing is never right, Claire, but the German army must be stopped. If that train got as far as the front line--' A second explosion was followed by a loud rumbling.

'The bridge,' Claire said. Together they watched as thick black smoke billowed into the sky. Like dense storm clouds, it blocked out the sun. Gripped by a feeling of dread, Claire shuddered. 'Shall we wait for them?'

'No, we'll see them at the safe house.' André hauled Marcel's rucksack onto his shoulder and started to run thought the wood. Claire followed.

Claire washed in cold water from pipes that banged as the water – rusty at first – ran slowly through them. She changed into a spare set of clothes. They were damp, felt cold against her skin, but they were better than the sodden bundle that lay on the scullery floor. Hearing voices, and eager to see Pierre and Marcel safe after their dangerous mission, Claire ran from the wash-house to the kitchen. Opening the door, she saw Pierre sitting at the table with his head in his hands, sobbing. Instinctively she looked round the room. Marcel was not there. She looked at André standing at Pierre's side. His face was ashen.

Closing the door behind her, Claire crossed the room and dropped into the chair next to Pierre. André pulled out the chair on the other side of their comrade and sat down. With tears falling from his eyes, the big Frenchman lifted his head and looked first at André, then at Claire. 'The second bomb,' he said. 'We knew the dynamite was damp.' He took a shuddering breath. 'I told him not to go back, that the fire from the first bomb would impact on the second, but he ran into the tunnel. I followed him, but the train was almost on us. I shouted to him to get out, that I needed to detonate. He shouted okay and scrambled up the embankment after me. The train entered the tunnel and I looked behind. Marcel raised his arm, brought it down again, and shouted, "Now!" I knew the train would soon be through the tunnel if I did not do it immediately, so I fell on the detonator.' Pierre put his head in his hands and sobbed again. 'Marcel must have slipped, fallen down the embankment,' he said, lifting his head. 'I ran to where I had last seen him. He lay on his back, his eyes open and staring. When the second bomb exploded the blast lifted him high in the air, dropping him onto the track like a rag doll. I wanted to go to him, but the tunnel collapsed. Bricks and fire and smoke spewed everywhere, burying Marcel. There was nothing I could do, so I ran.'

In their shared grief the three comrades sat in silence. Just before dark Émilie, a middle-aged woman with sad eyes and a lined face, wearing the traditional black headscarf and dress of a widow, brought a potato and onion broth, bread, and a very welcome bottle of wine. She left them to eat saying she would be back for the dishes in the morning. None of them felt like eating, but they knew they must. Later, in an attempt to take Pierre's mind off the death of his brother, Claire uncorked the bottle of wine and André took the map from his bag. They discussed briefly how they would sabotage the communication pylons to the north, but made no firm plans. They agreed they would have to wait several days, maybe longer, until the Germans had investigated the train crash and left the area.

Claire looked at Pierre, at his grief-stricken face, his red and swollen eyes. 'Why don't you go home to Yvette and your children? Go tomorrow, before the Germans start knocking on doors. And,' she hated saying the words that she knew were necessary, 'when you tell Marcel's wife that her husband is dead, be sure to tell her he died a hero.' Claire wondered how little that would matter to a woman who had lost the man she loved, or to children who would never see their father again. She thought about Aimée and wondered if she would one day have to tell her that her father had died a hero. She shook the thought from her mind.

That night the three comrades slept in the attic. Sleeping in their clothes on top of old rugs beneath what smelt like even older, but thick, blankets, they were warm enough. But as tired as she was Claire didn't sleep more than a couple of hours. Nor did her comrades by the sounds they made as they tossed and turned in the night. The following morning, before daybreak, Pierre left the safe house for home. Claire and André studied the map again, but again they made no plans.

News came in every day via Émilie, who brought them newspapers and food. Claire couldn't cook, or even make coffee. Smoke coming from the chimney of a derelict house would cause people to talk. According to Émilie, the nearby towns and villages were crawling with Gestapo demanding to know if anyone had seen strangers in the area – and threatening them with imprisonment and torture if they withheld information.

The Gestapo and a team of structural engineers

moved into the village while they swarmed over the crash site carrying out forensic tests. By the time they left, Claire was climbing the attic walls. She hated being confined to small spaces. She wanted to get out, do the job that she and André had stayed on to do, and get back to her daughter.

In the afternoon of the tenth day, Émilie arrived earlier than usual with their evening meal. She banged on the ceiling at the top of the stairs with a broom handle. 'The Germans have gone,' she called, laughing.

Relieved, Claire and André left the attic and followed the older woman downstairs. It was the first time Claire had heard Émilie laugh. It suited her. Seeing her now, almost dancing round the table as she laid it for supper, Claire realised how terrified she must have been every day, walking through a village overrun by Germans to bring them food. Some heroes wore medals. Some, like Émilie, Claire thought, did not. But they were heroes all the same.

'Today is a good day,' Émilie said, giving André a newspaper and Claire the clothes that she had taken without being asked, and washed and ironed.

'Thank you, Émilie.' Claire lifted the clothes to her face. They felt soft and smelled of soap. She left the room and changed. She felt warm for the first time in weeks. Enjoying the feeling of clean fabric next to her skin, she wondered how long it would be until she was wet and cold again. No matter. When she and André had blown up the pylons, she would go home to Aimée and Édith, and he would go home to Thérèse – and soon their baby. They had so much to go home to, and to stay safe for. She thought of Marcel and felt a lump in her throat. She closed her eyes. She must focus on the positive, not the negative. In the New Year, Claire promised herself – after she had spent Christmas with her daughter, and after Thérèse and André's baby had been born – she would go to Paris and seek out the leader of the Paris Centre Resistance. She would ask him where he saw Mitch, and if he knew where he was now. If he did, she would beg him to take her there.

After supper André packed his rucksack and checked the attic, while Claire packed and examined the other rooms in the house. It was important not to leave anything behind. When she was done, she arranged the old furniture in a slap-dash way so no one would suspect the house had been inhabited. She looked around. The rooms looked neglected and the furnishings run down, which was what you'd expect in a derelict house.

'All done,' Claire said. 'We've left nothing behind.' She felt a catch in her throat. Marcel had been left behind. He was still out there. Or had the Germans…?

Claire embraced the woman who had looked after them for almost two weeks. 'Thank you, Émilie, for all you have done for us.'

'It was my pleasure,' Émilie said. '*Vive la France*!'

'*Vive la France*!' Claire agreed.

When they came to a fork in the road they turned left. Soon the road narrowed to a dirt track ending at a gate. 'We are close,' André said. 'According to the map, the pylon is a mile north of this farm.' They climbed the gate. The pig farm, as it was described

334

on the map, looked more like a dairy farm. Surrounded by acres of flat grazing land, it gave no cover. André pointed to a low hedge in the distance and they ran for it. Staying close they half circled the farm and walked north. When they saw the pylon they fell to the ground. For twenty minutes they waited, scanning the area for a German presence. There was none.

'Let's do it,' Claire said. Together they got to their feet and approached the pylon. Taking the dynamite from her bag, Claire packed a quarter of it round one leg of the pylon and a quarter around the one next to it. André placed the detonators. From a safe distance they watched the pylon explode and topple sideways. The stench of burning rubber was followed by a loud ripping noise. Some cables snapped; others were torn from their fixings.

The second pylon was an hour's walk to the north, in an even more remote spot, but it was a clear night and they found it easily. The same action was taken; the same result ensued. It was time to go home.

They set off on the long trek to Gisoir. André had planned the route so they would return via the Loire bridge at Beaugency. They approached with caution, even though the Germans had surrendered it to the Resistance in September.

'The bridge is as free as France will be one day,' André said. He put his hand on Claire's shoulder and together they crossed the Loire and made their way home.

They arrived home exhausted, cold and hungry. Claire put her thumb on the latch of the door to the yard and pressed. It was locked. Leaning against the door, she groaned. André dropped his bag, climbed over the wall and opened it. Claire stumbled through with the rucksacks. 'The brick,' André said, pointing to the side of the kitchen door. He eased a brick out of the wall, took the key from behind it and opened the door. Claire followed him in, dropped the bags, and went to the range where she opened the oven door. The fire was still alight, just.

André sat down at the table and yawned. Keeping his voice low, he said, 'I should go up to Thérèse, let her know we're home, but...' He looked down at his muddy clothes.

Claire put a log on the fire and tuned to the sink. 'I'll put some water on,' she said, filling two of Édith's large pans. 'You can wash in the scullery. I'll wash in here.' André frowned through a yawn. 'Well, it's me who is doing all the work,' she whispered, taking coffee from the cupboard and cups from the dresser.

When the coffee was made, Claire poured two cups and sat down opposite André. They spoke quietly. 'I don't think I've ever been so pleased to be home,' Claire said, wrapping her grubby hands around her cup.

'I'll see what Mother has got to eat,' André said, struggling to his feet and opening the larder door. He came back with bread, cold meat and cheese. They ate eagerly and by the time they had finished the water was boiling. Claire hauled her tired body from the table, went to the range, and took a large pan from it. After adding cold water she gave it to André. 'I'll go upstairs to the linen cupboard and get us each a towel,' she said. 'Won't be a minute.' As she opened the door to the hall, she saw Édith coming down the stairs.

'My darling Claire,' she whispered.

'Édith.' Full of emotion, Claire was unable to hold back her tears. She bit her bottom lip and, aware that Aimée and Thérèse were asleep upstairs, ushered Édith into the kitchen.

'We have had a difficult time, Mother,' André said, putting down the pan of water and closing the door to the hall.

'Thank God you are safe. Thérèse will be so happy to see you.'

'Is she well?'

'Yes, she is like a flower in bloom. She is very well.'

'And Aimée?' Claire asked.

Édith smiled. 'She is also well. She talks to your photograph every day and tells me you will be home soon.' She looked at her son. 'André, wash and go to your wife. Claire and I will go to the sitting room. It is warmer in there and there is something I need to tell her.'

Fear gripped Claire's heart and it began to pound, taking her breath away. If it was bad news about Mitch, she wanted to run from the house, but she knew she must hear it. Trembling, she followed Édith into the front room.

'What is it, Édith?' Claire asked when they were seated by the fire.

'Alain--'

'No, Édith.' Claire felt the ground shift beneath her. 'Please don't say it,' she said, her eyes pleading.

'Let me finish, child,' Édith said, taking Claire's

hands in hers. 'Alain is here. He is in your room, asleep in your bed.'

'Here? I-- But I must go to him,' Claire said, jumping up.

'No, wait!'

'Why?' Claire began to tremble again. 'What's wrong?'

'Do not worry. Alain is strong, and will soon be well, but--'

'But?'

'But the doctor has given him morphine for the pain in his leg, and he sleeps all of the time. The bullet was removed from his leg by the doctor in the Pyrenees, but gangrene set in.' Claire gasped and put her hand over her mouth to stifle a scream. 'It wasn't the old man's fault, my dear. He and his wife risked their lives to save Alain's. He would not have survived if he had spent another night on the mountain. If the freezing temperature didn't kill him, the amount of blood he had lost would have. If the doctor hadn't got him to his house and operated on him...' Claire sat and listened. Everything Édith said after the word gangrene she was hearing down a tunnel that was a long way off. 'The bullet had been in his leg too long. When he realised this the doctor risked his life again and went in search of a Maquis group that he knew was in the mountains. I don't know the details but Pierre said--'

'Pierre?'

'Yes. Pierre and Father Albert brought Alain from Orléans.' Claire began to cry. Pierre had lost so much when Marcel had been killed, yet he had brought Alain home. 'Pierre will tell you, or Alain will tell you when he wakes. For now, know that the doctor in Gisoir has saved his leg, and he assures me that in time Alain will recover and will walk again. But you must be patient.'

Claire nodded. 'Of course,' she said. 'I'm sorry.'

'There is nothing for you to be sorry about,' Édith said, putting her arms round Claire and rocking her.

'I am going up to Thérèse,' André said, coming into the sitting room after having had a wash. He kissed his mother on the top of her head and turned to Claire. 'Claire, what is it?'

Claire looked up at her comrade and smiled as tears rolled down her cheeks. 'Alain is alive. He is here.'

'Thank God! Mother--?'

'I will tell you tomorrow. Now you should go to your wife.' Édith turned to Claire. 'Why don't you wash and I will make up your bed in here?' Claire looked at her old friend, her eyes pleading. 'You would like to see Alain, of course. André will have used all the hot water anyway,' she said, moving to the door. 'I shall heat more while you are upstairs.'

Claire crossed the room, opened the door, and mounted the stairs without making a sound. She opened her bedroom door and the dim light from the landing glowed pale yellow onto Alain as he slept in her bed. Tears of happiness fell from her eyes as she looked at the man she loved, but feared she would never see again. There was a support of some kind under the bedclothes to keep them from pressing on his injured leg. The bullet that had penetrated his leg was months ago, so why hadn't it healed? She crept into the room and, at the side of the bed, watched Alain sleep. His hair, long and greasy, lay lank on the pillow. His broad handsome face was gaunt, his lips dry and chapped. Dark patches beneath his eyes exaggerated the grey pallor of his skin. Claire wanted to lie next to him, put her arms around him and love him better. Instead she told him she loved him, kissed the fingers of her right hand and gently touched his forehead.

She had no idea how long she had been standing there when she felt a hand on her arm and turned. It was Édith. Reluctantly she left Alain and followed Édith across the landing. As soon as she entered Édith's bedroom joy swamped her. She knelt by Aimée's bed. She was asleep with her teddy bear in one hand and the thumb of the other hand in her mouth. Claire tucked the covers round her daughter and blew her a kiss. Leaving the room, she told Édith, 'I think my heart will burst with happiness.'

'I think first you should wash, and then you should sleep. I have made a bed on the settee. Sleep downstairs tonight and tomorrow we will clear Frédéric's things out of his room and-- Claire put her hand on Édith's arm and shook her head. She looked back at Aimée, 'We will see you in the morning, little one.'

Édith went into her room and Claire downstairs. She undressed and washed in the chilly kitchen, then scuttled back to the sitting room. Édith had laid her nightdress in front of the fire. She put it on and switched off the light. Falling into her makeshift bed, Claire cried with happiness. Finally, exhausted, she fell asleep.

CHAPTER THIRTY-ONE

Claire heard Édith talking to Aimée. She leant against the wall at the bottom of the stairs and listened. From what Claire could hear, Édith was counting Aimée's toys, and Aimée repeating the numbers after her. Some words sounded similar, but others, especially when Aimée lost interest, were gobbledygook. Claire put her hand to her mouth to stop herself from laughing when Édith began speaking in a whisper and Aimée copied her. She couldn't hear what her daughter was saying, but she sounded indignant. Claire hoped she wasn't being cheeky to Édith.

Quietly she climbed the stairs. The door of Édith's bedroom was open and Aimée was sitting on her bed. When Aimée saw her, her eyes lit up. With her forefinger to her lips, she crept across the room taking exaggerated steps, whispering, 'Shush Mummy. Man poorly.' Then she took hold of Claire's hand and tried to lead her downstairs.

Claire was torn between wanting to see Mitch and going with her daughter, until Édith said, 'Alain is heavily sedated; he will not wake until later today, maybe not even then.' Édith went into his room and dipped a flannel into a bowl of water that stood on the bedside table. She wrung it out and gently wiped Mitch's face. 'Spend today with your daughter; she has been waiting to see you for a long time. I will attend to Alain.' Smiling at her daughter lovingly, Claire picked her up. Then, sitting Aimée on her hip, she carried her downstairs.

That afternoon, when Aimée was having a nap,

Claire asked Édith how Alain had got from the Pyrenees to where Pierre found him.

'The Maquis group that the doctor asked for help took Alain to a nearby farm. Alain's leg had started to heal, but he could not walk, so they covered him with old seed sacks, borrowed a cart, and took him to the next farm. While farmers took Alain as far as they dare in the back of carts, trucks and trailers, messages went from one Resistance or Maquis group to another, as far as Paris. It doesn't matter when or how, but dirt got in the wound and it became infected.'

Tears fell onto Claire's cheeks. She took a handkerchief from her pocket and wiped her eyes. 'I'm sorry, Édith. Go on.'

'It was your friend Edwina who met Alain in Paris.'

'Eddie? Thank God she's safe,' Claire said, wiping her eyes again. 'I've been so worried…'

'She took him to the house of Madame Marron. But as you know, Paris is overrun with Germans, so it was too dangerous to keep him there.' Édith made a fist of her hand and lifted it in a sign of victory. 'The people are sick of being ruled by the Germans,' she said. 'They are frightened that the Allies won't get to them in time and the city will be defeated all over again, so they are challenging the authorities, fighting back. Railwaymen, policemen, even some medical personnel are on strike, which was lucky for Alain because one of Edwina's Resistance members is an ambulance driver and turned his back while she stole an ambulance.'

Claire felt a pang of love and admiration for her best friend, who had risked her life to save Mitch.

She shook her head. She didn't believe Eddie was experienced enough to take her place in Paris, but she was wrong – and she would tell Eddie when she next saw her.

'Eddie is a clever young woman,' Édith continued. 'She painted spots and hives on Alain's face and arms and taped quarantine notices to the front and back of the ambulance. Then, with Antoinette Marron driving, Alain unconscious in the back, and Eddie in a nurse's uniform and quarantine mask, they drove all the way to Orléans.'

'Where Pierre took over?'

'Yes. He and one of the Resistance group, an undertaker, brought Alain home in a hearse.'

Claire shivered at the thought of Mitch in a hearse. But it didn't matter how he got here. He was here.

Claire showed the doctor up to Alain's room. 'Aimée? What are you doing in here?'

'Reading to the man.'

Claire turned her face away from her daughter so she didn't see her laughing. It would be a while until Aimée would be able to read. 'Uncle André's maps? You mustn't play with this book, darling.' Claire took the atlas from her and put it in the dresser drawer. How she managed to lift the book onto the bed, goodness knows; it weighed almost as much as she did.

Aimée looked from the doctor to Alain, and then to her mother. 'Man awake, Mummy. Come on,' she said, 'wake up, Mister!'

Claire plucked Aimée from the bed. She began to protest, but Claire shushed her and tiptoed to the door. At the bottom of the stairs Claire put Aimée down and she ran into the kitchen calling, 'Grandma, Grandma, man awake.' Aimée tilted her head and tried to wink, but blinked both eyes.

'If you say so, little one.' Édith lifted Aimée up, sat her on a cushion and pushed her chair up to the table. She put a bowl of porridge in front of her and an apple that she had cut into half-moon shapes.

Aimée tapped Édith on the arm and when Édith looked at her she blinked again. Nodding, she picked up a segment of apple in her small hand and bit into it.

When the doctor came down he said, 'Alain is doing well. His leg has almost healed. I have taken the bandages off to let the air get to it.' He took a bottle of pills from his black doctor's bag. 'I think it best to keep the basket over his leg for protection. If he is in pain when he wakes, give him a couple of these,' he said, handing the pills to Claire.

'When do you think he will wake, doctor?' Claire asked.

'I'm surprised he hasn't woken already. Each day I give him less morphine than the day before. Today I gave him very little. He should wake soon.'

From the doorway, Claire saw Aimée put her book of numbers down and jump off Mitch's bed. 'More? Or Aimée sing?' she asked, putting her feet together and her hands out towards him in a gesture of offering.

'Sing,' Mitch murmured.

Claire held onto the door frame to stop herself from falling. Mitch was awake. He was awake. She could hardly believe her eyes, her ears. 'Will you go down and tell Grandma Alain is awake, darling?' Aimée nodded and, after taking her doll from Alain's side, went down to tell Édith.

'Hello China,' Mitch croaked.

Claire wanted to fall into his arms and stay there forever. 'Hello,' she said, before sitting on the side of Mitch's bed, taking care not to put pressure on it. 'How are you feeling?'

He took a shallow breath. 'Thirsty, hungry... I'm so hungry, I could eat a steak.'

Claire laughed though her tears. 'You can have soup. You need to start with food that is easy to digest.' Mitch tried to lift his head, but couldn't and exhaled loudly in failed effort. He had tears in his eyes. Claire leant over and wiped them away. Then she kissed him gently.

'Lie down beside me, China.' Claire kicked off her shoes and laid her head on the pillow next to his. Mitch closed his eyes.

When Claire told Aimée that Alain was her daddy – she still called Mitch Alain in case Aimée spoke of him when they were out – the little girl stared up at her wide-eyed, and then went upstairs to her bedroom. Claire followed and found her sitting on the edge of her bed telling Dolly and Teddy. Seeing her mother, Aimée put down her toys and reached out to her. Claire picked her up and rocked her. 'Shall we go down and see Alain, or would you rather we stayed here?' Claire asked after a few minutes. Aimée wriggled to be put down. Holding onto the banister, she took the stairs slowly with Claire following.

As they entered the sitting room, Claire saw

Mitch opening an envelope that Jacques had given Édith earlier that day. He put it down immediately. 'Hello Aimée,' he said, smiling at the little girl from the chair at the side of the fire. With a puckered brow, Aimée swayed from side to side before taking one tentative step at a time as far as the chair opposite. She climbed onto the seat and, sitting down, tugged the skirt of her dress until it covered her knees. Then she clasped her hands on her lap. 'Cat got your tongue?' Aimée shook her head. 'Then why so quiet?' Not taking her eyes off him, she lifted her shoulders. 'Aren't you going to read to me today?'

Suddenly smiling, she said, 'Yes!' and, jumping down, she took the envelope containing Jacques' message from Mitch's lap. She returned to her chair and leant against the arm. 'Once pon a time --' She stopped and looked across the room at Claire. Smiling, her mother nodded encouragingly and Aimée began her story again. 'Once pon a time was a daddy and--' Aimée stopped again and this time looked up at Mitch. A frown crept across her small forehead and her bottom lip began to quiver.

Mitch pulled himself out of his chair and, with the aid of a stick, took a couple of stumbling steps. Leaning heavily on the stick, he dropped onto his knees and took up the story. 'And they didn't know each other for a long, long time because the daddy had been taken to another place before the little girl was born. Then one day,' he said, 'some kind people found the daddy. He was very sick so,' he looked at Claire, 'Mummy's friend, your Aunt Eddie, and then Uncle Pierre, brought him home to Aimée's Grandma, and with her help, and Mummy's help,

Daddy was made well again. And,' Mitch took Jacques' envelope and put it in his pocket, 'they all lived happily ever after.'

Aimée clapped wildly. Then she threw herself into Mitch's arms. 'No go another place, Daddy,' she cried. Then she leant back and, shaking her head, looked questioningly into Mitch's face.' Daddy?'

'No, honey. I won't go away again. I promise I will never leave you and Mummy,' he said, hugging his daughter to him.

Claire slipped out of the room and put her hand up to her mouth to stifle her sobs. She walked quietly to the kitchen, to where her dearest friend Édith Belland was preparing the evening meal.

'Everything all right?' Édith asked, over her shoulder. Then, seeing Claire was crying, she stopped what she was doing and went to her. 'Now, now,' she said, putting her arms around Claire. 'What on earth is the matter, child? Why the tears?'

'Nothing is the matter. My tears are tears of happiness. Alain and Aimée have become friends. They are telling each other stories about mummies and daddies that have happy endings.' Claire laughed. 'Aimée has made Alain promise never to go away again.'

'She's a bright little one,' Édith Belland said with pride. 'Courageous too, like her mother.' She wiped Claire's face with the cloth she kept tucked in the front of her apron. 'Now go to your man and your child, so I can finish making dinner.' Claire began to protest. 'Go! It is already five o'clock; André and Thérèse will be back from visiting her parents at six.

'If you're sure--'

Édith Belland wiped tears from her own eyes and pushed the cloth back into her waistband. 'Also tears of happiness,' she said. 'Now go!'

The botched job that had been left after Mitch was shot in the leg had healed, but until the muscles were stronger he had to walk with a stick. The doctor said he may always need the stick, but Mitch refused to believe it and went walking every day.

'You are now trained in shopping, Alain,' Édith said, when he handed her the shopping bag.

Mitch half smiled and crossed the kitchen to where Claire was basting a joint of beef, a New Year gift from Thérèse's parents. He kissed her on the cheek.

'Is Aimée about?'

'She's upstairs having her afternoon nap.'

'That's good. I need to tell you something.' He put out his hand.

Claire's heart plummeted. What now? She looked at Édith. Her eyes were downcast. 'What is it, Mitch? You're frightening me.' She took hold of his hand and he led her into the sitting room.

'Sit down, darling,' he said, patting the cushion next to him on the settee.

Claire sat and looked into his eyes. 'What is it?'

Mitch took her hands in his. 'It's Eddie.'

Claire snatched her hands away. 'What about Eddie?' she asked accusingly.

'She's…' Claire looked at him defiantly, daring him to tell her what the sadness in his eyes was already saying. 'I'm so sorry, darling, but Eddie has been killed.'

'No, no, no!' Claire cried. 'Not Eddie. Please Mitch, say it isn't true?' She looked at him, her eyes pleading. 'Say it! Say it isn't...' she sobbed, collapsing into his arms.

There was a tap on the door and Édith entered. Claire looked up and saw her friend put a bottle of wine and two glasses on the shelf above the fire. 'Eddie is dead, Édith. My lovely, funny friend is dead.'

Édith poured a glass of wine and offered it to Claire. 'Drink, my dear. It will do you good.' Claire took the wine but didn't drink. 'I am so sorry,' Édith said, kneeling on the rug beside her.

The three of them sat without speaking for some minutes. It was Claire who broke the silence. She looked into Mitch's face and said, 'How did she die?'

'She was betrayed by someone at the ambulance station. The Gestapo were waiting for her when she took the ambulance back.'

Claire gasped. 'What about Madame Marron?'

'She is safe. Eddie insisted she took her home before she returned the ambulance.'

At that moment they heard Aimée call. 'I will see to her,' Édith said, pushing herself up. 'I'll take her to the kitchen and give her her tea. You come in when you're ready.' Édith bent down and kissed Claire on the head. 'Take your time, my dear.' She looked at Mitch, her eyes full of sorrow, and left.

Spring was turning into summer. The buds of April were beginning to bloom in the May sunshine. The Belland family left church straight after Sunday service, so they would be home in time to hear

General de Gaulle give his Victory Europe speech on the new wireless that Mitch had bought with redundant money from Colonel Smith.

As they walked along the streets and avenues of Gisoir, there was a celebratory feel in the air. People had taken down their blackout curtains and thrown open their windows. Flags flew from every house and the national anthem could be heard along every avenue. Claire laughed and began to sing *La Marseillaise*.

Édith caught up with her. 'I learned your national anthem at RAF Morecambe with Eddie,' Claire said, her voice hoarse with emotion. 'For you, Eddie,' she shouted and began to sing louder. Before she succumbed to tears, Édith linked arms with Claire and sang with her. Leaving André to push his son, Frédéric – who he and Thérèse had named after André's late brother, Édith's beloved youngest son – and Mitch to walk with Aimée, Thérèse joined them, and arm in arm the three women sang all the way home.

Édith took off her hat and hung up her coat. Claire and Thérèse followed her. 'Alain?' Édith called. 'Tune in the wireless for General de Gaulle's speech. And André, take the children into the sitting room, while Thérèse, Claire and I prepare lunch.'

Claire laid the table while Thérèse put the saucepan of vegetables on the stove. Édith took out a joint of beef, a gift from Thérèse's parents, and cut into it. 'Another half hour,' she said, spooning fat over it. 'Are we ready?' Thérèse and Claire nodded and Édith led the way to the sitting room. 'André, Thérèse's mother and father sent two bottles of very good wine to accompany the meat. They are under the sink.' André looked shocked. 'I didn't want anyone to drink it, so I hid it there. Go on son, we will drink a bottle while we listen to the speech.'

Thérèse followed André out of the room, returning with five glasses. André poured the wine as the programme began.

'Parisians are gathering in their tens of thousands at the Place de la Concorde, Tour d'Eiffel, Arc de Triomphe, and many other famous landmarks in our beautiful city,' the wireless presenter said. 'And now it is time to hear General de Gaulle give his Victory Europe speech.'

'The war has been won. This is victory. It is the victory of the United Nations and that of France. The German enemy has surrendered to the Allied Armies in the West and East. The French High Command was present and party to the act of capitulation.' Everyone cheered. 'In the state of disorganisation of the German public authorities and command, it is possible that certain enemy groups may intend here and there to prolong on their own account a senseless resistance. But Germany is beaten and has signed her disaster.'

'The Resistance will put paid to them! Sorry,' André said.

'While the rays of glory once again lend brilliance to our flags, the country turns its thoughts and affection first of all toward those who died for her and then toward those who, in her service, struggled and suffered so much. Not one single act of courage or self-sacrifice of her sons and daughters, not one single hardship of her captive men and women,' Claire thought of Eddie and closed her eyes, 'not one single bereavement and sacrifice, not one single tear will have been wasted in vain.'

'I'll check the meat,' Claire said, and, taking her wine with her, she left the room. In the kitchen she lifted her glass and made a toast to Eddie. 'Love you, Ed,' she said. 'Thank you for getting the Canuck out of Paris for me.' Drying her eyes, Claire went back to the family and the celebrations. De Gaulle's speech was over and everyone was in tears. Claire laughed inwardly. She needn't have left the room.

'Well,' Édith said, drying her eyes, 'the war is really over. We are free citizens again. *Vive la France*,' she sang out.

'*Vive la France!*' everyone echoed.

'Come on, precious,' Édith called to Aimée. 'Grandma needs you to help her in the kitchen.' She looked over her shoulder at André and Thérèse and, jerking her head, summoned them to come too. Looking bemused, they left baby Frédéric asleep in his pram and followed her.

As Claire got up to leave, Mitch caught hold of her hand and pulled her back down. 'I love you, China,' he said, looking into her eyes. 'Will you marry me?'

'Yes,' Claire said.

THE END

Outlines of the last books in The Dudley Saga

The last book in the Dudley Sisters Quartet, **The 9:45 To Bletchley**, is Ena Dudley's story. Ena works in a local factory, making components for machines bound for Bletchley Park, during World War 2. Ena finds herself involved in blackmail and theft. Is someone where she works setting her up? If so, who can she trust? Accused of breaching the Official Secrets Act, Ena must find out who is trying to incriminate her and expose them before it is too late.

I have had an idea for a fifth book, **The Foxden Hotel**, which begins ten years after Foxden Acres and brings the characters of the four novels together. The Foxden Hotel opens on New Year's Eve, 1948. Friends and family of the Dudley sisters are celebrating the opening of the hotel when a group of fascists gatecrash. Bess, Margot and several guests recognise one of the men from London during the war. Along with the other uninvited guests, he is thrown out of the hotel and chased off the property. When spring comes, the action of that night reveals shocking consequences.

ABOUT THE AUTHOR

Madalyn Morgan has been an actress for more than thirty years working in repertory theatre, the West End, film and television. She is a radio presenter and journalist, writing articles for newspapers and magazines.

Madalyn was brought up in a busy working class pub in the market town of Lutterworth in Leicestershire. The pub was a great place for an aspiring actress and writer to live. There were so many wonderful characters to study and accents to learn. At twenty-four Madalyn gave up a successful hairdressing salon and wig-hire business for a place at East15 Drama College, and a career as an actress.

In 2000, with fewer parts available for older actresses, Madalyn learned to touch type, completed a two-year course with The Writer's Bureau, and began writing. After living in London for thirty-six years, she has returned to her home town of Lutterworth, swapping two window boxes and a mortgage, for a garden and the freedom to write.

Madalyn is currently writing her fourth novel, The 9:45 to Bletchley, the last of four books about the lives of four very different sisters during the Second World War. The first three novels, Foxden Acres, Applause, and China Blue are available on Amazon – eBook and paperback.

Made in the USA
Columbia, SC
10 June 2018